The Wanderers of the Water Realm

D0107595

6 Petaluma Blvd. North, Suite B6, Petaluma, CA 94952
12 Strathallan Crescent, Douglas, Isle of Man IM2 4NR

First Published by M P Publishing Limited 2011

ISBN 978-1-84982-104-9
The Wanderers of the Water Realm

Book Design by Maria Smith
Cover Design by Dorothy Carico Smith

Lawton, Alan, 1938-
        The wanderers of the water realm : a novel / by Alan
    Lawton. -- 1st ed.
        p. cm.
        ISBN-13: 978-1-84982-104-9
        ISBN-10: 1-84982-104-6

        1. Sea stories, English. 2. Fantasy fiction,
    English.   I. Title.

    PR6112.A993W36 2011   823'.92
                                 QBI11-600178

The Wanderers of the Water Realm

A Novel by
Alan Lawton

I dedicate 'The Wanderers of the Water Realm' to my life partner Hilary Bargent and gratefully acknowledge the help and encouragement given to me by numerous friends, including Mrs. Barbara O'Hanlon OBE and Doctor Richard Hamm ... I give you all my heartfelt thanks.

Ruins of Hiram

South Lands

K'aa Nomads
&
Hixian Clans

Red Bank River

Mountains

Yam

Holy
Path

Port of
Ostla

Southern Sea

Deva

Empire of the
Kaa-Rom

Portal to
Earth

The Forest
Oblivion

K'aa Nomads
&
Hixian Clans

Mountains of the Kev

The Heart of Emerald

Wastelands
of the Hix

Great Thou
Forest

Portal closed
by the Hix

Saxmen
Barburians

Northern Sea

Great Life River

Celar of the
Mighty Wall

Narr
Herder's

Land of the
White-Skinned

City of the
Ancient Dead

A Map of the Water Realm. Owned by
Neor Balsam & copied by, Myra the Wise Woman
& modified during her wanderings.

Portal from
Earth

Chapter 1

Darryl Littlewood stifled a groan and jerked almost upright as Wise Hetty applied a steaming hot poultice to his badly bruised chest. "Easy there, Mother," he gasped, "are you intent on boiling me like one of your garden turnips?"

Hetty laughed, thrusting her son down with the palm of her hand until the young man lay prone upon the well-used couch that occupied a corner of her kitchen.

"Lad, what can you expect when you come here beaten black and blue, after fighting like a demon in them boxing halls and those so-called 'Gentlemen's Clubs!' I tell you plainly, son, I long for the day when you make the final payment upon that canal boat of yours then you can give up the bloody craft of prizefighting and make the whole of your living by plying an honest trade upon the navigations."

"Then tomorrow will be a memorable day for both of us, Mother," the young man answered with more than a hint of pride in his voice. "For yesterday's bout in Sheffield, the one that left me with this damnable bruising, has also given me enough cash to pay off the last instalment of Uncle Robert's loan. By tomorrow evening, the deeds to the Bonny Barbara will be in my possession and the craft will be mine and mine alone."

"I'm fair glad to hear it lad!" Hetty said with a deep sigh of relief. "For I feared that someday you would be made a cripple in the ring or driven daft through repeated blows to that poor head of yours."

She gently stroked his hair. "Now sleep, lad, and give the healing poultice a chance to do its work."

Hetty covered her son with a warm blanket and returned to the tedious yet important task of sorting out the heaps of freshly gathered medicinal herbs that lay upon her kitchen table. As she worked, she pondered the unavoidable circumstances of birth that had ordained she must inevitably become a healer of the sick, aye, and ultimately forced her son to become a pugilist, although it was the very last career she would have wished for him.

Even from her earliest childhood days, Hetty had known that she was destined to become the hereditary 'wisewoman,' or healer, to the little Pennine village of Elfencot, an isolated rural community nestled within the shadow of The Devil's Tor.

The Tor was a steep and sinister crag of naked granite overlooking the little hamlet, dominating its hinterland of small farmsteads and sheep pastures.

A woman bearing the Littlewood name had always treated sick humans and ailing farm animals in the district of Elfencot; daughter had followed mother, generation upon generation, with each wisewoman taking care to hand down the ancient secrets of her craft that were far older than recorded history. Each Littlewood female had inherited the very same plot of land upon which the present wisewoman grew her medicinal herbs and each healer had lived out her life in the same stone-built cottage that was situated on the outskirts of the village, a small four-roomed structure that lay hard by the towpath of the Marquis of Buckley's Canal Navigation.

Generations of grateful country folk had viewed their loved ones being skilfully tended and brought back to health by the wisewoman and her forbears, yet the influence of the church had always been strong in the district and the Littlewood women were often suspected of practicing witchcraft and the dark arts. Indeed, it was common knowledge that two of their number had once been burned as servants of the devil. Even in this far more enlightened year of eighteen seventy-one, folks were known to pay furtive visits to Hetty's cottage in search of some powerful charm to entrap a loved one, or simply to have their fortune told. Small wonder that many of the elders of the local church were known to suggest that the wisewoman's rumoured knowledge of sorcery was a threat to her everlasting soul, aye, and to the spiritual well-being of the community at large.

Not surprisingly, few local men could be induced to take a Littlewood woman to wife and for generations their children had been sired by passing travellers who begged for a night's lodging at their cottage, or by stalwart crewmen from the narrowboats that plied the nearby canal.

Hetty smiled with pleasure as she remembered the evening of her seventeenth birthday, when she had lain in the arms of a handsome boatman and conceived her son Darryl and his twin sister Myra. These were the only children she had ever been fated to bear.

Hetty's children were her pride and joy. But she had always realized that her offspring would suffer many social disadvantages due to her own unconventional lifestyle and occupation. For the knowledge that the twins were sprung from a witch's bloodline had effectively barred them from all church-run activates, including attendance at the local parish school, and no respectable tradesperson would ever consider teaching them a craft. Even so, a superstitious fear that Hetty probably possessed dark powers had ensured that they would always be treated with a kind of shallow civility, but they would never be 'citizens of the community' in the fullest sense of the word.

Hetty was proud of her daughter Myra, for she had proven to be a quick and intelligent girl who promised to become an even more competent healer than her mother. She had also been fortunate in acquiring a reasonable degree of education from a man of letters, whom she had nursed through a long and ultimately fatal illness.

Had the girl lived in an earlier age, she would undoubtedly have succeeded her mother as the village healer. But Hetty shook her head sadly; young Doctor Smithson was building up a good practice in the district and the day of the old-fashioned wisewoman was obviously drawing to a close. It was quite probable that Myra would eventually have to find a new way of earning her living, perhaps as a nurse or possibly a lady's maid. However, her son Darryl had far better prospects than his twin sister.

The wisewoman had only one close blood relative, a brother named Robert who was almost twenty years her senior. The elder Littlewood was master and sole owner of the narrowboat Bonny Barbara, a craft which for years had carried general cargo on the small group of narrow canals that linked Yorkshire and the Pennine hill communities to the rapidly growing industrial city of Manchester. The veteran boatmaster, upon the wisewoman's impassioned urging, had agreed to take Darryl aboard, at the early age of ten, and teach him the arduous trade of canal boatman--and never did her brother have cause to regret his decision, for the lad proved to be a willing pupil and had quickly grown to love the gypsy life of the waterways.

Two years ago, the elderly boatmaster had chosen to retire from trade, and the veteran had such confidence in his twenty-year-old nephew's ability, that he had offered to sell him the deeds to the Bonny Barbara, with repayments to be made by ten half-yearly instalments. Darryl had instantly accepted his uncle's offer, but Hetty shook her head disapprovingly, for the young man had subsequently decided to liquidate the debt as quickly as possible by engaging in the brutal and dangerous occupation of part-time pugilist. Small wonder that the preceding two years had been exceedingly worrying ones for the wisewoman, for she had been in constant fear for her son's safety. Even so, she was forced to admit that the young boatmaster had enjoyed a fair degree of success as a prizefighter in the city of Manchester, and the lad had even taken part in the occasional contest on the far side of the Pennines. Aye, and had successfully battered senseless every single one of the brutal 'Yorkies' matched against him.

Indeed, it was small wonder that Darryl had also succeeded in winning the vast majority of his bouts in Manchester and upon the Lancashire plain, for the lad had grown up as hard as teak due to the heavy physical toil that was an everyday part of a boatman's life, and had also become thoroughly inured to physical violence through taking part in the bitter brawls that often occurred between rival boat crews. In addition, the lad had been well schooled in the art of boxing, by a burned out old prizefighter who lived in a broken-down hovel near the Piccadilly wharves in Manchester. The old bruiser had taught him the intricacies of his violent craft for the price of a bottle or two of cheap gin and the odd plug of Navy Cut tobacco.

Hetty paused and glanced over to the couch where her son was now lying, fast asleep.

"Great Earth Mother," she muttered to herself. "I would never have believed that a child of mine would ever go by the ring name of 'Black Darryl.'"

The wisewoman shook her head. She had never liked her son's ring name, for it was borrowed from a famous Lancastrian murderer. But she also knew that 'Swift Darryl' would have been a more apt title, for he normally disposed of his opponents quickly and without receiving the flattened nose and the scarred features that were the normal hallmarks of his profession.

Wise Hetty felt happy and contented, as she hung the bundles of fragrant herbs from the rows of metal hooks that lined the ceiling beams, for she now knew that the debt upon her son's boat would be paid in full by the following evening and her son would be done with the prize ring. Her joyful mood was also accentuated by the knowledge that Myra had promised to arrive at the cottage by noon, and would keep her company until four o'clock sharp. The girl would then have to return to a nearby farmhouse with all speed and continue her ministry of an old horse dealer, who was far too ill to care if his nurse was a witch's daughter, or even Queen Victoria herself. Even so, an extremely faint yet disturbing thought began emerging from the farsighted portion of the wisewoman's brain.

"Beware!" It seemed to say. *"The pleasure that you are experiencing today - will perhaps be paid for by a deluge of pain tomorrow!"*

಴

The hour hand of Hetty's old grandfather clock was approaching twelve o'clock when the outer door of the kitchen suddenly swung open and a young woman entered the room with the weight of a well-filled wickerwork basket almost dragging her to the ground.

She dumped her burden upon the top of the kitchen table and turned to embrace the wisewoman.

"I'm fair glad to see you, Mother," she said quietly, in order to avoid waking her twin brother. "Old Mr Ramsbottom is sinking fast and won't live out the night. His son from High Fell farm is sitting with him in my absence. He sends you a dressed fowl, two loaves of fresh bread and some potatoes, in payment for the potions and salves that you prepared for his father."

"Coin would have been better," Hetty replied. "But never mind, lass, young Master Ramsbottom's provisions will furnish us with a fine dinner, for we have much to celebrate this day."

The wisewoman then told her daughter of the good tiding her brother had earlier brought to the cottage. Myra was delighted with the news, for she was extremely fond of her sibling, and the two women immediately set about preparing a sumptuous meal with which to mark the occasion. Myra busied herself with stuffing the fowl with breadcrumbs and herbs before setting it to roast in front of the kitchen fire, whilst her mother scrubbed the potatoes and then beat up the batter for the pancakes that would complete their unusually fine repast.

Soon, the savoury smell of roasting fowl filled the kitchen and the delicious odour began tantalizing the young boatmaster's nostrils as he slowly drifted back into wakefulness. He opened his eyes, but his vision was temporarily clouded by the effects of the strong painkilling potion his mother had administered when he first arrived at the cottage. Indeed, he was barely able to differentiate between the two women as they completed the preparations for the forthcoming meal, for they possessed many physical similarities. Myra had inherited her mother's long flowing red hair, her deep green eyes and her tall statuesque figure. But the younger woman's high cheekbones and slightly Asiatic features contrasted sharply with her mother's softly rounded Pennine face and was clear proof of the considerable measure of gypsy blood that the girl had inherited from her bargee father. The older woman's complexion, despite the onset of early middle age, was as smooth and unblemished as that of her offspring, and a complete stranger to that rural household would undoubtedly have taken them for blood sisters, rather than mother and daughter.

Myra raised her head from her work, and she noticed that her twin brother was now awake. She rushed across the width of the kitchen to embrace him.

"Oh Darryl," she said, clasping him tightly as he attempted to rise from the couch. "Mother gave me the good news and I hope that you keep to your resolve and fight no more in the ring."

"Have no fear, lass," he replied, as his sister slowly relaxed her grip. "I'll stay as tight as a tick to the navigations and leave boxing to the other fools who are willing to get their brains addled for the pleasure of others."

He reached for his jacket that was hanging behind the kitchen door and took a package from the inside pocket. He tore open the wrappings to reveal two pairs of finely embroidered silk handkerchiefs and presented one to each of the women.

"There you are, ladies," he said, kissing each one of them in turn as he handed over the gifts. "Please accept these handkerchiefs as a small memento of my good fortune, a token of my gratitude for all the help and support that you ladies have given me over the past two years. Now, for heaven's sake, serve up the food before I perish from sheer hunger!"

꧁

The little family group enjoyed a memorable dinner and then relaxed before the fire with a bottle of Hetty's excellent elderflower wine. The afternoon passed quickly and it seemed as though only a moment had gone by before the clock struck four and Myra was forced to depart upon her duties, leaving her mother and brother alone to keep the fire company.

Hetty poured the last of the wine into her son's glass.

"Will you stay the night?" she asked. "The poultice will have done its job by now and a good night's rest will take the last of the inflammation from that bruised chest of yours!"

But her son shook his head, reluctantly rising from his chair.

"Would that I could, Mother," he replied. "But my boat is moored alongside the towpath not far from your own front door. I must go aboard and cast off without further delay, for I'm carrying a load of bricks to be delivered to Thomas Brown, a builder in the town of Ashton-Under-Lyne; he expects us to be lying alongside the Ashton wharves by tomorrow morning at the very latest. It's my intention to begin the unloading of the cargo, then travel by railway to Manchester and conduct my business with Uncle Robert. George, my regular boat hand, will complete the off-loading of the bricks in my absence. Afterwards, he will load an assortment of Yorkshire-bound cargo and work the boat back to Elfencot with the help of a temporary boat hand. He can lay the Bonny Barbara up in the old mill branch to await my return, which will not be long, if everything goes well in Manchester."

Hetty wrapped up the leftovers from the meal in a clean linen napkin, together with a loaf of good wheaten bread, and handed the victuals to her son.

"That should keep young George going until evening," she said with a laugh. "He's a growing lad and he needs plenty of packing in his belly if he's to keep up his strength. Aye and God knows, you'll need all of his strength on that boat of yours." The wisewoman hugged her son fondly. "Give my regards to Robert," she said, as she escorted him to the kitchen door. "And look after yourself in Manchester!"

Darryl strode along the towpath towards the Bonny Barbara, moored about a hundred yards west of the wisewoman's dwelling. Looking beyond his craft he could clearly make out the crenulated entrance of the Devil Hill tunnel that lay about half a mile away. The boatmaster knew from long experience that each of the boat crews who entered its dark mouth faced a long two-and-a-half-hour journey beneath the barren Pennine moors, before emerging on the Yorkshire side of the long chain of hills that were often referred to as the 'Backbone of England.'

The navigation widened as he approached the mouth of the tunnel, and the boat-owner was just able to make out the beginnings of a narrow side-canal. The little waterway branched off from the main navigation, running for a distance of about one hundred yards before terminating at a dilapidated wharf that lay in the shadow of an old and long-disused corn mill. The mouth of the half-forgotten branch canal was shrouded by the same tangle of trees and undergrowth that also hid the ruins of the old mill from public view. Indeed, few villagers had ever seen fit to fight their way through the bramble thickets in order to visit the isolated and broken pile. Darryl had known about the branch canal and its derelict wharf since his earliest childhood, sometimes serving him as a quiet place to temporarily lay up his craft when trade was slack. He also used the wharf as a convenient place to regularly paint his boat and to carry out minor repairs whenever they became necessary.

Darryl turned his attention to the Bonny Barbara, which lay moored against the towpath, and he noticed that his barge horse was standing in full harness at the water's edge, with the long towing rope attached to the towing post situated just forward of amidships in the centre of the craft. George, his young boat hand, had obviously anticipated his imminent return and had prepared the boat for immediate departure, and the youth was already standing close to the bows with his hand upon the forward mooring rope in readiness to cast off.

The boatmaster jumped down into the cockpit of the craft, a sheltered area situated in the extreme stern of the vessel that housed the tiller and also gave access to the small cabin accommodating the boat's crew. His first act was to take hold of the tiller and order the waiting youth to cast off without a moment's delay. He placed two fingers into his mouth and blew a piercing whistle, the barge horse instantly responding by throwing the entire weight of its body against the padded collar encircling its neck. The towrope whipped taunt and the cargo vessel slowly began to gather way and started its journey down the Marquises canal--a journey that would take the narrowboat to the waterway's junction with the Peak Forest Canal and to its eventual destination, the commercial wharves at Portland Basin in the industrial borough of Ashton-Under-Lyne.

Only when the heavily laden narrowboat was making steady progress did the boat hand join his employer in the cockpit of the craft. Darryl immediately handed him the parcel of food prepared by his mother and pointed towards the door of the tiny cabin that served as communal accommodation for the young boat-owner and his crewmembers.

"In you go, lad, and get some food and rest, I'll give you a shout if I have need of you."

The youth nodded in reply and disappeared into the cabin, leaving the complete management of the craft in the hands of his master. Indeed, Darryl anticipated little need for the lad's assistance until the craft arrived at the junction with the Peak

Forest canal, near the village of Bugsworth. He would only need the lad's help if they unexpectedly met a boat coming in the opposite direction and were forced to cross the towlines in order to allow the craft to pass one another; but this was extremely unlikely, for the old Marquises' navigation was seldom used nowadays by commercial craft, due to the bitter competition from the trans-Pennine railway companies that had driven freight charges down to rock bottom. The few narrowboats still using the waterway were now forced to eke out a miserable living by carrying low-value commodities such as limestone and building sand. Darryl knew that he would also have been in desperate straits but for a precious agreement with a Yorkshire brickworks, allowing him to carry bricks and roofing tiles across the uplands and deliver them to their customers in Manchester and other towns situated upon Lancashire plain.

The young boat owner had further bolstered his financial position by purchasing boatloads of a reeking organic fertilizer manufactured at 'Corporation Wharf' from the contents of the privies of Manchester; this he took aboard as back cargo and sold by the ton to the farmers who cultivated the Pennine uplands. Even so, Darryl fully understood the financially precarious nature of his occupation and he knew perfectly well that his ability to continue carrying goods cheaply depended upon the blind loyalty of George, the young boat hand, who toiled relentlessly from dawn to dusk in return for only a few small coins per calendar month. However, the sixteen-year-old youth's loyalty had been well earned, for Darryl had originally found the lad, some two years before, lying upon the towpath of the Peak Forest canal, delirious with enteric fever and as close to death as mattered.

The boatmaster had taken the lad aboard the Bonny Barbara'and delivered him to Hetty's cottage, where his mother had saved the youth's life by a near-miraculous exhibition of her healing powers.

"Aye, near miraculous indeed!" Darryl reflected as he clung to the tiller of the boat. For the lad had been cold as a stone by the time they reached Elfencot and his pulse was almost undetectable. Fortunately, both his mother and twin sister had been at home; not for the first time, he had been bundled unceremoniously from the kitchen as the two women began practicing the most secret of their healing rituals. Once again, he had heard his mother singing a strange but haunting melody and again had smelt the acrid stench of the smouldering herbs that eventually forced him to leave the cottage and take refuge aboard his narrowboat.

He remembered returning to the cottage, some two hours later, and had re-entered the kitchen to find the youth breathing easily and obviously far from death.

Even so, it had required two months of careful nursing and a great many nourishing meals before the lad had been returned to full health and was able to leave the wisewoman's care. George had subsequently come aboard the Bonny Barbara, taking up the post of boat hand, and had proven to be a diligent worker and a true and loyal friend.

The Bonny Barbara progressed steadily along the line of the Marquises' navigation, and by early evening the craft had finally arrived at the head of the flight of locks marking the waterway's junction with the Peak Forest canal. Darryl then called his young assistant from the cabin and the two men had spent the remaining hours of daylight in working the narrowboat downwards until it rode safely upon the surface of the lower waterway. Afterwards, they secured the boat to its night mooring and attended to the needs of the hardworking old barge horse before gratefully retiring to their bunks for the night.

"A good day done," the boatmaster concluded, as he closed his eyes. "But tomorrow will be far better. For the remainder of the debt to my Uncle Robert will be fully discharged and the deeds to the Bonny Barbara will be mine and mine alone."

꧁

The big station clock was showing twenty minutes to nine when the morning train from Ashton-Under-Lyne drew to a halt in Manchester's Piccadilly Station.

Carriage doors crashed open and a flood of passengers poured onto the platform, flowing like a human torrent in the direction of the station exit.

Darryl waited a moment for the crush to ease and then stepped down onto the emptying platform. He caught his breath as he alighted, for his nostrils and throat were immediately assailed by the acrid air of the city. This gross atmospheric poisoning, he knew perfectly well, was the inevitable result of the dense clouds of coal smoke belching from the funnels of the numerous railway locomotives using the busy terminus.

Darryl grimaced at the nuisance, but he smiled to himself as he remembered the old northern phrase: 'Where there's muck there's money!' For he knew full well that the locomotive exhaust fumes merely augmented the huge volumes of coal smoke that daily poured from the forest of tall chimneys dominating the skyline of Manchester. The foul smoke-laden air was the price the city, together with its Lancashire hinterland, paid for becoming the greatest centre of textile production in the history of the world.

He was also familiar with the dreadful social cost of this industrial supremacy, namely the wretched slums housing a frequently hungry and often ill-paid workforce; the huge downtrodden and often ragged population, whose labours enriched the growing class of mill owners and entrepreneurs, men whose business acumen was held as being second to none in the world of British commerce.

The boatmaster stepped out of the station and onto a crowded sidewalk where men and women, drawn from almost every estate and occupation, hurried in every direction in order to reach their appointed places of work as quickly as possible. Darryl, by contrast, was in no great hurry. His original intention had been to conduct his business in Manchester upon the day following the departure from his mother's cottage. Unfortunately, a temporary shortage of horse transport at the Ashton canal wharves had slowed down the unloading of his cargo of Yorkshire bricks and it had been almost midafternoon before the Bonny Barbara was riding empty at the wharf-side. Darryl had therefore been forced to delay his departure for Manchester until the following morning. However, the young man had made the best of a bad situation and had used the extra time to gather and load a Yorkshire-bound cargo of scrap metal and general merchandise. He had then dispatched his craft upon the first leg of its return journey to Yorkshire, under the command of young George. The youth had been given a few coins to engage the assistance of a temporary boat hand and been given strict instructions to await his employer's return from Manchester at the old mill wharf in Elfencot. Darryl had then spent the night at the cottage of a former workmate before catching an early train to Manchester.

Darryl continued walking at a leisurely pace, for the doors of Downes and Sons, his bankers, would not open until nine o'clock sharp. He therefore had over an hour to wait before he could withdraw the twenty pounds lying in his bank account. A goodly sum, which, together with the twenty guineas that he had won in his last boxing contest, would enable him to clear the debt to his uncle and leave him in sole possession of the deeds to the Bonny Barbara.

He reached into his pocket and fingered a single silver shilling lying within its dusty depths.

"Plenty of cash for a good breakfast at Mother Cresswell's Ordinary," he muttered to himself. "Aye and why not? For a fellow doesn't become the owner of a narrowboat every day of the week!"

The young boatmaster turned down a narrow alleyway running behind the railway station and emerged inside the small courtyard where Mother Cresswell's eating house was situated. He crossed the courtyard, after picking his way between a column of heavily laden horse-drawn coal wagons, and was about to enter the eating house, when he felt a sudden tap on his shoulder. He turned and found himself looking into the face of a short, dapper man, who wore a rather old-fashioned stovepipe hat. Darryl immediately recognized the individual as being Sidney Arkwright, commonly known a 'Stovepipe Sid.' The man had an extremely dubious reputation and was said to earn a living by acting as an agent and runner for some of the bookmakers and publicans who operated their businesses in the districts of Piccadilly and Ancoats.

Stovepipe detained the boatmaster by grasping at his right arm.

"I'm right glad to have bumped into thee, Black Darryl," he said in a weak voice that was little more than a whisper. "Albert Pike's been asking after you for the past three days and he's let it be known that he wishes to have words with you over at his gymnasium."

Darryl frowned, for he knew Albert Pike only too well. Pike was the proprietor of the Sparta Gymnasium, an establishment that was situated only a few streets from Mother Cresswell's Ordinary. The gymnasium was a place where the unmarried sons of well-to-do businessmen met their friends and worked off the effects of their frequently damaging drinking bouts, under the watchful eyes of the group of ex-pugilists who acted as their instructors.

Pike often held boxing contests at the Sparta Gymnasium and at a number of other sporting venues in which he held a financial interest. Darryl also knew that Pike derived a considerable income from the numerous private contests that he was paid to secretly stage within the dwellings of his richest and most favoured clients. These were brutal encounters, with few rules to protect the contending fighters and where huge sums of money were routinely wagered upon the sad bloodstained figures battering each other to pulp inside the ropes of the makeshift fight rings.

Darryl had fought three times at the Sparta and had always won convincingly, and he knew, instinctively, that Pike intended to offer him further contests.

He shook his head. "Please tell Mr Pike that I have recently retired from the ring and will fight no more!"

Stovepipe looked worried.

"It's best that you tell him yourself," he replied. "Pike's no man to cross and I don't relish the task of bringing him bad tidings. Tell you what, he'll be over at the gym by now and it might be best for all of us if you slipped over there and had a word with him yourself."

Darryl reluctantly agreed to the runner's suggestion and the two men reached the Sparta Gymnasium in less than ten minutes, after passing through a perfect labyrinth of back-to-back houses and dirty alleyways.

The establishment was quiet, for the vast majority of the young bloods who formed its clientele would not begin arriving until almost midmorning and the only occupants were a pair of old pugilists sweeping the bare wooden floor with long-handled brooms.

A gaslight was burning inside the small office that occupied a distant corner of the gymnasium and Darryl instructed the runner to remain outside and await the outcome of the meeting. He then knocked briefly upon the door and entered without waiting for a summons from within.

The ex-fighter crossed the threshold and came face to face with a short, thickset man seated behind a large mahogany-topped desk supporting a stack of heavy brass-bound ledgers. The man quickly rose to his feet and grasped the ex-pugilist by the hand.

"Black Darryl," he exclaimed in a high falsetto voice that was little more than a squeak. "I'm glad to see you looking so well and obviously in perfect fighting trim."

He paused.

"Look," he said. "I'll not mess you about, but tell you at once why I had my lads keep a good lookout for you. The fact is that Silas Oldshaw saw you fight here the last time that I had you on the bill, and he's asked me to set up a contest between you and Bill the Boar. You know the man? That South-country bruiser who drives Oldshaw's coach-and-four, acts as his personal bodyguard and whom he keeps as his personal boxing fancy. He wants me to stage the fight in the basement of that big mansion of his. The one that stands high on the hill above Staleybridge."

The promoter smiled and jingled the spare coins in his right trouser pocket.

"There'll be a good purse to be won, a hundred guineas at least. What do you say to that, Black Darryl?"

The boatmaster shook his head. "I'm done with the ring, Mr. Pike. I fought my last bout four days ago, up in Yorkshire, and now I'm finished for good, for I've no intention of ending up beaten mindless like one of those poor nitwits who keep the floor of your gym clean."

Pike casually swatted away a fly that tried to alight upon his bald head.

"Can't say that I blame you for your sentiment," he replied. "For I remember you tellin' me that you only stayed in the boxing game in order to pay off the debt upon that canal boat of yours. So it seems to me that you must have reached the point of doing so, if I'm any judge at all!"

The promoter paused and struck at the persistent fly with a rolled-up newspaper. After squashing the insect against the surface of his desk, he turned his attention back to the young visitor.

"See here, Darryl. Cash is always useful to a man like yourself with bills to pay. Why not beat yon coach driver into the canvas and quit for good?"

Once again, the boatmaster shook his head, but the bald-headed boxing promoter was undeterred and looked the young man directly in the eye.

"I warned Mr Oldshaw that you might be reluctant to fight and that you wouldn't come cheap. He instructed me to offer you a fee of fifty guineas in gold. Win or lose. This would be in addition to the purse of one hundred pounds, if you should succeed in flattening yon coachman."

Darryl gasped in amazement at the generosity of the offer, but a feeling of suspicion crept into his mind.

"That's a lot of cash to offer a common fighter for a night's work," he stated. "Now where's the snag?"

Pike stared at the floorboards.

"Broughton rules," he replied in an almost inaudible whisper.

The young boatmaster cursed aloud and spat upon the floor in disgust.

"*Broughton rules!*" he shouted at the promoter. "A fuckin' bare-knuckle bloodbath until either me or yonder coachman is too crippled to move, or lose because one of us is too battered to stand upright. Well Mr Pike, my answer is that I'll have none of it, not even if you were to offer me the contents of the Bank of England." He spat again in disgust. "Aye, and furthermore, I'll take ample care not to have anything to do with you and your sort in the future!"

Darryl spun upon his heel then threw open the door and exited the office, only to be confronted by the waiting Stovepipe Sid.

"I hope that your business went well," the runner began. But his enquiry proceeded no further, for the angry boatmaster grasped the surprised runner by the waist, lifting him clear of the ground and flinging him bodily across the gymnasium, where he collided with a group of young gentlemen arriving for their morning exercise routine.

Darryl stood over the winded man. "I give you fair warning, Arkwright." He snarled. "Seek me out again, on one of your dammed crooked errands, and I swear that I'll bloody well kill you!"

Darryl quit the gymnasium and his temper quickly abated as he retraced his steps towards Mother Cresswell's eating house, and he was in a much better state of mind by the time that he crossed the threshold of the ordinary.

"Damned if I'll let my day be spoiled by yon pair of bastards," he muttered, as he seated himself before one of the scrubbed wooden tables. "I'll treat myself to the best breakfast the house can offer. Aye and I'll take my time about it for a bloody change."

❦

A nearby church clock had struck half past ten before the boatmaster settled his bill in the ordinary and began walking off his huge breakfast of bacon, eggs, sheep's kidneys, black puddings and fried potatoes. He stepped out briskly, with the taste of the sweet South American coffee still on his palate, and, within half an hour, he traversed the district of Piccadilly and was standing before the banking premises of Downes & Sons, the firm that managed his modest savings.

Young Mr Downes welcomed Darryl into his office, and as business was quiet, he entertained the boatmaster with tea and idle conversation for well over an hour. It was therefore almost midday before Darryl emerged from the bank with a total of thirty guineas stowed within the stout money belt that was hidden beneath his clothing. His next task was now to deliver the cash to his maternal Uncle Robert. This would require a substantial journey on foot, for the retired boatman lived on the extreme edge of the city in the district of Ancoats, his cottage being conveniently situated near the line of the Ashton canal navigation where the old man could sit and watch the boats sailing past.

For a moment, the young man considered retracing his steps through Piccadilly, but the cobbled streets were choked with traffic at this hour; instead, he settled upon a slightly longer but less strenuous route, one that would lead him past the nearby Castlefield wharves and along the towpaths and side-streets running eastwards in a roughly parallel line to the route of the Rochdale and Ashton-Under-Lyne canals.

Darryl felt perfectly safe from danger, as he tramped eastwards, even though his route took him through a poverty-stricken district where the cash in his belt would have been a sure invitation to robbery. However, the ex-fighter was a well-known and popular figure in the vicinity of the Manchester canals, and his progress was often delayed by friends and acquaintances who greeted him in the street. On more than one occasion, he was invited to share a beer with the day labourers who toiled on the canal wharves whenever work was available, and who spent the remainder of their lives in the rat-infested cellars lying below the level of the city's grimy streets, but he always declined their invitations and pressed onwards.

By midafternoon, the boatmaster had reached the outer limits of the city and was little more than a mile from his uncle's cottage, when the brutal and unexpected event occurred that was destined to alter the entire course of his life.

On the very edge of Ancoats, close to a newly constructed district of textile factories and terraced cottages, stood an isolated group of noisome hovels and temporary workshops that would soon be swallowed up by the ever-advancing suburbs of Manchester.

The hamlet was known to the local populace as 'Hells Corner,' and the boatmaster would certainly have been well advised to have given the place a wide berth, for its inhabitants were drawn from the dregs of the city workhouses, but Darryl also knew that he would shorten his journey by a good half a mile if he cut through this squalid district. He also recalled the fact that the broken and sick inhabitants of Hells Corner had never attempted to impede his progress in the past, and he resolved to run the slight risk of passing through the disreputable hamlet.

Darryl entered the tangle of buildings and was passing through a narrow alleyway running between a ruined hovel, a disused smithy and a rag-and-bone warehouse, when the attack suddenly occurred.

Without warning, a massively built man sprang from the gaping front door of the hovel and delivered a powerful shoulder charge, sending the boatmaster crashing against the wall of the smithy with sickening force. The young man's huge assailant, whose lower face was obscured by a thick woollen scarf, immediately stepped behind his victim and threw his left arm around the youth's throat. He instantly turned the move into a strangling hold by grasping his left wrist with his right hand, then hauling backwards upon Darryl's windpipe with the whole of his considerable strength. Meanwhile, a second man, whose features were similarly disguised, emerged from the door of the smithy and repeatedly drove his fist into the boatmaster's unprotected stomach. The second attacker was slightly built and the ex-fighters well-developed abdominal muscles enabled him to absorb the force of the blows without difficulty.

Even so, Darryl knew that he must react quickly before the stranglehold to his throat rendered him unconscious. The boatmaster was the veteran of a score of bitter wharf-side brawls, and twisting sideways he attempted to win enough room to drive his elbow backwards into his attacker's midriff.

Unfortunately, the move failed and the arm around his windpipe tightened alarmingly.

In desperation, he reached upwards, tearing at the hand that was locking-on the stranglehold, succeeding in forcing away his assailant's little finger. He summoned up the remainder of his strength and bent the digit back against the joint; his efforts were rewarded by a crack resembling the breaking of a twig. The attacker grunted with pain and Darryl immediately felt the pressure release from his throat, allowing his lungs to fill with gulps of life-giving air.

Darryl followed up this success by driving an elbow into his injured opponent's solar plexus with a force that would have felled most normal men. The man merely gasped and countered by grasping hold of the young man's right arm and delivering a whip-throw, sweeping him off his feet and crashing him to the ground.

The two attackers now closed in upon the helpless boatman, the slighter of the assailants drawing back his boot in order to deliver a finishing kick to the head. But Darryl's hand brushed against a pole-like object lying abandoned in the alleyway.

He desperately grasped the object, thrusting it upwards in an attempt to fend off the fatal attack. The assailant halted for a second as though frozen and then collapsed in a heap alongside the boatmaster, with blood pouring from a terrible rent in the side of his throat.

Darryl immediately glanced at the object that had delivered such a terrible wound and he perceived it to be a long-handled agricultural billhook, probably abandoned by some departed smallholder. The implement was dirty and covered with rust, yet the blade was as sharp as a razor and had cleaved through the man's neck without difficultly.

The remaining assailant lunged forward with the obvious intention of avenging his fallen comrade, when something very strange occurred.

A tiny dark-haired girl, wearing a white blouse and a long red skirt, suddenly appeared and interposed herself between Darryl and his massive attacker, rapping out a few words in a language that was totally unknown to the boatmaster. She took the man by his undamaged hand and quickly led him down the alleyway and out of sight.

Darryl rested for a few moments to regain his strength, then clambered to his feet and began examining his fallen opponent.

The man was quite dead, for the lifeblood had poured out of his body that was now surrounded by a veritable pool of gore.

The boatmaster, out of curiosity, bent down and pulled the scarf from the dead man's face, and he found himself looking at the pale features of Stovepipe Arkwright.

Darryl pondered upon his situation and decided that it was his duty to inform the local constabulary as quickly as possible. Yet another portion of his brain advocated immediate flight, for he had publicly inflicted physical violence upon the runner that very morning. Furthermore, only the unknown girl had witnessed the ambush and she was nowhere to be seen. He could not help fearing that he would be accused of murdering Arkwright out of sheer spite.

However, the boatmaster's dilemma was destined to be quickly resolved, for the door of the nearby rag-and-bone warehouse suddenly burst open and a flood of shabbily dressed humanity poured into the alleyway. The denizens of Hells Corner occasionally found casual employment by sorting out the piles of stinking rags that were stored inside the establishment, and the young man's presence in the alleyway had unfortunately coincided with the end of their working day.

The motley gathering halted as one at the very moment they spotted the blood-soaked body of the runner, with the boatmaster crouching over it and still holding the gory billhook that had inflicted such a terrible wound.

At first, they stood in silence, then a boy with a pockmarked face pointed at the corpse and then at the boatmaster.

"God help us!" he began, in a shocked whisper that grew into a shout of anger.

"There's been a right horrible murder and yon bugger with the billhook in his fist must be the one who's done it!"

"Aye, you're right," broke in another member of the crowd. "That's Stovepipe Arkwright lying there with the blood drained out of him. Aye, and I know the name of his killer. That's 'Black Darryl' standing there, I've seen him fightin' over at Pike's gymnasium on more than one occasion."

"It's Black Darryl right enough," shouted a third member of the crowd. "He's still armed, so we'd best soften him up a bit before we lay hands upon him." The man picked up a stone and flung it towards the boatmaster, narrowly missing his head. The remainder of the ragged group then joined in and began pelting the young man with stones, billets of wood and anything they could lay their hand upon. Darryl, with missiles flying around his head, had no choice but to take to his heels.

A portion of the tattered mob attempted to give chase, but the boatmaster was almost at the peak of physical fitness and he swiftly left them behind. The pursuers were soon out of sight but Darryl maintained a blistering pace, eating up the remaining distance between Hell's Corner and his uncle's dwelling that lay close to the banks of the Ashton canal.

Darryl was gasping for breath as he ran through the dense grove of oak trees surrounding his relative's cottage and found Robert Littlewood sitting in his front garden busily repairing the shaft of his broken spade.

The older man immediately realized that something was seriously amiss when the youth burst through his front garden gate and halted before him with his chest heaving from his exertions. He wisely allowed his nephew time to recover his breath before requesting the reason for the young man's hasty appearance, and waited patiently as Darryl recounted the events of that disastrous day.

Afterwards, Robert led him into the cottage, seated him at a stout table and handed him a mug filled to the brim with hot water and strong Navy rum. The old waterman made himself comfortable by the hearth, then lit his pipe and began reviewing his nephew's situation.

"You'll hang for sure if the constabulary takes you," he said quietly. "Or else they'll send you to the Dartmoor rock-pile for the rest of your life and you'll probably suffer a far worse fate than the rope, for there seems to have been witnesses enough at the gymnasium to prove that bad blood existed between you and

Stovepipe Arkwright. Aye, and there seems to be none who'll swear that you were the innocent victim, and not the assailant in that bloody ambush at Hell's Corner. Indeed, you can rely upon that bunch of rag-pickers to damn you as Stovepipe's killer and send you to the gallows without a single care in their drink-sodden minds. Best thing that you can do, lad, is cut and run whilst you still have a chance of staying alive!"

Darryl, however, was far from convinced.

"The police might find witnesses to prove my innocence," he suggested. "At any rate, I'm bound to receive a fair trial and..."

"A fair trial be buggered," shouted the old waterman angrily, striking his pipe against the side of the fireplace. "Remember that you're a boatman, living and working on the canals. Do you suppose that any of the property-owning shopkeepers who will make up the jury will consider you to be anything more than living slime? Why, a gypsy or a common felon would be afforded more respect. I tell you lad, those sanctimonious bastards would give you the 'nine o'clock drop' and then go to the chapel on the following Sunday and strut around as proud as punch, whilst boasting about making sure that justice was done and a felon hung."

Darryl was reluctantly forced to agree with his uncle's reading of the situation, for he had personally experienced the fear and hatred that a great many land-dwellers harboured for the boat people; folk whom many regarded as moronic thugs, whose itinerant lifestyle was often regarded as ungodly and an affront to civilized society. Indeed, it was not uncommon for some unfortunate bargee, caught poaching a rabbit to feed his hungry family, to become the recipient of a long and brutal prison sentence that far outweighed the gravity of his crime.

"Perhaps I can make it to Liverpool or Bristol and get aboard a ship bound for America," he suggested. But the old waterman shook his head.

"You'd never even make it to the docks, let alone get passage to America with the police being on your tail. No, lad, your best hope is to make your way back to Elfencot and seek your mother's assistance. Hetty will know how best to direct you to a place of safety."

The young man looked surprised.

"How on earth could mother possibly help me? And how could I return to Elfencot without bringing trouble to my family?"

The old man gently placed his hand upon his nephew's shoulder.

"Lad, Hetty and me sprang from the same womb and I know that she possesses depths of wisdom that ordinary folk could not even dream of. Get back to her as fast as you can, do it soon, for that scum over at Hell's Corner will have informed the constabulary and both the town and the countryside will soon be raised against you."

Darryl thought the matter over, whilst finishing off the measure of rum and water, and then agreed to go along with his uncle's suggestion, for he could see no alternative course of action. He took the money belt from his waist and handed it to the old waterman.

"There's the balance of the money that I owe you for the purchase of the Bonny Barbara," he said. "At least I won't die a debtor if they hang me!"

Robert agreed to bury the money belt and its contents deeply in the soil of his garden, in order to cover the young man's tracks, and then he quickly dropped a small loaf of bread, a wedge of cheese and half a bottle of rum into a hessian bag and handed it to his nephew.

"Take care to avoid human habitation until you reach the shelter of the Pennine hills," he advised."Then move as quickly as possible, for the constabulary will soon trace your birthplace. You must reach your mother's doorstep well ahead of them if you wish to live. Now go and good fortune be with you!"

≈

Darryl quit his uncle's cottage, moving with extreme caution as he crossed the eastern reaches of the plain lying beyond the outskirts of Manchester. He took care to keep to isolated country lanes and pathways, avoiding the small textile towns and mill villages that were springing up across the breadth of the Lancashire plain.

It was pitch dark before he was able to pause for a single hours rest in the shelter of a small wood near the tower of Harts Head Pike, a landmark standing high amidst the first range of the Pennine hills.

The boatmaster refreshed himself with a wedge of cheese and a drink of rum from his bottle and then pressed onwards until he crossed the line of the Tame Valley, near the village of Greenfield. By dawn, he had reached his first objective, the great expanse of heather-clad hills and deep peat bogs forming the backbone of Northern England.

The danger of immediate capture had now receded, but he continued to move with caution, for the uplands were patrolled by armed gamekeepers and Darryl had no wish to be apprehended on suspicion of poaching and summarily handed over to the police.

It was midafternoon of the following day before he stood high upon the crest of the Devils Tor and looked down upon his native village of Elfencot.

Darryl descended the hill with care, making use of every well-known bush and fold in the ground, until he reached the cover of the dense thicket of trees extending almost to the rear door of his mother's cottage. He passed noiselessly through the wood and crept silently to the kitchen window, to ensure that no strangers were present in the dwelling, but the only persons to be seen in the room were his mother and his twin sister Myra.

The young boatmaster announced his arrival by gently

knocking three times upon the door, his mother reacting instantly by opening the door and drawing him inside.

The two women hugged the youth affectionately and Hetty brushed away tears of relief.

"My inner eye warned me that you were in great trouble," she said, "and that you were probably a fugitive. Now lad, sit down and explain everything that has befallen you; then we can decide how best to bring you aid. But take care to tell us everything, for even the smallest detail may be of the greatest importance."

Darryl then related the events that had led to his ruin and threatened to rob him of his liberty and probably his life. Hetty, meanwhile, listened patiently to his every word, then uttered a deep sigh that might have been drawn from the very depths of her soul.

"My brother Robert was correct in urging you to return here and seek my assistance, for you will certainly be hanged if you are taken and brought to trial. You must therefore be placed beyond the reach of the constabulary until I can uncover the facts that will clear your name."

"We had best decide upon a course of action as soon as possible," Myra commented. "For I noticed two mounted constables riding up to the mouth of the Devil's Hill tunnel less than an hour ago, and then returning in the direction of Marple at a fair gallop. They were probably looking for the Bonny Barbara and it's not surprising that they failed to find her, for she's lying out of sight, alongside the old mill wharf, with George in charge of her. There's none to give away her position, for he told me that he discharged the temporary hand above the junction locks to avoid paying him an extra day's hire. Some old tramp, bound for Yorkshire helped him to work the boat to Elfencot for the price of a plug of tobacco."

The girl shook her head.

"Those two constables may have been frustrated in their search, but they'll certainly make further enquiries in the district and are sure to find out that Darryl's family resides in this village. They will surely return with plenty of reinforcements to back them up. They'll search this cottage and the surrounding countryside so completely that a single mouse would be unable to avoid detection."

Hetty acknowledged her daughter's words with a brief nod, then turned and stared into the flames of the kitchen fire. For a full five minutes she considered the situation, then turned to face her two children with tears in her eyes.

"There's no alternative," she said. "My son, you must flee from here and seek sanctuary within the Water Realm!"

The wisewoman's statement held no meaning for the boatmaster, but his sister gasped in amazement.

"Hidden powers save us!" she cried aloud. "Mother, you cannot mean it. The Water Realm is a violent and terrible place. He may not survive long, even if he should succeed in passing through the curtain unscathed."

"The Water Realm, Mother?" the young man queried. "I've never heard of this place!"

"My son," she replied. "We Littlewoods have always dwelt in the shadow of the Devil's Tor. Aye, since the days when our ancestors roamed these very Pennine hills dressed in animal skins and killed their meat with spears. Always the Littlewood women have been the healers of the sick and seers who would read a palm or sell a love potion to anyone who should demand it. Yet some were great adepts who could cast their inner selves forward into the future and foretell things that were still to occur; some were even able to use the immense power of their minds to converse readily with the wise ones who dwelt in other places."

The witch looked deeply into her son's eyes as though desperately willing him to believe her words.

"Aye lad, almost beyond comprehension were the mental powers possessed by many of our Littlewood ancestors, powers that could only be marshalled after long years of training, meditation and by dwelling in close proximity to the terrible

Devil's Tor. The hill above us, my son, marks the spot where the world in which we now reside comes into near contact with another reality, a strange place that we Littlewood witches call the Water Realm. This reality is normally separated from the planet Earth by vast distances in both time and space. But at the end of each recurring cycle of five years, the two realties draw close together in the vicinity of the Devil's Tor; for a few short weeks, they are only separated by a barrier of force as thin as gossamer. The greatest of the Littlewood seers knew the secret of tapping into the vast reservoir of alien power that exists beyond the barrier, and this reserve of energy enabled them to undertake the prodigious feats of the mind, that the ignorant and fearful call 'Witchcraft and the works of the Devil.' My son, both your sister and I are inheritors of this terrible gift!"

Hetty paused for a few moments to allow this startling information to sink into the youth's brain, and then she continued her explanation.

"The barrier of force is at its weakest at the end of each five-year cycle and may part without warning. At such times, any person or group of persons, near the vicinity of the breach can be seized and flung into the Water Realm to live and die as fortune pleases.

"Darryl, this is the reason why the Devil's Tor has such an evil reputation, for travellers throughout history have suddenly disappeared whilst crossing its barren slopes. Never to be seen again! Legend has it that a cohort of Roman soldiers once marched over the hill, in the direction of York, and disappeared to a man without leaving so much as a helmet or a discarded cloak to mark their passage. Why, in my grandfather's day, it was said that a group of canal navies working in the depths of the Devil's Hill tunnel also disappeared without trace, and they doubtless suffered the fate of being cast into the adjacent reality."

The witch leaned forward and squeezed her son's hand.

"Darryl, the last cycle of five years has recently come to an end and the curtain between our two realties is now as thin as spun silk. My knowledge of the secret arts is great and my powers have never been stronger. I have the ability to sweep aside the curtain and allow you to escape into the alien reality where the misdirected justice of our world cannot hound you. But only if you possess the courage!"

Hetty paused and drew a deep breath.

"Your sister mentioned that the Water Realm is a place where danger and violence are commonplace, yet it is also a home to folk who are not unlike ourselves. Some few are fellow seers whose minds I can reach with the aid of my powers. They have assured me that kindness is also to be found in great abundance within their world, and that persons with courage and intelligence may prosper and find happiness."

The witch forced a smile.

"Come lad; now say that you are willing to accept the only chance of survival that lies open to you."

Darryl slowly nodded and a wry smile tugged at the corner of his mouth.

"I doubt if I've got much choice, Mother, and I feel sure that you possess the power to transport me beyond the clutches of the constabulary. I always had a strong suspicion that you were more than a common healer when you pulled young George back from the grave, some two years ago."

"That's settled then," the wisewoman replied briskly. "Now take heed, for this is how we shall push matters forward. The reality that lies beyond the curtain is a world dominated by water, and boats are vital possessions for many of the folks who dwell there. It is my intention to pass the Bonny Barbara through the curtain whilst you are navigating her through the Devil's Hill tunnel. If I succeed in accomplishing this very considerable feat of magic, then your chances of surviving in the other reality will be greatly improved."

The words were hardly out of Hetty's mouth when the

younger woman joined her twin brother in the centre of the room.

"Mother," she said. "You once told me that it was possible for an accomplished seer to visit the Water Realm and return again to our own native reality. Was this true?"

"I didn't lie," the witch replied. "But to the best of my knowledge, only one person has accomplished such an incredible adventure."

She paused.

"Some three hundred years ago, this cottage was the birthplace of the greatest seer that our family ever produced; Rose Littlewood was her name. By the time that Rose attained the age of thirty, she had already served as a trusted adviser to some of the most powerful people of her day. Wealth and fame were hers for the taking. But her lust to explore the unknown knew no bounds, and one day she walked to the summit of the Devil's Tor and transported herself to the Water Realm. Her younger sister was serving as the wisewoman to the district of Elfencot at the time, and she never expected to see Rose alive again. Yet some ten years later, a crippled woman, prematurely aged by extreme suffering, walked into the village and knocked upon the door of this very cottage. That woman was Rose Littlewood. But she proved to be little more than a living shell, and she died only a few weeks later without giving a clear account of her adventures to the younger sister who was caring for her. However, she defiantly stated that a passage through the curtain could be made in one direction only. She insisted that any traveller wishing to return to this reality could only find the return portal after undertaking a long and frighteningly dangerous journey to remote portions of the Water Realm."

Hetty paused again.

"My son, to find this exit must be your prime concern; otherwise you can never return home. You must find it within the space of five years, so that you can re-pass the curtain when our two worlds are again in close proximity."

Myra laid her hand upon her brother's shoulder.

"That settles the matter," she said quietly. "I must accompany Darryl into the Water Realm, so that I may employ my wisewoman's knowledge to reopen the exit curtain-- otherwise he will have no chance of returning should he be fortunate in reaching the necessary portal."

"Aye, that fact had crossed my mind," the older woman added, "but it near breaks my heart to risk losing the pair of you. My daughter, I foresee that you will develop mystical powers far greater than my own and I feel that you would be of great assistance to your brother in the long and arduous journey that he must inevitably undertake."

Hetty wiped tears from her eyes. "Go with my blessing, children who shared my womb."

She paused and threw a log onto the kitchen fire.

"My inner eye advises me that a third wanderer should journey to the Water Realm aboard your narrowboat. Young George is devoted to you both and he would never suffer to be left behind. Indeed, why should he not plunge into another reality, for this one has shown him little mercy and you pair are amongst the few persons to have given him any real kindness."

Hetty turned away and began throwing medicinal roots and dried herbs into a hessian sack.

"Come, children," she said. "We have many preparations to make before you embark upon your journey and little time to make them, for it cannot be long before the officers of the constabulary arrive in the village and begin searching for their quarry."

🙐

The three Littlewoods immediately began work, and within the hour had transported almost the whole of the wisewoman's stock of preserved food to the old mill wharf and stowed it aboard the narrowboat. They also loaded a variety of other useful items, such as hand-tools, spare clothing and a stock of coal for the all-purpose stove that was situated in the craft's cabin. Myra, under her mother's supervision, had filled a heavy wooden chest with potions, charms and all the other paraphernalia of a wisewoman, stowing it beneath her bunk in the cabin.

Darryl also explained the gravity of the situation to his incredulous young boat hand and advised him to travel across the hills to Yorkshire and start a new life far away from the navigations, aided by all the cash that remained in the boatmaster's possession; but the young man would have none of it and expressed his firm intention to take his chances aboard the Bonny Barbara along with his friends.

The evening shadows were lengthening before everything was prepared for the boat's departure, with the old barge horse standing harnessed and ready to move at the quayside. Hetty then bade a brief farewell to her children as they boarded the craft, and to each one she gave a present that she knew would be of great value in the hard years that lay ahead.

She kissed her son lightly upon the cheek and presented him with a curved sword of Oriental design. The weapon was old and the deeply scored hilt showed that it had seen much service, yet the blade had an edge like a well-honed razor and the balance seemed to suit the young man to perfection as he practiced swinging it around his head.

"The sword is called 'Kingslayer,'" the wisewoman said. "It was given to your great-uncle Herbert by a Persian holy man whom he once saved from drowning. He warned your great uncle not to sell it to buy rum, for he prophesied that it would protect the life of a kinsman as yet unborn."

Hetty turned to her youthful witch-daughter and handed her a case containing an old parchment volume.

"This document is the grimoire of your ancestor Rose Littlewood. It contains a little of the magical knowledge that she gained whilst wandering through the Water Realm. Unfortunately, most of the text seems to be written in a code that appears indecipherable. Yet I feel that it may prove useful to you in the trials that lie ahead."

Finally, she strode down to the water's edge where George was making the final adjustments to the boat's towing line, and she pressed a small but beautifully worked spoon into his hand.

"George, my lad," she said. "Two years ago, I used all of my unseen arts to bring you back from the edge of the grave, but not for the sake of pity alone, for my inner eye warned me that you would someday be the instrument of my children's survival. In giving you this spoon, I may be presenting you with the means of helping them to continue living, for this object will turn black for the briefest instant, if brought into contact with any substance that is injurious to humankind."

Hetty Littlewood, the wisewoman of Elfencot, stepped back from the wharf-side and bade the three travellers a final farewell.

"I have cast my inner self beyond the curtain and contacted one who dwells on the other side. He will meet you and give you aid and protection when you reach the Water Realm."

She paused, describing a magical witch-sign with her right forefinger.

"Blessed be you all," she cried aloud. "Now go!"

꙳

The old barge horse strained at its harness and slowly the narrowboat pulled clear of the wharf with Myra at the tiller. Meanwhile, Darryl and George had scrambled up into the bows and prepared to pull aside the mass of foliage obscuring the entrance to the disused mill wharf. Within the space of a few minutes, the Bonny Barbara was clear of her former haven and moving down the last few yards of the main canal before plunging into the dark maw of the Devil's Hill tunnel.

Darryl now took over the tiller and steered the craft into the very heart of the hill, assisted by the light of a hurricane lamp suspended from a pole in the bows. George carried another lamp and led the nervous horse along the narrow towpath that hugged the right-hand wall of the tunnel. None of the crewmembers uttered a single word as the craft advanced into the depths of the hill, each being fully preoccupied with their own doubts and fears. The only sound that could be heard was the lapping of the water on the hull of the boat and the clip-clop of the horse's hooves echoing from the vaulted brick roof of the tunnel.

The wisewoman watched the craft depart and then plunged into the depths of the surrounding wood. She picked her way between clumps of prickly briers, skirting the trunks of numerous blackened oaks, until she finally entered a small clearing that was dominated by a huge moss-covered stone towering a good fifteen feet above the forest floor. She retrieved a leather bag from beneath the bush, where she had previously hidden it, and began the magical ritual that she hoped would place her son and his companions well beyond the reach of the constabulary.

Firstly, she drew a small brazier from the bag and placed it upon the ground in the shadow of the great stone and filled it to the brim with dry twigs and lumps of charcoal. She lit the brazier and blew upon its contents until they glowed red.

The witch took out a square of silk cloth that was decorated with ritual signs and spread it out upon the grass in front of the brazier. From the leather bag she also produced a small bowl of polished copper and filled it with clear water from a spring that surfaced in a corner of the clearing, and placed it in the centre of the silken cloth. Finally, she placed a bundle of scented herbs alongside the glowing brazier, then threw off her clothing and washed her body scrupulously in the waters of the nearby spring.

Hetty completed her ablutions, then knelt before the square of silk and began the strange and terrible ritual needed to open the portal to another world. She began the ritual proper by casting some of the herbs upon the glowing coals and inhaling the narcotic smoke that billowed upwards in a dense cloud. Then she began singing her witch-song.

The song that broke the silence of the surrounding woods bore no resemblance to any other music performed in the vicinity of Elfencot, for it had been composed by some long-dead minstrel who lived long ages past upon the edge of time itself, and whose lyrics were couched in the language of some ancient long-dead tribe whose very name was now forgotten.

The cadence rose and fell as Hetty piled more herbs upon the brazier, and slowly the brazier, the stone and even the surrounding trees began to fade from the wisewoman's view as the powerful narcotic took effect.

The witch-song died away and Hetty began concentrating her mental powers upon the water-filled bowl. Pain, agonizing pain began to stab through the wisewoman's head as she flung wave after wave of occult energy towards the bowl. Ripples now began forming on the surface of the water, for the liquid served as a conduit directing spear after spear of psychic energy towards the curtain separating the two adjacent realities.

The wisewoman screamed aloud as she sought to open the portal, suffering untold agonies as the frightful mental energies tore at the fabric of her brain. Her cries became animal-like in their intensity. Yet she knew that she was succeeding in her task, for the water in the bowl had turned an inky black and she began sensing the near presence of the alien reality.

A bright spot formed on the surface of the dark liquid, a spot that steadily expanded. Hetty knew the portal was opening, yet her feeling of triumph quickly evaporated, for her inner eye began warning her that an unfriendly force had entered the Devil's Hill tunnel and was in hot pursuit of her loved ones.

॰ஜ

Darryl first realized that a force of mounted constables had entered the tunnel when he looked back over the stern of the boat and caught sight of the flickering tongues of light cast by many lanterns. Soon, the clattering of hooves could be heard above the footfalls of his own barge horse.

The boatmaster shouted a warning to the other members of the crew and he immediately gave control of the tiller to his sister Myra. He then seized hold of a long pole and began thrusting it against the walls of the tunnel in an effort speed up the narrowboat's passage. Yet, despite his best efforts, the pursuit drew steadily nearer.

✤

Hetty, warned of the oncoming danger, gathered up her last reserve of mental energy and hurled it against the opening curtain. Slowly, the already expanding spot of light upon the dark surface of the bowl began glowing with ever-greater intensity until the whole interior of the receptacle was bathed in brilliant light.

The wisewoman, now totally exhausted by her tremendous effort of will, pitched sideways and lay prone upon the floor of the clearing. But she was perfectly happy as a black wall of unconsciousness engulfed her, for she knew the barrier between the two realties now lay wide open and her children's escape was quite certain.

✤

Myra was the first of the narrowboat's crew to notice that subtle changes were beginning to occur in the subterranean depths of the tunnel, for she could make out a number of orange spots of light sparkling in the wake of the fleeing boat and ragged sections of bright blue rock were mysteriously appearing amidst dull brickwork of the tunnel's vaulted ceiling. The young wisewoman did not require her inner eye to know that some stupendous event was about to take place. She cried out to George to abandon the barge horse and to jump down into the cockpit of the boat, then she flung open the door of the tiny rear cabin and thrust the two men inside.

"Onto the bunks and beneath the blankets," she cried, "if you both value your eyesight and maybe your lives, and don't even dream of emerging until I give you permission."

The two men followed the young witch's orders, whilst she cowered upon the floor of the cabin protected by an old feather mattress. The three crewmembers only managed to take cover with seconds to spare, for some incredible force suddenly seized hold of the boat and shook it until it appeared in danger of coming apart at the seams.

At the same moment, a brilliant flare of pure white light engulfed the craft. The strange phenomenon was over in seconds, but only Myra's timely warning had saved the three travellers from disaster.

Myra waited for several long minutes before allowing the men to climb from their bunks, and only then did the travellers emerge, taking in their new surroundings in wonderment.

Gone was the dark brick-lined tunnel. Instead, the Bonny Barbara was being carried along by some unseen current through a huge and partly flooded underground cavern whose walls and ceiling were fashioned out of some luminescent blue quartz of incredible beauty. Ahead of the craft was a semi-circle of light growing ever closer by the second, which doubtless marked the exit from this vast subterranean river system.

Myra pointed ahead of the craft.

"Well, gentleman," she said quietly. "Beyond yonder exit lies the Water Realm and the beginning of our journey. Doubtless many trials and adventures lie ahead of us before we return to our home in the village of Elfencot!"

Chapter 2

The current that carried the Bonny Barbara down the subterranean waterway slackened appreciably as the river neared its exit; the craft was barely making headway as it cleared the last jagged outcrop of rock and emerged into the light. It was the strange quality of the light that provided the travellers with their first vivid impression of the new reality. For the sparse rays of sunlight; penetrated a sky that was composed of wave upon rolling wave of crimson cloud had an orange-red appearance that immediately impeded the vision and baffled the intellect of the three newcomers.

The boatmaster's grip upon the tiller tightened convulsively as he fought to control the feeling of panic welling up in his breast, whilst George gave vent to his fears by reciting the beginnings of a half-forgotten prayer that he had first heard whilst taking temporary shelter in some church hostelry. "The Lord is my shepherd, I shall not want..." he intoned gravely, before bursting into a flood of tears, as he strove desperately to contain his terror and come to terms with the strangeness of his new surroundings.

But Myra, the young wisewoman, had often been forced to confront the inexplicable during her years of training in the occult and she remained perfectly calm.

"Take it steady lads," she advised. "Just take your time and let your minds become accustomed to what your eyes are telling you and recall that others have passed this way without harm and they certainly experienced the same kind of doubts and fears you are now feeling."

The two men followed the witch's advice and the crippling sensation of panic gradually subsided as their eyes became accustomed to the orange-red light. Soon they were able to begin making sense of their immediate surroundings.

The Bonny Barbara was riding gently upon the surface of a large lake, whose waters glowed with an all-pervading orange-red hue, an optical effect that was doubtless due to the strangely coloured beams of light constantly penetrating the crimson sky.

The lake, upon which their craft rode, lay at the foot of a huge mountain whose summit was lost in the crimson clouds rolling overhead. At the base of its rocky slopes was the mouth of the river-cavern through which the narrowboat had so recently passed.

Half a mile beyond the bows of their craft, the travellers were clearly able to make out the curving shores of the lake, and they were less than reassured by the realization that the nearby shoreline was occupied by a line of substantial structures, buildings that had obviously been erected by creatures possessing considerable creative ability.

"I wonder who lives in those bloody houses," George mumbled, openly expressing the same fear that was felt by his two companions. "But at least they don't seem over-keen on sailing around in boats," he said, surveying the empty surface of the lake. "Maybe they've no use for them?"

"Aye, there's certainly no craft putting out to meet us," agreed the boatmaster. "But I wonder what kind folk occupy yonder built-up shoreline and..."

"We must find a way of reaching land and take the risk of an unfriendly reception," broke in the wisewoman, "for we need to find the seer of whom our mother spoke. We must find him as quickly as possible, if we are to stand any chance of surviving in this unfamiliar world!"

George, now fully composed, took up one of the long poles lying upon the narrowboat's deck and thrust its point downwards into the waters of the lake. To the newcomers' surprise, the water proved to be little more than two yards deep and the lake also appeared to have a hard, unyielding bottom.

The young boat hand forced a laugh and threw his considerable body weight upon the pole. "This is how we'll shift the old girl," he said. "Two of us men can stand in the stern and push her over towards yonder shoreline without any trouble, whilst Myra steers."

The boatmaster nodded in agreement and climbed upon the roof of the cabin, studying the shoreline minutely for a good ten minutes. He eventually pointed to a spot where there appeared to be a wide gap in the line of waterfront structures.

"That's where we'll make our landfall!" he declared. "The water flowing into the lake from the underground river must make its exit somewhere; I reckon that gap marks the spot where the water overruns into a river or perhaps some kind of navigable waterway. Maybe we can use it as an escape route for the Bonny Barbara, should we receive an unfriendly reception from the inhabitants once we come ashore."

Myra held the tiller, whilst the two men took up their positions high in the stern and began polling the craft towards the gap in the shoreline. Both men were in excellent physical condition, but the work proved to be backbreaking and the narrowboat made only slow progress. They were also forced to take frequent rests due to the oppressive heat. It was during one of these breaks that the travellers witnessed an amazing natural phenomenon.

The crew of the boat were rapidly becoming accustomed to the beams of orange-red light that penetrated the crimson clouds constantly boiling overhead and they unthinkingly assumed that the light was generated by a single unseen heavenly body, doubtless a sun of similar appearance to the one illuminating their native reality. The travellers were therefore extremely surprised when the clouds thinned momentarily to reveal the orbs of five small suns, spaced in an absolutely straight line overhead. The three were able to view the phenomenon for only a few bare seconds before the rolling cloud cover thickened once again and obscured the five strange solar bodies.

The young witch at the tiller was the first to recover from this sudden revelation and she laughed out loud. "Not just one sun, but five to ripen the harvest," she joked.

"I wonder if they also harvest five times the crops in this strange world?" The two crewmen joined in her laughter, but the merriment was short-lived and it had a distinctively nervous edge to it.

The crew returned to the task of polling the craft along, but it required a further four hours of backbreaking labour to bring the Bonny Barbara to within a hundred yards of the shore.

Darryl, it transpired, had been correct in assuming that the gap in the line of waterfront buildings marked the beginning of an exit river, for a ribbon of orange-red water broke from the confines of the lake and passed beneath the remnants of a once-mighty bridge before disappearing into the far distance. The three companions also noticed that all of the riverside buildings were in an advanced stage of disrepair; for the roofs of almost all of the structures had fallen inwards and many of the buildings were no more than piles of broken stones. Nothing moved in the rubble-strewn avenues lying beyond the long waterfront promenade, and the absolute silence that lay over the ruined city suggested that it was completely deserted and had probably been abandoned for long centuries.

George shuddered. "Gawd what a place," he muttered. "I wonder if the ghosts of the dead ever return to the ruins and molest the likes of us who come here to trespass."

"Keep hold of your wits lad!" the young wisewoman answered sternly. "However, my inner eye suggests that we take care, for I do feel that a number of malevolent influences exist in yonder ruins. Yet I also feel that we are in no immediate danger, whilst we continue to lie out here on the water."

She paused. "I think that I would know if it were otherwise, for my occult powers seem to have been strangely augmented since we arrived in this reality and ..."

The witch fell silent, as did her two companions, for they noticed that the sky had suddenly begun to darken and it was obvious that night was almost upon them. It was also apparent that night fell with great rapidity in this strange new world.

"Quickly George," shouted the boatmaster. "Lend a hand and we'll lash two lengths of cable to a couple of the heavy iron bars that are lying amongst our cargo of scrap metal, then we'll chuck em' over the side and we can use them to anchor the boat; for I'm damned if I want us to drift close to them ruins during the hours of darkness!"

Half an hour later, with the narrowboat securely anchored, the three crewmembers retired to the craft's tiny cabin and barred the door with balks of timber.

Darryl had also briefly considered setting a watch in the cockpit of the boat, but he had quickly abandoned the idea, for the darkness in this new reality was like a thick black ink.

A guard would have been completely blind and have added nothing at all to their security.

In addition, he knew that the strenuous physical and mental exertions of the day had brought them all to the point of near exhaustion and it was evident that they needed all of the rest the night would allow. He therefore made a determined effort of will and pushed all of his fears to the back of his mind, concentrating upon cooking a pottage of fresh vegetables on top of the little stove standing in the cabin.

Very soon, the tired travellers were well fed, fast asleep and quite oblivious to any possible dangers that might exist within the utter darkness of the Water Realm night.

The orange-red light of the Water Realm dawn struck with a sudden intensity through the windows of the narrowboat's tiny cabin and roused Darryl from his slumbers.

He thrust aside his blankets and, checking his old pocket watch, learned that night in the new reality had lasted a mere six and a half Earth hours.

The boatmaster peered cautiously through the windows of the craft for any sign of danger, before removing the protective balks of timber from the door and stepping out into the vessel's cockpit. Once again, he carefully perused the nearby ruins for any sign of movement before returning to the shelter of the cabin. Both of his companions were still asleep in their bunks and he decided to let them rest for a little while longer, in order to allow them to recover from the terrible stresses of the previous twenty-four hours.

He stirred up the embers in the stove and added more fuel before setting a pan of porridge to cook upon the rapidly heating hotplate. Soon, the smell of grilling bacon began to permeate the cabin, the tantalizing fragrance quickly coaxing the two remaining sleepers into full wakefulness, and only a little time elapsed before the company were enjoying a leisurely breakfast at the cabin's folding table.

Darryl was the last to push away his empty plate and drain his mug of strong tea.

"Now is the time to make decisions!" he said. "Are we to lie here offshore and await the man who Mother says will meet us and give assistance? Or do we venture ashore and seek out our guide and mentor?"

Myra topped up her companion's mugs with fresh hot black tea.

"Our guide is still a good distance from us!" she said quietly. "The man who is to help us is evidently a seer of great ability, for he reached into my mind at the very moment that I awoke from my deep sleep, but our minds were imperfectly linked and we were able to converse for only a short time."

"Who is he? Where can he be found?" the boatmaster asked anxiously.

"I know very little," the young wisewoman replied. "For my psychic power still has limits. All that I can tell you is that he is approaching us from the direction of the Exit River and he is moving through the ruins with extreme caution."

She paused. "Perhaps he needs to take care! Yesterday, my witch's intuition comforted me and told me to have no fear. Yet I feel that danger now exists, out there, amidst the ruins."

The boatmaster nodded in agreement. "Well then, sister, it's quite evident that our best course of action is to meet with our helper as quickly as possible. That Exit River looks navigable. I suggest that we ride down upon its current and hope to make contact with him. We shall be riding upon the water for most of our journey, but we had best arm ourselves as well as possible, in case we have need to sally ashore."

"Aye, that does appear to be our best course of action, brother," the young witch replied. "And there will be no chance of passing him unawares, for my occult senses will tell me when we are near. Then we can anchor the boat in the safety of the river whilst you and I go ashore to meet him.George can stay aboard and watch for our return."

Darryl swallowed the last dregs of his black tea and stood up. "Well, if we are all agreed, then we had best make a start, but first we'll arm ourselves as best we can, for only fools confront danger empty handed."

The boatmaster buckled the sword Kingslayer to his waist and made sure that the blade was free in the scabbard, whilst George opened a locker and selected a blunt and battered meat cleaver from the tangle of utensils stored within.

"Not much of a weapon," he reflected as he tested the cleaver for balance. "But it will serve to split the skull of anyone who attempts to clamber aboard the Bonny Barbara whilst the pair of you are absent."

Myra took charge of the only firearm which the crew possessed; this was an ancient flintlock fowling piece that had been the property of Robert Littlewood until he had sold the boat and its contents to his younger kinsman. The weapon had seen little recent use, due to the severity of the game laws, and indeed there was only enough powder and shot to load it with a single charge. The three crewmembers then quit the cabin without further delay and prepared to navigate their craft to the mouth of the Exit River.

Darryl and his young boat hand hauled up the makeshift anchors and returned to their labour at the long poles, whilst Myra took up her former station at the tiller. Slowly, the Bonny Barbara began making headway and their progress quickened appreciably as the current from the Exit River began taking hold of the craft. Soon, the toilers were able to ship their poles entirely and rest as the narrowboat passed beneath the remnants of the great bridge and began making headway down the mainstream of the river.

Darryl dispatched his young assistant to the bows of the craft, in order to give ample warning of swiftly running rapids or any other danger to navigation they might encounter, but the current bore them along at a steady walking pace and this portion of the waterway appeared to be free of obstructions as far as the eye could see.

The travellers were able to relax and view their surrounding at leisure. But Myra noticed another strange phenomenon, for the narrowboat was responding readily to every touch of the tiller although the craft was being carried forward by the power of the current alone. No helmsman would have this much control whilst navigating a river in her home reality, she thought before shrugging her shoulders, for this was not the river Mersey and she was no longer on the planet Earth.

As the craft advanced, it became clear that the Exit River was taking them through a district that had once been the city's main docklands area, for abandoned wharves and ruined warehouses lined both banks of the waterway; numerous secondary canals, now largely obstructed by fallen debris, branched out in every direction and having obviously once carried a vast commercial trade to every portion of the city.

"Heaven preserve us!" Muttered the boatmaster, as he viewed row upon row of ruined structures, "yon place would have made the Manchester canal wharves look like some country parcel-stop by comparison. I doubt if the Liverpool docks could have competed for size with this place, at least, when it was occupied and at the height of its prosperity."

The narrowboat proceeded steadily for almost an hour, until Myra suddenly winced and clasped a hand to her forehead.

"Our helper is very near," she said. "It's time to steer over to the right bank and find ourselves a safe and secure mooring."

Darryl took over the tiller and with practiced skill he steered the craft alongside a long jetty that jutted out into the river for a considerable distance. He then ordered George to moor the craft by a single cable, which he secured to the vessel's stern.

"Now lad," he instructed as he prepared to accompany his sister ashore. "Keep a sharp lookout whilst we are gone. If danger threatens, then don't hesitate to cut yonder cable with your cleaver and save yourself. We will rejoin you further down river, if we are alive and able to do so."

Darryl and the young wisewoman strode down the length of the jetty, picking their way through the debris littering the riverside wharf before entering the city proper.

"He's close, very close!" Myra said and pointed towards the remains of a large single storey structure that might once have been a warehouse. "My inner eye tells me that our friend is to be found on the far side of that building!"

The pair advanced towards the structure, but Darryl had now taken the lead with his sword held at the ready, whilst Myra brought up the rear with the loaded fowling piece held in the crook of her arm. The twins had advanced only a short distance when the boatmaster halted and pointed towards a huge doorway that was set in the gable of a nearby building.

"Sister," he said. "Yonder door space must be a good fifteen feet in height. Just look at the width, you could lead a pair of horses through it." He pointed to a number of doorways leading into other nearby buildings and the air whistled through his teeth.

"Can you imagine the size of the people who built this city? Compared to us, they must have been veritable giants."

"Then let us hope that they are as dead as the rest of their city," the young witch replied. "Now let's get a move on," she added impatiently, "for I sense that our friend is extremely close now, but I also feel that he is afraid and I know that we must link up with him as quickly as possible."

Myra pointed toward a door space that was set in the side of a nearby building.

"Come," she said. "Through that door and keep your sword handy."

The pair entered the building and began picking their way across the breadth of an enormous room, occupied by row upon row of stone workbenches; at least they appeared to have been made of stone, for they felt as cold as granite when touched by the hands of the travellers and yet the material had a grained appearance reminding them of English oak. Indeed, the entire building seemed to have been constructed from the same strange material.

"A factory," the boatmaster thought as he threaded his way through the wreckage of the fallen roof. "This place could have been nothing else. But who or what toiled here?"

Myra suddenly halted, gave a sharp cry and clasped her hand to her forehead.

"Oh the terror," she gasped. "Quickly, our friend is in the greatest danger."

She leapt into the lead and ran towards a door-opening that was situated in the far wall of the room, clearing the aperture with a single bound, and Darryl in close pursuit. The pair were brought to a sudden halt by the sight that met their eyes.

The twins had entered a small annex to the main building, a room that had probably served as a factory office, for every wall was occupied, from floor to high ceiling, by rank upon rank of deep stone shelves that had undoubtedly been used for the storage of rolls of parchment and works ledgers.

Midway up the far wall, an old man could be seen precariously clinging to the edge of the shelving with his hands and feet, and he was desperately attempting to evade the clutches of two bizarre and terrifying creatures that were attempting to reach him from the floor below. It was the grotesque appearance of the old man's attackers that brought the couple to a sudden halt.

The two creatures were definitely humanoid in appearance, each having a head and two arms. But there the resemblance ended. For the heads that turned to view the old man's would-be rescuers were both triangular in shape. Huge jawbones occupied the horizontal base-lines and supported the sharply canting cheekbones reaching upwards to the peaks of their sharply pointed skulls. The beings had no necks and their triangular heads swivelled grotesquely above massive muscled shoulders. The creatures' torsos were almost human in appearance, and the whole of their bodies were supported upon powerful muscular legs that obviously enabled their owners to cover long distances without undue fatigue. However, the beings' arms were probably the strangest part of their anatomy, for they were long and supple and divided into three separate segments through the possession of two sets of elbow joints; their claw-like hands were also multi-jointed and doubtless endowed the creatures with great manual dexterity. The appalling vision that confronted the newcomers was compounded in horror by the two pairs of eyes that turned to gaze upon them, for they were set high up in the creatures' triangular foreheads and resembled dark glass orbs, being quite devoid of pupils and irises. Below each pair of eyes were two narrow slits, which presumably served as nostrils, and their terrifying appearance was completed by gaping mouths, set with flat teeth, suggesting that the twin apparitions normally ground their prey rather than ripping it apart.

The two beings had obviously intended to remove the old man from his perch and then dispatch him without the use of weapons, for two long spears stood upright in a corner of the room and their immediate response to the unexpected arrival of the newcomers was to launch themselves forward in an attempt to rend them apart with their many-jointed talons.

The first of the apparitions closed with the boatmaster and attempted to break his neck with a single blow from one of his multi-jointed arms, but Darryl used his boxer's reflexes to sway out of the path of the slashing limb, delivering an upward cut from Kingslayer and opening up the creature's blue-skinned body from crotch to chest. As the apparition fell, the boatmaster saw that the torrent of blood pouring onto the floor along with the creature's intestines was as red as that flowing in his own veins.

Myra, meanwhile, had waited until her opponent was almost upon her and then discharged the fowling piece directly into its face. The creature halted with the left hand side of its head carried away by the impact of the charge of buckshot, but the apparition had not fallen and the young woman moved forward purposefully to club it down with the butt of her weapon. Fortunately, this form of *coup de grace* was not required, for the old man swung down from his refuge with surprising agility, retrieving a crossbow-like weapon from the dust and launching a needle sharp dart into the creature's spine. The monstrosity fell forward with a hissing groan and was dead before hitting the floor.

The old man brushed away some of the dust that had clung to him during his frantic scramble for safety and greeted his rescuers.

"Arr," he grunted. "All be well that end well ... as you folk say ... now we best get to your boat ... pretty quick ... in case these ones we kill got friends nearby."

He pointed to the pair of long spears that had belonged to the dead creatures.

"Good weapons ... bring!"

The three victorious combatants headed for the narrowboat's mooring with all possible speed and the twins were able to take a good look at their new companion as they moved through the ruins. He was short, only about five feet in stature, and clad in a brief loincloth that had been woven from some type of course material. His head and body were quite hairless and his deeply lined features were dominated by a hooked nose that would have done justice to a Bedouin Sheikh. His only possessions appeared to be his crossbow-like weapon and a small skin pouch, both accoutrements being slung over his shoulder and suspended from stout leather thongs. Yet it was his red skin colour that riveted the attention of the travellers.

The man noticed their inquisitive looks and he burst out laughing.

"You ain't seen any red-folk like me before," he stated. "Arr ... but you see plenty now ... all folk in Water Realm coloured like me ... cept' folk from beyond Northern Sea who be mostly white like you and perhaps a few others in distant parts ... you got plenty questions ... you wait until safe on boat."

Once the travellers had reached the safety of the Bonny Barbara they cast off the single mooring and continued their gentle voyage down the Exit River, but now under the directions of their new helper.

"No ... danger now," shouted the old man as he stood quite naked in the bows of the boat and sluiced the filth of his journey from his body with a bucket of river water.

"Hix can't swim ... frightened of deep water so ... can't reach us out here."

He replaced his loincloth and joined the other crewmembers, who were preparing to dine on bread and cheese in the cockpit of the boat. He refused to share their food and chewed with apparent relish upon a fragment of dried flesh from his pouch.

"The Hix," Darryl enquired. "Who or what are they?"

"Arr ... same race as them pair ... we kill back there." The old man struggled to form his next sentence. "De... de ... dea..." He paused and shook his head.

"I speak no Angle for many sun-cycles," he explained and tried again with greater success.

"Dea ... desert dwellers ... the Hix ... most hate water." He paused again and washed down the last morsel of dried flesh with a draught of liquid from a small flask drawn from his pouch.

"My name is Thom!" he continued, "Thom Jak's! ... I be wizard and healer ... in valley called ... Fruitful Stream ... a settlement two darkenings march ... from City of Ancient Dead ... where we kill Hix."

He pointed towards Darryl and his twin sister. "Hetty ... your mother ... my mind friend ... she ask me to protect and council you ... we take this boat to my valley ... there you live until you understand ways of Water Realm."

He looked at them sharply and touched his hooked nose.

"You much to do ... much to learn!"

❦

The Bonny Barbara continued its voyage downriver and the long-abandoned port area was soon left well astern. The craft began passing through what appeared to have been the city's residential suburbs, for the surviving structures were much smaller and less well preserved, with the vast majority being little more than heaps of debris. The mounds were invariability covered by a low growing red moss, which Thom called 'Nulla'. He explained that the plant was the commonest form of none-sentient life in this part of the new reality. A fact that became self-evident, once the last remnants of the City of the Ancient Dead were left far astern, for the Exit River began passing through a vast rolling plain where every inch of ground space was covered by the all-pervading red plant.

The course of the river also became less predictable and the old wizard stationed himself in the bows of the narrowboat in order to give the crew ample warning whenever a rock or shoal-bank hove into view. He also gave the crewmembers adequate warning when it became time to anchor their craft in the middle of a quiet stretch of the river, in preparation for the onset of the inky-black Water Realm night.

Darkness fell and the newcomers cooked an evening meal of salt beef and dumplings before preparing to spend the night in the narrowboat's tiny cabin. However, the old wizard spurned the comforts that the travellers offered to share with him and simply chewed upon another fragment of dried flesh before retiring to sleep upon the open deck.

Darryl stretched out upon his bunk, anxious to gain as much sleep as possible during the Water Realm night. But sleep eluded him for a good hour and he spent the time pondering the responsibilities that were heaped upon his shoulders.

The Water Realm, he knew, was a dangerous place in which to venture. The brutal clash with the Hix had dispelled any doubts that he might have harboured on that score. He also knew that he would have to exhibit firm leadership if they were to survive the dangers that undoubtedly lay ahead. Yet he was dreadfully inhibited by his complete lack of knowledge of the new reality and knowing that every decision he would be forced to make had the potential to bring complete disaster upon the little expedition.

"Three heads are better than one!" he mused, as he tossed in his blankets. "Whenever possible, everyone must be consulted on the best course of action." Even so, he realized that survival for the group would often depend upon the split-second decisions that he would be forced to make when danger arrived without any prior warning. But that resided in the future, for their immediate security now rested in the hands of the little wizard who was sleeping soundly in the bows of the Bonny Barbara.

❧

Dawn broke and the narrowboat continued its voyage downriver. The task of the navigator at the tiller, however, became ever more difficult as the current of the river gathered speed. Sharp rocks often jutted out from the banks and the course of the waterway frequently twisted and turned alarmingly, often catching the craft in dangerous back-eddies causing the vessel to pitch and roll almost uncontrollably.

The nature of the countryside through which the Exit River ran also began changing. The trackless moss covered plain began giving way to a vista of rolling hills and narrow valley's often containing dense groves of trees. Streams sometimes flowed from these wooded glades and poured into the main river, greatly augmenting its flow.

The difficulties of river navigation gradually increased as the day wore on and none of the travellers were disappointed when Thom pointed towards the mouth of a sizeable tributary and told them to steer in its direction.

"That be the way ... to The Valley of the Fruitful Stream," he said. "My home and now yours."

A group of about forty young red-skinned men and women were standing near to the mouth of the stream, and, under the wizard's direction, the three crewmembers prepared a long towrope, which they threw to the people waiting onshore. The shore party immediately grasped the line and began bow-hauling the Bonny Barbara up what appeared to be a large navigable tributary of the main Exit River.

The bow-haulers uttered a low rhythmic dirge that helped them to keep up a steady pace as they executed their arduous task, and thanks to their efforts, the narrowboat made swift progress up the course of the stream.

By midafternoon, the party entered a small valley that seemed to be enclosed on three sides by gently sloping hills. The nulla moss that covered the hillsides was copper coloured and of a finer texture than the similar vegetation covering the plain outside the City of the Ancient Dead.

Groups of strange two-legged creatures, which bore a slight resemblance to kangaroos, could be seen grazing upon this new strain of nulla moss. A few of the animals wandered down to the stream to drink and the newcomers quickly realized that the resemblance to the marsupials was purely superficial; for their heads and the upper portion of their long necks were covered with fine red scales and the lidless eyes, gleaming in their narrow heads, gave the creatures an almost reptilian appearance.

Also, their slender red-coloured bodies were supported upon legs and hips that were certainly bird-jointed and doubtless gave rise to their curious hopping gait, whilst their stumpy forelegs appeared to be only useful for giving support to their forequarters when they bent down to graze upon the bronze nulla moss.

Thom pointed towards the creatures. "Narr," he said shortly. "We breed plenty narr in Fruitful Valley." He waved his hand towards one of the animals whose body was covered with a thick red mat of wool. "Wool narr," he explained, and drew a warm sleeping cloak from inside his travelling pouch.He ran his hand over the soft material. "Warm ... light ... keep you dry ... if you sleep outside on ground ... during rain-time."

The wizard pointed towards another larger narr whose body was covered by a much thinner coat of red hair. "Meat narr ... plenty wool and meat narr ... here in valley ... bronze nulla moss ... here ... good for grazing narr."

Even as he spoke, a larger and more powerful example of the curious species emerged from behind a rock, and the travellers were amazed to see that an adolescent girl was strapped to the creature's back and controlling the creature with apparent ease. The girl wielded a long whip and used it mercilessly to drive back a group of wool narr who were straying away from their fellows. She was obviously controlling her strange mount by the pressure of her knees, for in her left hand she carried a slender javelin with a wickedly barbed head that undoubtedly had the capacity to inflict a terrible wound. Moments later, two young boys, similarly mounted and armed, emerged from behind a hillock and silently observed the passage of the narrowboat.

The old wizard laughed at the perplexity of the newcomers.

"Riding narr swift ... but what you call bird-jointed ... riding narr too weak in the hips to support man-rider ... so children herd domestic narr ... children also watch for Hix."

"Do those demons whom we met in the ruins also attack your people?" Darryl asked.

"No," the old man replied. "Most Hix live in tribes ... far away in Great Western Wasteland ... here just a few families live ... in ruins like City of Ancient Dead ... perhaps steal odd narr for food ... if Hix become too bold ... children kill with javelins."

"Your children are able to kill those monsters?" Myra asked.

"Aye ... but we also lose ... maybe ... one ... two or even three children each time," answered the wizard, with a look of sadness in his eyes. "Myself lose ...one good son ... most here lose same."

The old man moved up into the bows of the craft, and, for a while was lost in his own thoughts and the newcomers were left in no doubt of having inadvertently stumbled upon one of the many painful facets of life in the Water Realm.

The bow-haulers stuck doggedly to their task and the Bonny Barbara continued to make good progress for the stream remained easily navigable for the narrowboat. As the day advanced, the bronze nulla-covered slopes began to recede and eventually gave way to a flat valley bottom. The land in the valley appeared to be extremely fertile, for every inch of soil was subdivided into small fields hedged with banks of nulla moss and the travellers were able to make out numerous homesteads, each one constructed from overlapping planks of rough hewn timber.

The Water Realm night was almost upon them when the bow-haulers finally drew the narrowboat into a small flooded basin and the travellers were able to moor their craft alongside a stoutly built wharf. The sweating haulers then scattered to their various homesteads without waiting for a single word or gesture of thanks from the newcomers.

Thom pointed towards a substantial cottage standing in the centre of the settlement.

"My home," he said. "You my guests ... come ... we eat ... sleep." The wizard, however, noticed the boatmaster's reluctance to leave his craft unattended and laughed. "No worry ... boat," he said, "children always on guard."

The night was dark as pitch by the time the travellers crossed the threshold of the wizard's dwelling and they were immediately greeted by a plump elderly woman who was dressed in a simple shift-like garment, dyed a brilliant shade of green.

Thom introduced them to the woman.

"This Erda, my living mate," he explained and seated them before a warm fire burning in an inglenook-style fireplace. Erda then dipped a ladle into a cauldron hanging over the flames and served them with a thin soup that she distributed in small earthenware bowls.

"Eat slow!" the wizard advised. "Get used ... Water Realm food and water ... take little to begin with ... along with boat food ... then you no get ill."

The travellers consumed their food as instructed and then Erda led them to three self-contained sleeping cubicles occupying the far wall of the cottage. Each of the cubicles contained a simple wooden bedstead, with a base made from strips of leather. Blankets and pillows of soft narrs-wool were also provided in abundance and the newcomers were soon enjoying their first night of rest upon land, since escaping through the depths of the Devils Hill tunnel.

The sudden arrival of the Water Realm dawn signalled the start of many busy days for the trio, for the old wizard immediately instituted a course of intensive schooling that was intended to equip the newcomers with the skill and knowledge needed to survive in this new and strange reality.

Thom Jak's, they quickly discovered, was the wizard and healer of a people who called themselves the 'Narrs-folk' in honour of the creatures whose husbandry formed the basis of their simple agrarian economy; they also discovered that the term 'Folk' was generally used to describe all the inhabitants of the Water Realm of human appearance.

'Folk' was also the name given to the common language that was spoken by most of the human inhabitants of the new reality. From the very first morning, Thom had insisted upon spending long hour's doggedly imparting knowledge of the tongue to his new charges. He repeatedly estimated their chances of survival as virtually nil if they were unable to communicate with other humans.

'Folk,' it transpired, contained numerous elements of the many languages commonly spoken on Earth, and Myra, who was far better educated than either of her two companions, declared that she could recognize words that were of German, French and even Latin origin. The tongue had definitely received important contributions from the many luckless individuals who had stumbled through the curtain and unwittingly entered the new reality. Yet, many of the words and much of the language structure was unfamiliar and had certainly been created within the isolation of the Water Realm.

Thom also said that a few Earth languages were spoken in their entirety by a few persons dwelling in isolated portions of the Water Realm and it was fortunate that he was able to speak to them in 'Angle,' a bastard form of English.

One evening, as they relaxed after a day of intensive study, Thom stated his belief that the entire human population of the Water Realm were descended from the people who had passed through the curtain at various times in the past. His own grandfather, he told them, had been an itinerant knife-grinder called Tom Jackson, who inadvertently wandered through the portal whilst crossing the wilds of the Devil's Tor, some eighty cycles ago. One moment he was passing over the moors above Elfencot, the next instant he found himself wandering along the shores of the great lake near the City of the Ancient Dead.

As their grasp of Folk increased, the newcomers were able to converse and socialize with many of the inhabitants of the village and they sometimes accompanied Thom when he travelled abroad to minister to sick and injured men and animals in the outlying homesteads. In this manner they were able to learn much about the everyday life of the Narrs-folk.

Almost from the beginning, they became aware of the central importance of children in this pastoral society. Infants were introduced to riding narr at birth and were placed upon the beast's backs almost before they were able to walk. As they grew older, they were soundly instructed in the skills required to ride and tend their charges and trained in the casting of those terrible barbed javelins their principle weapon.

Each child eventually took its place in the ranks of the narr-riders, at the age of about six cycles, and retained this position until it became too heavy for the strongest of the creatures to bear upon its back. This generally occurred between the ages of twelve to fourteen, assuming that they survived the attentions of the Hix or were not killed by a crushing fall from their speeding mounts.

The youthful narr-riders were carefully tended by their parents, who lifted their offspring from the backs of their mounts, on completion of each spell of patrol duty, and carefully bathed their tired bodies and massaged them tenderly with liniment and soothing herbal oils. The parents also made sure that their children received adequate rest and the very best food available. Moreover, the young narr-riders were honoured and respected by all of the Narrs-folk, irrespective of village or clan allegiance. Each child knew that it occupied a revered place in the life of its people. The narr-riders inevitably lost this exalted social position once they became unable to ride the narr and were forced to embrace adulthood.

The adults, who made up the vast majority of the population, appeared to be extremely industrious. They carefully tended the narr breeding females who were always housed near the homesteads and constantly waited upon the strange animals as they incubated the clutches of eggs that would hatch into another generation of narr. This was an important task, for almost the whole wealth of that rural society rested upon the wellbeing of the narr-herds. When time permitted, the Narrs-folk also cultivated a variety of seeds, herbs and tubers in the small fields that lay close to their homesteads and contributed to the simple meat and vegetable broth, together with a type of nutty flatbread that formed the people's staple diet. The newcomers often dined upon this simple fare at the tables of these hospitable farmers and they quickly became accustomed to the local food; this was just as well, for the stores aboard the Bonny Barbara were diminishing rapidly and would soon disappear altogether.

The wanderers also learned an important lesson in tact and survival, whilst accompanying Thom during a trip to one of the isolated farmsteads. The group had been passing along a narrow track leading through a patch of woodland, when Darryl suddenly tripped over a length of exposed root and fell forward onto his face.

"Damn that cursed root," he shouted aloud. "The bloody thing could have crippled me."

The old wizard spun round with a glint of anger in his eyes and for a moment it looked as though he was about to strike the boatmaster, but he quickly regained his composure and addressed his three guests.

"These are Thoa trees!" he said quietly, taking hold of a handful of dry twigs. "As yet they are small and of little value, but someday they will grow tall and provide wood for our homesteads and fuel for our fires. Far to the south, there are Thoa trees growing in vast forests that sometimes reach three hundred hands in height; the largest of the Thoa trees produce nuts that can be ground into flour and from this our daily flatbread is made. Some varieties of the Thoa tree give us a sweet fruit that can be eaten fresh, or boiled down and used to produce a syrup, which is the only sweetening agent to be found in the entire Water Realm; also the bark from Thoa trees can be stripped down and pounded to produce a fibre from which ropes, tent-cloth and even garments can be manufactured."

The old man paused.

"In your ignorance, you cursed a gift from the Gods that makes human life in the Water Realm possible. Here we call the tree 'The Holy Thoa' and we give it due reverence. To pour scorn upon the tree is deemed to be a deadly insult to the Gods and to the gift of life itself."

He paused again.

"Do not repeat this mistake. None will forgive you as I have!"

Thom then turned upon his heel and resumed the march as though nothing had occurred.

A little less than three months were destined to pass before the newcomers became reasonably conversant in Folk, the common tongue of the Water Realm, and before Thom declared himself satisfied with their level of competence.

One morning, the old wizard told them that the time had now arrived for them to master the various types of personal combat needed to survive in the many lawless regions of the new reality. He told them that he had dispatched a runner to a distant clan and had begged for the services of a retired mercenary soldier named Noor-Balsam to be their tutor. The retired mercenary, he explained, had served in the armies of a number of the warlords who ruled the lands lying adjacent to the distant Northern Sea and that no other man in the realm of the Narrs-folk had a greater knowledge of weaponry and warfare. The runner had now returned with the news that the retired mercenary had agreed to the wizard's request and would arrive on the following day to begin training the three travellers without delay.

The man who introduced himself to the newcomers at first light on the following morning, was taller and more powerfully built than most of the other Narrs-folk, and walked with a vigorous and purposeful stride that almost belied the fact that he was well over sixty cycles of age. He wasted no time on pleasantries, but had immediately ordered them to parade outside the wizard's homestead, addressing them using the tone of a disgusted drill sergeant.

"May all of the Gods of the Water Realm spare me!" he growled before spitting copiously into the red dirt. "I thought that I had seen some poor material when I trained the infantry of Chief Sorltoft the Slime-eater. But you are the worst I have ever encountered. Nevertheless, I will turn all three of you into formidable fighters, even if it kills me!"

The old mercenary immediately imposed a strict regime of physical exercise upon the newcomers, which, the boatmaster stated, was more arduous than anything that he experienced during his time as a pugilist. Many hours were also spent in becoming skilled in the various types of weaponry that were commonly employed in the Water Realm.

Firearms, they discovered, were never used. Not because the relevant technology did not exist, but because many of the materials needed to manufacture guns and explosive propellants were unavailable in the new reality.

Instead, various traditional weapons of warfare had been constantly refined until they were capable of inflicting slaughter on a vast scale.

The most commonly used weapon in the Water Realm was
a heavy scimitar-like sword called a gill, and a finely worked
example of its type always hung from Noor-Balsam's belt.
Rapiers, daggers and hand-axes were also in regular use and
the old mercenary declared them absolutely indispensable
in the brutal hand-to-hand combats that often took place in
the darkness of the Water Realm night. However, the most
technically sophisticated hand-weapon in common use was the
darter a weapon that resembled an Earth crossbow; it was a
darter that Thom had used to finish off the wounded Hix in
the City of the Ancient Dead. But the Water Realm weapon
differed from its antiquated Earth cousin in having a magazine
containing four deadly bolts and a folding tensioning lever
enabling it to be loaded and discharged with extreme rapidity.
The darter was also extremely light and Myra had no difficulty
in carrying and discharging the weapon. Indeed, she mastered
the weapon to such a degree that Noor-Balsam had made the
girl a present of the darter upon which they practiced. He also
made a sarcastic suggestion to her male companions "that they
might shoot better if they wore skirts instead of trousers!"

The mercenary also introduced them to a spring-loaded
weapon resembling a native Indian blowpipe projecting a tiny
feathered dart that was tipped with a deadly toxin.

"No narrsman would use such a weapon," he declared, but
he also warned them that the 'perm' was a widely used weapon
in some remote parts of the Water Realm, and was the favourite
weapon of the numerous paid assassins who plied their deadly
trade in many portions of the land.

After the passage of some twenty darkenings, the old soldier
consulted Thom and said that Myra would gain little further
benefit from continued military instruction, being already fully
conversant in the use of the darter and the concealed dagger.The
wizard thereafter took the young wisewoman under his wing and
taught her the trade of healing as practiced in the Water Realm.
Myra, being extremely quick and intelligent, rapidly absorbed

the lore of the unfamiliar herbs and medicines that Thom daily used to treat sick humans and ailing farm animals. She also mastered many of the complicated spells and incantations used by the wizard to summon occult energy, thus bringing help and comfort to his unfortunate patients. Occult energy, she quickly realized, could be gathered and concentrated far more easily within the Water Realm than in the bounds of her home reality. Furthermore she was often bewildered by the sheer speed at which her own psychic powers were developing under the wizard's expert guidance. She was also amazed by the fact that she had quickly learned to converse with Thom by the use of telepathy, a skill that had taken her mother long years to acquire.

As the days past, she noticed that the vast majority of the wizard's human patients were pregnant and nursing mothers, and it became obvious that child-bearing in the Water Realm was a far more difficult and dangerous occupation than on the planet Earth. Indeed, the mothers and young children of the Water Realm appeared to run a far greater risk of sickness and premature death even than the unfortunate families who dwelt in the fever-ridden slums of Manchester. She often assisted Thom in the nurturing of farm animals and quickly noted the sharp contrast between the difficulties suffered by birthing mothers, and the comparative ease experienced by the egg-laying narr in reproducing themselves. She was swiftly forced to conclude that the strange environment of the Water Realm was definitely unfavourable to mammalian life forms. The old wizard had readily agreed with her deductions and he drew her attention to the fact that the do-fowl a relative of the Earth-bred domestic duck, plus some small birds and a few minor species of plants and fungi were the only life forms from Earth, to have successfully adapted themselves to life in this portion of the Water Realm.

"But remember child," the old man had warned. "This world is immense, and who can tell what manner of creatures have succeeded in making their homes in its furthest reaches.

It has even been rumoured that a strange blue-skinned people dwell far beyond the Northern Sea, people who ride terrifying creatures with cavernous jaws and six pairs of legs" He had laughed aloud at his own words. "I do not believe they exist, but I don't discount the legend entirely."

Darkening had followed darkening and the young witch's occult powers continued to grow, aided by the strict disciplines imposed upon her by the old wizard, and her senses became so finely attuned that she doubted if any danger could possibly escape detection by her inner eye. In addition, she began developing an almost uncanny skill in predicting events that were due to happen in the near future.

One day, Myra had retrieved the grimoire of Rose Littlewood from her belongings and showed it to the wizard, but the old man has simply shaken his head as he leafed through its pages, for like all of the Narrs-folk, he was completely illiterate.

"I can only enlighten you on one point," he said. "Your mother was wrong in believing this volume to be written in some form of code, for it is mostly scribed in temple script, a type of ancient written language now used only by the priestly sects who dwell to the east. I cannot read a word of it, but it resembles a short prayer-text that I was once shown by a wandering monk who dwelt amongst us for a while, until he insulted one of the narr-riders and got himself speared."

"Perhaps I will strive to read this script," the young wisewoman surmised. "For my inner eye tells me that we must soon leave this hospitable valley and continue our journey far to the south."

"Aye, your mind's eye does not deceive you," the wizard agreed sadly. "You and your two companions will soon be capable of continuing your wanderings beneath the five suns of the Water Realm. Tomorrow we shall hold a feast beneath my roof and Noor-Balsam and I will advise and direct you as best we may. Afterwards, you and your comrades must begin making plans for your journey through the vastness of the Water Realm and my obligation to your mother will be discharged in full."

※

Thom belched and wiped the narrs-fat from his mouth. "Erda, my beloved mate," he said, playfully slapping his wife's ample bottom with the palm of his hand. "The Gods take me if that wasn't the best meal that I have ever tasted. Now let the unseen ones have their portion." So saying, he tore the remainder of the joint from the spit and dropped it into the midst of the fire burning in the hearth. He then turned his attention back to the three crewmembers, who, apart from Noor-Balsam, were the sole beneficiaries of the old couple's hospitality.

"Honoured guests," he began. "Almost half a cycle has passed since you arrived in the Valley of the Fruitful Stream. Now only four and a half cycles remain for you to discover an exit that will allow you to re-cross the curtain and regain the shelter of your own reality. I tell you plainly, I have no idea where this exit portal is located."

He paused.

"However, traditional folktales suggest that it can be found at the foot of a stupendous mountain that stands alone and in perfect isolation, far beyond the waters of the Southern Sea."

The wizard paused again and took a long drink of herb wine from a tumbler standing at his elbow.

"Only the priests, who dwell in the Palace of the Ancient Lore, in the Holy City of Ptah, can furnish you with the necessary information. The journey to Holy Ptah is both long and extremely perilous. Even if you should reach the city in perfect safety you will be required to offer the priesthood some fabulous gift, or render them some inestimable service, in order to win the privilege of questioning those priestly clerics, for their greed and avarice are said to know no bounds."

The old man shook his head. "Even so, you have no choice but to go hence and beg their aid."

Thom laid his hand upon the old mercenary's shoulder.

"Of all the Narrs-folk," he said quietly, "only Noor-Balsam has looked upon the Holy City of Ptah and returned alive to his own land. He will now furnish you with whatever advice he can."

The old soldier cleared a space on top of the dining trestle and unrolled a large map.

"This," he said, "is a map of the Water Realm, or such portions of our world as are generally known to us."

"As you can see," he said, indicating the position of the Valley of the Fruitful Stream with his finger. "We are presently located upon a tributary of the Exit River that runs from the City of the Ancient Dead to its junction with the Great Life River, certainly the largest and most important waterway in the whole of our world."

He swept his hand across the face of the map.

"The Great Life River is connected to the Northern Sea and continues southwards until it meets with a similar stretch of water that is located far to the south."

The mercenary pointed again with his finger. "Here is Holy Ptah, standing on the banks of the Life River at approximately the midpoint between the two great seas."

Darryl peered at the map with interest.

"Where exactly does our own Exit River connect with this Great Life River?" he asked.

"Here is where the waters unite," answered the old soldier and he pointed to a river junction, that lay at no great distance from the place where the Life River met the Northern Sea. "Nearby lies the great trading city of Calar... Calar of the Mighty Walls. Jarl is the prince of Calar and rules over a city that is renowned for the size of its markets and the cunning of its many merchants. At Calar, the narrs-wool from our western plains is exchanged for Thoa flour, sweetener and also the metal products that we cannot produce for ourselves."

Noor-Balsam took a mighty draft from his tankard of herb wine and then resumed his speech.

"Yes, my friends, to Calar come the white-skinned people who dwell beyond the Northern Sea. They exchange their fine iron and timber for pretty slave girls and the like. Aye, rich is the city of Calar and so are its merchants, who travel the length and breadth of the Water Realm in search of profit."

The old soldier ran his finger from a circle on the map, marking the position of the city of Calar, to a huge rolling plain lying upon the eastern side of the Great Life River.

"This plain is the home of the Saxmen tribes who dwell under the stern rule of their brutal warlords; here chaos and constant warfare prevail. Once, long ago, the Saxmen crossed the Great Life River and put Calar to the sword and the torch. Afterwards, the citizens of Calar surrounded their city with walls of enormous height and strength and garrisoned it with many fighting men. In addition, the princes of Calar periodically carried fire and slaughter into the lands of the Saxmen to keep down their burgeoning numbers.

"Forty cycles ago," he mused, "I took service as a mercenary in the army of Prince Jarl's grandfather who was planning a great incursion into the Saxmen lands. "Arr," he growled. "For five terrible cycles, we marched and counter-marched through the territory of the Saxmen and countless were the numbers of people that we butchered, until we finally returned home and celebrated our triumph in the streets of Calar."

He paused again and drank deeply from his tankard. "It was during the fourth year of that frightful campaign that I gazed upon the shining walls of Holy Ptah for the one and only time, although it was from a distance, for no body of troops are permitted to venture close to the holy city." He sighed. "How brightly the rays of the five suns shone from the polished yellow metal of the city walls! Never shall I forget the wondrous way the bright sunlight glinted in the waters of the great protective moat; a body of water fully a thousand paces wide that surrounds the entire city and is said to be inhabited by terrible flesh-eating monsters and other frightening creatures…"

"But what lies beyond the City of Ptah and the plains of the Saxmen?" Myra asked.

"The Empire of the Kaa-Rom lies to the south," the mercenary answered, "of which I know little; however, to the east, far beyond a mighty belt of Thoa forest, are situated the barren wastelands of the Hix where none may venture and return alive."

The old fighting man slammed his empty tankard down upon the top of the trestle with an air of finality. "This is all that I can tell you," he said. "Further knowledge you must gain from others!"

The wizard refilled his guests' tankards with wine and turned his attention to the three travellers. "My friends, only one course of action lies open to you if you seriously wish to regain your own reality. You must re-embark upon the craft that brought you to this world, and then you must navigate down our little stream and then the Exit River until you reach the city of Calar. You must then sail down the Great Life River until your craft lies under the walls of Holy Ptah and somehow persuade the priests to furnish you with the help that you will need to cross into your own world."

He looked into the eyes of each of the travellers in turn. "I repeat. No other course of action lies open to you!"

George was the first of the newcomers to reply to the wizard's suggestion and made no attempt to disguise his fear and apprehension.

"In God's name," he breathed. "How can anyone possibly survive a journey through lands and peoples as barbarous as those our armsmaster has just described?"

"Simply by remaining upon the waters of the Life River," the wizard answered.

"The first law of the Ancient Lore, imposed by the priests of Ptah upon pain of death, states that no king or chieftain may interfere with, claim or control, or in any way attempt to impose his jurisdiction over the traders who navigate the waters of the Life River. Nor must traders who come ashore be molested unless they stray over a thousand paces from the bank!"

The old man paused and drew breath. "Commerce is necessary for human survival in the Water Realm and the high priests of Ptah will not have it interrupted by over ambitious warlords. However, pirates and thieves desperate enough to break the priests' lore are said to be a constant menace."

"Do the craft which navigate the Life River proceed under sail?" the boatmaster inquired, anxious to gain as much knowledge of navigational matters as possible.

"No," broke in the old mercenary, "shipping movement is assisted by the fact that the current of the Great Life River flows in both directions. From the North Sea towards the south, it flows close to the western shore. Whilst the current from Southern Sea hugs the eastern bank until it reaches the waters of the Northern Sea."

The boatmaster shook his head and laughed in disbelief."A river that flows in both directions! I've seen some strange things since I took refuge here, but I cannot believe that any river can behave in such a bizarre manner!"

The wizard smiled.

"Not a river that follows the laws of nature perhaps, but many consider that the Life River was a product of the very same people who built the City of the Ancient Dead. Yet who under the five suns will ever know the full truth of it?"

The old man topped up their tankards.

"Your boat, the Bonny Barbara was never built for service upon fast-flowing rivers, for the craft is far too long and narrow on the beam to be of any use in choppy waters. However, your boat can be adapted for use on our Water Realm rivers by having airtight outriggers fitted to the hull to widen its beam. Security would also be improved if the canvas sheets protecting the cargo hold of your boat was replaced with a deck made of stout Thoa planking with sealed hatches for access. Our village carpenter and his two assistants are perfectly capable of undertaking the task, but it will take a good twenty darkenings to complete. The work must begin immediately, for the season of rains will soon be upon us and you must reach Calar before the Exit River becomes a raging torrent."

Thom emptied his tankard at a single gulp and slammed it down upon the top of the trestle with an air of finality.

"Let us sleep," he said, "for there is much to do before the Bonny Barbara rides the waters to Calar!"

The wizard's household rose early on the morning after the feast, and preparations for the narrowboat's departure began at once. The first task that Thom and the three travellers undertook was to carry out a complete examination of the Bonny Barbara and to compile an inventory of the cargo that had been taken aboard the craft at Ashton-Under-Lyne, for delivery to Yorkshire. A single hour sufficed to carry out an examination of the narrowboat's hull. Afterwards, George and Darryl drew back the heavy canvas sheets protecting the contents of the hold from the elements and they followed the old wizard down into the body of the craft.

Thom ran his hands over the long sections of worn-out railway line that had been destined for smelting in some Yorkshire furnace and nodded in approval.

"Good iron." He muttered, "Very good iron. There is enough value in this metal to pay the carpenter's fee and to keep you in provisions until you reach the city of Ptah, or even as far as the Southern Sea."

The wizard ventured further into the depths of the narrowboat's hold and he tripped over a pile of twisted metal sheets that been salvaged from the roof of some old parish church. He cast aside several lumps of lead and then he paused to stare intently at the remainder of the mangled sheets.

"Copper," he cried excitedly, pulling out sheet after sheet of the material. "Enough to ransom a dozen chieftains if I be any judge!"

"Aye, there was a bit of copper amongst that scrap lead that we took aboard," George observed. "But I didn't think it had that much value."

Thom waved them up into the light of day and took a tiny disc of copper from his pouch.

"This is how copper is utilised," he said. "Copper is scarce and very precious in the Water Realm, and discs, such as this, are the common means of exchange between people. We simple narr-herders have little need of it, but down in yonder hold you have a treasure worth thousands of these discs!"

He grasped the boatmaster's hand. "This metal may prove to be your salvation," he said. "For you have easily enough wealth in that hold to bribe the Priests of the Ancient Lore and gain their assistance."

The wizard paused for a moment in thought.

"My friends, the best way of protecting your wealth is to hide it away from the eyes of those who may wish to rob you. I suggest that we instruct the carpenters to seal this precious metal in a secret compartment in the bottom of the craft; let it lie there unseen until you dock in the city of Ptah and make ready to approach those greedy priests!"

"A good beginning," mused the wizard, as he climbed out of the hold and brushed away the grime. And he quietly resolved to sacrifice a pair of fat narr to the Goddess of Fortunate Occurrences and to dedicate the offering in the name of his three young guests; for he knew the travellers would need all the celestial assistance they could muster, if they were to overcome the fearful trials that lay ahead.

The village carpenter and his assistants were soon hard at work on the Bonny Barbara and day after day the sound of hammers and saws echoed through the hamlet, whilst the travellers made the final preparations for their journey.

Myra, under the direction of the old wizard, packed all manner of herbs and charms into skin bags and stowed them in a small cabin erected by the carpenters in the bows, for the young wisewoman had complained about her lack of privacy and the gross overcrowding in the craft's existing accommodation. She also began compiling her own grimoire, and the young wisewoman spent long hours recording all the wisdom and occult knowledge the old wizard was prepared to divulge. Indeed, she knew this to be necessary, for her newly acquired gift of foresightedness had left her in no doubt that her witch-skills would often be called upon to save her own life and that of her travelling companions.

Meanwhile, Darryl and the young boat hand completed their military training under the stern direction of the old mercenary. The pair became perfectly accustomed to running, stalking and fighting in the metal-studded leather tunics and trousers, together with a stout iron helmet that served to protect most Water Realm warriors during combat.

Darryl's skill with the sword Kingslayer became almost uncanny and the weapon's razor-sharp blade hissed through the air with frightening speed upon the occasions when Noor-Balsam ordered him to attack a row of stout practice targets. He also augmented his already considerable boxing skills by receiving instruction in many of the unarmed combat methods that were in common use within the Water Realm.

"What a prince's champion you would make!" the old soldier had remarked, in grudging praise after a particularly gruelling training session, "for I declare that few warriors could face you in single combat and survive the encounter."

George also became skilled in weaponry and he developed into a deadly marksman with the longbow. However, he professed no great liking for either the sword or spear and he chose to wield a long-handled war-axe, a weapon that promised to utilize the enormous bodily strength that he had developed under the old mercenary's brutal regime of physical training.The young boat hand also retained the old meat cleaver he found on the narrowboat. The implement-cum-weapon was now sharp and lovingly polished and could always be seen hanging from his belt.

One morning, as the modifications to the Bonny Barbara'were nearing completion, the old soldier appeared on the training ground and called out to the two boatmen who were practicing marksmanship with a pair of darters.

"Rest yourselves!" he cried. "Your training is now over and you are both ready to face the perils of your journey. Aye, and may the Gods receive the spirits of your enemies, for they will surely die swiftly beneath your steel."

He paused. "I shall return to my clan-folk without further delay, for my work here is completed. But first I will present you with gifts and give you your war-names--that is my right as your tutor."

Noor-Balsam unfastened a narr-skin bag, producing a small circular shield, made from hardened leather, with a razor-sharp iron spike protruding from its central boss.

"This target is called 'Gut-ripper'," he said, handing the shield to the boatmaster.

"I carried it throughout the long wars against the Saxmen barbarians and six enemies have had their guts split upon yonder spike. I pray that it will serve you as well!"

He laid his hand upon the boatmaster's shoulder. "I name you Black Darryl, for no title that I can bestow will fit you better than the name you have already won in your own reality."

He turned to George and handed him a tiny dagger with an inch-long flattened blade.

"Hide it in your stocking," advised the old mercenary. "Use it to cut open the jugular vein of an unsuspecting guard, should you ever have the misfortune to be taken prisoner."

Once again he paused and placed his hand upon the young man's shoulder.

"Your war-name is Twin-axe. A name that celebrates the two weapons that you will wield in battle, the long-handled skull-smasher that rests upon your shoulder and its deadly helper that forever hangs from your waist-belt."

"Finally," he said. "I will give you the name of a man who dwells within Calar of the Mighty Walls, a man who will give you assistance, should the need arise. He is Ali son of Grom, a whore-master who can be found in the Street of Women, beneath the sign of The Crimson Nipple. He is an old comrade from the wars who owes his life to my skill with the sword."

Without saying another word, the old mercenary spun upon his heel and disappeared into the gathering mist.

❧

Three darkenings later, the modifications to the Bonny Barbara'were completed to the satisfaction of the boatmaster and the old wizard. A further day was required to provision her and also to take onboard a hundred bales of pure narrs-wool, which Darryl had agreed to deliver to a trusted merchant in Calar; the fine wool that would be exchanged for the Thoa flour ensuring that the hospitable villagers would not go short of bread during the following cycle. Thom had also suggested to the travellers that if they were stopped and questioned during their voyage to Calar, they would be well advised to claim to be Northland merchants who had business to transact upon the Exit River, for the Northlanders were as white-skinned as the three crewmembers of the narrowboat.

Three narrsmen, who knew the river route to Calar, were also persuaded to serve aboard the craft, but only as far as the great market-city and no further. The boatmaster wondered how the extra hands could be housed within the craft's tiny cabin, but Thom Jak's laughed and stated that narrsmen required only a simple square of canvas for shelter. Finally Darryl breathed a sigh of relief and declared the expedition to be fit and ready to sail.

A great feast was held at the travellers' expense, on the night before the narrowboat departed, and many a fat narr and much wine disappeared down the throats of the friendly clansmen. The following morning, almost six Earth months after their arrival in the Water Realm, the crew of the Bonny Barbara'said their final farewells to Thom the wizard and the hospitable population of the Valley of the Fruitful Stream to embark upon the next stage of their great adventure.

Chapter 3

H etty stepped out of the old wooden bathtub and began towelling herself vigorously in front of the kitchen fire; then, with her body tingling from the friction, she strode across the room and carefully took stock of her appearance in the mirror that hung from the wall.

Her flowing red hair, still damp from the bathwater, was lustrous and entirely free of the slightest hint of grey. Her features, she noted, were still pleasantly rounded showing few of the marks associated with early middle age, but her fingers touched a few tiny wrinkles in the corner of her eyes, an inevitable result of the terrible mental effort needed to pass the narrowboat, and its youthful crew, through the portal and into the Water Realm. She allowed her hands to move downwards, over her full and perfectly formed breasts, then gently over her tightly muscled stomach, until they came to rest alongside her generously curved hips.

The witch smiled with satisfaction, for she knew that she could still pass as a woman in her late twenties or perhaps thirty on one of her worst days. She viewed her prominent nipples with their generous crimson aureole and then lowered her gaze to the gently curved Mount of Venus, which nestled between her thighs and felt sure of her ability to use the power of sexual attraction to bend men to her will, if needs must. Indeed the wisewoman was quite sure that she would be forced to use all the attributes in her possession, both mental and physical if she was to succeed in penetrating the seedy underworld of Manchester and find unquestionable proof of her son's innocence.

Six long months had passed since that terrible day when she had torn open the curtain allowing her children to escape the clutches of the constabulary. She shuddered in remembrance at how she had been forced to crawl back to the shelter of her cottage in a state of complete exhaustion and the subsequent weeks of rest and relaxation needed to rebuild her strength to fully regain her occult powers.

Jenny Bowyer, she reflected, had been of considerable help to her during this unavoidably long period of recuperation.

Jenny was the youngest daughter of Lill Bowyer, a wisewoman who practiced her craft in a secluded hamlet deep in the Forest of Dean. Hetty and Lill were mind-friends of long standing and frequently communicated with each other by means of their occult skill.

Hetty, still suffering from the debilitating effects of the curtain-opening ritual, had summoned up the dregs of her mental strength and begged her friend to dispatch one of her many daughters to assist her in looking after the sick of the district, until she herself was fully recovered. Jenny had duly arrived, after a long rail journey, and had immediately taken over the burden of caring for the wisewoman's patients.

The girl was hardly turned fifteen and still lacked most of the occult powers of her witch-mother, but she had a keen brain and had already acquired a deep knowledge of herbal medicine almost equivalent to that of the wisewoman. In addition, her nursing skills had won the gratitude and admiration of all the patients she had attended.

Jenny had recently agreed to remain in Hetty's service indefinitely, an arrangement that greatly satisfied the wisewoman, for Hetty knew that she would be absent from Elfencot for quite long periods, due to her resolve to dwell in Manchester and establish a completely new identity amongst the less than respectable portion of the city's populace. For the witch knew that buried deep amidst the mire of pickpockets and thieves, ale-house masters and brothel keepers, dwelt the people who would lead her to her son's enemies.

Hetty had made the girl party to most of her plans, for she relied upon Jenny to protect her interests in Elfencot, and she had even hinted at the terrible secrets lying hidden beneath The Devil's Tor. But she knew that the girl would divulge nothing to any stranger, not even under torture or the threat of death, for she had ensured the girl's silence by making her take the witch's blood oath and the wisewoman knew that no power on earth could force the girl to open her lips.

Even now, Jenny was away visiting a cottage on the high fells, in the faint hope that her herbal skills would save the life of an old stockman who was suffering from a chronic lung infection, whom young Doctor Smithson had predicted would be stone dead by morning.

The wisewoman entered her bedroom and, after covering her nakedness with a woollen robe, began packing a few personal belongings and some warm clothing into a well used carpet bag. After a while, she looked at the face of the clock on the mantelpiece that informed her it was almost ten in the evening.She hoped against hope young Jenny would be able to return home before morning, for she desperately wished to bid farewell to the girl and give her a few last minute instructions, before she departed for Manchester aboard a heavily laden narrowboat that was moored alongside the nearby towpath for the night after working its way through the length of the great tunnel.

Hetty had planned to spend a few more days with the girl before journeying to Manchester, but the previous night, Thom, the wizard of the Narrs-folk, had thrust his mind through the curtain dividing the two realities, and informed her that the Bonny Barbara had now departed upon its voyage into the heart of the Water Realm. The news had immediately galvanized the wisewoman into action, instantly deciding to depart upon her quest at the soonest possible opportunity.

The wisewoman had barely finished packing her bag, when she heard the back door bang, sending a sudden blast of ice-cold air sweeping through the cottage, for it was now mid-February and the outside temperature was only a little above freezing.

Hetty hugged the robe around her body and re-entered the kitchen in time to see a tiny hooded figure splaying itself in front of the kitchen fire in an effort to catch the remaining heat from the dying embers.

"The fates have mercy on you, girl. You're frozen to the bone!" the wisewoman exclaimed as she stirred up the ashes and threw more wood upon the fire.

"Did they not send one of the young herdsmen with you, to see you safely down from the fells?

"No, mistress, they did not," Jenny replied in a rich and melodic voice that belied her youth and diminutive appearance. "The old man's sons said something about going after stray sheep at first light, least ways, I managed to keep their father alive with my strengthening potions until the hot poultices had done their work; I reckon he'll live out this winter and a few more besides, I shouldn't wonder."

Hetty frowned. "Those two lads won't have thanked you for keeping them out of their inheritance, so it's no small wonder that yonder pair of scoundrels left you to struggle home through the cold."

The wisewoman helped to unfasten the heavy cape and from its voluminous folds emerged a tiny girl who could scarcely have been more than five foot in height, even standing in her studded boots. She was dark-haired and her face, like the remainder of her body, was extremely thin and this tended to give her features a slightly mousy appearance. Yet piercing blue eyes suggested that the girl possessed a sharper than average intellect.

The girl put her right hand into the pocket of her plain woollen gown and drew out two florin pieces, which she offered to Hetty.

"Got paid, Mistress, I cornered one of the lads and said, 'How it would be a pity if some mischievous spirit was to enter his bed and put blight on his private parts.' He couldn't part with his silver quick enough!"

Hetty laughed. "Keep the money lass," she said. "You've earned it right enough. Now Jenny, my girl, tomorrow I shall depart aboard yonder stone-boat and you'll be left here quite alone. I know the sick of the district will be perfectly safe in your hands. But I council you to be wary of strangers, for you do not possess the inner eye that enables me to separate friends from enemies. So treat all newcomers with suspicion. If folks ask you to state the reason for my absence, then always remember to say that I have departed from the district in order to nurse a sick relative."

She paused. "Tomorrow I will be gone lass, but the skill of reading and writing we both possess has fortunately given us the means of contacting each other, should it become necessary. It will be a simple matter to post a letter to you from Manchester, and I will eventually send you a secure postal address enabling you to reply in confidence.

"Even so, lass, you must be careful to read and then destroy all my correspondence, only giving your own letters to the old postmaster in the village and to none other. Remember that my very life may depend upon your diligence."

The girl leaned forward and embraced the wisewoman. "Have no fear, Mistress," she said. "Everything will go well here in Elfencot, for I was not born lacking between the ears and the oath that I swore to you will hold me securely in your service. Now Mistress, please retire to your room, for dawn will presently arrive and you will have a hard day ahead of you upon the morrow."

※

The hour was well past midnight and the weather was bitterly cold when Hetty arrived at the door of her brother's cottage near Ancoats, and young Jenny's words had proved to be perfectly correct when she had prophesied that a hard day lay in store for the wisewoman.

The day had started gently enough, for Hetty had been able to spend the entire morning within the heated cabin of the stone-boat, as the craft worked its way down the Marquis of Buckly's navigation and onto the line of the Peak Forest Canal. By early afternoon, however, the temperature had fallen drastically and the thin skin of ice that lay upon the surface of the canal had thickened alarmingly, reducing the craft's progress to a bare crawl. The wisewoman had intended to remain aboard until the boat had tied up alongside the main wharf in Ashton-Under-Lyne, but her patience had finally run out by late afternoon, as the vessel was approaching the outskirts of the town. She had chosen to step ashore under cover of the gathering darkness, hoping the night would shield her progress from prying eyes. The remainder of her journey to Ancoats had been a difficult and slow hike; for Hetty had used paths and quiet back lanes as far as possible in an effort to avoid human habitation. However, this extra measure of security had inevitably added miles to her journey, contributing greatly to the late hour of her arrival.

Robert Littlewood responded immediately to the sharp tapping on his bedroom window and Hetty was soon comfortably seated in the old waterman's kitchen with a glass of dark navy rum in her hand.

The old man stirred up the ashes of the fire and placed a pot of soup to warm on the hob before addressing his sister.

"I've been expecting you to arrive here anytime during the past few weeks!" he said. "For I know you well enough lass, and I expected you to travel to Manchester to seek redress for your son's situation; you can be rest assured that I will do everything in my power to help."

But Hetty shook her head.

"I tell you plainly, Robert," she replied. "I have no stomach for exposing my own brother to needless danger. All I ask is that you give me all the information you possess on those villains who branded my son a common murderer. Then I'll quit your roof, this very night, and you'll not set eyes on me again until this business is over and done with."

The waterman looked slightly relieved when he heard his sister's statement.

"I must admit, lass, I was far from looking forward to crossing swords with some of the worst characters hereabouts, but I did take steps to discover as much as possible about the folk who may have had a hand in your son's undoing. Take yon Stovepipe Arkwright, him that finished up dead. I can vouch for the fact that he differed not one whit from a thousand other small cheapskates who scratch a living by fetching and carrying for fish far bigger than themselves."

He paused.

"True enough, Stovepipe might well have planned that ambuscade at Hells Corner simply to pay your son back for the rough handling that he received earlier in the day. But why should he care? After all, a quick dustin' from some irate client must have been a risk-in-trade to a small no account creature such as Arkwright."

Robert lit his pipe and drew in a lungful of smoke.

"No sister," he continued. "You can be sure that a far bigger man was standing behind him and pulling the strings that made him jump about. I reckon that man is Albert Pike, the gymnasium owner and boxing promoter!

"Young Darryl, if you recall, flatly refused to take part in a private contest with Silas Oldshaw's pet bare-knuckle fighter and you can bet your life that Pike stood to lose plenty of cash if he failed to stage the meeting. Aye, and it was no secret that Darryl only fought to pay of the dept upon his boat; so it's quite possible that Pike somehow discovered that the lad would be carrying most of his cash on the day that he was attacked, and ordered Stovepipe to organize the robbery as a means of driving Darryl back into the prize ring."

"There could well be something in what you say," the wisewoman admitted. "But can you really believe that a substantial man of business, such as Albert Pike, would take the risk of playing the felon, simply to regain the services of a part-time pugilist, when a score of other competent fighters could be hired in his place?"

Robert blew a cloud of blue tobacco smoke towards the ceiling.

"Perhaps he had good reason to do so, lass," he replied. "Black Darryl was becoming a well-fancied boxer in the Manchester halls and some rich sporting toffs were beginning to wager heavily on your son. Pike might have thought the lad was capable of earning him a tidy amount of brass and it seems that yon bugger can use all the cash that he can lay his hands upon, if my information is correct!"

The old waterman laid aside his pipe and filled a bowl with the hot soup that was now bubbling on the hob.

"I have a mate of mine working as a drayman for one of the larger breweries," he said, handing her the steaming bowl. "Those draymen get all over the city in order to do their deliveries and they see plenty of what's going on. They also do plenty of talkin' with potmen and landlords and the like. Well, that mate of mine tells me that a man called Joe Pasco, a fella who used to run a small pub in Bury, has recently set up in a fair way of business in Manchester. The man has bought two commercial inns and a large eating house close to the Cotton Exchange, a place where the better-paid clerks often take their midday meals. Recently, the man has spread his wings even further and has opened up a new combined public house and music hall at a spot near Prussia Street, about midway between the Rochdale Navigation and the Lancashire and Yorkshire railway station."

He paused. "The place is called The Cleopatra and it's reckoned to be patronized by a mixture of well-to-do rakes and groups of young clerks doing the town on payday."

He paused to relight his pipe.

"Yon Pasco is Albert Pike's brother-in-law, him being

married to Pike's sister Mildred. But the draymen say that Albert Pike's always about the place and that Pasco, himself, is no more than a puppet. Think now, sister, if Pike's stood paymaster for all these new investments; then its small wonder that he's being forced to milk all the profit that he possibly can from fighters such as Darryl."

Hetty nodded. "There could be much in what yon drayman says," she replied. "That boxing agent certainly appears to be more than he seems. Now, please tell me everything that you know about that giant bruiser who helped Stovepipe to attack my son, and have you identified the girl who led him away?"

Robert shook his head.

"I've discovered nothing. The ground might well have opened up and swallowed the pair of them."

Hetty stood up and laid her hands upon her brother's shoulders.

"I can never thank you enough for the help that you have afforded my son. But your relationship to Darryl and myself could put you in great danger. It would be best if you quit the district for a while until matters are satisfactorily resolved."

The old waterman laughed. "Well, I'll have no problem in letting out my cottage for a few months, and the coinage earned will take me to some secluded portion of the canal system where no one will find me in a hundred years."

The wisewoman kissed her brother fondly upon the cheek.

"Once again, I give you my thanks. Now I must rest a while, for I must depart well before dawn!"

*

The wisewoman was tired and footsore, for she had quit Robert's cottage about two hours before dawn, and the long walk into Manchester had given her ample time in which to digest the full significance of her brother's words.

Albert Pike was implicated in her son's downfall. Of that she was sure. Although the manner of his involvement still mystified her. Yet, even as she trudged through the dark streets of the city, she became ever more convinced that the fight promoter held the precious key that could unlock the deepest secrets of the whole affair. She had quickly realized that nothing would be gained by confronting the man openly; she had resolved to find employment in some part of his business empire and patiently ferret out the proof of her son's innocence from within. Dawn had found the witch standing outside one of Pasco's commercial hotels, but this hostelry, like its sister establishment that was situated only a few streets away, had a very unwelcoming feel. This had warned the wisewoman to avoid the place like the plague and she hurried across Manchester to her alternative point of entry, namely the solid-looking eating house called 'Masterson's Pie and Pudding Emporium,' having a much more welcoming feeling.

"Nothing ventured, nothing gained!" she muttered to herself as she followed a narrow alleyway leading her into a substantial courtyard lying to the rear of the establishment. Hetty knocked vigorously upon the door of the restaurant's kitchen and her summons was answered by a burly man who wore a blue striped apron and casually cleaning a bloodstained meat cleaver with a piece of linen rag.

Hetty bowed her head. "Please sir," she began. "I am in desperate need of work, washing, scrubbing, anything...."

The man abruptly curtailed her plea. "Come on in, wench, for today must be your lucky day! One of my kitchen hands got knocked down by a cab on her way to work this morning and it's left us short of help."

He drew her into the kitchen and pointed towards a bench, where a dark-haired and rather slightly built girl was busily rolling dumplings from a mound of suet dough.

"Wash your hands and put on a clean pinny and give Mary-Helen a lift with the dumplings. But remember, no talkin' at all. I won't have it in my kitchen!"

Hetty began rolling dumplings as fast as she was able and laid them out on the floured trays that were periodically removed by a male cook. As she worked, she was able to steal a few swift glances to familiarize herself with her new surroundings that at first glance, resembled a scene from some madhouse.

The kitchen was not large, being about thirty feet square, but it was packed with workbenches and sinks, at which a score of women worked without pause and where puddings, pies and stews were constantly being made ready for cooking. The far wall of the room was completely dominated by the long coal-fired range, where Masterson's much vaunted pies were baked; together with the bread cobs and jacket potatoes that satisfied the hunger of the young clerks who laboured in the nearby offices and warehouses. On the top of the long range stood a row of copper pots, in which simmered the hundreds of beef puddings and many of the suet dumplings the wisewoman was now helping to prepare.

At the very end of the range stood a massive cauldron of shredded cabbage that bubbled endlessly and filled the kitchen with its acrid fragrance.

After about an hour, the mound of suet dough that had stood upon the top of the workbench had disappeared entirely and Mary-Helen led the witch over to a sink standing in a distant corner of the room. The two women began washing up the discarded pie tins casually flung in their direction by the sweating cooks who laboured at the ovens.

The dark-haired girl leaned over and began talking quietly to her new helper.

"Don't worry yourself, lovie," she said in broad Cockney accent. "Mr Simister can't see us in this corner, so bugger him and his no talkin' rule. Me name's Mary-Helen Jones, but most folks just call's me Marsie 'cept for that gafferman. But he's not such a bad old cove is Simister, for all his stuck-up chapel ways. Even he needs to come to heel when the owner shouts, for he has to make a livin' like the rest of us; him with nine hungry young mouths to feed at home."

She laughed quietly. "Me. I was born and bred in Bermondsey, London, but I took the train north, about a year ago, after me fella started beating me about something awful. He was threatening to put me on the game after he got sacked and blacklisted from the docks."

Marsie chuckled. "I reckon scrubbing pie tins ain't so good, but it beats havin' to flog me arse for a tanner a go to them bloody stinkin' fish porters over on Billingsgate market."

She laughed again. "Well girl, if we gets done with this washing up, then we might get the chance to have a good chinwag, for we usually gets a break once the waiters start serving the first of the customers."

The two women continued washing up kitchen utensils and to Hetty's inexperienced eye, it appeared that the mad confusion in the kitchen could get no worse. However, a little before midday, a group of white-coated waiters and waitresses suddenly burst into the kitchen and began shouting out their customers orders to the sweating cooks; the cooks immediately responding by loading the dining room staff's serving trays with bowls and plates of steaming food.

"No break today!" Simister shouted above the din. "The dining rooms near full already and the toffs are still flooding in through the front door. So you must all grab a bite of food and a drink of tea as you work!"

"Aw Christ," Marsie' groaned in response to the gaffer's words. "No time for a moment's rest, only more piles of dishes to wash."

Soon, heaps of dirty crockery began joining the used pie tins in the sink and the two women were hard pressed in keeping up with the demand for clean plates and kitchen utensils.

The clock on the wall struck one o'clock and the chaos in the kitchen continued unabated, with the overworked operatives pausing only for a few seconds to swallow some broken pie and wash it down with a mouthful of black tea.

The clock struck two and the waiting-on staff began entering the kitchen at a rather more leisurely pace as the clerks in the dining room began returning to their places of work.

By half past three, the women at the sink had cleared the backlog of dirty crockery and were ordered to move across the kitchen to assist some other workers who were washing and preparing the vegetables that would be needed on the following day.

Afterwards, they scrubbed down the workbenches until they were perfectly clean and their last task of the day was to swill down the stone-flagged kitchen floor with buckets of boiling water mixed with strong washing soda.

It was well past seven in the evening before Simister declared himself satisfied with their day's endeavours and dismissed his tired kitchen staff to their homes and families.

The gaffer walked over to Hetty, who was putting away the mops and buckets in an outside closet.

"You worked well enough today, lass," he commented, "you can count on the skivvying job as being yours, if you still want it. But first tell me a bit about yourself, for I've never seen your face around here before and I wouldn't care to find myself employing someone who's known to the constabulary!"

Hetty smiled to herself, for she had anticipated the possibility of being asked to account for her origins and had taken the precaution of concocting a plausible story.

"Please sir; I am a respectable working widow," she said, bowing her head. "My husband was a labourer working in one of the quarries above Kendal, but he was killed in a rock fall over a year ago. Havin' no close kinfolk, I had no choice but to leave my home village and seek work elsewhere."

Simister nodded sympathetically, appearing to be satisfied with her explanation, for dispossessed country women were often found seeking work in the factories and households around Manchester.

"Very well," he said. "You may continue here. You may also bed down above the vegetable store along with Mary-Helen, if you have no adequate lodgings. You will be paid four shillings per week and you may eat your fill of the leftovers from the kitchen. Now I bid you goodnight."

The gaffer clamped a bowler hat upon his ample head, locked the door of the kitchen and then disappeared into the darkness.

Marsie' took the wisewoman by the hand and led her across the courtyard to a small storehouse lying against the boundary wall. The building had evidently been originally intended as a stable, for the girl led Hetty up an external staircase and into a disused hayloft that had once held the provender for the animals below.

The young woman lit a candle and the witch was able to make out pair of straw-filled pelisses, two rickety chairs and an upturned box that evidently served as a table.

"Ain't no palace," the Cockney woman remarked, "but I've cleaned the place up and no rats get up this far. It gets cold at night, right enough. But we're not short of blankets and I reckon that hundreds of homeless folk around Manchester would give a year of their lives to be as well fixed up as we are this night."

Marsie' removed a cloth from the top of the cane basket that she was carrying and drew out a pair of steaming hot beef puddings, a fruit pie and a bottle of warm black tea.

"Best thing about working in a kitchen," she said with a laugh,. "is that you ain't likely to starve, and old Simister isn't above turning a blind eye if we take a bit of good stuff along with the slops. Now get stuck in before this lot gets cold and then we had best get under the blankets and catch some sleep. For we have to get the grates cleaned out and the fires lit before half past five in the mornin'. Aye, and God help us if the ovens ain't hot when the cooks arrive for work at six o'clock sharp!"

Hetty quickly became accustomed to the routine of the kitchen in the days following her arrival. The work was hard and the long hours of unremitting toil often brought her to the point of almost complete exhaustion. Even a good night's sleep was sometimes difficult to obtain, for the unheated hayloft was cold and draughty. One evening, the temperature suddenly plummeted and the two women had been forced to pile all of the available blankets onto a single pelisse and spend the night clinging together for warmth.

Marsie, however, proved to be an excellent workmate, for she was invariably good humoured and possessed all of the irrepressible wit of her Cockney ancestors.

The girl would always crack a joke when the drudgery of the kitchen became unbearable and Hetty's face would then contort with silent laughter.

The eating house, she soon discovered, was closed on Sunday and the operatives were relieved of their duties for the day. On her first free Sunday, the wisewoman walked through the quiet streets until she came to a boat-chandler's store that was situated on the banks of the Rochdale Canal. The owner, it was said, often allowed his premises to be used as a postal accommodation address by the itinerant boat crews who plied the waterway for the payment of a small fee.

The establishment was closed, but the proprietor responded to the wisewoman's knocking and after a short bout of haggling, the man agreed to receive and hold her mail for the sum of three pence per week. The wisewoman's inner eye warned her that the chandler was shifty and unreliable, but she desperately needed to keep in touch with Elfencot so had little choice but to reluctantly trust in the man's honesty. However, she took the precaution of giving her name as Hetty Walters, rather than Littlewood, and she also resolved to make sure that she was always alone and unobserved whenever visiting the store.

Hetty had been working in the restaurant for almost a fortnight before she set eyes upon Joe Pasco, the official owner of the establishment.

The man had entered the kitchen about midmorning in the company of Mr Simister and began giving the workplace and its edible products a rapid and far from searching examination.

None of the operatives dared to pause for a moment as they worked under the eye of the proprietor. Yet the witch had no difficulty in observing the man out of the corner of her eye, and she was soon able to make a tentative evaluation of both his character and his appearance.

Joe Pasco was tall, being over six feet in height, and possessed a lean and athletic build that would have done justice to a professional sportsman. In addition, a shock of shining blonde hair fell almost to his shoulders and his unusually loose hairstyle tended to act as a backdrop to his remarkably handsome features.

'Indeed, a man born to turn the heads of the ladies,' tThe wisewoman concluded.

But she also noticed that the man's shallow blue eyes did not carry that sharp telltale glint of intelligence that invariably suggested an advanced intellect; whilst she knew that it would be dangerous to consider Pasco a fool, she was already convinced that some other person was directing and controlling the growing business empire that bore his name.

'Aye, someone pulls the strings and makes that handsome puppet dance,' she thought.

'Probably his wife Mildred, or perhaps the draymen are quite right and it's Albert Pike, the fight promoter who owns the property and keeps a firm grip upon the purse-strings.'

The wisewoman kept her eye upon Pasco as he threaded his way between the workbenches and she turned her body sideways as he approached, giving the young man an ample opportunity to notice and admire the outline of her breasts.

As she hoped, the man halted before her workstation.

"You're new here!" he exclaimed. "I hope that you find the work to your liking?"

Hetty smiled at him before dropping her gaze.

"Yes indeed, sir," she replied. "And I wish to express my deepest gratitude for the opportunity to earn my bread. Life can be hard for a poor woman such as myself."

Pasco rapped the top of the workbench with his walking stick.

"In that case woman," he replied sternly. "See that you carry out your tasks diligently, and continue to obey the commands of your masters and then you can be assured that you will continue to receive our support!"

Joe Pasco disappeared into the dining room and the wisewoman almost laughed aloud.

'It certainly doesn't take much to set that young stallion sniffing around a woman's skirts,' she thought. 'Aye and I'll bet a pound to a shilling that not many days will pass before he tries to get between my thighs. Well, all to the good, I might as well play that young treasure along and see if he leads me to something interesting.'

Only four days elapsed before Pasco again visited the kitchen, and on this occasion he lingered for a few minutes in the vicinity of Hetty's workbench; ostensibly testing the quality of a batch of pies that were being prepared to a new recipe, but the wisewoman knew instinctively that her employer was using this task as a pretext for gaining a closer and clearer view of her body. She stretched even further across the top of the work bench, as she kneaded a mound of suet dough, thus tightening the rear of her skirt and further accentuating the curve of her shapely buttocks.

'Take a good look you bloody ram,' she thought as she stretched out and pummelled the dough. 'Get yourself good and randy and then let's see what you try to do about it.'

Hetty did not have to wait long to discover to result of her womanly ruse, for the following morning, Simister strode across the kitchen and addressed the two women as they toiled at their workbench.

"See here, ladies," he said. "Mr Pasco has instructed me to offer you both the opportunity to wait-on, part time, in the dining room. You will work in the kitchen in the mornings and relieve some of the dining room staff in the afternoon. You won't receive any increase in pay, but you will have the chance of gleaning a few tips and the work is also lighter. Well, ladies, what do you both say?"

Hetty smiled at the young London girl, who appeared to be slightly hesitant.

"Shall we give it a try?" she asked.

Marsie' nodded. "Swore that I would never wait on table again, after toilin' away me childhood working in one of them boarding houses near Brick Lane. Still, it will give us a break from all that washing up, so let's say... yes!"

Mr Simister then instructed the two women to be washed and presentable by a quarter past twelve, and then report to the head waiter who would assign them to their new duties.

'So Pasco thinks enough of me and Marsie' to grace us with a small promotion,' the wisewoman pondered, as she returned to making suet dumplings. 'Yet I wonder if a good tumble is all that he expects in return? Or has he another reason? However, time will tell, of that there can be no doubt!'

※

Waiting upon tables in a public dining room was a new experience for Hetty. But Marsie' nursed her companion through the first few days until she became fully conversant with the work, and she even began to enjoy the interlude from the drudgery of the kitchen.

The two newcomers, now dressed in clean white linen aprons, had begun their new careers by waiting upon the rows of benches and tables that ran along the rear wall of the dining room and only brought into use when the lunchtime trade was at its frantic height. The normal clientele, Hetty soon discovered, were the young clerks and tellers who worked in the surrounding offices and warehouses. The young men could normally afford to dine in the restaurant once or twice a week, and they were invariably a merry crowd, for a hot beef pudding with vegetables was frequently the high point of their working week.

A smaller number were senior clerks and various types of commission agents, who dined on a daily basis, whilst a handful of the diners were the sons and close relatives of factory and warehouse owners, residing in the city whilst being taught the skills of management. The latter invariably occupied the best tables and were far more fashionably dressed than their more lowly colleagues who sat upon the rear benches. These privileged diners often ordered expensive none standard items from the kitchen, such as beefsteak, fresh oysters and port wine. Yet even the ones known to be heirs to substantial fortunes had to quit the restaurant in haste when their lunch break drew to a close, for the discipline of the mills and trading houses was strict and extreme punctuality was required of everyone.

The common clerks, the wisewoman noted, consumed every last morsel of the food placed before them and seldom had a single spare coin to slip under their plates as a tip, but their senior colleagues sometimes deposited a halfpenny before departing the establishment. The well-to-do sons of the mercantile families, by contrast, were often generous to the dining room staff. One lucky waiter was rumoured to have once caught a half sovereign that had been casually flipped in his direction by some extremely generous diner.

Marsie' was very adept at loosening the wallets of these young gentlemen. A knowing smile and a few words of her Cockney banter often earned her a tip from the young gentlemen. One youthful toff, anxious to gain the approbation of his fellows, once pressed a silver florin into the palm of the London girl's hand.

Days passed into weeks and the routine of kitchen and dining room became second nature to the wisewoman.

One morning, she noticed an old ash tree struggling for life in a corner of the courtyard was beginning to burst into leaf, and realized that winter was rapidly giving way to spring. She could not help pondering upon the fact that she was making little progress with her inquires into the affairs of Messer's Pasco and Pike and their associates. Indeed, only one small item of interest had come her way since she had begun working in the dining room. The male waiters, it transpired, were under strict orders to recommend the Cleopatra Music Hall as a lively evening venue to any of the young gentlemen who expressed an interest in going out on the town with their friends.

Yet, even this instruction could well be perfectly above board, for would not Pasco's various business enterprises be expected to support each other whenever possible? Indeed, no entrepreneur would turn his back on such an opportunity to increase his trade.

Joe Pasco never spoke to the wisewoman during his subsequent visits to the eating house, yet he still seemed to be sexually attracted by her voluptuous form and Hetty sensed that the young businessman was feasting his eyes upon her whenever he was in her presence.

On one occasion, the man had reason to pass close behind her as she was clearing away a pile of dirty crockery and she felt his fingers sliding lightly across her buttocks as he brushed past. Pasco then paused momentarily by the door of the restaurant and glanced for a second or two in her direction, but quite long enough for her to reward him with a coy smile, before he averted his gaze and disappeared through the door of the establishment. However, the entrepreneur made no attempt to cement a closer relationship between them, and the wisewoman began to suspect that Pasco was little more than a rather nervous voyeur. So her scheme to seduce the man and wheedle her way into his confidence was unlikely to succeed.

Indeed, as the weeks passed by, Hetty became less sure that her enquires could be advanced by remaining in Pasco's employment. But her inner eye warned her to persevere and she resolved to remain at the eating house until late May at the very least. Yet the month of April had not even drawn to a close when Hetty's occult intuition proved to be correct and a door opened that was destined to lead her into the murky depths of the Manchester underworld.

꒰ℒ꒱

On the morning of the last day of April, the two women were called into Mr Simister's tiny office where the kitchen gaffer was waiting to receive them. He invited them to be seated and poured them two cups of tea from an old china pot. Hetty accepted a cup, but she noticed, at once, that Simister was far from being his stern confident self. In fact, he appeared to be strangely troubled and unhappy.

"Ladies," he began. "This morning, I received an urgent message from Mr Pasco, who, as you probably know, owns the Cleopatra public house and Music Hall. In the message, he states that the Cleopatra is desperately short of a pair of barmaids and that I am required to hire a horse cab and send you two ladies there without delay!"

Simister paused for a moment and the wisewoman knew instinctively that the man was struggling with his conscience.

"There are many who hold that a place where strong drink is sold is no place for respectable women. And I confess that I am among that number. But ladies, you must either accept Mr Pasco's orders or leave his service immediately."

The kitchen gaffer paused. "If you both decide to leave, then I will give you excellent references and seek to find you alternative employment amongst the members of my chapel congregation. I shall now leave you both for a few minutes and I expect your answer when I return."

'The man is trying to give us a warning,' Hetty decided, as Simister left the room, 'and as openly as he dares, without risking his position and the livelihood of his large family.' But the wisewoman knew that she must disregard the kitchen gaffer's words and enter service at the Cleopatra, if she was to continue with her current line of enquiry.

'Yet what of Marsie,' Hetty thought and she turned and faced her workmate.

"You know, lass," she said. "Simister's quite right about some of those drinking dens; they are no place for a respectable woman to be! Me, I'm going to give it a chance, for I'm fair sick of makin' dumplings. I might get more tips from buttering up drunks than I receive from serving dinners to hard up clerks with empty pockets, but you are still young lass! Perhaps you should leave and start a new life as Simister suggests."

The London girl laughed loud enough to make the teacups rattle.

"Bless you for your concern." she replied. "But I'd sooner serve ale to Old Nick himself, than scrub floors for one of Simister's stuck-up chapel cronies! No, Hetty, I'm going along with you for better or worse and that's the end of the matter!"

꙳

The horse cab deposited the two women on the pavement outside the Cleopatra Music Hall. The building occupied a corner position where two streets met and the structure was obviously brand new, for the chimney smoke which begrimed the air of Manchester, had not yet removed the shine from the ornate marble cladding that decorated its facade.

The hall was closed at this early hour, but the billboards already carried the names of the various artists who would be performing there during the coming week. The Cleopatra public house stood immediately adjacent to the music hall; this was a much older building and its soot-blackened exterior stood out in sharp contrast to its newer companion.

The wisewoman and her friend passed through the glass panelled front door of the public house and gazed across the sea of tables and chairs that occupied the floor of the spacious front saloon. They were also able to make out a long bar, made from polished mahogany running the entire length of the room. This ornate bar, together with the polished glass mirrors, the gleaming brass fittings and the mass of gilded stucco work, suggested that the Cleopatra pub belonged to the huge family of gin palaces that had sprung up in every industrial city from London to Glasgow.

It was still early and the handful of customers, who had arrived for a late morning drink, were being attended to by a single bored looking girl who was lounging behind the bar.

"You'll be the new ones," she remarked, hardly sparing them a second glance.

"Go through the back of the bar and into the rear passageway then knock upon the door marked Office."

The newcomers did as they were told and they were ushered into the office by a powerfully built woman of about forty years of age and who stood a good six feet in height. The woman was no classical beauty and her plain features were far from improved by the livid purple scar that ran across her forehead and down her right cheek, until it petered out alongside her heavily squared jaw.

The woman gave the London girl little more than a cursory glance, but her dark piercing eyes wandered over the wisewoman's face and form for almost half a minute.

"So you're the one they call Hetty! Well, I can make out that you're much older than your face and figure suggests, you could doubtless give most of the girls who work here a good ten years. But you carry your age well and most of the toffs will take to you as readily as your younger friend here."

The scar-faced woman treated the two newcomers to an almost malevolent stare.

"My name is Mrs Pasco. Mrs Mildred Pasco and I run this pub and music hall along with my husband Joe. Work hard and obey every order without question and you'll both do well here. But if you cross me, it will be at your peril!"

She handed Hetty a room key.

"The pair of you can take the attic bedroom at the head of the stairs. You may also make free with the dresses that you find in the wardrobe. But be sure that you are both on duty in the saloon bar at six o'clock sharp, tonight."

The newcomers were about to leave the office, when a sharp word from Mrs. Pasco halted them on the threshold.

"A word of warning," she hissed. "That husband of mine has an over fondness for the ladies and I care not a fig if you let him finger that thing you keep beneath your petticoats. But if I catch him with something else pushed right up yer skirts, why then I'll put a scar on yer faces that will be the twin of the one the brickfield hussies put on me, when I was but a feckless girl. Now get out the pair of you!"

"Gawd help us!" the London girl breathed in alarm as the office door closed behind them. "I'd not have a tumble with Joe Pasco, not even for a king's ransom. Not if it means havin' yonder battle-axe after me blood and no mistake!"

❧

At precisely six o'clock upon the same evening, the wisewoman and her companion began working in the saloon bar of the Cleopatra public house. At first, the two women found the complexity of the work bewildering, for they had to tackle the necessary task of memorizing the complex range of alcoholic drinks, which the establishment sold and the accompanying list of prices. Even so, only a few days were needed for them to become fully conversant with the duties expected of them.

The task of serving pints of beer and measures of spirits to the Cleopatra's thirsty customers was often hard and hectic, especially in the early evenings when the nearby offices and warehouses were closing for business and the city's reasonably affluent class of foremen and scribes were free to consume alcoholic beverages in the company of their friends. Yet the work was far less exacting than the grinding toil of the eating house kitchen and the two women were seldom exhausted when the big glazed doors were locked behind the last of the evening's revellers. In addition, the meals served to the staff were of excellent quality and the attic room, shared by the two women was clean and comfortable. Indeed the wisewoman quickly noticed that all of the barmaids who worked in the Cleopatra public house were enjoying a standard of life that would have been the absolute envy of their sisters who toiled in the city's shops and factories.

Yet, Hetty noticed that little camaraderie existed between the numerous female employees who worked in the establishment. True, the customers were always greeted with a smile, but the maids only conversed when trade was slack and they seldom attempted to strike up friendships with the other members of the establishment. At first, this strange absence of social intercourse puzzled the wisewoman, but she shrugged the matter off and put it down to the fact that most of the women appeared to be quite new to the City of Manchester and had little in common with each another. However, the reason for this lack of sociability was revealed at the beginning of her third week of employment, when she and her young companion were ordered to leave the bar and report to Mildred Pasco's office without a moment's delay.

The two women entered the office and were confronted by Joe and Mildred Pasco and two other men who were unknown to them. One of the strangers was a short middle-aged man who wore the uniform of a sergeant in the Manchester Constabulary; whilst the other was a broken-nosed individual whose powerful build and cold dark eyes gave him a frighteningly menacing appearance.

"Sit yourselves down, ladies," Mildred said, pointing towards a pair of chairs that stood in the middle of the office. "And listen carefully to what I have to say. Now both of you two ladies have done well by us since you entered our service and we feel that the time has now arrived for you both to profit personally from this association. Tomorrow, you will both begin working as waitresses in the Cleopatra Music Hall at a weekly wage of fourteen shillings cash!"

Mildred Pasco paused for a moment, in order to give the women an opportunity to grasp the full generosity of an offer equalling the earnings of many skilled tradesmen. "To earn this money," she continued "you must wait upon table and see that our customers get the very best of service. We also have a dozen private boxes, set high up above both wings of the hall, from where our special visitors can get an uninterrupted view of both the stage and the performers, yet still remain completely hidden from the majority of our customers who are seated in the main body of the hall. Each box fronts an entertainment room where our special friends can dine in complete privacy. Or do anything that takes their fancy!"

Mildred then looked sternly into the eyes of the two seated women and uttered her next sentence very slowly and with considerable emphasis. "You will sometimes be expected to wait upon these very special guests, and provide them with any service which their hearts may desire!"

Marsie' gave a sudden start. "You mean that we must lie back and let em' ride us sore, if that's what the buggers want to do!" Mrs. Pasco smiled broadly and the livid scar on her face twisted into a grotesque pattern. "Precisely my dear," she said quietly.

"Yet our special guests are often old and burdened with cares and wish for nothing more taxing than an evening of pleasant conversation with a beautiful young woman. Occasionally, our guests are men in the prime of life and require a rather more intimate service. But all are men of substance and are usually generous to the ladies who please them."

She paused.

"Consider my proposition, ladies. A year or perhaps two, here at the Cleopatra, then back home with nobody the wiser and with nest eggs to set you both up for life. Or better still, a voyage to Australia, with enough cash to start up your own businesses." The smile suddenly vanished from Mildred's face and her voice took on a much harsher tone.

"You ladies are newcomers to Manchester and have had only a mere taste of the hard living that this city can inflict upon women without adequate means. Sleepin' under a railway arch ain't so good, but it can be even worse if the Sergeant here chucks you into jail for vagrancy!"

Mildred nodded towards the policeman who stroked his chin before speaking.

"Aye, prison for certain," he surmised. "Maybe six months or a year, if I manage to get you both charged with stealin' wallets or some other crime!"

Mrs. Pasco then pointed towards the broken-nosed bruiser who stood at the policeman's side. "You might even be glad to be in jail, if I was to put my head minder on yer trails!"

Once again, the scar-faced woman's tone softened. "It ain't as though you're a pair of innocent virgins, so don't you think that an odd tumble with a well-heeled toff is a small price to pay for a jolly good livin' and the chance of a prosperous future? Now go up to your room and give thought to what's just been said. If you agree, then both of you can start working in the music hall tonight. If the answer is no, the Sergeant here will put you on the next fast train for London, with a pound in each of your pockets to tide you over until you both get new situations. Now go away and think about it and be back here with your answers inside half an hour!"

Everything was now clear to the wisewoman as she climbed the stairs towards the attic bedroom. It appeared that she had succeeded in penetrating a carefully organized brothel-keeping operation that prospered with the aid of corrupt members of the local constabulary; an operation existing to serve the carnal needs of the city's large and prosperous male middle class. She had already discovered that Pasco's eating house, together with his two commercial hotels, supplied the Cleopatra Music Hall with many of its customers. Now she also knew that the three linked businesses also provided his brothel-keeping enterprise with a constant supply of fresh young whores. Indeed, she had also experienced, at first hand, the means by which desperate young women could be frightened and beguiled into embracing the life of a prostitute. Now she fully understood the meaning of Mr Simister's cautiously expressed warning.

However, the fact that the wisewoman had successfully uncovered an elaborate high-class brothel-keeping enterprise appeared to have done nothing to help clear her son of the charge of murder. Once again, her logic told her that her present line of enquiry was leading her up a very dangerous blind alley, and that her interests would be best served if she was to slip away from the Cleopatra and continue her inquiries by other means.

Yet her generally reliable witch's inner eye urged her to be patient and remain close to the Pascos for a little while longer. The wisewoman uttered a sigh, as she reached the top of the stairs, and once again she resolved to place her whole trust in her well-tried intuition.

The two women entered the attic bedroom and Marsie' threw herself onto the bed.

"Gawd' help me," she said. "I runs away from London to stop me fella from putin' me on the game. Now I finishes up by walkin' into a brothel all by myself. Seems like I'm destined to become a whore, no matter what I do!"

"Aye, providence moves in strange ways!" agreed the wisewoman, "but I'm determined to give this place a try. After all, it can't be worse than sleeping in that bloody freezing hayloft and rolling dumplings for a living!"

The London girl burst out laughing.

"Well. Hetty, I reckon that I'll stay here with you. If I'm fated to become the plaything of men, then I might as well be ridden on a nice clean bed, by a succession of well-heeled toffs, as being stretched out over the back of some cart by a bunch of stinkin' London sewer cleaners every night!"

Marsie' leapt from the bed and embraced the wisewoman.

"Hetty, Hetty, Hetty," she repeated, still laughing. "We'll both stay here and become whores together. Perhaps we'll both be lucky and service some crown prince and both make our fortunes!"

Chapter 4

Myra stood bolt upright in the bows of the Bonny Barbara as the craft drifted gently down the Exit River, anxiously scanning the rolling nulla-covered plain occupying both banks of the river and stretching away as far as the eye could see.

Nothing moved on that vast ocean of moss, with the exception of a pair of wild narr, drinking at the water's edge, and a group of do-fowl busy scavenging for food in the muddy shallows. Once again, she ran her eyes over the featureless plain, but the repeated search of her surroundings yielded nothing tangible to account for the deep intuitive feeling of menace that she had experienced for the last hour. The young wisewoman shrugged her shoulders in frustration, but remained alert, for she knew that danger was close. Very close.

Six darkenings had passed since the modified narrowboat had cleared the mouth of the Fruitful Stream and begun riding upon the waters of the main river. For the next four days, the river current had carried them through a landscape dominated by low crimson hills and numerous straggling Thoa groves clinging precariously to the banks of the many fast flowing streams; but two days ago, the vista had suddenly changed and the broken countryside had given way to a wide nulla-plain that seemed to stretch into infinity.

Fortunately, the danger from rocks and other impediments to navigation had receded, once the hill country had been left well astern, but a careful watch had still to be kept from the bows, for shoals and the wreckage of long-abandoned river-works occasionally hove into view. Indeed, it sometimes required all of the knowledge of the three native crewmen, allied to the skill of the young boatmaster at the tiller, to avoid a catastrophe.

On several occasions, The Bonny Barbara passed the ruins of small towns that had evidently been originally constructed by that extinct race the Narrs-folk referred to as the 'Ancient Dead.' Once, on the far horizon, the travellers had been able to make out the remains to a pyramidal structure, whose apex stood a good thousand feet above the surrounding plain; indeed, it almost seemed capable of piercing the dense banks of crimson cloud rolling endlessly overhead.

Yesterday, about midmorning, the lookout in the bows had sighted another craft approaching them from down-river and the crew of the narrowboat had immediately armed themselves, in case the strange vessel proved to be hostile. As the two craft converged, the crewmembers quickly realized that the vessel was little more than an open barge, with less than half the cargo-carrying capacity of the Bonny Barbara. They also noticed that the barge was being drawn, upriver, by a gang of about a dozen emaciated men, wearing little more that ragged loincloths as they staggered painfully along the opposite bank of the river.

Clem, who was the oldest of their three native crewmembers, had thrown aside his loaded darter and waved frantically as the craft came within hailing distance.

His greeting had been returned by a grey-bearded man who stood at the tiller.

The small barge, Clem had later explained, was commanded by his great uncle Tem-Haspar and was carrying a cargo of Thoa flour from the city of Calar to the vessel's home village, lying about six days march North of the Valley of the Fruitful Stream.

"Those poor men at the ropes, who are they?" Myra had enquired.

"Bow haulers," Clem had replied, and explained that such men could be hired by the day in most of the larger riverside settlements. They were, he emphasized, quite indispensable in moving laden craft upriver against the power of the current. He also added that slaves and criminals were occasionally used for the task; but the haulers were generally poor freemen, who undertook the arduous duty in order to feed their families.

Clem had then spat over the side and said, "A freedom-loving narrsman would sooner kill his wife and children and then hang himself, rather than endure such a dire indignity."

The small cargo barge had barely disappeared from view, when they sighted another similar vessel approaching from downriver, and the crew of the converted narrowboat realized that they must encounter craft, in ever-growing numbers, as the Exit River carried them eastwards, towards the great trading City of Calar.

Myra chewed upon a fragment of dried narr-flesh, as she continued her watch from the bows of the craft, but nothing remotely threatening could be seen within the surrounding sea of crimson moss. Even so, her witch's inner eye constantly warned her that both the craft and its occupants were in imminent danger of destruction. Finally, unable to contain her fears any longer, she made her way to the stern and consulted her brother, who was manning the tiller, accompanied by Clem, the senior narrsman.

Darryl allowed his sister to voice her worries and then turned to Clem asking if anything of a particularly hazardous nature lay immediately ahead of them.

The narrsman pondered for a moment before answering. "Soon we shall encounter a place that has long been called The Pirates' Leap. Here, the remains of an ancient bridge lie fallen across the breadth of the river. To pass safely, one must steer close to the left-hand bank and pass under a section of broken arch that reaches out over the water. The place gained its cursed name because bands of pirates had once leapt down from the broken arch and landed upon the decks of passing vessels, prior to slaughtering the crews and pillaging their goods." Clem's face assumed a grim aspect. "No gang of river pirates has ventured this far west since my father was a child, but if your witch-sister's fears prove to be correct and we are attacked, then it will most probably happen at Pirates' Leap.

Blood surged through Darryl's veins experiencing the same build-up of tension that he felt when entering a boxing ring. He immediately began making the preparations needed to repel a possible attack. The narrowboat, he realized, was almost seventy feet in length and it would obviously be impossible for his small crew to prevent a determined body of attackers from getting aboard the vessel. He therefore ordered George and two of the narrsmen to arm themselves with darters and lie hidden beneath a tarpaulin in the bows of the craft. Clem and the young wisewoman would be similarly armed and lying in wait in the shelter of the narrowboat's stern cabin to pick off any pirate who survived. If an attack did occur, Darryl reasoned most of the pirates, after successfully landing upon the vessel's deck could then be decimated by darts launched from both front and rear. The boatmaster firmly resolved to remain at the tiller and personally steer the craft into the ambush; he also donned one of the long red robes often worn by prosperous river merchants in the fervent hope that such a guise would lull the attackers into believing that the intended prey was both weak and defenceless. The loose-fitting robe also served to hide the boatmaster's military garb and the sword Kingslayer, intending to engage any borders who escaped the attentions of the darters. His final precaution was to conceal a short javelin beneath the cockpit's wooden seat, in case he needed a missile weapon.

The crew's defensive preparations were barely completed when the remains of the old bridge hove into view. Great piles of masonry could be seen obstructing the flow of the river and the rushing waters became flecked with foam as the current strove to force its way over and between the piles of fallen debris. Close by the left-hand bank, however, the waterway was still quite passable, for the stub of the bridge's first arch had remained largely intact and the river beneath was quite free of wreckage. The boatmaster instinctively put the tiller hard over and guided the craft beneath the broken span.

The bridge must originally have been constructed to carry a considerable volume of traffic, for the stub of the arch was at least three hundred feet in width and everything beneath the broken span was shrouded in deep shadow. It was therefore small wonder that Darryl failed to catch sight of the river pirates, who were hiding in deep clefts within the underlying masonry, until a dozen figures suddenly dropped out of the gloom landing upon the narrowboat's central hatch cover.

"Now!" Darryl roared, and the hidden crewmen in the bows emerged from hiding and poured a hail of needle-sharp darter projectiles into the bodies of the surprised boarders, the snipers in the stern picking off any survivors.

The boatmaster's counter-ambush worked with deadly effect, and within a few seconds the entire force of would-be freebooters were pouring out their lifeblood upon the narrowboat's wooden deck.

The crew of the Bonny Barbara gave vent to a loud cheer, but their triumph proved to be extremely premature, with a second group of attackers dropping out of the gloom, this time landing dangerously close to the stern of the vessel.

The second group was only six warriors strong, but they were far better organized than the first, heading directly for the cockpit in a solid body, with the intention of destroying the force in the rear of the craft and killing the remaining crew at leisure.

Darryl was the first to recover from this fresh assault. He cast the merchant's robe aside and called for his sister to take the tiller. Seizing the hidden javelin he leaped out of the cockpit meeting the new attackers head-on.

The leading boarder was a tall redheaded man wearing a padded tunic covered in iron studs, but the protective garment served the man ill, for Darryl's javelin tore its way into the man's vitals and hurling him back amongst his fellows. Within seconds, the ex-boxer was amongst the remainder, thrusting Kingslayer into the stomach of his nearest adversary and withdrawing the blade to ward off a blow from a heavy gill. With a twist of the blade he completely severed the hand that grasped it. Clem threw himself forward with a light shield upon his arm to protect the boatmaster's vulnerable left side. Yet Darryl was still in grave danger of being cut down by the three able bodied pirates still confronting him. Fortunately, George arrived from the bows in the nick of time.

He smashed into the enemy's rear and his friends witnessed a facet of the young man's character unknown to them. Howling like some wild animal, he hewed a pirate's legs away at the knees with a single sweep of his long-handled axe, before burying the head of the weapon between the shoulders of another. Still howling like some creature possessed, he tore the cleaver from his belt, slashing and battering the last remaining pirate until the man was little more than a pile of mangled flesh. Indeed, it required all of Darryl's considerable strength and the efforts of two narrsmen to overpower the young boatman and pinning him to the deck until the berserk-madness left his brain.

The Bonny Barbara finally drifted clear of the broken span emerging into the crimson daylight and the scale of the slaughter now became evident, for dead and dying pirates now lay upon the deck of the narrowboat all the way from its midsection down to the edge of the stern cockpit. Nor had the victorious crew of the vessel escaped unscathed, for Clem had received a dagger thrust in the thigh and a sword cut had opened up a shallow gash in the boatmaster's left forearm.

George, now recovered from his bout of berserk-madness, took over the tiller from Myra, and the young wisewoman set about the task of treating the Bonny Barbara's wounded.

Darryl's first act was to give the clothes and weapons of the fallen pirates to the narrsmen, as a reward of their loyal service, and the two unwounded clansmen immediately began stripping the dead and dying pirates naked, before rolling them unceremoniously over the side. But one of the wounded pirates, a relatively young man, groaned piteously and hauled himself up into a sitting position against one of the hatch covers. The boatmaster, seated on the edge of the cockpit whilst having his wounded arm dressed, witnessed the man's plight, ordering him to be spared and carried down into the cockpit for questioning.

Darryl recognized the young man as the one whose hand he struck off during the fight and he ordered his sister to staunch the stream of blood flowing endlessly from the man's severed stump. He also requested Myra to give him a draught of medicine to ease the pain.

At Myra's suggestion, the robber was given a little time to recover his strength before the interrogation began and the boatmaster also assisted the process by pouring a draught of strong wine down the man's throat.

Darryl waited awhile and then addressed the pirate.

"Tell us all we wish to know and you may be surprised at our mercy," he began. But the wounded robber immediately interrupted him.

"Ask away," the man said, in a dialect that Darryl had difficulty in understanding. "For I be one-handed now…I be finished up anyhap."

"Where do you and your comrades come from?" the boatmaster enquired. "Why did you take the risk of attacking a craft so far up the river from Calar?"

The pirate strove to answer, in a voice that was still thick with pain.

"From banks of…Great Life River…south of Calar City… we come."

He paused to draw breath.

"Turning finger at family meet-house...say me...and many of us...must go!"

He paused and raised his one remaining good hand.

"We come here to ... where old people say...robbing once good!"

The pirate turned his head and looked past the boatmaster to where Clem was propped up against the far side of the cockpit, gingerly nursing his wounded thigh.

"Not good choice...I think...old man who breeds running animals."

The young robber then closed his eyes and fell silent, apparently exhausted by the questions.

"Can you manage to make any sense of what the man was trying to tell us, Clem?" Darryl asked, "For I confess that I don't understand a word of it!"

The elder narrsman smiled. "Yes, yes. I understand the man's speech well enough. Although it must sound like some kind of mad gibberish to a newcomer like yourself.

"I think the man told us about all that he's capable of telling us. To begin with, the man's shaven head and his tattooed arms tell me with certainty that he belongs to one of the great robber families who have infested the banks of the Great Life River since time began. Now that young devil told us that he and the gang that attacked us were selected by 'The Turning Finger.' I've heard of this ritual from the old sailors who drink in the taverns of Calar. The sailors used to say the pirate families divided their loot into separate lots and then stood in a large circle around the chief of the clan. The chief would then call out the number of a particular lot and then spin a wooden finger that was balanced upon the top of a metal spike driven into the ground. The number of the lot called then became the share of the pirate to whom the finger pointed when it came to a halt!"

The old narrsman paused for breath and then continued.

"The sailors also said that pirate families sometimes grew too large and it became needful for some of their members to depart and try their luck elsewhere. Once again the Turning Finger was used to select those unfortunate individuals who must leave the shelter of the clan-house."

Clem smiled. "It seems that the band we wiped out was trying to establish itself in a new territory alongside the Exit River. They must have heard of the Pirates' Leap and decided that it was still a good ruse to try!"

"Are we still in danger?" the boatmaster asked.

"Aye, in all probability," the wounded narrsman answered, "for it has been rumoured that many newcomers are taking to the trade of piracy upon the Great Life River, and that many of the old robber families have been displaced, forced to seek their livelihood in distant pastures. It seems that our adversaries were one of those groups and where there's one band of desperate pirates, there can also be others!"

Clem moved slightly in order to relieve the discomfort from his injured thigh.

"So we had best be on our guard until we reach the territory patrolled by soldiers from Calar."

Darryl turned and faced the wounded pirate.

"I promised to be merciful if you answered our questions. You will therefore be put ashore at our first opportunity."

The young robber managed a single harsh laugh and pointed with his sound hand towards the sea of crimson moss. "Mercy... you call...that mercy! Freedom for man with one hand to starve slowly on plain...or maybe get took by Hix. You tell animal keeper...here...to kill me like he kill narr!"

The pirate staggered across the cockpit and knelt before the old narrsman, with his neck bent and fully exposed. "Cut," he muttered. "Cut quick!"

Clem drew his knife and looked questioningly towards the boatmaster, who nodded reluctantly. With a casual flick of his blade, the narrsman opened up the crippled robber's main artery, and, a few moments later, his lifeless body joined those of his comrades in the waters of the Exit River.

꙼

The narrowboat continued its descent of the river and once again, the nature of the waterway and its surroundings began to change. Small rushing streams no longer joined the main river to quicken its current, and the ruined river works of the Ancient Dead ceased to threaten the travellers with shipwreck and death. Indeed, hardly a single slab of masonry could be seen reaching out into the water or rearing itself alarmingly above the level of the endless crimson plain.

Three days after their encounter with the pirates, the travellers anchored their craft for the night within a stone's throw of a small riverside village, the first of the many they were destined to encounter as the group began navigating the lower reaches of the Exit River. The village was situated on top of a small mound on the right bank of the river and comprising a mere six small huts. Each dwelling was rudely constructed from balls of river mud and roofed with clumps of the ubiquitous crimson moss. The hamlet was protected on the landward side by a high wall, built from the same readily available materials.

A handful of poorly clad villagers stared at the narrowboat as it come to anchor and a number of prematurely aged women watched over a small group of emaciated children playing in the dust. A coracle, made from narrskin and animal bones, put out from the wretched settlement and its sole occupant, a skinny near-naked individual, engaged Clem in a bout of sharp haggling and eventually succeeded in exchanging two braces of freshly killed do-fowl for a measure of salt and a small bag of Thoa flour taken from the narrowboat's stores.

"This village wasn't here the last time that I passed this way," the elderly narrsman said, as he and the boatmaster plucked the birds and dropped the feathers over the side.

"I doubt if they will survive here for very long. Those people are wild-fowlers who make a precarious living through bartering part of their kill to passing river craft and hopefully gain some of the necessities of life such as flour and oil. They also manage to trap the occasional wild narr and the women are able to grow a few vegetables on small patches of river silt. But these people are always living on the edge of starvation, always!"

The narrsman laughed. "Don't worry, newcomer," he said, after noting the look of dismay upon the boatmaster's face. "These people are not typical of most of the folk who dwell in the Water Realm. Once we travel a little farther downriver you will see many settlements that are infinitely more prosperous!"

His words proved to be quite correct, for two days later, the narrowboat drifted past a village where the huts were built to a far better standard and where the men and women could be seen working together in the small fields, whose fertility, Clem explained, was renewed each year by the rich silt carried down-river during the annual flood. The Bonny Barbara frequently passed by similar villages and the trading coracles that put out from the shore enabled them to supplement their diet with crisp fresh vegetables and eggs from the flocks of domesticated do-fowl, tended by the children whilst their parents laboured in their little riverside fields. On one occasion, they were invited to tie up alongside one of these villages and spend the night ashore, but the memory of their clash with the river pirates was still fresh in their minds. So they allowed the craft to continue drifting downriver until a safe and secluded anchorage could be found.

One morning Clem pointed ashore towards a line of blue uniformed warriors who were marching along the left bank of the river. "Soldiers from Calar, he said, and explained that the narrowboat had now entered territory that was under the direct rule of the great trading city. The 'Bonny Barbara' now began encountering other trading craft with greater frequency and Clem was often found hanging over the side of the narrowboat and shouting either greetings or insults towards familiar vessels passing them on their way upriver.

The travellers also encountered the first of the great undershot waterwheels, that turned slowly and sedately, providing the power for a number of substantial riverside mills. These mills, the old narrsman explained, were the personal property of the rulers of Calar. Within the factory walls, the nuts of the Holy Thoa trees were crushed and then ground into the nutritious flour that was the staple food of most of the humans who dwelt in the Water Realm.

"There is a saying," Clem had said to the boatmaster, as the narrowboat passed one of the slowly turning wheels. "The mills that grind out flour also grind out money!"

And he went on to explain that it was the boundless wealth produced by these mills, together with the taxes paid by visiting merchants at the wharves of Calar, funding the formidable army of mercenaries holding the terrible Saxmen barbarians at bay.

One evening, just as the five suns disappeared from the sky plunging the Water Realm into pitch darkness, the old narrsman appeared on deck and slapped Darryl boisterously on the back. "Well, friend from another world," he said. "Tomorrow morning, exactly twenty-nine darkening after the day we sailed from the Valley of the Fruitful Stream, you will be able to stand in the bows of your craft and feast your eyes upon the City of Calar. Calar of the Mighty Walls."

❧

A light mist hung over the water as the crew of the Bonny Barbara raised the anchor from the bed of the Exit River and began the final stage of their voyage to Calar.

The mist was slow to lift and the day was half done before the sunlight succeeded in breaking through the banks of rolling cloud to burn away the last of the cloying vapour so the travellers were able to catch their first glimpse of the great trading city's colossal walls. Indeed, the narrowboat had been less than a mile from the city when the visibility cleared, and the newcomers were stunned by the enormous scale of the city's defences. The main walls of Calar must have stood at least one hundred and fifty feet in height and each section of the wall was reinforced by projecting bastions jutting out from the main defences and threatening the flanks of any force foolish enough to attempt a direct assault upon the city. As the narrowboat drew closer the crew were also able to make out the line of the wide moat that protected the landward side of the city and they clearly viewed the long rows of catapults and other casting engines, standing sentinel upon the walls and bastions, dominating every possible approach to the city.

A narrow strip of land lay between the great wall of the city and the river's edge, and every available inch of this precious ground was occupied by the dockyards and warehouses that handled the valuable commodities shipped to Calar from almost every portion of the Water Realm.

A number of trading craft were in the process of entering and leaving the harbour complex, their strenuous manoeuvres assisted by a number of small galleys that towed their charges in and out of the narrow dockyard basins. Twice a towing galley drew alongside the Bonny Barbara and its captain attempted to strike a bargain with the elderly narrsman, but Clem simply refused to pay the fee demanded, and the vessels sheered away with their captain's uttering loud strings of curses. However, the owner of a third galley grudgingly accepted the three mcagrc discs of copper held by the narrsman in the palm of his hand. Soon, a stout hawser made from Thoa fibre was hauling the narrowboat into the wharf of Agar-Marduk, a merchant and factor who had won the trust of the Narrs-folk by years of honest trading on their behalf.

The mercantile establishment of Agar-Marduk was large, even by the opulent standards of Calar, for the Bonny Barbara'was towed into a spacious basin containing six other craft already comfortably berthed. The basin was flanked by a number of tall warehouses and gangs of sweating labourers could be seen moving bales of goods between the stationary vessels and the extensive onshore storage facilities. Like an army of ants, the dock labourers worked hard, never pausing for a single moment to catch their breaths and view their surroundings.

An old grey-bearded man, wearing the conical hat of the merchant class, stepped aboard the Bonny Barbara as she drew alongside a vacant stretch of wharf and offered the crew the traditional welcoming gift of bread and wine. Clem immediately introduced him to the boatmaster as Agar-Marduk, the owner of the establishment and suggested that the merchant was best fitted to handle their affairs in Calar.

Darryl took to the old man immediately, for the merchant's rounded features and jovial appearance seemed to suggest infinite reliability. Furthermore, an almost imperceptible nod from Myra informed him that Agar-Marduk had also satisfied the close scrutiny of the witch's inner eye.

The boatmaster replied graciously to the merchant's act of welcome and then quietly informed him that the Bonny Barbara was carrying goods of an extremely unusual nature.

Agar-Marduk then gave orders for the narrowboat to be drawn into a secluded covered wharf, where her cargo could be examined well away from prying eyes.

The move was swiftly accomplished and a number of trusted labourers quickly removed the hatch covers and unloaded the bales of narrs-wool, thus exposing the sections of worn railway line that lay beneath.

The old merchant descended into the hold and he ran his hands over the dark metal.

"Good iron!" he exclaimed. "As good as or even better than the top quality metal that is occasionally shipped here from the forges of the distant North-folk."

He turned and looked enquiringly at the boatmaster. "I can get you a good price for the iron, if you wish to dispose of it here in Calar."

But the boatmaster shook his head.

"You may sell some of the iron," he replied. "But we shall need most of the metal to exchange for supplies during our intended voyage south, along the line of the Great Life River."

He pointed towards a few fragments of scrap lead that had been hidden along with the copper. "That you may sell, and give the proceeds to the three narrsmen who have served us so well."

"A generous sentiment," the old man replied. "I shall do as you say, but I must point out to you that I think it would be very unsafe for you to venture along the Life River, with such a wealth of iron aboard your craft. Pirates abound, as you have already discovered, and the head of one of the robber families would undoubtedly risk his entire clan to capture only a fraction of that wealth." He paused. "But the decision is yours, good master. However, you can be sure that your vessel, and its cargo, will be quite safe whist they lie under guard alongside this wharf. On that I give you my word."

The trader chuckled, his grey beard shaking with merriment. "Now rest my friends. Tonight, you will be the guests of Agar-Marduk the merchant, and I believe that you will find the hospitality provided by my wife to be very much to your liking. Rest my friends," he repeated. "I will return for you a little after dusk, when the working day is finished, and I will personally conduct you to my house that lies only a little way from the docks."

Finally, his voice took on a more serious note, and he warned them that carrying personal weapons of war was strictly forbidden within the gates of Calar and only a small dagger, worn openly in the belt, was allowed by the city authorities.

The travellers rested aboard the narrowboat for the remainder of the afternoon, then rose and bathed themselves in a tub of fresh water that had been lifted aboard the craft by two of the merchant's slaves.

The three newcomers took considerable care with their appearance, as the evening approached, wishing to make the best possible impression when they met the family and the close friends of their host. Darryl wore a pair of trousers tailored from the best Yorkshire broadcloth and a jet black caftan made from the softest narrs-wool, whilst George donned a matching shirt and trousers made from multicoloured strands of the same material. Myra, however, easily eclipsed the appearance of her two companions and drew gasps of admiration from all who set eyes upon her. She had chosen to wear a long red velvet dress that had once belonged to her maternal grandmother. The garment fitted her like a glove and it displayed her sensuous young body to perfection.

The witch woman smiled to herself as she answered the old merchant's summons and stepped onto the wharf, for she knew full well, that her beauty had flowered in the months since her arrival in the Water Realm.

Agar-Marduk led the group towards the nearest gateway in the city walls, where about a dozen spearmen were supervising a milling throng of porters, sailors and numerous other citizens who were seeking to enter or leave the city. Fortunately, one of the guards instantly recognized the old merchant and he led the party through the opening in the walls without delay.

A short walk across a public square brought them to a plain wooden doorway set into a high stone wall that Agar-Marduk declared was the one and only entrance to his dwelling. This unassuming entrance, however, gave no indication of the luxury that lay within. A tall slave answered the merchant's summons and the group passed through the wooden doorway to enter a stone paved courtyard giving way to a spacious and elegant colonnade. Flowers grew in abundance in well-tended beds, whilst miniature versions of the ubiquitous Thoa tree wound their way up the many fluted columns and hung in garlands from the lintels they supported. The merchant's house that lay adjacent to the colonnade was both large and sumptuously furnished and the travellers were greeted at the threshold by six women of various ages whom Agar-Marduk introduced as his wives and concubines.

The old merchant noticed the look of surprise that was evident upon the newcomers' faces and he quickly explained that polygamy, whilst uncommon in the Water Realm, was by no means illegal and often practiced by the members of privileged social groups such as landowners and wealthy merchants.

"Why be satisfied with a single pair of thighs?" he said with a laugh, as the women knelt to wash the newcomers' feet, "when one has amassed enough wealth to possess five women, or even six!"

Ura, the merchant's senior wife, let the guests into a large dining room, where the newcomers were invited to be seated upon the soft cushions arranged around a long low table occupying the middle of the floor.

Two other men were already seated before the table. One was a short hawk-nosed man who wearing a turban, whom the merchant introduced as Enki-Baal, the trustworthy overseer of his warehouses. The other was a diminutive man with wizened features whom Ura briefly introduced as Carl Hems, and, as his white cowled robe indicated, was a senior priest at the temple of Dumteck, a deity devoted to the task of health and healing the sick.

The woman of the household began the feast by passing around the customary offering of bread and salt. They busied themselves in presenting a succession of spicy dishes created from narrs-flesh, do-fowl and a wide selection of fresh vegetables, most being quite new to the palates of the travellers. The specialty, concluding the feast, was a steaming platter of black-red crustaceans that, to the newcomers, resembled a strange cross between starfish and the edible crabs dwelling in the oceans of their own reality.

Agar-Marduk and his local guests fell upon this new marine delicacy with relish. At first, the crewmembers from the Bonny Barbara were somewhat wary of the strange crustaceans, but, after a single taste of the creatures' sweet and tender flesh, they found themselves digging into the contents of the platter with a will.

"Eat your fill," the old merchant advised. "Rossfish are only to be found in the shallow waters of the Northern Sea. They are brought here in the holds of our swiftest trading galleys and are kept alive in tanks of fresh sea water. We are lucky to be able to enjoy this delicacy, for only the dried flesh of the rossfish can be purchased by those who dwell at any greater distance from Calar."

Sweet wine was passed around and the members of the company began to indulge themselves in conversation. George and the boatmaster listened with interest as the old merchant described the long trading journeys he had undertaken to the Northlands, in the days of his distant youth. They were fascinated by his stories of the dangerous trading ventures into the lands ruled by the white skinned iron-masters whose furnaces could be seen glowing along the shores of their storm-swept Northern homeland.

Myra, meanwhile, had soon forsaken the wine and sought out the priest of the god Dumteck. The pair had quickly found a secluded corner and fallen into a long, earnest and very private conversation.

The feast finally came to an end when the guests had consumed as much wine as they were capable of drinking. Agar-Marduk's women had then conducted the travellers to a suite of rooms where they passed the hours of darkness in comfort. Indeed, they had little choice, for the gates of Calar were now closed against both friend and foe, and would not be opened again until the light of the morning suns once again illuminated the sky of the Water Realm.

⚓

Daylight struck through the high windows of an upper clearstory and roused the three newcomers to a new day. They washed their faces in bowls of warm water and then breakfasted together from the platter of fresh fruit and cakes of warm Thoa bread, brought to them by the old merchant's youngest and prettiest concubine.

Myra broke a cake of bread in two and passed half to her brother.

"Last night," she said, "I talked for a long time to Enki-Baal, that old priest who serves the healing god Dumteck. He seems to know a great deal about us and he certainly knew that I was a wisewoman from another reality."

She paused.

"Enki-Baal has invited me to visit the refuge for the sick in the temple of Dumteck. He says that he, and his brother priests, will be happy to teach me many of their healing secrets that may stand me in good stead in the future. He informed me that a litter, borne by four young priests, would call at this house an hour after dawn and bear me to their precinct, if I should take up his offer. He also said that I would be their guest for at least three to four days!"

The boatmaster looked worried.

"Do you really believe that you will be quite safe under the roof of these priests?" he enquired. "Where you can receive no help or support from your friends?"

Myra smiled and nodded emphatically.

"Yes, yes without doubt. For the priests of Dumteck are sworn to uphold all life and to harm no member of the human race." Her voice then assumed a far more sombre tone. "Even so, you are right to be cautious, brother, for my inner eye tells me that a great deal of evil lurks inside this city and my witch's sense warns me that the sooner we are gone from this place the better it will be for all of us."

Darryl paused for a moment and gave the matter some thought.

"Go to yonder temple," he said. "And learn anything that may be of value to us. Meanwhile, George and myself will prepare our craft for the voyage down the Great Life River. Aye, and perhaps see something of this huge city whilst we have the chance. For in four days time or a week at the most, we will certainly be departing for the Holy City of Ptah and the next leg of our long journey home!"

The young wisewoman had barely time to acknowledge her brother's words before a servant entered the room, announcing the arrival of her litter. Myra bade farewell to her companions and departed upon her latest quest for knowledge.

Darryl and the boat hand finished eating a hearty breakfast and then accompanied Agar-Marduk back to the dockyard. They spent the morning supervising the wharf labourers as they unloaded the portion of the iron rails that had been promised to the old merchant. A little before noon, they walked over to a nearby wharf to say goodbye to the three narrsmen who had been such good shipmates during the dangerous journey down the Exit River. They watched, with a hint of sadness, as the men boarded a chartered river boat, heavily laden with bags of Thoa flour and other commodities needed by the people of the Fruitful Stream. They continued watching as the craft cleared the mouth of the dockyard and departed upon its long journey upriver.

The boatmaster spat upon the ground and shook his head.

"To the devil with work," he declared. "We'll make the rest of today a holiday and see something of yonder city."

The two men then sought out Agar-Marduk who was busily employed in his house of accounts and stated their intention. In reply, the old merchant ran his hands over a pile of scrolls and ledgers and declared his inability to accompany them. However, he gave orders for Carl Hems, the overseer of his warehouses to go in his stead and act as their guide for the day. He also detailed two of his strongest dock labourers to accompany them and provide some much needed protection when they ventured into the crowded streets of Calar.

"Enjoy yourselves,." he advised, as the group turned to leave. "And view the breadth of our city, for you will not see its like anywhere else in the Water Realm."

Carl Hems led the group back through the gate and into the city, but this time he took a sharp turn away from the direction of the old merchant's house, leading them into a quarter of the city that was given over to its great marketplaces.

First, he took them to the leather market, where the factors stood cheek by jowl and argued over the prices that were to be paid for the great stacks of narrs-skins standing on every side. Afterwards, a short walk down a narrow crowded street led them to the square of the woollen merchants, where other factors wearing conical hats, were busily engaged in selling this season's crop of fleeces to the city's rich spinning magnates.

The party then visited the corn exchange, the rope emporium and many other commodity markets, until the newcomers were heartily tired of fighting their way through crowds of stinking porters and requested to be taken to a quieter part of the city.

Carl Hems led them to a tranquil quarter where large and opulent mansions stood amidst broad parklands and flower decked decorative gardens.

"Here," the overseer explained, "is where the ruling aristocracy of Calar have their town houses and where they live when they come to Calar on business from their various country estates."

By midafternoon, the five suns were shining down mercilessly and the overseer led the little group to a wayside tavern where they took shelter beneath a fabric awning and ate a light meal of bread and small do-fowl egg omelette's delicately flavoured with aromatic herbs.

Carl Hems ordered flagons of light Thoa-beer to wash down the repast and then addressed his charges.

"My master suggests that you spend another darkening as guests at his house near the dockyard gate. If this plan meets with your approval, then you will have no need to exit the city before the gates close after nightfall. This will give us ample time to visit the oldest quarter of Calar and still rejoin

Agar-Marduk and his women for the last meal of the day." He paused. "The landlord here has a passenger cart for hire and we can travel to the old quarter in comfort and avoid the worst of the late afternoon heat."

Darryl wiped the sweat from his forehead and readily agreed with the suggestion, for the heat was extremely oppressive to the two travellers. Comfort, however, proved to be a relative term, for their conveyance turned out to be a crude two wheeled un-sprung cart drawn by four malnourished slaves, poor creatures who clung to the rough towing shaft like a covey of displaced scarecrows. A pair of hard wooden forms served as seats and the travellers were soon in danger of developing bruised posteriors as the vehicle bumped laboriously through the potholed streets.

The old quarter of Calar, the place where the very first settlement of the city had taken place, was a visual revelation to the newcomers as they finally climbed out of the cart. Gone were the elegant villas of the city rulers; instead, this portion of the city seemed to resemble some ancient Earth cleric's description of purgatory.

Tall spider-like buildings seemed to wind their way ever upwards, from the narrow stinking alleyways lying adjacent to the ground floors, to the upper stories of the tallest buildings that almost reached to the height of the massive city walls and enclosed the old quarter of the city on three sides. Darryl gasped in amazement at the sight, for the very tallest of the eccentric buildings even eclipsed the line of the great walls and the structure must have stood a good two hundred and fifty feet from street level up to its crowning spire.

Nor were the buildings isolated from each other, for countless timber causeways reached out from one building to its neighbour and the entire old quarter had the appearance of having grown skywards, like some mad organic entity, striving to climb ever upwards in search of fresh air and heat from the life-giving suns.

"By all that's holy," breathed the boatmaster. "Can human beings possible live within yonder hell?"

"Yes indeed," replied the overseer, as he dismissed the passenger wagon. "More than two out of three of the citizens of Calar call this place home."

He pointed towards an alleyway that ran between two of the gimcrack towers.

"We will not venture far, because robbers abound in this portion of the city, but there lies the 'Street of the Bone-carvers' and no one should visit Calar without viewing the work of the artists who dwell within. Even so, I caution you to keep together for your own safety."

The Street of the Bone-carvers was long and dark and was little more than two arm-spans in width. The flaring torches, set in brackets in the surrounding walls, were absolutely indispensable in supplementing the faint trickle of daylight filtering down from the distant upper levels. However, the newcomers were impressed by the sheer quality of the art works that were on display in the tiny booths lying on every side, and they marvelled at the array of geometric and organic ornaments, which the artists of Calar had fashioned from fragments of polished bone.

Darryl haggled determinedly with one of the artists for the possession of a piece of bone upon which the craftsman had depicted a wild narr hunt and had eventually succeeded in obtaining the artefact for the price of three copper discs. George, meanwhile, had successfully obtained a tiny bone sculpture of a Thoa tree. Unfortunately, the men had become so engrossed with their bargaining that the overseer's words of warning were forgotten, and the travellers were taken completely by surprise when the ambush suddenly occurred.

The incident began when a small urchin darted from the shelter of one of the booths and snatched the newly purchased sculpture from the young boat hand's grasp. George had instantly flown in pursuit of the diminutive thief. But this action had dire consequences, for he immediately became separated from his companions and was hopelessly vulnerable when unseen hands thrust a heavy wagon out of a side-alley and blocked the narrow passageway behind him. Six burly thugs then flung a net over the young man, and, despite his struggles, they quickly bore him to the ground and dragged him inside one of the spider-like towers.

George's companions instantly recognized his plight and attempted to clamber over the stalled wagon and come to his aid, but even as they did so, a line of darter projectiles were launched from the shadows above them and thudded menacingly into the woodwork of the wagon. A second flight followed the first and there was no mistaking the message they brought.

"Hold! We can do nothing to help our friend!" shouted the overseer, who was white as a ghost and visibly shaken by the episode. "Except return to my master's house, as quickly as possible, and apprise him of the situation."

Darryl ground his teeth in frustration, but there was nothing that he could do and he was immediately forced to agree.

Carl Hems managed to hire a pair of twin litters from a portage establishment that was situated close to the Street of the Bone-carvers and the four men reached the merchant's dwelling about half an hour after darkening.

Darryl and the overseer were immediately conducted into a small reception room where Agar-Marduk was waiting to receive them.

The boatmaster was about to speak when the merchant raised his hand and forestalled him.

"I already know what has befallen you." he said quietly. "For a messenger boy reached my house about an hour ago, bearing a written message from the young man's abductors. They state that we must surrender all of the iron that remains aboard your vessel, if we wish him to be returned to us alive! The rogues have allowed us the space of this present darkening, then another full day from tomorrow sunrise, to make up our minds. At the second dawn from now, the very same boy will arrive at my door and receive our reply."

"There can be no question as to what our answer will be," stated the boatmaster. "The iron must be given up to obtain George's release."

But he merchant looked doubtful. "The decision is yours my friend. But the criminals of Calar generally kill their hostages, even when payment is made in full, simply to safeguard their own identities. You had best prepare yourselves for the worst, even if you comply with their demands!"

Agar-Marduk paused and rubbed his chin.

"The criminals obviously know the nature of your cargo meaning that I have a traitor in my employ. I will find him, for there are many petty jealousies amongst my slaves and wharf labourers and someone will know his name."

He paused again.

"But such enquires will take time and there is very little chance that I will be able to discover the names of George's abductors, or their whereabouts, before the criminal's deadline expires." The merchant shook his head. "I must sadly admit, that I cannot think of a way of ensuring your friend's safety!"

Darryl cradled his head in his hands and almost wept in despair. But at that very moment, his brain seemed to give a strange and almost inexplicable lurch and the parting words of old Noor-Balsam, the master-at-arms, flashed into his mind as though implanted there by some outside agency...

... I will give you both the name of a man in Calar of the Mighty Walls, who will give you assistance, should the need arise...

He is Ali, son of Grom, a whoremaster who can be found in the Street of Women, beneath the sign of the Crimson Nipple...

Say who sent you... For he is an old comrade from the wars, who owes his life to the skill of my sword...

The boatmaster's head cleared and the feeling of black despondency evaporated, for he now knew what he must do. He gave a rapid summery of Noor-Balsams words to Agar-Marduk and requested the use of a litter to take him immediately to the Street of Women. However the old merchant pulled at his white beard and stated that this request was quite impossible to fulfil, for the Street of Women was situated in the Quarter of All Pleasures, and this quarter could only be reached by passing through the portion of the city were George's abduction had taken place. Litter-bearers, it transpired, could not be induced to traverse this lawless district at night, no matter what financial inducements were offered to them.

"You must depart at first light and with an armed guard to see you safely through the old quarter," the old merchant said firmly. "You will still arrive at the Street of Women well before midday, and you will have ample time to seek out this whoremaster of whom you speak. Meanwhile, eat and sleep, for tomorrow you may need all of the strength that you can possibly muster!"

The boatmaster lay back inside the cushioned interior of Agar-Marduk's personal litter, as the conveyance was borne as swiftly as possible through the dangerous old quarter of Calar. He could clearly make out the muffled footfalls of the six burly guards who protected the litter, but he still kept a firm grip upon the hilt of his dagger in case a sudden attack by street robbers should overwhelm his escort.

It was still early morning, for Darryl had insisted upon leaving the merchant's house a good hour before dawn, in order to cross the old quarter a little after first light and reach the Street of Women as early in the day as possible.

The ex-boxer was in a far from jovial frame of mind, for he held himself partly responsible for George's abduction. 'If only he had prevented Myra from visiting the Temple of

Dumteck,' he thought. 'Then she would have been present and her inner eye would have given us ample warning of the attack in the Street of Bone-carvers.'

He even chided himself for leaving the Bonny Barbara yesterday morning, instead of continuing the preparations for their journey to Holy Ptah rather than allowing George and himself to go wandering about Calar like a pair of choirboys on a church outing.

He even began to doubt his fitness to command the party, but he summoned up his remaining confidence and thrust his doubts aside, for he realized that his actions alone held the best chance of saving the young boat hands life. He therefore bit his lip and resolved to continue with the plan of action that he had carefully formulated the evening before. George's abductors, he reasoned, were probably keeping a close watch on the merchant's house and he believed that it was quite possible that the litter and its escort would be followed from the moment that it left Agar-Marduk's residence. Darryl had therefore instructed the senior bearer to pass by some secluded spot, near to the Quarter of All Pleasures, where he could slip away from the conveyance, unobserved, thus leaving the litter and its escort free to return to the merchant's house by a circuitous route and hopefully drawing away any observers who might be following upon their heels.

The senior bearer had stated that he knew of a secluded alleyway, not far from the Street of Woman, where the boatmaster could leap from the shelter of the litter and hide in one of the many dark side-alleys, without much chance of being detected. Darryl had rewarded the man with a copper disc and the bearer had also agreed to inform the boatmaster when they had safely passed through the dangerous old quarter of the city and give a sharp tap upon his carrying handle once they drew abreast of the side-alley where the boatmaster planned to alight.

A further half an hour elapsed before the head bearer quietly whispered that the litter was now clear of the old quarter and, a short time later, the boatmaster heard the bearer clearly say that they were now approaching the place where he must alight with all speed.

Darryl's left hand was upon the curtain and his right hand was grasping his naked dagger when the head bearer gave the anticipated tap upon his carrying handle; without a moment's hesitation, the young man hurled himself from the litter and then lay quite still amidst the shadows of the side alleyway. He looked back into the main passageway and waited. Moments later, he witnessed two dark figures flitting briefly past the mouth of the side alleyway. Darryl smiled grimly to himself, for he now knew that his suspicions had been correct and both the merchant's town house and its occupants were being kept under constant observation by George's abductors.

The boatmaster waited a little longer and then he rose and brushed the dust from his clothing. He listened for a moment and then he followed the narrow side-alley until it opened out into a wide avenue called 'Happiness Road', which, according to the head bearer, led directly to the heart of the Quarter of All Pleasures.

As directed, he turned left and walked at a brisk pace along the neatly flagged pavement that flanked the main road, and, as he walked, he realized why this quarter of Calar had received its particularly descriptive name, for the entire avenue was lined with opulent establishments offering a wide range of entertainments. In the space of a few hundred paces, the boatmaster passed an amphitheatre where the hoarding advertised a wide range of sporting events. Theatres were exotic music and dancing was performed on a daily basis. A public bathing establishment that was flanked by numerous gambling halls and restaurants of every shape and size, offering a range of elaborate dishes that made Darryl's head spin. However, few customers were to be seen, for the trading day was only just beginning and this was exemplified by the large number of heavily laden tradesmen's carts using the roadway to replenish and re-victual the district.

After a further ten minutes of brisk walking, Darryl came to an intersection where another avenue branched sharply to the right that he immediately recognized as the infamous Street of Women because of a large obscene mural on the side of a nearby building, which depicted naked men and women performing a wide variety of sexual acts.

It was early and only a few jaded prostitutes could be seen disporting themselves on the numerous first floor balconies, in the faint hope of attracting the attention of some stray pedestrian.

Darryl had no difficulty in finding the establishment known as the Crimson Nipple, for it stood only about a hundred paces from the intersection and, like most of the adjoining establishments, it was shuttered up and closed for business. Indeed, the only human activity that could be seen was that of a male servant who was energetically scrubbing the long flight of steps leading up to the brothel's front entrance.

The boatmaster confronted the man.

"Greetings friend," he said. "I wish to speak with Ali, son of Grom, who I believe resides in this house."

The man did not pause in his task or even bother to look up at the newcomer.

"Then you had best return this evening, master," he replied, "and you can have your pick of Ali's women."

Darryl grasped the man by the shoulder, hauling him upright and then showed him the disc of shining copper that lay in the palm of his hand.

"I wish to speak with Ali, son of Grom," he repeated.

The man looked fixedly at the coin and the bitter battle between greed and fear was plain to see upon the man's features, but greed won and the man took the copper coin.

"In the name of the Gods!" he exclaimed. "Don't tell anyone who gave you the information, but Ali dines at the Blue Do-fowl Tavern at this time of day and you may catch him there if you can find a fast litter."

The boatmaster slipped his dagger halfway out of its sheath.

"You wouldn't be cheating me floor-scrubber?" he hissed, but the man shook his head vigorously.

"No master," he replied, shrinking away. "Follow my directions and you will find the man that you seek. You will certainly recognize him, for his face would stampede a whole tribe of Hix!"

Darryl waved down a fast passenger litter at the junction with Happiness Road and he was quickly borne across the quarter to a small tavern lying in a secluded avenue.

The tavern, he noted, was fronted by a garden containing a number of tables and chairs, doubtless for the use of those of its clients who valued the open air and who enjoyed the perfume from the beds of aromatic herbs growing on every side. It was still only an hour before midday and only a single customer was to be seen relaxing in the pleasurable surroundings.

Darryl drew closer and a single glance told him that he had found the man he was seeking, for the individual's face looked as though it had been smashed in by some red hot object. The cheekbone on the right hand side of the man's face had been flattened inwards and a good half of his nose was missing, along with a sizeable portion of his lower jaw and this vision of disfigured humanity was horrifyingly completed by a mass of crimson burn tissue covering the remainder of the man's face.

The man looked up at the boatmaster with eyes that were as cold and expressionless as those of a dead fish.

"Stranger, what do you want of me?" he spat out abruptly.

"I know you to be Ali, son of Grom," Darryl replied. "Noor-Balsam, the armsmaster to whom you owe your life, told me to go in search of you if I was ever in need of help in the city of Calar."

Ali, the son of Grom, drew up a chair and shouted for the landlord to fetch two tankards of the strongest Thoa-nut beer.

"I had a feeling that today would be cursed," Ali said, stroking his disfigured face.

"Many long years have passed since I last set eyes on Noor-Balsam. Now you have arrived, stranger, and reminded me of the debt that I owe the man. Aye, and of everything that happened in the old days. Well, no man can say the son of Grom ever evaded his obligations, so tell me, how I can be of service to you?"

Darryl swallowed a deep draught of the powerful brew and related the happenings of the previous day whilst his cruelly disfigured companion listened intently.

The boatmaster eventually fell silent and Ali shook his head.

"Your friend can thank the Gods if he lives for more than another darkening, yet something may perhaps be done. Now think hard, young man, and tell me if you noticed anything peculiar about the dress of the men who carried off your friend."

Darryl cast his mind back to the previous day and thought hard before answering.

"I was a good distance from George's attackers, but I caught a fair glimpse of them as they passed beneath one of the street-torches; but I can tell you they were all dressed differently, except for the last three who wore black skullcaps with long red tassels hanging down the back."

Grom struck the table with his fist.

"I thought as much. This abduction was the work of one of the old pirate families and the black skullcap with a red tassel hanging down the back, is the hallmark of the old and much-feared Blood-spill clan."

The boatmaster looked surprised. "I was told that all of the pirate families dwelt close to the great rivers and shunned all heavily populated settlements."

"Most do," the disfigured man replied. "But a few families, who were driven from the river by their fellow robbers, have managed to settle in the old quarter of Calar in recent times. The demons have become a perfect menace and even the city guard has difficulty containing them."

He paused.

"The Blood-spill clan has a stronghold on top of one of the highest towers and that is where your friend will be held. Tonight we will attempt to rescue him. I keep a room at this beer-house and you must rest here until evening. I must go now for I have many preparations to make. Tomorrow, your friend will be a free man or we shall both be as dead as fresh narrs-meat!"

ﯼ

The hours of daylight passed with agonizing slowness for the boatmaster. He attempted to catch some sleep on the bed in Ali's room, but he was unable to do so and he was heartily glad when the Water Realm night fell with its usual suddenness.

The son of Grom arrived an hour later, carrying a large bundle wrapped in Thoa-cloth.

Without uttering a word of greetings, he cast his burden upon the bed and opened the wrapping. First of all, he drew out a razor-sharp gill, which he handed to his companion, and his face gave a convulsive twitch, the nearest the man could get to a smile.

"If Noor-Balsam was your armsmaster," he said, "then you will certainly be able to handle one of these toys and you are likely to have need of it before this darkening is over."

Ali then produced a long cylindrical weapon that resembled an African blowpipe that Darryl knew to be a spring-powered poisoned dart throwing weapon called a perm. He gently caressed the weapon with the palm of his hand.

"Many a life have I taken with this little pet," the whoremaster mused. "But never did I expect to have use of it again!"

The man looked at Darryl with his cold fishlike eyes.

"Perhaps you are wondering how I came to owe my life to Noor-Balsam," he said.

"Well, we have sufficient time to satisfy your curiosity. Once, long ago, I was employed as a military assassin by the old Prince of Calar during one of his bitter wars against the Saxmen barbarians. One ill-fated day, I was ordered to sneak into a Saxmen village and shoot a death-dart into the body of a chieftain who was becoming a particular threat to my master. A fighting patrol, commanded by Noor-Balsam, was ordered to follow on behind and wreak as much havoc as possible in the confusion that was expected to follow the chieftains killing. Unfortunately for me, I was apprehended and captured on the outskirts of the village by a Saxmen picket. I was put to the torture for the entertainment of the populace and that is why I sport a face uglier than an aged Hix female.

"As I was suffering away the last few hours of my life, Noor-Balsam and his men crept up to the edge of the village, set fire to some huts, and rescued me under cover of the ensuing confusion. Noor-Balsam even avenged my pain, for he split that damned chieftain's stomach open with a single blow from his gill. And that, stranger, is how I came to be in debt to your armsmaster."

The old assassin paused for a moment.

"The old prince of Calar was a decent man. He engaged a priest from the Temple of Dumteck to treat my wounds and he gave me a good present of copper when I left his service. I used this wealth to buy a string of girls, and that stranger, is how I came to be a whoremaster in the Street of Women. "It was fitting, for hadn't my father and grandfather been whore-masters before me?"

"Well, enough of my history," he said, looking at Darryl with his dead-fish eyes. "It is now time to apprise you of my plan to rescue your comrade. He will certainly be held in the Blood-spill clan's headquarters situated at the very top of one of the highest towers in the old quarter. The internal stairways are always heavily guarded and no access is possible from ground level. However, the building is adjacent to the city wall and the roof of the tower is almost exactly level with the highest ramparts."

Ali paused and drew a deep breath.

"We must make our way along the ramparts until we are opposite the building that contains the Blood-spill headquarters. Then we shall gain access to the roof by crawling over the intervening void by way of a long thirty hand-span ladder. We shall then enter a skylight, rescue your friend and return by the same route, if the Gods are willing!"

Darryl gasped at the sheer audacity of the scheme.

"Will the city guards not apprehend us once we step upon the battlements?" he asked. "And surely the pirates will not have neglected to place some guards upon the roof of their headquarters tower?"

The old assassin's ruined face twitched.

"The guards are already bribed and will be nowhere to be seen. As for the Blood-spill sentries, leave them to me!"

Ali pulled the bundle completely apart and drew out two black-hooded garments and a pair of brightly coloured cloaks.

"Put on this black creep-suit," the assassin ordered, handing him one of the long black garments. "You will be almost invisible in the darkness and then put one of the coloured cloaks over the top. Folks will take us for a pair of evening revellers and that will be our disguise until we reach the base of the ramparts. The coloured cloaks will then be discarded having served their purpose. Now hurry, for the precious hours of darkness are quickly ebbing away!"

꿀

The two men moved swiftly through a maze of side-alleys and back lanes, until they reached a portion of the city walls where a circular stairway led upwards to the top of the darkened ramparts. Darryl expected a soldier to emerge from the guard post standing at the base of the stair, but nothing moved and the two men began their ascent without being challenged. The walkway at the top of the ramparts was likewise deserted, although burning torches illuminated the guard posts that stood at regular intervals.

Ali, the son of Grom, took the lead and the two men moved along the walkway as silently as possible, cautiously flitting from one patch of dark shadow to another.

Finally, they came abreast of a tall tower whose roof was almost level with the walkway. A gap of about fifteen hand-spans separated the edge of the parapet from the flat roof of the tower and the void between the two buildings was terrifying to the imagination.

The assassin pulled the younger man back into the safety of a deep pool of shadow, then drew out his deadly perm and began to carefully scan the roof of the Blood-spill headquarters.

Five minutes passed, then ten, and the boatmaster witnessed nothing. Then he noticed a slight movement behind the head of a rooftop ventilator, in the same instant he heard a faint 'Phut' from the assassin's weapon and all movement on the roof ceased immediately.

Ali did not waste time admiring his marksmanship; instead he dived into a nearby guard post and emerged carrying a long ladder, which the two men pushed out across the void until it rested upon the very edge of the pirate's tower. Ali crawled out along the ladder with the boatmaster holding it firmly. The old assassin soon reached the roof of the tower and then it was the boatmaster's turn to cross the ghastly void. Inch by inch, Darryl forced himself to crawl forward until he too was standing upon the top of the flat roof.

The pair stepped over the corpse of the guard, whom Ali had slain with the poison tipped perm dart and searched until they found an open skylight with a ladder leading down into a deserted attic room.

The son of Grom took the lead and quietly climbed down the ladder until he reached the floor of the room. He crept over to a single door and listened intently for a few moments, before gently easing it open just sufficiently to take a quick look outside.

The door, it transpired, opened out into a dimly lit corridor and the assassin was just able to make out the indistinct silhouette of a guard who was stationed at the far end of the passageway. Ali eased the muzzle of the perm through the crack in the door and shot a single dart into the man's leg. The Blood-spill guard uttered only a single strangled gasp as the deadly nerve toxin took effect and a second later his lifeless body slipped noiselessly to the floor. With the killing accomplished, the assassin safely entered the room with Darryl at his heels, holding his razor-sharp gill at the ready.

It quickly became clear that the two intruders had successfully found the pirate's prison complex, for a number of cells, each equipped with a heavy wooden door, lined the sides of the passageway, which they had just entered. Darryl whispered his friends name outside several of the doors before George replied in a gruff voice and the boatmaster was relieved to know that his young comrade was still alive.

Darryl threw aside the bolts and the rather dishevelled boat hand stepped out into the passageway. However, George's whispered greeting quickly turned into a shouted warning, for the cell door opposite crashed open and a second Blood-spill guard, who had been apparently disturbed whist taking an illicit nap, appeared with his heavy war-axe raised and ready to strike. Fortunately, Darryl reacted with the lightning speed of a trained fighter. Spinning upon his heel, he instantly laid the man's midriff open with a single stroke from his gill, then decapitated him with a second blow.

Unfortunately, the man's brief cry for help brought a shouted response from the floor below and the thunder of feet could soon be heard upon the lower stairs.

"Quickly, back onto the roof," the assassin ordered, but his instructions were interrupted by a shout from one of the cells.

"In the name of all the Gods, don't leave me here to die. Take me with you and I swear that I will be your man forever!"

The plea for help came from a cell lying close by and Ali cursed furiously as George disobeyed his orders and darted to the man's assistance. He grasped the battle-axe from the dead guards hand and smashed open the door of the cell with a single blow. He pushed the occupant of the cell into the attic-room and towards the base of the ladder leading to the roof and he ordered the man to climb for his life.

Combat with the Blood-spill clansmen, who were streaming up from the floor below, was now inevitable and Darryl immediately ran to the head of the stairs and cutting down the first of the pirates to emerge. Ali joined him and quickly launched three poisoned darts down the stairwell in rapid succession, whilst George turned from his mission of rescue and lifted the body of the boatmaster's first victim above his head, hurling it downwards amidst the attackers attempting to ascend the stairs.

"Come now," the old assassin cried, as the press momentarily slackened. "Back onto the roof whilst we still have a chance of escaping."

Ali then ran back into the attic room, with his companions in close attendance and jammed the door shut with a chair.

"Back onto the roof and across the ladder to the battlements," he yelled, diving for the skylight. "And hurry if you value your lives, for that door won't hold for more than a few seconds."

The men obeyed and quickly reached the sanctuary of the battlements, although the man whom George had rescued from the cell fainted at the very moment he reached the roof of the tower and had to be dragged bodily across the groaning ladder.

"Push the ladder into the void!" the assassin cried, as the last man reached the ramparts, but a darter projectile struck the edge of the walkway as George attempted to obey the order, and he was forced to join his companions in the shelter of one of the deserted guard-posts as a veritable hail of darts followed the first.

The situation was now becoming critical, for some of the pirates were attempting to cross the ladder, heedless of Ali's poisoned darts that picked of two of their number, when help suddenly arrived from an unexpected quarter.

A wind that was no product of nature howled across the battlements and shook the guard-post were the party were hiding from the darter projectiles. It grew in strength and picked up the ladder and flung it, together with its burden of doomed pirates, downwards into the terrifying void. The wind grew in strength until it screamed across the old quarter of the city and plucked the remaining darter marksmen from the roof of the tower, as though they were ripe fruit hurling them to their deaths in the streets below.

At the same instant, an irresistible mental command exploded inside the boatmaster's brain...

"Run... Escape now... Whilst you have a chance!"

The other members of the party had presumably heard the same command, for they all bolted from the guard-post with Ali sprinting in the lead. On they ran, along the walkway and down the spiral stairway, until they reached the safety of the street.

Yet even as Darryl fled in near panic he spared a single second to glance over his shoulder. Standing upon the battlements and silhouetted by the light of a single torch, he spotted the solitary figure of a man who was wearing the dark robe of a priest. And the man's right hand was still pointing towards the roof of the tower where his magical powers had wreaked such havoc. The boatmaster did not venture a second look, he simply ran like a man possessed.

※

The boatmaster lay upon his bunk in the cabin of the Bonny Barbara and listened to the comforting sound of the water lapping against the hull.

Almost three days had gone by since the terrible events that accompanied George's rescue. Days of constant activity as the narrowboat completed her fitting out for the long voyage down the Great Life River. Darryl, however, had found time to reflect upon his recent experiences in the city of Calar and upon his young boat hand's abduction.

He recalled his meeting with Ali the grim assassin and above all, his vivid recollection of the dark priest pointing the finger of death towards the luckless Blood-spill pirates.

He remembered the headlong flight and the hasty scramble to board the fast litters that Ali had caused to have waiting for them in the darkness below the city walls.

The boatmaster also pondered upon their bumping, swaying journey through the mass of revellers in the Quarter of All Pleasures and their exit through a little-used gate in the city walls. Indeed, Darryl had almost wept with relief when the party had reached the docks and the sanctuary of Agar-Marduk's wharf buildings.

Ali, son of Grom, had refused to enter the dockyard area and taken leave of the travellers by the city gate. He had grasped the boatmaster by the arm, in the now-familiar Water Realm gesture of farewell.

"I wish you only the best of fortune," he had said. "But I thank the Gods that I am not accompanying you, wherever you are bound. I also looked to the rear, as we fled along those accursed ramparts and I viewed the figure of the Dark Priest as we ran for our lives." He had laughed grimly. "Life has taught me that fortune seldom smiles upon those whom the Dark Priests favour. For that reason, Black Darryl, I pray that I never set eyes upon you again."

The assassin had drawn his cloak tightly around his body and disappeared into the depths of the city.

Agar-Marduk had welcomed the returning navigators like a pair of long lost brothers and roasted a whole narr on the quayside in celebration. At the height of the festivities, a man whom Darryl knew to be an assistant wharf-master was led before him in chains. The old merchant had informed him that he was the man responsible for betraying them to the Blood-spill pirates. He would now face a lifetime of slavery aboard one of the Prince of Calar's war-galleys. The man's wife and two weeping children were also led forward in chains. The sad trio, the old merchant had explained, would also be sold into bondage. In addition, their offspring for perhaps a thousand generations would be fated to toil under the pitiless lash. Such was the price of betrayal in Calar of the Mighty Walls.

Darryl had not been tempted to plead for clemency on behalf of the criminal's wife and two children, and he began to wonder if the harsh usages of the Water Realm were beginning to affect his own sense of humanity.

Preparations for the narrowboat's departure had continued apace, but one of the boats pontoons had developed a slight leak and needed to be repaired and re-caulked; this had taken two full days to complete.

The merchant again suggested the disposal of the remainder of the boats cargo of iron rails, here in Calar, for the metal was an obvious magnet for pirates. This time, Darryl had agreed willingly and had received, in return, a number of sealed merchants' bonds that could be exchanged for good copper coinage in any of the many trading establishments lying along the banks of the Great Life River.

A cargo of good Northland timber, a commodity much sought after in Holy Ptah had also been taken on board in place of the iron and this would help to reinforce their cover as being ordinary river traders. Extra protection would also be provided, during the first leg of their voyage, by the presence on board the Bonny Barbara of six of Agar-Marduk's best security guards; men who were taking leave in their home village that lay some twenty days' sailing to the south.

Another sound began assailing Darryl's eardrums as he continued to rest in his bunk, the sound of heavy rain beating down upon the roof of the narrowboat's tiny cabin; he knew that cooler weather had now arrived in this portion of the Water Realm.

The boatmaster was also comforted to know that Myra was again occupying her cabin aboard the narrowboat, having returned from the Temple of Dumteck on the previous evening. He had been eager to converse with her and to give her a full account of his recent experiences in the old quarter of Calar. But his twin sister was extremely tired and he reasoned that a mutual exchange of knowledge would be best undertaken at leisure, once they were sailing upon the waters of the Life River.

Meanwhile, his sister was comfortably bedded down and fast asleep.

The Bonny Barbara had also acquired a new pilot for the coming voyage down the great river. The prisoner whom George had rescued from the Blood-spill prison was still deeply unconscious when the party had reached the shelter of Agar-Marduk's wharves. Indeed, it was little wonder, for the man's body was covered with the livid marks of numerous branding and the deep cuts upon his back showed that he had been mercilessly scourged with heavy whips.

Agar-Marduk had recognized the man as soon as he set eyes upon him.

"By all the Gods!" he had said. "That's Wilakin of the River, one of the best young pilots who ever sailed upon the Life River. You are indeed fortunate to have him swear allegiance to you, for you need a person with his navigational abilities, if you are to reach Holy Ptah unscathed!"

The pilot had been tended by the merchant's own physician and had quickly recovered consciousness, although it was quite certain that he would need some time to recover his full strength after such a terrible ordeal. Even so, he had insisted upon repeating his oath of allegiance to the boatmaster and had willingly agreed to serve as the Bonny Barbara's sailing master for the coming voyage.

Wilakin, it transpired, had been abducted by the Blood-spill clansmen in order to force him to betray a valuable cargo.It said much for the young man's bravery through successfully resisting every torture inflicted upon him.

The light of the Water Realm dawn began penetrating the windows of the tiny cabin and Darryl knew that he must rise at once, for the narrowboat was due to depart within the hour. He quickly dressed and stepped out into the cockpit of his vessel and looked out over the waters of the dock to where a towing galley was already manoeuvring to pass them a line. Darryl would have climbed up into the bows to lend George a hand with the towing line, but his attention was distracted by a call from the wharf, where Agar-Marduk and his entire family were waiting to wish them a safe journey.

"May all of the Gods be with you!" cried the old merchant, casting handfuls of flour and salt upon the water to propitiate the water spirits, "and may the rivers upon which you sail always stay calm and friendly!"

Darryl acknowledged the merchant's well-wishing with a wave of his hand. His eyes swept out over the docks to the city of Calar. Calar of the Might Walls.

"A place where much evil dwells!" he concluded. Yet he also surmised that good people such as Agar-Marduk and his hospitable family also dwelt there and thankfully prevented evil from having full reign. But how did that dark priest who had stood upon the battlements, fit into the picture? And what vital knowledge had Myra managed to gain in the Temple of Dumteck?

The boatmaster shrugged his shoulders. "Only the future will provide the answer to those questions!" he decided as he concentrated upon casting off the stern mooring. "For we begin our voyage to the Great Life River, then onwards to Holy Ptah, the fabled city with walls of shinning copper."

Chapter 5

Hetty relaxed luxuriously in the steaming hot bath and rested after her lover of the night had departed. The young man had been good, a real stallion and the wisewoman had enjoyed herself immensely. Hetty liked sex for her occult beliefs venerated both nature and procreation and she was quite uninhibited by the narrow-minded restrictions of the Christian Church.

Over the years, Hetty had entertained many lovers in her cottage by the canal. Usually her beau for the night had been a passing boatman or a waggoner, and even the occasional herdsman driving his charges to the Manchester slaughterhouses, all pausing to spend the hours of darkness in the wisewoman's embrace. Hetty, however, was no slave to the demands of her loins and seldom welcomed the attentions of local men who could prove troublesome if she wished to abruptly end an affair.

Instead she preferred to allow her sexuality to lapse for weeks or even months at a time and had occupied herself with the ills of her often desperately sick patents.

She stretched out and let the hot water caress her body. The youth had been her first client for over a week and she knew that she was unlikely to lie in the embrace of another man for several more days. Mildred Pasco, despite her fearsome appearance, took great care over the day-to-day welfare of her girls and she made sure that none of them became overtaxed through entertaining too many lovers in too short a space of time; for she knew well enough that her wealthy clientele could not be fobbed off with listless and jaded merchandise. Even the hours spent waiting upon table in the Cleopatra Music Hall were carefully limited and Mildred also kept a close eye upon the way the girls dressed and frequently examined their personal hygiene. Heaven help the hapless waitress-cum-whore who betraying the slightest trace of body odour.

Almost six weeks had elapsed since Marsie' and the wisewoman had begun working at the Cleopatra and both women had now become quite used to the routine of the establishment. The women were roused at about nine o'clock in the morning by one of the maids and were usually free to do as they pleased until midday, unless they were required to take an occasional early turn behind the public bar. Afternoon duties occurred about twice a week, but every woman who was not entertaining a client in one of the private rooms, was expected to be on duty in the public house or the music hall, from seven o'clock in the evening until about midnight when the last client had departed. Waiting upon the tables in the body of the music hall could be hectic in the extreme, for the clientele were mostly drawn from the same social class as those who frequented the pudding and pie establishment, and they often filled the music hall to the doors when 'out on the town' for their Saturday night's entertainment. Even so, there were many nights of the week when the artists on the stage were performing to thin houses and Mrs Pasco would give half of her staff the evening off. Sunday, of course, was a day of rest.

Mildred placed no restrictions upon the movement of her female employees and Marsie' and the wisewoman often spent some of their free time wandering around the city. They admired the expensive wares within the shops and the newly constructed shopping malls and viewing the houses of the well-to-do merchants where copies of classical sculptures stood amidst colourful beds of flowers, giving visual evidence of their owner's prosperity. However, Hetty always planed a route that never took them close to the canals, where there was always a slight possibility that she might be recognized by some passing boatman.

She picked up a tablet of scented soap and reflected upon the men who had been her clients for the past six weeks as she rubbed the fragrant oils into her skin. A mixed bunch of men, she concluded. The majority had been middle-aged businessmen, possibly bankers and leading merchants, a fact the wisewoman had been easily able to define from their general lack of physical fitness, their slack muscles and smooth uncallused hands.

Some had been quite explicit and openly stated the nature of their businesses without divulging their names. "Had a good day in the Cotton Exchange," one had said, as he leaned over the supper table and freed Hetty's ample breasts from her bodice. "Made a thousand pounds in the first hour of trading, lass, so I deserve a good tumble here in the Cleopatra." The cotton factor had been a competent lover, she recalled, despite his rather prominent beer belly, but some of her clients, strange as it might seem, had no wish to indulge in sex and contented themselves with an evening of quiet conversation, sadly recounting their fears and frustrations to a prostitute rather than burdening the deaf ears of their unloving wives. Once, a thoroughly distraught man had spent the hours of darkness, weeping in her arms as he grieved for a dead friend, and the wisewoman had quickly realised all the ills of the world were not confined to the poor of Manchester.

A great deal of unhappiness was to be found beneath the thin veneer of middle-class respectability.

One of the waitresses-cum-prostitutes was occasionally expected to visit a client at his own residence and was given an extra remuneration for providing this service. Only once had Hetty been required to undertake this duty. On that occasion a private coach had taken her to a large house near Didsbury, where she graced the bed of a grey-haired old gentleman who had once been a magnate in the coal trade. The man had wined and dined her on champagne, beefsteak and oysters, and had sent her home in his coach with two golden guineas in her purse.

Hetty stepped from her bath and towelled herself vigorously. She was far from satisfied with her enquiries within the Cleopatra, for despite keeping her eyes and ears open, she had been quite unable to discover anything of Albert Pike's affairs, or indeed gain any information that might help to clear her son's name. However, by discreetly questioning some of the girls, she had learned that Pike occasionally indulged his carnal nature by spending a night with one of the women. The fight-promoter's habit was to sit in the body of the Cleopatra with a group of his drinking friends and select the woman whom he would visit the following evening. Pike, it seemed, frequented the establishment for sex about once a month and a visit was now well overdue; these few facts, however meagre, had been sufficient to stimulate the wisewoman's curiosity, and she had devised a plan to uncover the fight-promoter's secrets. Hetty covered her nakedness with a nightshift and a heavy bathrobe and followed the stairs and passageways that led to the bedroom she shared with Marsie' her companion.

"Beware, Albert Pike," she muttered sleepily to herself, as she slipped between the warm bed sheets. "You are a man with well-kept secrets, but fate has now decreed that you will share your knowledge with Hetty, the wisewoman of Elfencot."

The day was overcast and rain was falling upon the city of Manchester in sheets, as Hetty entered the side door of the Cleopatra. She removed her soaking wet cape in the hallway and hurried up to her bedroom and began stripping off her drenched undergarments. It had been no fit day for a person to be abroad on the streets. Yet the bad weather had suited the wisewoman's purpose, for it had concealed her movements when she visited the boat-chandler, to collect the small package that Jenny had dispatched by post from Elfencot, in accordance with her written instructions.

She dried herself and donned fresh clothing before opening the package that had been wrapped in sailcloth to protect it from the rain. The package contained a small wooden box, no more than three inches long and with a sliding lid. Inside, cushioned in lamb's-wool, lay a tiny glass vial and a small bundle of needle-sharp blackthorns tied together with a strand of cotton thread.

Hetty carefully picked up the vial and pondered momentarily upon the green liquid. 'Aye, this will loosen your tongue, Albert Pike,' she thought. For the liquid contained within the vial was a potion known only to a handful of the most adept herbalists as 'Truth.' The potion was prepared from a tiny blue flower that was only found upon a few of the highest crags of the Pennine hills.

'Truth' had once been a common flower growing in the primeval uplands, but only a few roots of the plant now remained and the species must soon disappear into extinction. Indeed, the potion Hetty now held in her hand, had been prepared by her grandmother half a century ago. A long-dead Shaman had named both the plant and the drug 'Truth,' because a person who was pierced by a thorn, dipped in the potion, would become semiconscious, and in that condition would truthfully answer any question put to them. In addition, the subject would have no recollection of the unwitting indiscretion.

Hetty smiled grimly as she replaced the vial in its container, for the time had now arrived for putting into action the plan that had slowly been maturing in her mind ever since her arrival some eight weeks ago. She intended to meet Albert Pike during one of his visits to the Cleopatra and then play upon the man's sexual appetite until he was in the grip of uncontrollable desires. She would then administer the drug whilst the fight-promoter lay locked in her arms. In this manner she hoped to discover the hidden details of the man's relationship with her son, Darryl. The strategy, however, was not without risk to herself, for the potion had dangerous side effects and could mentally impair the subject or even kill him. Indeed, it was not beyond the realms of possibility for the wisewoman to hang for murder.

The drug had arrived at the boat-chandlers store just in time to serve Hetty's purpose, for only yesterday evening she learned that Albert Pike would be at the Cleopatra this very night.

Mildred had called together the five waitresses, including Hetty, who were required to be on duty the next evening. "Now see here, girls," she had said, in her usual authoritative voice. "My brother Albert is comin' to the music hall tomorrow night so as to celebrate his birthday. He and his friends are to be given anything they desire and I want to hear no complaints afterwards."

"No bloody complaints," a blonde girl called Rose had muttered in a low voice. "I waited on yon bugger's party, last year, and me arse got pinched so bad that I couldn't sit down for near a week."

'It will be you who needs to watch your arse, Albert Pike,' the wisewoman thought, as she hid the container away in her dressing table. 'Time you got punished for pinchin' ladies bums, you bastard.'

❧

The second act of the night, a troupe of Italian tumblers, were performing on the stage of the Cleopatra when Rose nudged the wisewoman gently in the side and told her that Albert Pike and his party were entering the main body of the music hall. Hetty turned and noticed the group in question were seating themselves at a number of tables being the responsibility of the two women. Rose, who was free at that moment, hurried over to the visitors and took an order for some fifteen pints of strong ale and a varied assortment of wines and spirits. "Best get yer present order done with," she said to the wisewoman as she loaded her tray with brimming tankards, "for that bugger Pike and his crew seem well drunk already, and might turn nasty upon us if we keep them waiting over-long." Hetty nodded and delivered her current order of drinks, then hurried over to the bar to collect some of the wines and spirits required by the birthday revellers. She paused, momentarily, at a long mirror by the bar and quickly checked over her appearance. She smoothed her long red hair falling around her shoulders and viewed the reflected image of her breasts swelling out from the plunging neckline of her low-cut black velvet dress, an outfit that she had chosen especially for Pike's benefit. Hetty smiled. "Not bad for an old lass," she concluded with satisfaction.

She carried her tray with its load of bottles and glasses, over to the half a dozen tables, situated close to the stage where the fight-promoter's party had chosen to sit.

Hetty quickly ran her eyes over the birthday gathering. Pike she immediately recognised from her son's description, but the remainder were a very motley crew.

Four of the guests were muscular young gentlemen who appeared to be professional fighters, probably from the Sparta Gymnasium, whilst two more were dressed in smart dark suits and might have been country clerics, had not the scars on their faces betrayed them as being hired thugs. The remainder were obviously middle class friends of the fight-promoter, men who probably frequented his numerous venues and possibly sought his company for the sporting entertainment that he was certainly capable of providing; some might even have been close businesses associates of the man. One thing was obvious: with the exception of the scar-faced minders, they were all on the way to complete intoxication. Hetty unloaded some of the bottles and glasses at the first table, and then moved on to the next where Pike and some of his cronies were drinking ale like drowning men. "Here's part of your order Mr Pike," she said, smiling sweetly as she transferred the bottles and glasses to the tabletop and stretched over the table to collect some empty glasses giving the fight-promoter a close-up view of her very ample cleavage.

"I'll be back soon with the rest of the order," she said, and strode back to the bar, knowing instinctively that Pike's eyes were now riveted upon her.

She placed the tray upon the bar and reaching behind her back with both hands. She deliberately began smoothing out the wrinkles in her velvet dress, allowing her fingers to run seductively over her well-formed buttocks. She turned her head slightly and out of the corner of her eye she noticed, with satisfaction, that the fight-promoter's eyes were still fixed upon her.

Hetty served a number of other customers and then returned to the fight-promoter's party, bearing a tray loaded with steaming bowlfuls of pig's trotters and freshly cooked marrow-bones. She placed some of the bowls on Albert Pike's table, but as she did so, he reached out and took hold of her by the wrist. "You must be one of my sister's whores," he said with beer dribbling down his chin. "I think I'll take you upstairs right now, and celebrate my birthday by givin' you a bloody good rodgerin...."

The fight-promoter proceeded no further with his drunken threat, for Mildred appeared at the wisewoman's side as though conjured by magic. She pulled the man's fingers from Hetty's wrists. "Steady there; Albert," she said in a steely voice. "Not even me own brother is goin' to maul me girls. You can have her tomorrow and ride her raw; besides, you couldn't screw yer own shadow the state you're in right now."

Mildred's final comment drew a burst of laughter from Pike's immediate companions and the manageress ushered Hetty back to the safety of the bar. "Get yerself up to yer room," she ordered. "The rest of the girls can manage and get ready to give Albert a bloody good bouncing tomorrow night. Now shift yerself!"

A lady singer wearing a vivid scarlet dress was finishing the last of a medley of sentimental songs as the wisewoman left the hall. 'Enjoy the singing, Pike,' she thought. 'Tomorrow night you'll be singing a different tune. Aye and I'll be the one doing the listening.'

꒰

Fabric ripped as Albert Pike burst open the wisewoman's bodice in his eager desire to fondle her breasts. Hetty's dress, petticoats and drawers already lay in shreds alongside the bed, whilst she herself was stretched out across the embroidered coverlet, as the sexually aroused fight-promoter began licking and sucking her nipples with the eagerness of a child in desperate need for sustenance.

Pike had knocked upon the door of the private room less than ten minutes earlier and, upon being admitted, had completely ignored the champagne, oysters and other delicacies spread out upon the dining room table. Instead, the man had dragged Hetty, his woman for the night, into the adjoining bedchamber and stripped himself stark-naked before roughly tearing the clothing from her body.

Hetty continued to endure the fight-promoter's initially brutal attentions, until his mood began to change into one of languid passion as he feasted avidly upon her breasts, whilst the wisewoman encouraged Pike's mood-change by gently stroking his back with the tips of her fingers. The man groaned, then ran his right hand down the length of her body, parting her pubic hair with his fingers and began expertly massaging her pelvic area with the tip of his index finger. Hetty responded to the man's arousal technique by arching her spine and driving her fingernails into his back until she drew blood

The wisewoman's action further stimulated the fight-promoter, who forced her legs apart and drove his penis into her body in a single movement. Hetty moaned in response and raked the man's back with her fingernails, then, as the fight-promoter began ploughing into her she reached out with her right hand, retrieving one of the six drug impregnated thorns lying hidden beneath a napkin on her bedside table. Again, she raked the man's back, using his pain to mask the prick of the thorn, which she slipped beneath his skin.

Pike grunted and continued pushing into her vigorously for another minute, then his movements slowed to a stop and his once rampant penis became flaccid and slipped out of the wisewoman's body. Hetty laughed quietly in triumph, then slipped from beneath Pike's body and turned him over onto his back. She took another of the thorns inserting it into the man's arm close to an artery.

Pike was now quite unable to move and his eyes wandered aimlessly as the wisewoman began her interrogation.

"Do you know Darryl Littlewood, the ex-boxer?"

"Yes," he answered.

"Were you responsible for the ambush leaving him branded as a murderer?"

The man's eyes focused upon her face for a moment. "No," he grunted.

"Tell me, who was to blame for the attack at Hell's Corner?" she said, pressing the thorn a fraction deeper into the man's flesh.

"Silas Oldshaw," came the reply.

Hetty was amazed by the answer, and she began to realize the plot that had ruined her son was deeper and far more complex than she had ever imagined.

She paused and visited the dining room to retrieved a glass and a bottle of Champagne, for it was now obvious that the interrogation would be long and complicated.

"We have the whole night before us, Albert my lad," she said, looking down upon the prone form of the fight-promoter. "I'll know all of your secrets, even if the drug should leave you stone dead."

꙳

Hetty opened the curtains and allowing the dawn light to flood into her bedroom. She was tired! The interrogation had taken most of the night, and had required all of the wisewoman's wit, plus five of the six drug-impregnated needles to glean the information that she required.

Albert Pike lay unconscious on the bed and his face was ashen white, yet his pulse was strong and the wisewoman had no doubt that two or three days' rest would restore him to his usual self.

Hetty poured the last of the champagne into her glass and pondered upon the importance of the information that she had extracted from the fight-promoter.

Joe and Mildred Pasco, as she had suspected, were people of straw, who, despite their undoubted managerial expertise, held only a small financial interest in the eating house, the two commercial hotels and the music-hall-cum-brothel.

Overall control of the group, Hetty had learned early in the interrogation, was vested in Albert Pike, who owned a profitable quarter share in the venture. However, long and careful questioning was needed before the wisewoman was able to discover that Silas Oldshaw was the fight-promoter's silent partner and the real power behind the two men's various legal and illegal businesses enterprises.

Silas Oldshaw, it transpired, had also been directly responsible for her son's ruin.

Stovepipe Arkwright, the fight-promoter had disclosed, had sometimes undertaken small tasks for the mill owner, and after his bitter clash with Darryl at the Sparta Gymnasium, Stovepipe had picked himself up off the floor and followed the young boatmaster to the premises of Downes And Son's, his bankers. He had then hurried to Oldshaw's townhouse and given the man a first-hand account of all that had occurred. The mill owner, Pike had revealed, had flown into a rage at being denied the bare-knuckle contest that he so desired, and had detailed one of his minions to accompany the runner and give the boatmaster a beating that would leave him half-crippled. Robbery as a means of forcing Darryl to return to the ring had not, as the wisewoman had suspected, been the real reason for the brutal attack at Hells Corner. Instead, the motive had been the thwarted whim of a man with the power to hurt those who attempted to resist his will.

Hetty was now in possession of most of the main facts. Even so, she realized that she still had much to accomplish before being able to clear her son's name.

At first, she had considered reporting both Albert Pike and Silas Oldshaw to the police, but the fight-promoter was sure to deny everything, once he regained full control of his faculties, and a possibility also existed that she would fall foul of a member of the constabulary who was already in the men's pay.

'No,' she thought, she must bide her time and somehow find her son's second assailant and his female accomplice and persuade them to provide evidence of Darryl's innocence.

Pike, however, appeared to have no certain knowledge of their whereabouts, but he believed them to be creatures of the mill owner and members of his household.

Hetty splashed water from a ewer upon Pike's face and applied smelling salts to his nostrils. As she worked she considered what her future course of action should be. One thing was certain; she must gain a greater knowledge of Oldshaw's affairs.

Yet her witch's inner eye, which had remained dormant during her residence at the Cleopatra, had suddenly come awake, and she was now experiencing a deep feeling of menace whenever matters concerning the mill owner crossed her mind.

Indeed, there was a great deal about Silas Oldshaw that she did not fully understand. Why, for instance, should a prosperous industrialist who owned a large cotton mill in Stalybridge and reputed to have shareholdings in a number of other factories, have need to invest in a music hall that also doubled as a brothel? Only one explanation suggested itself to the wisewoman. Perhaps Silas Oldshaw had invested in the Cleopatra in order to discreetly provide himself with a supply of women who could be made to satisfy his sexual appetites in any way he pleased. She gasped with horror as she began to suspect the nature of the man's desire.

The wisewoman had kept her ear to the ground, during her stay in the Cleopatra, and she had discovered that several of the women had experienced varying degrees of physical abuse whilst visiting clients in their own homes. In most cases the injuries sustained were scratches and light bruises occurring during bouts of boisterous sex-play. However, some of the women had suffered far more serious forms of injury. For during the eight weeks that she had been in residence, two women had been excused duty for periods of ten days or more and another girl had needed a much longer period of treatment in a nursing home at Buxton Spa.

The three unfortunate women who experienced such levels of brutality were tight-lipped with fear and would say nothing, but a drunken doorman, whom the wisewoman had engaged in conversation, had divulged that all three girls had been absent from the Cleopatra for periods of two or three days at a time, and had been transported in a black coach. The driver of the vehicle had been a burly man with the battered face of a pugilist and Hetty realized that it could only have been Oldshaw's coach driver--the prize-fighter whom the mill owner had wished to match against her son.

The drunken doorman had also mentioned that about a year ago, a buxom redhead called Claire, with whom he had been extremely friendly, had disappeared one night in the black coach and had never returned. Hetty had wished to question the man further, but the doorman suddenly realized that he was being dangerously indiscrete and departed to sleep off his head full of whisky fumes.

Silas Oldshaw, the witch now strongly suspected, was a psychopath who derived his pleasure from witnessing the brutalities of the boxing ring, and enjoyed personally inflicting pain in the bedroom. She now realized that she must seek proof of his perversions in order to clear her son's name, and rid the world of a monster.

However, to accomplish this task, the wisewoman knew that she would have to become a member of the mill owner's household, if she was to gain a closer knowledge of the man's affairs; but as yet, she had no idea of how this might be accomplished.

Meanwhile, she resolved to remain at the Cleopatra and gather as much additional information as possible, and plan her next move.

Pike groaned and opened his eyes. "For pity's sake, what happened to me last night?" he asked in a weak voice.

"You overdid yourself, that's what you did," Hetty answered, placing a tumbler of brandy and water to his lips. "You might have been the freshest young ramrod in Manchester once upon a time, but you ain't anymore. Best get yourself home to bed and lay off drinkin' and jumping on top of whores for a while."

The wisewoman dispatched a skivvy to find a horse-cab, then helped the sick fight-promoter to dress and supported him as he descended the stairs into the main hall. Finally, she placed him into the care of the burly cab-driver who had arrived to take him home.

"Sleep well, Pike," she said to herself as she watched the horse-cab depart. "I swear that I'll not rest until both you and Oldshaw are sleeping in prison cells. Then may the devil rot the pair of you forever!"

Chapter 6

Rain fell in sheets from an angry red sky, as the mighty walls of Calar fell astern of the Bonny Barbara."Darryl cursed the water penetrating his battered old oilskin coat, as he manned the tiller and carefully steered the vessel close to the left hand shore as Wilakin, the river pilot, had instructed him to do.

"Keep well away from the middle of the river," the man had warned him. "Or you may possibly collide with a vessel that's being towed upriver from the junction with the Great Life River, you would hardly see an approaching vessel in all this mist and rain!"

The boatmaster was happy, despite the weather, for it was good to feel the narrowboat moving beneath his feet and he was glad to have left the anthill of Calar behind.

Another figure, likewise dressed in oilskins, joined him in the cockpit and he recognized the newcomer as his twin sister, Myra.

"We need to talk, Darryl," she said. "for many of the events of the past few days are almost beyond my comprehension, but first, tell me everything that happened to you after I left for the Temple of Dumtek."

The young boatmaster nodded and swiftly related every detail of George's capture and release, without taking his eyes off the river for a single second.

Myra listened quietly until her brother had finished speaking.

"So one of the Dark Priests intervened to save the lives of your party upon the battlements of Calar," she said. "Well, it doesn't surprise me after what I've experienced in the Temple of Dumtek. For the litter that took me from Agar-Marduk's house bore me directly to the temple precinct situated close to the far walls of the city. At first, I was placed in the care of three cheerful young lay-brothers of the medical order, who took me through the hospital wards and instructed me in many of the treatments and remedies commonly use to aid the sick. Later, I was placed in the hands of two priests wearing dark robes with hoods spun from black narrs-wool. These priests led me to a small room lying within the bowels of the temple and they kept me company for two full days, although I swear that it felt like a veritable eternity!"

The wisewoman paused for a moment to brush away the rainwater that was running down her face.

"At first, I believed the two priests were going to give me further instruction in the medical arts. Instead, they ordered me to carry out exercises that were designed to strengthen my mental powers and give me the ability to converse with other individuals by the power of the mind alone. For hours, they had me seated before a crystal ball, saying it would act as a mental conduit allowing me to communicate without a single word ever passing my lips."

Myra looked her brother straight in the eye. "I tell you, Darryl, never again do I wish to endure such a terrible strain, for I truly thought that my brain was going to burst.

"Yet, after a while, I was able to read some of the thoughts they projected towards me. Later, they required me to cast my own thoughts abroad, eventually, the three of us were able to converse without speaking within the narrow confines of that small room. After what seemed like another eternity, they gave me back into the keeping of the same young lay-brothers; they fed me and allowed me a little rest before continuing my instruction in the medical arts. Eventually, I was dismissed without a word of farewell and returned to the dockside to be reunited with you and the rest of the boats company."

The young wisewoman extended her right hand, and in her palm lay a small transparent sphere of crystal.

"The Dark Priests gave me this crystal and ordered me to give you regular lessons in the art of thought transfer. They said that it should be possible for us to communicate with each other, to a limited degree, for we both have witch's blood in our veins and are twins of the womb!"

A spine of rock jutted out from the shoreline a little way ahead of the boat and the boatmaster thrust the tiller hard over in order to pass the obstruction at a safe distance.

"Those black-hooded Priests of the Ancient Lore seem to be taking a fair lot of interest in us," he said, "and I would give all of our supply of copper to know why. However, I daresay that time will show whether they mean to help or do us harm."

At that moment, the twins' conversation was interrupted by George, who emerged from the cabin to relieve Darryl at the tiller. At Myra's suggestion, the twins made their way forward, so as to avail themselves of the privacy of her personal cabin situated in the bows of the craft. Once inside, the pair stripped off their oilskins and continued their conversation.

The young witch put her hand inside a storage bag and drew out an old book that Darryl recognized as the grimoire of Rose Littlewood. She also produced a roll of soft narrs-leather that was inscribed with long columns of unfamiliar words.

"I showed the grimoire to one of the senior priests and he gave me this roll. It is a dictionary of the temple script, which the priests sometimes use in their devotions. This dictionary should allow me to translate the temple script portions of Rose's grimoire into a form of English that I can understand. It may take weeks of hard work, but my inner eye tells me the book contains knowledge that may well save our lives."

Myra paused. "The senior priest also told me that Rose Littlewood is known to have stayed for a while in the Temple Of Dumtek when she first arrived in the Water Realm, and was taught the temple script by one of the institution's most able priests. He also whispered that she was brought to the temple by a Priest of the Ancient Lore, and had eventually departed in his company."

Darryl had no time to reply, for at that very moment, a look-out in the bows shouted that a line of mooring-posts had just hove into view. The boatmaster hurried onto the deck for this was the place where Wilakin had suggested they moor for the night. At first light, they would cast off again and proceed to the waterway's junction with the Great Life River, which the pilot was certain would be reached by mid-morning of the following day. Darryl again took charge of the tiller and eased the craft into its night berth. Afterwards, he set a strong guard to watch out for pirates, for Wilakin had warned him that bands of the marauders were active in this area and could attack at any time.

The boatmaster personally took command of the first watch and he sat in the bows with the sword Kingslayer resting across his knees.

"Tomorrow will be a memorable day," he pondered, as he peered into the gathering darkness. "The Bonny Barbara will breast the waters of the Great Life River for the first time. Another waterway to sail, another shoreline to see, may the night pass swiftly and roll on the dawn."

⚘

The Bonny Barbara'quit her moorings at first light and carefully nosed her way out into the river with Darryl at the tiller. The rain had temporarily cleared and the visibility was good. Only the occasional squall disturbed the surface of the river, and the boatmaster was glad to have taken Wilakin's advice and flung a sack of the best Thoa flour over the side, as an offering to the Gods.

As the morning wore on, the banks of the Exit River fell away and the current slackened considerably. George, who was standing watch in the bows, reported that he could see a long shoreline on the horizon, which, the boatmaster realized, could only be the eastern bank of the Great Life River and Darryl knew the craft was nearing the junction of the two great waterways.

Suddenly, there was a commotion in the cockpit and Wilakin emerged supported by one of the temporary crewmembers. He groaned with pain and steadied himself by gripping the edge of the cabin roof.

"The currents and eddies are dangerous where the two rivers meet," he gasped. "It would be for the best if I was to go up into the bows and direct you."

The pilot painfully made his way forward and Darryl began steering the craft according to the man's instructions, relayed back to him by George and one of the temporary crewmembers. Ahead of them and now in full view flowed the Great Life River.'

The waterway was positively enormous and it must have been well over a mile and a quarter wide at its junction with the Exit River and many craft could be seen navigating its waters. Some of the vessels near the western bank of the Great Life were being carried south by its current, but, close to the far shore, the boatmaster was able to make out the hulls of numerous other craft moving in an opposing northerly direction and he was intrigued by this strange phenomenon.

The boatmaster's attention was momentarily distracted by a towing-galley that sped past them with its oars threshing the water into red foam, as it made for a vessel that was leaving the Great Life and attempting to enter the mouth of the Exit River.Darryl also noticed that several heavily laden trading craft were already being towed into the Exit River by other galleys and beginning their laborious journey upriver to Calar of the Mighty Walls.

Suddenly, they entered a stretch of turbulent water that made the "Bonny Barbara" pitch violently but a stream of urgent orders from the pilot enabled Darryl to steer the narrowboat through the seething belt of water where the two rivers joined.

Then, almost by magic, the craft was clear of the influence of the Exit River and was being carried south upon the flowing waters of the Great Life River.

Wilakin, now ashen faced with pain, was helped from the bows by a crewmember and also by Myra, who gave the man a powerful draught of a strengthening potion from her medicine bag.

"Keep her steady and her bows before the current," the pilot advised, as he was taken back into the shelter of the cabin, "and we shall fare well enough, until we reach our night mooring, for I know of a riverside village where we shall be well received!"

Darryl remained at the tiller in order to familiarize himself with the characteristics of the new waterway. After a while he realized that handling the craft was mere child's play, for the great river appeared to be largely free of the dangerous spits, sand banks and meanders that had plagued their descent of the Exit River. Even so, it was necessary to keep a look-out constantly stationed in the bows in order to give him early warning of an impending collision, for large numbers of other craft were also heading south in the left-hand portion of the mighty river. About a quarter of a mile ahead of them was a big open-decked barge that appeared to be carrying blocks of stone, doubtless for some large construction project; whilst unpleasantly close to the stone-barge's stern was a raft of massive Thoa logs, that was being held in station by a pair of brightly painted towing galleys. Immediately astern of the Bonny Barbara was a gaggle of tiny river craft that, one of the temporary crewmembers explained, were small vessels plying a local trade between the villages and hamlets lying at regular intervals along the banks of the mighty waterway.

A veritable cavalcade of vessels moved Northwards in the opposite direction. Once again, the vessels were of every type and design imaginable and varied from small boats with a single crewman, to a huge twin-decked cargo and passenger ship that must have been of six or seven hundred tons burdened. Most of the craft navigating the waterway were borne to their various destinations by the multi-directional flow of the river alone, yet a few of the smaller vessels that served a purely local trade, carried a simple sail allowing them to tack amongst the larger craft and also to make a landfall on the riverbanks with comparative ease. On one occasion the boatmaster had been forced to thrust the tiller hard over so as to avoid running down one of the smaller local craft that had ventured beneath his bows. Darryl had cursed violently at the boat's dangerous manoeuvre, but one of the temporary crewmembers, a squat, muscular individual called Dromon, had burst out laughing.

"You think the river is crowded today, master," he chuckled. "Yet this is the season of rains, when many of the merchants who normally sail these waters are safe at home with their friends and families. Why, my master, when the rains depart and the five suns are again strong in the sky, then the surface of the Great Life River will be so thick with shipping that you will need the sharpness of a riding-narr to avoid a collision, or worse, a fatal sinking."

"Are vessels often sunk?" Darryl enquired.

"No," Dromon replied. "But when this happens, a local overseer, appointed by the Dark Priests, sends a gang of men to raise the sunken craft and charge the full cost of the operation to the owners of the lost vessel. Aye, many a thriving merchant has been rendered poor by such a disaster."

The boatmaster smiled. "Then I must take care when I'm standing watch at the tiller and make sure that no incompetent fool takes charge of the steering in my absence."

The day wore on and rain began to falling in torrents. In late afternoon Wilakin was helped back into the cockpit of the boat and pointed towards the safe village that he had spoken of earlier. Under the pilot's direction, the boatmaster put the tiller over and gently steered the craft towards the left-hand bank of the river where there was little movement from the current.

A quarter of a mile ahead of them was a small settlement occupying a high artificially constructed mound that reared up sharply from the water's edge dominating the surrounding territory. At its base was a small quay, whose riverward approaches were protected by a squat tower mounting a pair of very lethal-looking missile-casting engines.

Darryl was a little surprised by the sight and he turned to the pilot.

"Wilakin, I was led to believe that no military preparations were allowed close to the Life River, on the direct orders of the Priests of the Ancient Lore who administer this great waterway?"

"Aye, that is generally the case," the river-pilot answered. "Any prince holding sway over a portion of the riverside lands would risk heavy punishment if he sought to gain control over the waterway itself. Yet, the Dark Priests allow some of the riverside villages to establish 'Night Harbours,' as we call them. Here vessels plying their legitimate trade on the river can lie in perfect safety during the hours of darkness and their crews do not run the risk of having their throats cut by river-pirates while they sleep."

"Why do the Dark Priests tolerate the existence of these bloody freebooters?" Darryl asked, without taking his eyes from the quay that was now looming large before the narrowboat's bow.

Wilakin replied with a bitter laugh.

"Why master, the pirates are like the weeds that grow in a Thoa plantation, the more you cut them down, the more they multiply! However, the priests occasionally order a prince or chieftain to wipe out the pirates within his domain. Less frequently, the priests order the Overseers of the River, the officials who are charged with the day-to-day running of the great waterway, to hire mercenaries and carry out the task themselves.

"Perhaps once in a man's lifetime, a group of pirate families will become overconfident and combine to conquer a riverside district. On those rare occasions, the priests will conjure up a sickness known as the 'The Shaking Death' and the miscreants will perish to a man. But much of the time, the pirates are simply ignored by the authorities."

A small towing boat, propelled by six oarsmen, put out from the quay and shepherded the Bonny Barbara into a vacant berth and the vessel was soon securely roped to her mooring.

"My wounds pain me still," the pilot said as he struggled towards the door of the narrowboat's cabin. "So my suggestion is that I remain aboard with two guards for company, whilst the remainder of you spend the night ashore as the paying guests of the villagers." He nodded towards one of the temporary crewmen. "Dromon here knows the village well and will be a competent guide in my absence. A word of advice: arm yourselves, for weapons are a mark of personal esteem in these riverside communities, and take plenty of discs of low denomination with you, for you will certainly need them!"

The shore party stepped onto the quay and took stock of their surroundings. The quay itself was constructed from blocks of stone and balks of rough hewn timber and was surfaced with a layer of compacted clay that was now becoming slippery due to the falling rain. A number guard fires burned upon the quay and they provided warmth and comfort for the village sentries who patrolled the landing and protected the numerous visiting craft throughout the hours of darkness.

The light was now fading fast. Even so, the newcomers were clearly able to define the nature of the mound upon which the village stood, for huge blocks of masonry lay heaped upon one another, and it was immediately obvious they were viewing the collapsed remains of one of the huge buildings constructed by that long-extinct race known as the Ancient Dead.

The little group ascended the mound until they reached a well protected village occupying its slopes. Near to the first of the huts, they were met by a jovial looking man bearing a copper-tipped stick, which, Dromon informed them, was the emblem of office of a village council member.

"Two lead discs each!" the man said, shaking the leather moneybag that hung from his belt. "Two lead discs is the price of a night's accommodation inside the communal barracks. It costs three lead discs to sleep in a private hut!"

On Dromon's advice, they each paid over the sum of three lead discs and the party was conducted to a spacious hut where a number of clean beds were laid ready for use. A young girl, who could not have been aged more than three cycles, attended them and presented Myra with a posy of blue flowers.

"Perhaps my mistress wishes to enjoy a steam-bath?" she said, clutching at the hem of the wisewoman's dress. "Only one small disc to have your aches and pains soothed away by the hot vapour. But with no immodesty," she quickly added, "for we have separate cubicles for both men and women."

Dromon threw his padded tunic onto one of the beds.

"I have a yearning that must have come from the Gods," he said, as he turned to face the newcomers. "I suggest that we all agree with the child's offer without further delay for a steam bath in this village is an experience not to be missed."

The party stripped of their outer garments, stacked their weapons and left them in charge of a crewman who agreed to bathe later, then followed the child to a nearby garden where the bathing establishment was situated.

A row of cubicles occupied one end of the garden and in front of them stood one of the strangest contraptions that any of the newcomers had ever set eyes upon; a huge iron cauldron stood upon four pillars of stone, and beneath its base their roared a wood fire that was tended by two smoke-blackened young boys. The mouth of the cauldron was hidden beneath a round wooden cover, from which odd spurts of steam were constantly escaping. From the top of the boiler there ran a number of leather pipes conveying a supply of steam to a number of nearby cubicles.

A group of muscular young women appeared and one of the attendants attached herself to each of the bathers. Darryl was led into one of the cubicles and was requested to strip naked and lie prone upon a smooth wooden bench, where every inch of his muscular body was rubbed down with handfuls of thick purple leaves producing a crimson pith. The woman attending him drew out the plug from the end of the steam-pipe, allowing the hot vapour to flood into the chamber, causing the temperature to rise until it was almost unbearable. The boatmaster lay upon the bench for about half an hour, whilst the woman massaged his body and wiped away the sweat and grime that his body excreted in considerable quantities. Finally, the woman concluded the ablution by washing him down with containers of ice-cold water.

Darryl moved with supple ease as the attendant led him back to the night hut where he rejoined his companions.

"Now we must eat!" Dromon said, as they adjusted their outer clothing and re-armed themselves; once they were all respectably attired, he led them to a small public square situated at the very summit of the mound.

One side of the square was completely taken up by a number of open-fronted booths, from which there drifted the appetising smell of cooking food and the irresistible aroma reminded the crewmembers that they were all extremely hungry.

"One lead disc," shouted the proprietor of the first booth they approached.

"One disc only, for a bowl of my vegetable and narrs-flesh stew. Yes, and with all the Thoa bread that you can eat!"

Dromon led the group past the first booths, to one that sported a green awning protecting the diners from the constantly pouring rain.

"Now you will sample a dish beloved of all sailors upon the Life River," he said. "Joints of smoked do-fowl, served upon a salad of fresh water-leaf. You will have to pay no less than five discs each to obtain this delicacy, but I swear that you will not be disappointed!"

Darryl, George and Myra each paid over their lead discs and each received a broad platter containing a number of tan-coloured pieces of do-fowl, served with a side-salad of water-leaf, a vegetable peculiar to this portion of the Water Realm.

The newcomers seated themselves upon a bench situated beneath the protective awning and began sampling the rather unsavoury looking concoction. Yet, despite their early reticence, they were soon digging into the contents of their platters with a will. The smoked do-fowl, they quickly discovered, had a slightly peppery flavour, but the flesh literally melted in the mouth, whilst the purple water-leaves had a sharp fresh taste that provided the perfect accompaniment to the preserved meat.

As soon as their dishes were empty, their guide conducted them to another booth where they ate bowls filled with narrs-head stew, served with steaming dumplings made from Thoa flour and dried herbs. George, however, was still hungry and proceeded to demolish a huge bowl-full of vegetable broth and a dish of slightly astringent green berries that he demanded from the proprietor.

Once the entire group was replete with food, they made their way to a tavern standing at the head of the square and began sating their thirst with tankards of foaming Thoa-nut beer.

"That was a fine meal," the boatmaster declared, after swallowing half a tankard of beer in one single draught. "And a man would not fare badly if he never ate worse!"

"The food in this village is very good," Dromon agreed. "But not uncommonly so. The folk who ply the Life River are as hard-working as any within the Water Realm, and their needs are simple. Good plain food, at a cheap price and a clean bed under a roof that doesn't leak, aye and an occasional steam-bath to ease pain in their weary bodies."

Dromon paused for a moment, before continuing.

"Wilakin informed me that you are newly arrived from the Northlands, as your white skins suggest. Perhaps you should learn the ways and customs of the river as soon as possible."

He pointed towards a group of roughly dressed men sitting around a table and playing a board game that had a distinct similarity to draughts.

"Those men are the crew from a stone-carrying barge moored alongside the village quay for the night. Now blocks of stone are of little interest to river pirates and the craft carrying them would certainly be bitterly defended by their crews!" Dromon emphasized the fact by pointing to the iron-spiked clubs propped against the side of the Stone-carriers table. "Stone-carrying barges can therefore tie-up for the night, almost anywhere along the river, with very little danger of attack. Yet Stone-carriers have their personal needs, like other men who dwell upon the Great Life River, and they must come ashore and enjoy themselves once in a while. Night-harbours are therefore often used as places of entertainment by many people, as well as being vital sanctuaries for others!"

He pointed towards a thin woman in a blue dress, who was sauntering provocatively between the tables. "Yes," he added. "A woman's body is also available along with the food and drink; all of the pleasures of the flesh can be had for the price of five lead discs or even less, if one bargains hard enough."

Dromon also explained that Stone-carriers had a well-earned reputation for being the toughest group of sailors upon the river; yet, his sage warning arrived too late.

For George, filled with all the inquisitiveness of youth, allowed his gaze to remain over-long upon a group of game-playing Stone-carriers at a nearby table.

One of the Stone-carriers, a powerful looking individual with a massive barrel chest, stood up and walked across the room and confronted the young boat hand.

"Who do you think you're staring at, you lump of Northlander narr-shit?" he growled. "Are you willing to wrestle with me, or are you going to crawl out of here lickin' the floor clean of dirt as you go?"

"Peace and good health to you, my friend!" Dromon answered in a quiet tone. "The young man is new to the ways of the river and had no intention of giving offence. Perhaps a round of drinks will suffice to..."

Unfortunately, at this point George's irascible temper took control of him and he leapt to his feet.

"To hell with giving away beer," he shouted. "I'll rip the head off that bastard's shoulders and ram it up his arse." The young man's angry retort had been shouted out in English, but the Stone-carrier understood perfectly well that his challenge had been accepted.

"Now you must fight," Dromon said to the youth with a sigh and a shake of his head. "Now remember, there are no rules in these contests, save that you cannot punch or kick your opponent. You will fight within a circle of spectators until one man cannot stand or else breaks the circle and flees. Now strip, young man, and prepare to fight harder than you have ever fought before!"

Benches and tables were cleared away from the centre of the room and a ring of spectators quickly formed and the two combatants stood glowering at each other like a pair of fighting cocks. No signal was needed to begin the contest, for the barrel-chested Stone-carrier hurled himself across the room and attempted to head-butt his younger opponent in the stomach. George was taken by surprise, but slipping sideways at the last moment he tried to get a headlock on his adversary. He failed, for the man twisted out of the hold and skipped away to the far side of the ring. The fighters sparred for a few moments whilst they took a close measure of one another.

George was younger and possibly a little stronger than his opponent and had the advantage of a much longer reach. Unfortunately, his experience in this form of combat was limited to a few brawls with bargees on the Manchester canals, plus some basic instruction in the art of wrestling from old Noor-Balsam.

His opponent, by contrast, was a skilled veteran of the many bitter contests fought during his long years spent upon the river. Several times, George attempted to get a head- or an armlock upon his opponent, but the Stone-carrier had either broken the hold or wriggled clear with consummate ease, whilst constantly head-butting, elbowing and kneeing his younger opponent until he could barely stand upright.

"Keep away from him, you confounded idiot!" the boatmaster roared from the edge of the ring. "Use your long legs and keep away from him and let him wear himself out from chasin' you!"

George must have heard Darryl's cries, for he began swiftly backing away from his opponent, using the speed of his young legs to keep himself out of trouble. Even so, the barrel-chested river-man continued chasing his opponent relentlessly, but his breathing rate began increasing visibly and it became obvious that he was gradually tiring. Twice, the Stone-carrier charged head-down at the young man, only to miss, crashing into the ring of spectators; but on the third occasion George stood his ground and delivered a sickening body-check, sending the river-man spinning into the crowd. The man was still dazed as the crowd thrust him back into the middle of the ring and George immediately took his chance to finish the contest. He dived forward and grasped the Stone-carrier around the waist, swinging him over his head and sending him crashing to the floor. The impact would have finished most fighters, but the river-man was brave and attempted to rise again, only to slump down unconscious.

The fallen man was hauled away by his crewmates, whilst George received the congratulations of the entire gathering. The youth turned and faced Darryl without showing the slightest concern for the blood trickling from superficial cuts to his face and forehead.

"I beat him like I said that I would!" he said triumphantly.

"Yes, you beat him all right," the boatmaster snarled in reply. "But I swear that one day, your temper and your damned impetuosity will be the death of us all. I had my doubts about bringing you with us to the Water Realm, now I wished that I had possessed enough sense to leave you with my mother in Elfencot."

"Easy brother," Myra said quietly. "Only experience will rid the lad of his impetuosity, and I may help him to control his berserk temper. In any case, brother, the time for recriminations is long past, and we must either work together as a team or perish as individuals."

"So be it," the boatmaster replied. "Do what you can to instill a sense of caution into the lad, for he sorely needs it!"

The conversation between the three travellers came to an abrupt end, for the crowd parted and the defeated Stone-carrier appeared, still reeling slightly from the effects of the savage punishment so recently received. He came face to face with George and grasped his wrist in greeting.

"I salute my conqueror," the man said with some difficulty, for blood was still running like a river from his mouth. "For only the best of men can beat a Stone-carrier in the sport of wrestling."

He paused and raised his arm in salutation to George and the remainder of the Bonny Barbara's crew.

"You are now the guests of the Stone-carriers for the remainder of this evening. Landlord, bring beer and only the best--let us see which of our two ships' companies can drink the most."

"Lord help us," muttered the boatmaster under his breath. "Not only must we beat them at wrestling, but we must also get the better of them at boozing, as well!"

≈

Darryl's head was pounding like a trip-hammer as he manned the tiller and steered the Bonny Barbara away from the quay and into the midst of the current. Soon the vessel was being carried away from the village upon the mound, the scene of the previous night's revelry.

The Stone-carriers, for all their rude customs, had been extremely hospitable hosts, and for the remainder of the evening the party from the narrowboat had been feted like kings. Round after round of Thoa-nut beer was purchased by the Stone-carriers for the consumption of all, without a single disc of lead being deemed acceptable from the pockets of the newcomers. More food had been ordered from the booths in the square and they had been introduced to the staple dish of the Stone-carriers: narrs-liver, fried in a pan with lumps of bread, and sprinkled with a seed that had all the sharp acidity of pure lemon juice.

George, the hero of the night, had been plied with strong drink from all quarters and had finally collapsed into a state of complete intoxication during the early hours of darkening. Myra, helped by two of the temporary crew-members, had put the youth to bed in the night-hut and the young wisewoman had remained with him to make sure that he came to no harm.

Darryl, however, had remained in the company of the Stone-carriers for a little while longer before seeking his own bed, in order to gain additional knowledge of their water-borne society and also details of the other peoples dweling along the banks of the Life River.

He recalled that an old one-armed man had introduced himself as the owner of a stone-barge, and the man had quietly warned him that he might be wise to dispose of his cargo, as soon as possible, and return to his own distant land without delay.

"We seldom have time to put into night-harbours now," he had explained. "For never in my lifetime have there been such a demand for heavy stone blocks, aye and Thoa-logs and all manner of building materials. Most of the towns and cities, from Calar right down to Holy Ptah seem to be overhauling their defences; old collapsed walls are being rebuilt, whilst new towers and bastions are being planned and constructed. Even fairly large villages that formerly placed their faith in a solid wooden stockade to protect them from the ravages of marauding pirates can sometimes be found building stone ramparts."

"What is the reason for all this defensive activity?" Darryl asked, as he forced down another tankard of Thoa-nut beer.

"The threat of war," the old man had replied. "I cannot tell you why this fear of an imminent conflict stalks the river-lands, for little seems to have outwardly changed, but the hammers in the forges of the armouries continue to ring and I fear that some great catastrophe is hanging over us."

The barge-owner's son had overheard his father's words and had poured scorn upon the older man by suggesting that he must be approaching senility. Yet Darryl had clearly remembered the veteran's warning, despite the large quantities of alcohol that he had consumed in the course of the evening and he resolved to keep the old man's comments in mind.

By midmorning the boatmaster's hangover had largely subsided, due to a relieving potion administered by his twin sister. The young witch had also given George a similar measure to relieve his thundering head and the three travellers were now standing in the cockpit of the narrowboat, viewing for the first time, the complicated manoeuvre enabling a sizeable vessel to be extracted from the south flowing portion of the Life River and placed under the influence of the opposing current moving in an ever northerly direction.

An open barge, heavily laden with a cargo of Thoa-logs, moving with the southerly flow of the river, suddenly changed course and began steering towards the centre of the waterway. Dark smoke from a signal fire rose from the vessel's deck and a pair of fast-towing galleys responded by darting out from a creek in the riverbank and steered for the heavily laden barge. One of the galleys moved ahead of the log-carrier and passed over a stout line and began towing the craft into an area of disturbed water lying between the two opposing currents. The second galley, which had a fender made from some leathern material attached to its blunt prow, manoeuvred carefully until its padded prow was thrusting against the forward hull of the log-carrier. Slowly, the barge began to turn, until she was caught in the grip of the opposing current and began moving in a northerly direction. At this point, the two galleys fell into station on either side of the log-carrier and the three craft were soon receding from view.

"Those craft are bound for the mouth of that small river, over on the eastern bank; the one that we passed some time back," Wilakin said, as he clambered into the cockpit without the aid of another crewmember, for he was recovering quickly from the injuries he received at the hands of the criminals in Calar of the Mighty Walls.

"The village of a powerful Saxman chieftain is situated on the banks of that river, about half a day's hard towing from the line of the Great Life River," the navigator explained. "I expect those logs are for the construction of a new tribal meeting hall, or some other project. The boat-turning manoeuvre that you have just witnessed may seem strange to you who are newcomers to the river, but you will see it repeated many times before we reach the Holy City of Ptah. Indeed, we may need to use this technique ourselves, should we be required to make a landfall on the opposite shore."

Wilakin pointed to a small local boat, with a single sail made from some rough fabric, driving hard before the wind.

"Yonder craft can use the power of its sail to carry it into the opposing current, but larger vessels have difficulty in doing this, and the towing galleys are therefore essential and can easily be summoned by a simple smoke signal, such as the one that you have just witnessed."

"Who owns the towing galleys?" Darryl enquired.

"Independent masters for the most part," the pilot answered. "The craft usually lie in some creek and wait for a fire-signal to summon them. Some galleys, however, are the property of ambitious riverside communities who maintain them in order to promote trade."

The boatmaster frowned. "What would happen if some group of pirates seized a towing galley and used it to attack trade?"

"Then absolute havoc would be let loose upon the river!" Wilakin said. "But it rarely occurs, for the towing galley's are not crewed by slaves, but by heavily armed freemen who can be relied upon to fight for their lives."

"Have no fear, master," he continued. "If we are destined to be attacked by river pirates, then the assault will be launched from a small fast-moving, oar-propelled craft, and it will come under cover of darkness. Such attacks are difficult to repel and we shall live or die in a matter of seconds!"

'So much to learn,' the boatmaster thought, as he bent over the tiller. 'So much new knowledge to gain, if we are to stand a chance of surviving this journey!'

᠁

Day followed day, and the crew of the Bonny Barbara fell into a regular routine as they navigated along the Great Life River in the direction of Holy Ptah.

Each of the crewmembers stood regular watches, both at the tiller and as forward lookouts in the bows, whilst those without duties cooked, cleaned, or simply sat on deck and viewed the seemingly endless array of craft plying the river in both directions.

At the approach of most darkenings, the vessel put into one of the many night-harbours and the travellers slept under the protection of sharp-eyed village guards, but on a number of occasions they were forced to lie at anchor in the shadow of the western bank. During those dangerously long nights, half the crew stood on watch, whilst the remainder rested fully armed and ready to spring into action at a moment's notice.

Darryl was deeply concerned with the safety of his craft. Each day, he required every member of the crew to spend two full hours in arms drill and martial exercise. The wisdom of the boatmaster's defensive policy was fully demonstrated on the eighteenth day out from Calar, when the entire crew of the narrowboat witnessed a pirate attack at close quarters.

A small barge had put out from one of the riverside villages, and had taken station about three hundred yards ahead of the Bonny Barbara when the pirates suddenly struck without warning. Two fast oar-propelled craft suddenly darted out from the shoreline and drew alongside the doomed barge in a matter of seconds. A wave of armed men then swept over the side of the craft, and moments later, the lifeless bodies of the barge's crew were unceremoniously flung into the river. The captured barge was then taken in tow and hauled off towards the western shore for beaching and pillage.

"A sharp object lesson," the boatmaster remarked, viewing the bodies rolling about in the current, "but the murdering bastards won't find us such easy meat, if they try to come aboard our vessel."

"No master, they will not," Wilakin agreed, as he sheathed his naked gill. "But it's quite unusual for those devils to attack in broad daylight, when they have no chance of achieving complete surprise; and it's even more unusual for them to bother capturing a small vessel, whose cargo is likely to consist of firewood and cheap foodstuffs!"

Wilakin shook his head. "Trading upon the Great Life River is certainly becoming far more dangerous, and I shall not be sorry when we draw closer to Holy Ptah and reach a part of the river patrolled by the war galleys of the Dark Priest's overseers."

Darryl made no reply, but he respected the navigator's opinions and resolved to station an extra lookout amidships, during the hours of daylight. For it was now quite obvious that the Bonny Barbara's small tonnage could not be relied upon to deter the attack of some desperate band of freebooters.

George and the boatmaster spent a great many of their off-duty hours inside Myra's makeshift cabin in the bows. The young wisewoman encouraged George to learn a number of mental exercises, which she hoped would help him to control his impetuous behaviour in times of stress, for his berserk temper was a potential danger to the entire company.

On other occasions, Myra and her twin brother followed the priest's instructions and spent a great deal of time before the crystal sphere, in the hope of establishing a psychic link allowing them to converse with one another without the need of speech, but all of their initial efforts ended in hopeless failure. Yet they persisted, and after many sessions of intense concentration, each twin began to develop a strange ability to mentally read the basic feelings and impressions generated within the others sibling's brain. Pleasure, danger, pain, temperature, colour and the like, but they utterly failed to develop any semblance of conversational ability.

"We must persevere, Darryl," the witch had insisted as the boatmaster became disillusioned by their constant failure. "For a means of silently communicating with each other might well save our lives!"

On the twenty-second day out from Calar, the Bonny Barbara docked near the home village of the temporary crewmembers who had joined them at The City of the Mighty Walls, and the returning mariners were joyfully greeted by their families and friends.

The same evening, a celebration was held in the village where food was consumed in great quantities and Thoa-nut beer was dispatched by the cask-full. Early upon the following morning, the boatmaster rose and swallowed a draught of his sister's hangover potion and set about the task of replacing some of the ex-crewmen, who were now dwelling happily at home with their families.

Dromon, it transpired, was landless and unmarried and immediately volunteered to serve aboard the Bonny Barbara until the craft reached Holy Ptah. In return, the boatmaster promised him enough copper coinage to enable him to purchase a small plot of land upon his homecoming.

"Master, never in all my years upon the river have I ever journeyed as far as Holy Ptah!" he remarked to Darryl, after agreeing to his terms of service. "Yet it is often said that all river-men should view the copper walls of the Dark Priests, on at least one occasion, before they die!'

Dromon also introduced the boatmaster to a pair of youthful blood cousins called Tess and Tom-Tess. The pair were young and neither could have been aged more than sixteen cycles, yet they were both strong and agile and when their battle-craft was put to the test, they both proved to be deadly marksmen with the darters they carried. In addition, the youngsters were extremely adept with the short-handled pike, a weapon much favoured by crewmembers on this portion of the Great Life River. Myra had also secretly scanned the young cousins with her witch's inner eye and she had no doubt that the pair were honest and likely to be a great asset to the narrowboat's company. Darryl had then hired the youths for the duration of the voyage to Holy Ptah and the pair had pledged their personal loyalty to him without hesitation.

The narrowboat resumed its voyage after the travellers had spent a comfortable four days ashore. On the thirty-second day out from Calar they sighted the walls of a substantial town situated close to the western bank of the river. The defensive walls protecting the town were minute in comparison with those encircling Calar, but the guard towers bristled with missile-casting engines, and there was little doubt the folk dweling within its bounds were extremely mindful of their own security. The narrowboat came abreast of the town and the travellers caught sight of numerous stone-built warehouses and many rows of neat workmen's cottages, each with its own patch of garden. Upon a small knoll, close to the eastern edge of the town, the travellers were clearly able to make out a number of larger buildings that could only be temples or possibly the dwellings of the town's richest citizens.

Suddenly, the wind veered slightly and the boat-crews nostrils were assailed by a disgusting odour almost causing the three newcomers to vomit over the side.

"Don't worry!" Wilakin said, holding an improvised cloth pad over his face. "The smell will not bother us, once the river-current carries us past this town!"

"What in all creation could produce such a vile smell?" the young witch asked, pressing a handkerchief to her nose

"Why, the shit-filled pits in which the inhabitants of that town soak raw narr skins," the navigator explained. "Some of these riverside towns have trading specialties and that stinking place, over there, manufactures narrs-leather as soft as your arse. Aye, my friends, many towns, such as this one, are sited close to the western bank of the river, and we shall pass several of them in the days that lie ahead."

"Are there many towns situated on the eastern side of the river?" the boatmaster enquired.

"Not a single one," Wilakin answered. "For beyond yonder shoreline lies the territory of the Saxmen barbarians; men who have no use for towns, cities, or any type of structure built from stone. Yonder barbarians are country dwellers to a man; a hovel or a farmhouse of rough-hewn timber is all they ever require. A squalid village might well spring up around the wooden hall of some powerful chieftain, but it will never grow to resemble a town!"

"Do the Saxmen control all of the eastern side of the river?" George asked, taking a rag from his nostrils, for the stench of the tanneries was beginning to slacken as they left the town astern.

"Not entirely," Wilakin answered. "The Wizards of the Ancient Lore will not allow any single power to rule the territory immediately adjacent to the waters of the Great Life River. Indeed, a great many river-folk eke out a living on the eastern fringes of the river, and some do well enough by trading with the Saxmen who dwell a little way inland. Yet it is a precarious existence, for the barbarians are dangerous and unpredictable and the edict of the Dark Priests is barely sufficient to ensure the safety of those river-folk who choose to dwell by the water's edge."

The navigator smiled and pointed far beyond the bows of the craft.

"My friends, we must fare along this river for at least another sixty days, before we draw clear of Saxmen territory and can land in safety on the far shore."

The boatmaster laughed. "Then we must continue to seek our food and pleasure on this side of the river, and that suits me well enough, but I sincerely hope that all of our landfalls don't smell quite as badly as that putrid town we have just had the misfortune to pass!"

Darryl drew a bucket of water from the river and poured it over his head and body, thus washing away the sticky leaf sap that served the river-folk as a personal cleansing agent. He then stood upon the deck of the narrowboat and dried himself with a towel, before returning to the stern cabin to prepare for his next spell of duty at the tiller. The boatmaster opened the cabin door and his nostrils were assailed by the acrid fumes issuing from a pot of a caulking compound that Dromon was boiling upon the top of the stove. One of the outriggers had recently developed a slight leak and the boat hand had sworn that a single application of his home made caulking mixture would immediately take care of the problem. Darryl had readily agreed with the man's suggestion, but the stench from the mixture was rendering the cabin almost uninhabitable and its foul smell reminded the boatmaster of the reeking town of the narrs-skin tanners they had passed exactly two Earth months ago.

The river's south-flowing current had subsequently carried the narrowboat past thirty-two well-built towns lying in close proximity to the western bank of the Great Life, and the travellers had also viewed the battlements of three large cities, each fronted by quays swarming with river craft of all descriptions. Darryl had occasionally become slightly bored with the humdrum routine of life afloat and had once suggested that the crew should be allowed to spend an odd evening ashore in one of the larger settlements, but Wilakin had opposed him vigorously, saying that landing charges at the town quays were inordinately high and that food and accommodation was far cheaper and of superior quality in the smaller riverside villages and night-harbours. However on two occasions they had been forced to visit larger town settlements, allowing the boatmaster to cash some of the merchants' bonds he had received from Agar-Marduk, in return for the Bonny Barbara's cargo of railway iron.

On the first occasion, the travellers had come ashore and taken great pleasure in sitting upon the sunlit plaza of a small town, and watched the woman and children weaving the brightly coloured Thoa-fibre matting that was the prime product of the settlement. The second town they visited stank like a veritable brewery, and the numerous barrels of Thoa-nut beer, standing upon its riverside quay, left them in no doubt as to the town's principle manufacture. Indeed, Wilakin had laughed aloud as they drank the foaming brew, and had persuaded the boatmaster to purchase three kegs of the finest beer to supplement the narrowboat's stores.

Darryl had often gazed across the Life River to the distant eastern shore, but the boatmaster had never been tempted to visit the narrow strip of land bordering the territory of the Saxmen barbarians. Furthermore, Myra had stated that an aura of menace lay over the distant shoreline, and she felt sure that terrible acts of cruelty were frequently perpetrated upon its soil.

"Never be foolish enough to land on yonder shore," she often said, "or it may well be our undoing, for I feel that a terrible evil lurks there."

The boatmaster quit the reeking cabin and stepped into the cockpit, for it was now time to relieve Wilakin, who was coming to the end of his watch at the tiller. His first act was to review the progress of his vessel and he immediately realized that the pilot had steered the craft out into south-flowing currant, until it was riding only a stone's throw from the centre of the river, and he looked quizzically towards the man at the helm.

Wilakin smiled. "Master, I have steered our craft as near to the centre of the waterway as possible, so that you will be able to gain a clear view of an artefact that will interest you greatly." He pointed across the river towards a short spit of land jutting out from the eastern shoreline.

The boatmaster let out a gasp of surprise, for his gaze fell upon a small promontory supporting a grove of giant Thoa trees, some of which, he perceived, stood a good two hundred feet in height. But the feature that really caught his eye was the upper portion of a huge obelisk reaching upwards for a further hundred feet above the existing treeline. The structure had been engineered from some strange material that bore a close resemblance to burnished copper, for intermittent beams of light from the five suns were caught upon its polished surface and reflected in every direction.

Darryl knew at once that he was viewing yet another artefact of that mysterious race,The Ancient Dead, and his respect for their physical achievements grew immeasurably.

The river pilot seemed to read his thoughts.

"An impressive sight, Master,. The reason for its original construction is well beyond our understanding. Yet, for long ages, it has served as the marker defining the outermost limit of Saxmen power. So far and no further is the rule. A few inland clans do have settlements to the south, but it is generally understood that no Saxmen chieftain may send his troops beyond that shining marker without incurring the wrath of the Dark Priests, and even the wildest barbarian would be loath to take such a terrible risk."

Wilakin paused. "That obelisk is also a welcoming landmark to all river-folk who are faring south along this waterway, for they know the shining walls of Holy Ptah can be reached in forty more days, if the Gods are willing, and the long and hard journey is coming to an end; also, from here and until we reach Holy Ptah, the river is patrolled by the war-galleys of the priests overseers and few pirates are foolish enough to raid shipping on this well-protected stretch of the Life River."

"That's good to know," Darryl said, as he took over the tiller from the pilot. "Now perhaps we can sleep safe in our beds at night, and it's especially good to know that we are nearing Holy Ptah, for I have only two of the merchants' bonds remaining. Soon we must exchange these bonds for copper discs and somehow purchase enough food to last us until we reach Ptah and find a buyer for our cargo of timber."

Wilakin smiled.

"Have no fear on that account, Master. By tomorrow noon, we shall be nearing the Island of Plenty, situated on the eastern side of the river. There you can obtain the very best rates of exchange for your merchants' bonds, and you can also purchase all manner of provisions at extremely low prices."

"There is an island amidst the waters of the Life River?" Darryl asked incredulously.

The pilot shook his head. "No, Master, not in the way that an island stands in the middle of a lake. Let me explain. A sizeable river flows down from the eastern hinterland and then divides into two separate waterways, at a point about one day's march from the bank of the Great Life River. The two waterways then discharge themselves into the Life River by separate mouths that are situated about one good days sailing from each other. A great triangular tract of fertile land is thus enclosed that we river-folk call 'The Island of Plenty.' The farmland is certainly the most productive in this portion of the Water Realm and grows enormous crops of vegetables, but most especially a type of nutritious tuber that is called 'ginna.' The vegetable cannot be grown anywhere else but upon this Island. Ginna tubers are traded along the length and breadth of the Life River, either fresh to the settlements lying close at hand, or in a dried form to markets that lie further afield."

Darryl looked keenly into the pilot's face. "Are you sure this island is a safe place for strangers to visit?" he asked anxiously.

"Unquestionably," Wilakin replied. "The inhabitants are prosperous and extremely hospitable and it has long been their custom to welcome strangers with open arms."

The pilot drew a long breath and continued.

"We are doubly fortunate, Master, for tomorrow begins the festival of Persephone the local goddess of agriculture, and celebrates the divine gift of the ginna. Three whole days will be given over to holiday-making by the entire population of the Island, whilst people from other riverside communities also arrive by water to join in the revelry."

Wilakin smiled and winked knowingly.

"Aye, Master, the first day of the festival of Persephone is entirely given over to feasting and all the many pleasures of the flesh. On the morning of the second day, a great ceremony will be held at the temple of the goddess, when naked priests will sacrifice fat narr in the flames of the sacred fire. Afterwards, beautiful virgins will copulate with handsome athletes and take the men's seed into their bodies as an offering to the powers of nature."

Darryl appeared doubtful.

"Are you sure that we can exchange our merchants' bills and purchase provisions during this season of celebration?"

"Without the slightest difficulty," the pilot immediately replied. "For a great many factors ply their trade throughout the festival, in order to serve the needs of the numerous visitors. Why I know of a merchant who will cheaply supply us with..."

"Coffins, perhaps," a woman's voice broke in, and the two men looked up to see Myra standing upon the cabin roof. She slipped down into the tiny cockpit and faced her brother.

"Wilakin gives you sound advice, as far as it goes. Yet my brother, I beg you to remain on our side of the river and go on half-rations, if needs be, rather than visit this Island of Plenty. My witch's inner eye has constantly warned me that danger lurks on yonder eastern shore, aye, ever since we first rode upon the waters of the Life River. I tell you plainly, that feeling still remains with me, ever though we are now clear of the territory of the Saxmen barbarians."

Darryl turned and faced the pilot.

"The delights of that island certainly attract me, Wilakin, yet I have come to respect and heed my sister's warnings, for without them I would have been dead and forgotten by now. It is therefore my resolve, as leader, to continue upon our present course and eke out our remaining provisions until we lie beneath the shining walls of Holy Ptah!"

"A wise choice, my brother," the wisewoman said with a smile, "and one that might well save us from some terrible catastrophe. Now let us speak no more of the matter!"

❦

Despite the boatmaster's best intentions, the Bonny Barbara was destined to put into the Island of Plenty, for the reeking compound that Dromon had applied to the leaking outrigger failed to hold and the stabilizing pontoon began taking on water almost as soon as they attempted to resume their voyage at first light. The river-pilot had immediately stated that no alternative existed but to put into one of the boatyards on the aforementioned island and have the leak attended to by professional tradesmen.

Darryl discussed the matter with his sister, but it was quite obvious that a forced visit to the Island was inevitable and she reluctantly agreed.

About midmorning, the lookout in the bows of the craft, pointed towards the eastern shore and shouted out that he had sighted the mouth of the northern waterway marking the beginning of the Island of Plenty. Darryl took charge of the tiller, and, under the pilot's careful direction, he headed for the middle of the Life River, whilst Dromon lit a smoke signal, which they knew would eventually attract a towing galley. A great many other vessels were also attempting to obtain a similar service and some two hours were destined to elapse before a sleek multi-oared craft nosed alongside and passed them a stout towing-line, in exchange for a number of copper discs. A further hour passed before the Bonny Barbara was riding in the north-flowing current and fast approaching the gaggle of docks and wharves serving as the Island's river port.

As the narrowboat nosed its way landwards, the newcomers were soon able to view the Island of Plenty from close quarters and they were forced to admit that it bore no resemblance to anything previously seen in the Water Realm.

Docks, warehouses and the dwellings of the common folk did indeed line the water's edge. Yet beyond the built-up area, the crewmembers clearly viewed rank upon rank of terraced fields seeming to stretch as far as the eye could see. Nor were the fields of a similar colour, for the predominantly red hue of Water Realm crops was interspersed with patches of unfamiliar green, yellow and brown vegetation. In addition, small irrigation canals could easily be seen following the contours of the ground. With difficulty, they were even able to make out the vast web of narrow ducts carrying the life-giving water to the crop-laden fields, and the three newcomers quickly came to understand why this great tract of fertile land was known as 'The Island of Plenty.'

The narrowboat was soon berthed in a small repair dock, and Wilakin, after much protracted haggling, persuaded the owner of the dock to forgo some of the pleasures of the public holiday and immediately begin work on the faulty outrigger, upon the guarantee of a substantial bonus once the repair was completed.

Darryl viewed the nearby quays and noticed that very little commercial activity was taking place, but, here and there, an odd merchant was selling food to newly arrived boat crews. It was quite obvious that most of the men who would normally have been found toiling in the dock complex were absent and enjoying the public holiday.

The fact that a celebration was taking place was easy to define, for many of the structures near the docks were decorated with bunting and fronds of freshly cut creepers; occasional groups of revellers could be seen leisurely threading their way between the riverside buildings. Some of them were festooned with sprays of freshly cut flowers and singing loudly as they moved, and it was obvious that Thoa-nut beer was already being consumed in considerably quantities.

Wilakin hailed a young urchin and instructed the child to run swiftly to the chambers of a factor with whom he had previously done business. The message invited the man to immediately attend the Bonny Barbara and bid for the boatmaster's last remaining merchants' bonds. The urchin returned half an hour later, followed by a rather portly factor riding in a light one-man litter. Wilakin formerly introduced the man to his master and, after an hour of intense haggling, a suitable deal was struck and the bonds were exchanged for an ample supply of copper discs. In addition, the factor agreed to deliver enough cheap provisions to feed the entire crew of the narrowboat until they reached the Holy City of Ptah.

"How long will it take for the supplies to arrive and be stored aboard our craft?" the young wisewoman asked anxiously.

"An hour from now and no more," the merchant replied, and Myra sighed with relief for it appeared that nothing could prevent their departure, once the leaking outrigger had been repaired.

The crewmembers sat upon the quay and consumed an impromptu meal of roast ginna tubers purchased from the handcart of a passing food vendor and waited impatiently for the boat repairer to complete his work. Unfortunately, they had barely finished their repast when the boat-repairer reappeared and declared that the damage to the outrigger was much worse than had previously been suspected, and the craft could not possibly be made river-worthy until the following morning, even if work continued throughout the hours of darkness.

Darryl received the news and was reluctantly persuaded to make the best of a bad situation, but Myra clenched her fists and it was obvious that she was extremely frustrated by this further delay. However, some of the hired crewmembers, including Dromon the boat hand, were far from put out by the news and made no secret of their wish to attend the festival of Persephone. The young wisewoman noted this fact, and taking her brother by the hand, she led him into the privacy of the narrowboat's cabin.

She turned and faced him, brushing back her long red hair as she did so.

"Darryl," she said. "My intuition tells me that you are about to grant the hands leave to visit the festival, aye, and perhaps go yourself. My advice is that you should confine the men on-board, then keep a good watch on deck and be ready to repel any danger that may threaten us. Finally, we should push off into the river and get away from this place, the very second that yonder boat-repairer has made our craft watertight."

Darryl did not answer his sister immediately, but paused to wipe the sweat from his brow with a coloured handkerchief.

"Myra, lass," he said quietly, "you know, well enough, that I value your advice and that I put great store upon your gift of second-sight. But I command this vessel and must give due consideration to everything that concerns both our craft and its crew. If danger does exist, then it cannot be as serious as that ambush on the Exit River." The boatmaster paused, and took a deep breath.

"I must confess that I find this island more peaceable and far less threatening than almost any place we have visited since arriving in the Water Realm. No sister, I feel that I cannot risk harming the morale of the crewmembers by confining them aboard this craft, on the unlikely off-chance that some danger might arise before we leave. Therefore, my decision is to allow most of the boat's company, including George and myself, leave to visit the Festival of Persephone, until the second hour after dawn tomorrow morning, and then we shall all depart for Holy Ptah aboard our newly repaired vessel!"

Anger blazed from the wisewoman's eyes, but she suppressed her rage and gently placed her right hand upon her brother's chest.

"Strange are the ways of providence," she said quietly. "You have a gift enabling you to be a leader of men. But you will not follow the advice of one who would shield you from harm!"

"Go to the Festival!" Myra continued. "I will cast a luck-spell to help protect you and I shall remain here with Wilakin to watch over the boat. Yet be sure that you all carry arms and wear full battle garb when you go ashore and, for your lives, do not become separated for a single moment."

The young witch kissed her brother on the lids of both eyes, and then departed from the cabin without uttering another word.

Darryl watched his sister leave, then he donned his iron studded protective tunic and trousers and buckled on the sword Kingslayer. He then strode out into the cockpit of the boat and proceeded to name the members of the crew who were to be allowed ashore. The boatmaster ordered the men to arm themselves, as Myra had suggested; as an afterthought, he revisited the cabin and added a tight fitting iron skullcap to his military equipment, together with the spiked shield Gutripper.

George also joined the shore party on the dockside, wearing a protective tunic and trousers and a close fitting helmet. His massive long handled axe rested upon his right shoulder and the murderous butcher's cleaver hung menacingly from his belt. The other leave-taking crewmembers were also gathered upon the dockside wearing protective clothing. A heavy gill swung from Dromon's waist, whilst the two young blood-cousins, Tess and Tom-Tess, carried the short boarding pikes that were their favourite close-range weapons. The boatmaster finished by giving firm instructions for the shore party to remain within close proximity to each other at all times. Led by the knowledgeable Dromon, they moved inland towards the scene of the revelry.

The party stepped out briskly, and quickly cleared the dockland area fringing the river. Soon, they began making their way through a district of small cottage type dwellings, each fronted by an ample patch of garden that invariably contained a pen of domesticated do-fowl and a nut laden Thoa tree.

"The homes of common day-labourers," Dromon explained causally. "Not royal palaces by any means, but far better than anything that landless river-folk can normally aspire to own!"

The boat hand had hardly finished speaking when a procession of revellers, about five hundred strong suddenly appeared from a side-road and the boat's company was soon engulfed in a flood of humanity. Fortunately, the crowd were in no way threatening and the travellers were soon at ease in their midst. Even so, the newcomers were amazed by the appearance of many of the individuals who surrounded them.

The procession was made up of members of both sexes, and they ranged in age from adolescents who were undergoing the effects of puberty, to elder citizens with deeply lined faces. But young adults in the fertile years of early maturity were present in overwhelming numbers. All were in various stages of semi-nakedness and their bodies were adorned with freshly cut fronds of crimson vegetation; this scant covering was certainly not intended to ensure the privacy of individual revellers, for the breasts of most of the females were prominently displayed and decorated with brightly painted symbols, as were the lower organs of both sexes.

Dromon noticed the look of surprise upon the boatmaster's face and burst out laughing.

"You are shocked, Master," he said. "But please remember that you are witnessing a celebration of the reproductive powers of nature and the open nakedness, that you see before you is but a visible manifestation of these people's devout faith."

The crowd advanced in an easterly direction and Dromon suggested that it would be best if they accompanied the throng, for he understood that the shrine of Persephone was situated a little way inland and was a place where much interesting ritual activity could be observed.

Darryl took the boat hand's, advice and the company marched eastwards amidst the crowd of revellers. At first, he wondered if the military appearance of his group would arouse the animosity of the islanders, but the only attention they received from the semi-naked populace was a few ribald comments, such as. "Hey, you white-skinned Northlanders, are you looking for a fuck or a fight?" Or: "Get rid of your axes and spears, newcomers, and start waving your baby-makers around instead!"

In general, however, the revellers were friendly towards their uninvited guests and offered them draughts of Thoa-nut beer from the skin flasks that many of them carried, a kindness much appreciated by the newcomers, for the day was warm and the protective clothing they wore was hot and made them sweat profusely.

The column, in which the newcomers marched, was eventually joined by multitudes of other worshippers and the entire mass of humanity flocked into a huge stadium, hewn out of the gently sloping hillside.

The sides of the stadium were terraced and covered with a soft purple moss, upon which the revellers reclined and waited for the ceremonies to begin; the uninvited group were also glad of the opportunity to rest and neglecting to bring their own refreshments proved to be of no concern, for a group of nearby worshippers handed them ample supplies of food and drink.

"Eat and drink your fill, strangers," they cried. "No worshipper must go hungry or thirsty, if Persephone is to be properly venerated!"

Far below them, in the body of the stadium, was an open arena of considerable size that had been liberally strewn with fronds of the same purple creeper that adorned the bodies of the worshippers. Suddenly, a single booming drumbeat echoed across the entire stadium and the enormous gathering fell silent. From the mouth of a wide tunnel situated at one end of the arena, there appeared a tall woman dressed in a long deep purple robe that covered her from head to foot. She paused in the centre of the arena and clapped her hands. Immediately groups of musicians, situated in the farthest reaches of the stadium, obeyed her signal and struck up a strange rhythmic melody, throbbing and pulsing over the entire gathering.

Darryl eyed the scene with interest and saw that most of the worshippers had begun to sway the upper portions of their bodies in time to the music, whilst a few were seen leaping briefly to their feet and executing some impromptu dance steps before subsiding, once again, onto the soft purple moss.

Again, the great drum sounded, but this time it echoed over the beat of the other instruments and from the tunnel there emerged a double line of figures, all dressed in a similar fashion to the priestess who was now standing motionless in the centre of the arena. The two lines of figures separated upon reaching the open air and each line began circling around the other from opposite directions. Gradually, the tempo of the music increased and the circling figures began executing the steps of a rhythmic processional dance as they moved. Faster and faster grew the tempo of the music and soon the two lines of figures were crossing at an ever increasing speed. As they moved, their robes flared open, and the newcomers noticed that one of the lines of dancing figures was made up entirely of handsome youths, whilst the other was comprised of beautiful young girls who were all in the first flush of early womanhood.

Darryl viewed the surrounding worshippers and he noted, with surprise, that many of them had paired off and were copulating vigorously upon the soft moss of the terraces.

Dromon burst out laughing. "The lovemaking surprises you, Master. Yet it is quite normal for the worshippers of Persephone to pay homage to their goddess in this fashion. For during the festival, all vows of marriage and chastity are set aside and anyone can lie with whom they please. The children who are conceived during these couplings, will be born during the next season of rains, and be collectively called 'The Children of 'Persephone,' in honour of the deity."

The great drum sounded for a third and final time; at that point the two lines of dancers merged together forming themselves into mixed couples, who proceeded to copulate frenziedly upon the floor of the arena.

The music throbbed for a further ten minutes, whilst the young couples honoured the Earth Goddess before the vast adulating throng. Then the officiating priestess, who had remained motionless throughout the entire proceedings, suddenly threw up her arms and the music ceased abruptly; the young couples in the arena sprang apart, disappearing into the tunnel as quickly as they had appeared. The purple-robed priestess followed, and the official ceremony came to an end the moment she disappeared from view.

The vast throng of worshippers, however, had obviously no intention of departing to their respective homes, for the feasting, drinking and lovemaking continued apace.

But the lure of the beer-flask appeared to be assuming precedence over all other activities, for white-robed slaves began circulating amongst the revellers with skins of the common Thoa-nut beverage hanging from their shoulders and they distributed measures of the brew to all who extended a drinking vessel in their direction.

Darkness fell with its usual swiftness, but the celebrations continued as before, with numerous lanterns and torches illuminating the proceedings. Singers and dancers, jugglers and clowns, performed to the delight of the crowd, yet Darryl gradually became tired of the scene and he began considering the wisdom of a return night-march back to the dock were the Bonny Barbara lay under repair. Then a soft female hand began to gently stroking his cheek with the softest possible touch, and, turning his head, he beheld a young woman kneeling at his side. The woman was of statuesque build, with sharp dark nippled breasts that jutted out beyond the garlands of vegetation adorning the upper portions of her body. She was obviously a person of considerable wealth, for bracelets of burnished copper encircled her wrists, and a pin of the same material restrained her long dark hair.

She placed a finger upon the boatmaster's lips in order to maintain his silence.

"My name does not matter Northman." She whispered softly. "But during this darkening, you may call me Surri, the fair one!" She giggled. "It has always been my wish to lie with a man of your skin-colour. You may possess me until the last hour before dawn, if it is your wish."

Darryl hesitated. "We must leave here soon. Also my friends are..."

"Do not worry over the well-being of your men," Surri interrupted. "My hand-maidens are four in number and will take good care of your comrades. Whilst you and I travel to paradise beneath my love-shroud!"

So saying, the woman swiftly unfolded a voluminous sheet of some light purple material, which she drew over the boatmaster and herself, thus shielding them both from the prying eyes of the throng. Darryl began protesting and he attempted to rise, but the dark-haired woman thrust him down with surprising strength.

"Easy, my lover of the night," she whispered. "Would you offend the Great Goddess by refusing a gift of love? Will you not lie with me and thank nature for all the lavish gifts that she bestows upon mankind?"

Surri kissed the boatmaster on the cheek, and nibbled at his right earlobe, whilst simultaneously moving her left hand down to the crotch of his protective trousers, where her nimble fingers began to deftly release the leather fastenings.

Darryl groaned with frustration, for he had not made love to a woman since entering the Water Realm and the cloying perfume worn by his present companion played upon his senses like a drug. His determination evaporated like a drop of water upon a glowing hob.

"No danger can possibly exist here," he decided, as his hand reached out for the women's moist sex. "We can have our fill of these wenches until dawn and still reach the Bonny Barbara"before she's repaired and ready to depart. Aye, and that will be time enough and no mistake!"

⁂

A strange birdlike sound, carried upon the breeze, brought Darryl back to full consciousness and he cast off the woman's love-shroud that was still covering him. He rose to his feet and found that he was able to view his surroundings without undue difficulty, for the first glimmer of light from the five suns was beginning to illuminate the stadium.

He ran his eyes over the moss-covered terraces and beheld the sleeping forms of last night's revellers. Some rested in each other's arms, totally drained by their frantic bouts of lovemaking, whilst others lay prone amidst pools of stinking vomit, after over-indulgence in Thoa-nut beer had rendered them incapable of movement.

Surri and her four hand-maidens were nowhere to be seen, but George and the three other crewmembers lay upon the ground, fast asleep, with the women's discarded love-shrouds roughly draped over their bodies.

Once again, a distant high-pitched cry drifted over the stadium and Darryl was instantly alarmed, for he knew it to be a scream of terror issuing from the throat of some terrified human. He immediately kicked his comrades into full conciseness.

"Hurry up, you idle buggers," he growled, closing up the fastenings of his protective garb and buckling the sword Kingslayer to his waist. "Rise and arm yourselves for some danger is approaching and we must be prepared to meet it!"

The travellers did not have to wait long for the danger to openly reveal itself, for the cry of terror was quickly followed by many others, until the very air echoed with the sound of screaming. Another sound also began manifesting itself, the growl and roaring of rapidly advancing fighting men. Indeed, the four companions had barely time to cloth and arm themselves before a flood of terrified figures poured over the rim of the stadium.

The wave of panic-stricken fugitives was composed of human beings of both sexes and of all ages. Some were clad in flimsy night attire, or in garments hurriedly seized up at the commencement of their wild flight, but the vast majority were stark naked.

The fugitives trampled upon the existing occupants of the stadium, who awoke in terror and joined the fear-stricken rush to escape. Indeed, they had great need of instant flight, for hard upon the heels of the fugitives, there appeared a solid wall of heavily armed warriors, who drove forward with levelled spears and mercilessly slaughtered all who came within stabbing range of their weapons. Behind them came numerous groups of tow-haired fighting men, in winged and crested helmets, who completed the act of butchery and robbed the corpses of their victims of anything of value.

None were spared! Even children, carried in their mother's arms, were sliced in two halves by the pitiless cut of the sword, their bodies joining the red carpet of quivering human flesh that was remorselessly covering the terraces of that doomed place of worship.

"Saxmen warriors," Dromon gasped. "They must have taken advantage of the festival to launch a surprise attack. Now we shall pay for our night of screwing with our lives."

"To hell with dying here," Darryl roared. "Listen, all of you. Adopt the arrowhead formation that we have practiced so often, and then we shall smash our way out of this confounded trap."

The tiny group quickly formed themselves into their well rehearsed combat formation. George, the giant axe-wielding boat hand, took the point position, whilst Dromon and the boatmaster stood immediately behind him in order to protect his vulnerable left and right flanks. Finally, the two youths, Tess and Tom-Tess, levelled their boarding spears and guarded the exposed rear of little battle formation.

Terrified fugitives poured past them, as they began advancing towards the rim of the stadium, and upon more than one occasion, they were compelled to use the flat of their weapons to beat the panic-stricken rabble aside, enabling them to continue their advance. Suddenly, the press of fugitives slackened, and they found themselves in open ground and closing rapidly upon the first rank of advancing enemy spearmen.

A clash between the tiny arrowhead of desperate fighting men and the spear-tipped line of Saxmen infantry should have proved fatal to the former. But the Saxmen formation became ragged as it descended into the stadium, for gaps had begun appearing in the ranks of the spearmen, due to a number of undisciplined warriors pausing to strip the bodies of the dead. Darryl spied one of these gaps and ordered George to make for it as quickly as possible. The huge boat hand immediately did as he was bidden, but a knot of fierce spearmen still confronted the mariners as their arrowhead formation reached the Saxmen battle-line.

A spearman thrust his weapon at George, who twisted violently sideways to escape the razor-sharp point. A split second later, the giant boat hand's long-handled axe flashed downwards, rending open the body of his adversary from shoulder to thigh. Simultaneously, another spearman attempted to stab George in his right side, but Darryl caught the spear-point on his target. Kingslayer darted out once and the Saxman warrior fell with blood pouring from a gaping wound in his throat.

Three more spearmen died. Two fell before the whirling axe of the giant boat hand, whilst a third was beheaded by a slash from Dromon's gill. Then the press slackened as the arrowhead formation burst through the front line of Saxmen spear-carriers.

The rim of the stadium was only two hundred paces away, but upwards movement was slow, for the intervening ground was thick with corpses and the purple moss of the terraces was copiously lubricated with the blood of slaughtered Islanders.

Even so, it seemed likely that the little group would reach open ground without further fighting; unfortunately, a Saxmen war-band, some forty strong, suddenly leapt into the stadium and charged headlong at the escaping mariners.

"Hold formation!" Darryl yelled above the screaming war cries of the oncoming enemy. "Remember to keep moving forward. It's our only chance!"

Moments later, the leading member of the Saxmen war-band died beneath the young boat hand's axe. A second later, every man in the little arrowhead formation was engaged in combat and fighting for his life. Some of the Saxmen warriors began working their way around the mariner's formation to attack its vulnerable rear, but help came from an unexpected quarter. About a score of the worshippers had witnessed the river-farer's penetration of the Saxmen spear-line, and taken station at the rear of the arrowhead formation, in a desperate effort to escape from the death trap. The mariner's new allies had armed themselves with staves, shards of broken pottery, anything that could be used as a weapon and they fought with a savagery born of desperation; but their naked bodies were open to the steel of the Saxmen, and, one by one, they fell writhing in their own gore. Yet they protected the rear of the tiny formation, as it neared the lip of the stadium.

The fighting crewmembers were close to their immediate goal, when a man of Herculean proportions suddenly appeared and pushed his way through the ranks of the attacking Saxmen warriors; the forward step of the mariners faltered slightly as they set eyes upon the monstrous new arrival.

The man was of colossal stature, standing a good seven feet in height and his legs, chest and shoulders were in perfect proportion to the remainder of his body. He wore a breast-plate made from iron and burnished copper, the winged helmet surmounting his heavily be-whiskered features, was made from some polished copper alloy that shone brightly in the morning light.

Upon his shoulder there rested a huge long-handled axe.

Dromon groaned. "May the Gods have mercy upon us! I have heard of this man. He is Tor Skull-splitter, the greatest of all the Saxmen chieftains. A warrior who has never known defeat, he..."

The boat hand's baleful warning came to an abrupt end, for the Herculean chieftain suddenly swung his axe above his head and, leaping forward, he brought the weapon down in a glittering stroke that was intended to split George's body wide apart. The young man reacted by twisting sideways and warding off the blow with the flat of his own weapon. Unfortunately, the shaft of his own axe was unable to withstand the impact of the stroke and shattered, leaving him holding only a small portion of the splintered handle.

Tor Skull-splitter swung his mighty weapon with the intention of delivering the coup-de-grace. The blow never fell. Darryl, having killed his immediate opponent, realized the young boat hand's peril and dropping upon one knee he executed a sideways cut severing the tendons behind the chieftain's right ankle.

Tor Skull-splitter lurched sideways and the head of his axe buried itself harmlessly in the ground, sticking fast. George instantly seized his opportunity. He tore the butcher's cleaver from his belt, dashing the weapon three times into the crippled chieftain's face. As the man fell, he drove the Sheffield steel blade down through Tor Skull-splitter's winged helmet and into his brain.

The survivors of the Saxmen war-band fell back aghast, after witnessing the death of their greatest leader and the tiny formation crossed the rim of the stadium without further molestation.

A terrible scene met their eyes, as they looked out across the surrounding countryside. Houses, villages and homesteads, were in flames and dense clouds of black smoke drifted across the once bounteous landscape. Even the fertile soil was being destroyed, for the Saxmen vandals had breached the irrigation canals, and the terraced fields were being swept away by the raging waters. Groups of the murderous warriors could also be seen quartering the ravaged countryside and hewing down the last of the peasantry, hopelessly trapped between the waters of the Great Life River and the swords of the barbarians.

Darryl viewed his small command and was relieved to note that all had won clear of the stadium, although blood from superficial wounds could be seen seeping from numerous rents in their protective clothing. Of the worshippers who had attempted to escape along with his party, only a solitary individual lived. The survivor was a short, stocky young woman, with a shock of sleek silver blonde hair that fell to her shoulders and contrasted sharply with her rounded and rather plain features. Yet, she clutched a sword, taken from the hand of some dead barbarian and the blood dripping from its blade proved that she had welded it to grim effect. The woman was virtually naked, like most of her dead companions, but the boatmaster had no time to examine the strange blue and black tattoos decorating much of her body, for he realized that he must quickly tighten up the little arrowhead formation and order a resumption of the march towards the Great Life River.

Darryl was about to give the order, when an urgent mental command smote his brain.

"Quickly... Abandon your present formation... And run for the docks... Run for your lives!"

The boatmaster knew instantly that the mental instruction

had been placed in his brain by one of the Dark Priests and he reacted without a moment's hesitation.

"All of you," he shouted. "Take to your heels and make for the safety of the Bonny Barbara. Keep together, but run as you have never run before."

The group fled in the direction of the river, avoiding numerous burning buildings and the pitifully twisted corpses of the butchered field-workers that lay everywhere.

Fortunately, most of the Saxmen warriors were busy looting the bodies of their victims and they had little interest in molesting the fugitives as they traversed the stricken countryside. Only once did a pair of barbarians attempt to cross their path, and the unwise duo died in an instant beneath the sword of the boatmaster and the flailing cleaver of his huge boat hand.

Half an hour later, the survivors entered the blazing dock area, with their lungs at bursting point, their feet raw from running and they were almost pulled up short by the sight meeting their eyes. Two huge black galleys were lying against the quayside, the big casting engines mounted on their main-decks hurling pots of some highly combustible liquid at nearby groups of Saxmen warriors. The effect was deadly, for entire groups of barbarians were immediately incinerated whenever the weapons succeeded in achieving a direct hit.

Close to the water's edge was ranged a battle-line of fighting men dressed in black protective clothing, and whose spear-points were stained red with the blood of the Saxmen barbarians who had unsuccessfully tried to drive them back to their ships.

"Mercenaries, mercenaries from the galleys of the Dark Priest's overseers," Dromon gasped. "We shall find safety once we pass through their lines."

Strong but gentle hands grasped the survivors as they reeled, totally exhausted into the ranks of the mercenaries, and they were quickly carried aboard their newly repaired narrowboat, where a very angry young wisewoman awaited them with a flask of restorative cordial to ease their fatigue.

"You bloody fool!" Myra whispered, as she poured a draught of the liquid down her brother's throat. "You risked the lives of your men, not to mention your own, in order to play giggle-bum with some slut, I shouldn't wonder, instead of being here, attending to your duties."

"I realize my stupid error, sister," the boatmaster replied in a penitential tone. "But I swear that I will never ignore your sage warnings in the future."

The wisewoman's attitude softened slightly, as she helped her brother to discard his blood-stained protective jacket.

"Well, what's done is done!" she said. "Yet I see the hand of the Dark Priests in all of this. Consider well, brother. They helped you to survive the evils of the City of Calar, and they also assisted me in refining my occult arts. Now they have dispatched their armed minions to rescue us from a situation that should have meant the death for us all. The Dark Priests interest in us goes deep, very deep. I have a feeling that we are being deliberately preserved to fulfil some greater purpose, and my witch's intuition tells me that all will be revealed to us very soon."

Darryl was about to reply to his sister's statement, when he suddenly felt a hand clutching at his ankle, and he found himself looking downwards into the distraught face of the woman who had assisted the travellers in their bitter conflict with the barbarians.

She now lay at his feet in a desperate act of supplication.

"Master," she said. "I owe my life to you and I beg you to take me into your service, so that I can repay my obligation." She paused. "My name is Whiteflower and I am a daughter of the Chief of the Kev Sword-Clan. We of the Kev dwell beyond the farthest reaches of the great Thoa-forests lying many long marches to the east of the Great Life River. My travelling companions are all dead and I humbly beg your permission to become a member of your boat crew!"

Darryl hesitated. "My vessel is small and another woman would be difficult to accommodate ..."

Myra halted her brother's speech by gently squeezing his arm, and she leaned over and quietly whispered in his ear. "The girl can share my cabin in the bows and she can take her turn on watch with the other crewmembers. Remember, brother, she has proved herself to be a worthy comrade in battle and my inner-eye suggests that she will be crucial to our survival in the future."

The young wisewoman viewed her brother sternly. "Brother, you must not cross me in this matter!"

The boatmaster slowly nodded. "Rise to your feet, Whiteflower of the Kev." He said. "From this moment hence, you are a member of our company!"

Myra continued to treat her brother's wounded crewmen, but a few minutes later, an officer from one of the overseers war-galleys boarded the Bonny Barbara and advised them to get underway at once, for he stated that the force of mercenaries, on shore, were being heavily counter-attacked by the barbarians and would soon be forced to re-embark on the two warships.

Darryl reacted to the news by leaping into the cockpit of the narrowboat, where he took charge of the tiller.

"Move yourselves," he roared to the exhausted crew. "Prepare to take aboard a line from one of the towing galleys and cast off. The sooner that we are clear of this place the better, for the only people to remain here will be the dead, and those who are going to die. Now, look sharp and get to your posts!"

※

Two hours later, the narrowboat was riding upon the south-flowing current of the Great Life River and Darryl gratefully surrendered the helm to Wilakin the navigator, who climbed down into the cockpit after casting off the line from the towing-galley.

Over to the east, across the breadth of the river, the boatmaster clearly viewed the raging fires and the dense clouds of smoke, marking the position of the once-fertile Island Of

Plenty. A place that was now reduced to uninhabitable cinders and where only the corpses of the dead and a few broken ruins remained as an epitaph of a once thriving society.

Darryl examined the dark hulls of the overseer's wargalleys, which had taken station to port and starboard of the Bonny Barbara, and he knew that his little company would be well protected until they reached the Holy City of Ptah, in some two Earth months' time.

"A bitter day to live through," he murmured, as he turned away to seek the comfort of his bunk. "Yet live we have and I believe that we shall survive to enjoy many better days in the future!"

Chapter 7

J enny Bowyer was preparing medicinal herbs upon the kitchen hob inside the wisewoman's cottage in Elfencot, when she was disturbed at her task by an unexpected knocking upon the front door. The crippled healer set aside her wooden spoon, and, opening the door she found herself staring at a well-built man who sported a bushy ginger-coloured beard and a carefully waxed handlebar moustache. Despite the warmth of late summer, the stranger wore a suit made from the heaviest woollen tweed and in his right hand he held a walking stick with a head made from a single polished ram's-horn.

"What can I do for you, master?" Jenny enquired.

"Och, little enough lass," the man answered, in a soft Scottish accent. "My name is Inspector Angus Smith, of the Manchester Constabulary, and I would have words with Hetty Littlewood who I believe is your employer."

"I be ever so sorry, but I am unable to help you," Jenny answered hesitantly. "For my mistress is far away, tending to a desperately sick relative, but if you need treatment for some simple ailment, why then, I will happily assist you as best I may."

"No lass," the Scotsman replied, stroking his beard. "I need no medical attention, yet I would speak with your mistress; aye and I ken well enough that she's no tending a sick relative!"

The inspector made a subtle movement with his left hand, a movement the young healer recognized as a secret occult sign, known only to those who possessed some knowledge of the magical arts.

"I'll no bother ye further, lass, for I know that Wise Hetty will have bound you with the witch's blood-oath and that hot iron would not suffice to loosen your tongue. Contact your mistress and tell her that I will return to this cottage in a week from today, at this very hour, aye and you may also tell her that I may be willing to assist her in clearing her son's name."

"Remember now," the policeman repeated, as he turned away from the threshold. "I will return at this hour, in a week's time. Do not fail to inform your mistress!"

✺

Jenny did not waste a single moment in penning a letter to the wisewoman carefully describing every detail of the inspector's visit and posting it without delay.

Hetty, upon reading the letter, decided that she must meet with this strange policeman, who appeared to have knowledge of the occult arts and discover what was on his mind. The wisewoman had already decided that no more useful information could be gained by remaining at the Cleopatra, and she resolved to find an excuse for leaving the music hall without delay, thus giving herself ample time to return to Elfencot and meet this Inspector Smith, whom Jenny had so carefully described in her letter.

The wisewoman sought out Mildred Pasco and asked to be allowed to leave her employment immediately, for she had grown to dislike the great city and wished to return to Kendal without delay.

Mildred, much to Hetty's surprise, accepted her request without the slightest hesitation and gave the wisewoman her accumulated earnings down to the very last farthing.

"Older women seldom prove satisfactory in this business," Mildred remarked, as Hetty turned to leave her office. "But you've served the Cleopatra well enough. Now remember to keep your mouth shut about all that you've seen and heard within these walls. Else things might go ill for you, even in faraway Kendal."

Hetty ignored the woman's threat and sought out Marsie' who burst out in a flood of tears the moment that Hetty announced her imminent departure.

The London girl begged her to return as soon as possible.

"I ain't never had many friends," she moaned. "And now you're going too. However am I goin' to manage on my own?"

"Oh, you'll do well enough," the wisewoman said, giving the girl a comforting hug. "Time will pass quickly and then you can depart for America, and find yourself a kind husband. So I council you, don't despair!"

The wisewoman left the Cleopatra at dawn on the following morning and she exercised extreme care in case she was followed from the establishment. Instead of taking the steam-train to Ashton-Under-Lyne, she begged her passage upon a coal barge that took her across the Lancashire plain to the town of Wigan. From there, she made her way overland to the village of Marple, and thence to Elfencot, where she arrived the day before her intended meeting with Inspector Smith.

Jenny was overjoyed by her mistress's return, but she immediately found herself being questioned in great detail by the wisewoman, wishing to gain all possible knowledge of her forthcoming visitor. However, it soon became obvious that she had little further information to add, and Hetty realized that she would have to contain her curiosity until her meeting with the policeman on the following day.

※

Rainclouds had drifted in during the night and it was a wet and rather bedraggled Inspector Smith who knocked upon the door of the witch's cottage.

Jenny answered the front door and removed the policeman's long waterproof cape and hood before ushering him into the wisewoman's sitting room. Hetty invited the man to rest in the most comfortable chair in the room and ordered her young helper to fetch a plate of wholemeal scones and a pot of freshly brewed tea, before leaving them to their discussion.

"I'll no beat around the bush!" the Scotsman said, the moment the pair were alone. "And I'll state from the very beginning, that I believe your son to be quite innocent of the murder of Stovepipe Arkwright, and he likely killed him in order to save his own skin. Yet I also ken that many in the Manchester Constabulary would certainly not agree with me."

He ran his fingers through his rain-moistened ginger beard. "Aye, yon Arkwright was well known to me, for I've been keeping a close eye on that man for quite a while. He worked as a runner for Albert Pike, a sometimes boxing promoter, and a few others of a similar ilk. I also know that Arkwright occasionally worked for Silas Oldshaw, the Stalybridge mill-owner, another body who's perhaps more than he seems to be."

"Then why have you not investigated these men much more closely, in order to get at the truth?" the wisewoman asked sharply, but the policeman simply shook his head in reply.

"Proof lassie--Proof, some of these people are well respected and prosperous. I can't go beatin' upon folks' doors with nothing but a few vague suspicions to justify my actions. No, lassie, I must proceed with great caution when enquiring into the affairs of men like Silas Oldshaw!"

The inspector tasted one of the whole meal scones and brushed away the crumbs before continuing.

"I know that your son, Darryl, didna' escape through the Devil's Hill Tunnel under his own steam, lass," Smith said quietly, whilst looking the wisewoman straight in the eye. "I ken that you used your witch-wiles to spirit him into a refuge that my old granny used to call 'The Place O' Muckle Water.'"

Hetty was almost dumbfounded by the accuracy of the policeman's statement, but she managed to utter a few words in reply. "Your grandmother ... She knew of ..."

Inspector Smith interrupted with a gentle laugh. "My family hails from the Island of Skye close to the west coast of Scotland. My father was taken to Edinburgh to live when he was but a ween, where he served in the constabulary for all of his working life, but when I was very young, I was often sent to spend the summer on Skye, to keep my old granny company."

"Aye lass," he continued. "I ken that you will have heard of her, for other witches used to call her Meg One-Eye, on account of the fact that she had lost her right eye when she was a very young girl."

The wisewoman quickly regained her composure and took a sip of tea from her cup.

"Yes, Inspector," she answered. "I certainly recall hearing of your grandmother, for it was said that she was one of the most accomplished healers of her day. I suspect that you know many of her secrets!"

The policeman nodded. "Aye lassie, many were the nights when I fanned the embers beneath her cauldron, whilst she chanted her spells and prepared one of her curing potions. One dark night in midsummer, she sat me on the grass by an old stone circle, whilst she danced, naked as a baby, with the other members of her coven."

He sighed. "But I myself never danced around the fire, in honour of the forces of nature, for I never inherited my granny's occult powers. Yet I was a clever young bairn and I still recall much of what I saw and heard. Like the location of the portal by which a body can return to our world from the Place O' Muckle Water. The place whose exact position you must learn, if you're ever to assist your son in returning to his own world!"

Hetty was unable to disguise her excitement. "You know were such an exit lies?" she asked.

"Och, aye," he said slowly. "I know it well enough, but I keep its location secret, together with the remainder of my granny's occult knowledge, for I've no wish to be hauled off to the Manchester Bedlam and shut up with five hundred

'Laughing Cavaliers' for company. Or at the very least, I wouldn't be believed and my career with the constabulary would be over and done with."

Inspector Smith leaned over and took Hetty's hand. "Lass, I'll put my cards on the table, plain for you to see. I've known for the past two years that Albert Pike and that Pasco couple have been involved in a brothel-keeping operation at the Cleopatra Music Hall, and they were well protected by some corrupt members of the local constabulary. I could have brought them all to justice, with the aid of my superiors, had I so wished, but I wouldn't have netted Silas Oldshaw, and I strongly suspect that he's the man behind the whole rotten crew."

The policeman paused and drew breath. "We both have corresponding interests, lassie. I suggest that we pool our knowledge and cooperate, in order to bring these villains to justice and also to clear your son's name. Think about my proposal, lassie, but be sure to give me your answer before I leave your cottage."

Hetty called out to her young assistant, and requested her to bring another pot of tea.

'Could I trust this man?' she wondered. Her inner eye gave her an explicit 'Yes,' and an added incentive was the fact that the policeman was connected, by blood, to the fast-disappearing witches' fraternity. The wisewoman had also begun to realize that her personal enquiries were unlikely to bear further fruit and she was certainly in need of assistance from another source.

Hetty put down her tea-cup and gripped the policeman firmly by the hand.

"Well, Inspector Smith," she said decisively. "I'll agree with your suggestion and join forces with you, so now you had best settle back and listen carefully whilst I tell you everything that I have discovered in the City of Manchester."

The tea in Inspector Smith's cup was quite cold by the time that Hetty had finished relating her experiences within the Cleopatra Music Hall. When she had finished, she called out to

Jenny, who visited the larder and produced a bottle of her finest gooseberry wine and two glasses.

"You've done well, lassie," the policeman remarked, as he carefully sipped the powerful beverage. "The information that you gleaned at such a considerable personal cost serves to substantiate everything that I have long suspected--aye, and it has also brought many other previously unknown facts to my notice." He looked at her with fresh admiration. "You're determination itself lass," he said, "aye and sharp as a razor!"

The inspector took another sip of the gooseberry wine and his face took on a grim aspect. "Would you risk yourself, even further, in order to clear your son's name and bring him home safely?" he asked.

"I would do anything!" the witch answered, without a moment's hesitation.

"Well, lassie," Smith said. "It is my feeling that we should delve even deeper into the heart of Oldshaw's organization, and that heart unquestionably beats within the walls of Westdyke Grange, an old mansion house standing upon the hills overlooking Stalybridge, and that he presently owns and occupies. True enough, the man has a townhouse in Manchester, but he spends most of his time at the Grange, at least when he's not travelling between his various businesses."

"You seem to have learned a great deal about Oldshaw's affairs!" the wisewoman reflected.

"Aye lass," the inspector replied. "But I know next to nothing about what goes on inside that damned house of his. Silas is extremely careful; none of the servants that he employs are local folk, and all are well paid and know how to keep their mouths shut when not on duty. Quite a few have prison records. Oldshaw tells his chapel cronies that 'Heaven requires him to be charitable to such unfortunates,' but the truth is, they must be loyal to the man or starve in the gutter!"

Smith paused. "An informant of mine, an ex-felon called George Piggins, has managed to gain himself a position at the

Grange as second gardener, and he believes that it would be possible for him to persuade Oldshaw's butler to engage his 'sister' as a scullery maid in the main house."

The inspector hesitated for a moment.

"Lass, my suggestion is that you should play the part of Piggins sister, in order to worm your way into Oldshaw's household and discover what you can of the man and his affairs!"

Hetty was initially surprised by the audacity of the man's suggestion, yet it immediately fired her interest.

"What if I should be recognized as an ex-whore from the Cleopatra?" She asked.

"It would undoubtedly have serious consequences for you, lass," the policeman replied. "But I doubt if Oldshaw would ever consider the possibility that a lowly cleaning skivvy, working in his mansion-house, could once have been the beautiful woman who delighted the customers in that Manchester music hall of his; as for his associates at the Cleopatra, he seems to keep them at arm's length and won't have them anywhere near the Grange."

The inspector stroked his chin.

"Lassie, I can't deny that it's a risky venture that I'm suggesting, yet it's perhaps the best hope we have of bringing these people to book and of clearing your son's name!"

The wisewoman never hesitated. "Very well, Inspector, I will enter Westdyke Grange in the guise of a servant--and I have little fear of being recognized, for a witch can do much to alter her appearance. Now tell me, when should I present myself at Oldshaw's mansion?"

Smith thought for a moment. "I expect that it will take Piggins a good two weeks to arrange for your employment, so you'll need to present yourself at the Grange in about a fortnight's time, but be sure to see Piggins before you try to enter the house. Remember, the gardener will be our only means of maintaining contact between ourselves, for the inside servants are seldom allowed to leave the house, but Piggins is an outside worker and can come and go as he pleases. He will serve as our postman!"

The policeman picked up his walking stick and prepared to leave the cottage.

"I wish you the best of luck lassie," he said. "And I freely admit that never in my career with the constabulary have I ever met another woman with your depth of courage and intelligence. Now I bid you good-day."

⚘

Hetty spent the following ten days resting and making the necessary preparations for her departure to Stalybridge. Indeed, the policeman had hardly quit the cottage, before she had entered her kitchen and brewed a bitter herbal potion that she swallowed at a single draught. The effect of the drug was that she instantly began losing her appetite, and in the following days, the flesh fell from her body and face, giving her an unfamiliar gaunt appearance. In addition, the witch dyed her hair with a vegetable concoction turning her into a rather dark brunette.

The wisewoman also undertook some additional precautions. Into the hem of a heavy woollen skirt, she stitched a number of tiny vials of liquid, each one having the particular ability to either blind, paralyze or stupefy. One vial contained a bright coloured liquid that possessed the appalling capacity to render the recipient permanently insane. Hetty also impregnated a long hat-pin with a poison that would kill its victim with a single scratch, and finally she concealed a potential bribe of twenty golden sovereigns inside the heels of a pair of her walking shoes.

"Not bad!" she said to herself, as she took stock of her preparations, during her last evening at Elfencot. "I've done all that I can. Now providence and my own wits must be responsible for the rest!"

❧

The textile town of Stalybridge was basking in the weak autumn sunshine, when Hetty alighted from the narrowboat that had delivered her to a coal-wharf lying in the shadow of a huge cotton mill, a vast industrial structure whose tall chimney belched forth clouds of black smoke into the soot-flecked atmosphere.

Hetty picked up a large carpet bag containing the few possessions she had brought with her from Elfencot and made her way across the centre of the town, until she came to an old pack-road that wound its way up into the heather-clad hills overlooking Stalybridge and its outlying villages.

The wisewoman had travelled only a little way along the roughly surfaced road when she was offered a lift upon a vegetable cart that was returning to one of the small farms lying close to the edge of the moorlands. The driver was a stout red-faced fellow, who stated that he was passing within a quarter of a mile of Westdyke Grange, and would willingly carry her as far as the long drive leading up to Silas Oldshaw's residence.

Two stone pillars, topped with carved lions, marked the beginning of the mill-owner's property, and Hetty thanked the driver for his kindness before starting the final trudge towards the mansion house. The drive was well maintained and free from pot-holes, yet the carpet bag was heavy, and the wisewoman was extremely relieved when she finally arrived at the door of a gate-house, which, together with a large iron gate, was set into the high wall surrounding Westdyke Grange and its extensive gardens.

Hetty knocked upon the gate-house door and a short sallow-faced man appeared and abruptly asked the wisewoman her business.

"I've come to seek employment with Mr Oldshaw," she answered. "I am sister to George Piggins, the second gardener, and ...."

"Oh aye," broke in the sallow-faced man. "I've been told to expect thee!" He opened the gate and pointed to a path following the inside of the boundary wall.

"Keep to yon path, and you'll come to the row of conservatories lying to the rear of the great house. There you will find your brother at his work."

Hetty followed the path as she was instructed; as she walked she was able to take a good look at the boundary wall protecting the Grange. It was newly constructed from local brick and stood a good twelve feet in height, whilst the parapet, that overhung the wall by a good six inches, was covered with a double row of razor-sharp iron hooks.

"Yon bugger Oldshaw certainly wishes to keep himself secure," the witch muttered to herself. "For a wall of that size would cost a pretty penny to build."

Hetty breasted a small rise and caught her first glimpse of Westdyke Grange and she gasped as she noted its forbidding appearance.

The building was a good four stories in height, with two oval towers flanking its front elevation and the exterior masonry was dark in colour, blackened by time and the chimney smoke drifting upwards from the factories in the valley below.

Hetty shuddered slightly. Even the bright autumn sunshine failed to relieve the gloomy appearance of the place. She knew the Grange had a bad history, for Inspector Smith had told her that the main house had originally been constructed, two centuries earlier, by a local landowner who dwelt in constant fear of his ill-used tenants. However, a separate wing jutted out from the eastern elevation of the house, and its archaic appearance suggested that it was older than the rest of the structure and was perhaps of monastic origin.

The wisewoman's inner eye counselled her to turn upon her heel and flee without further delay, but she gritted her teeth and advanced towards the cluster of glass conservatories nestling in the rear of the main house.

Hetty found George Piggins working in a glasshouse filled with potted palms, and Piggins, a short rat-faced individual, quickly drew her inside and closed the door so as to avoid any chance of them being overheard.

"So you be the woman who Inspector Smith wants me to slip inside the Grange!" he began. "I don't like it, I can tell yer, for Oldshaw's bad to them who cross him. I likes me job and I'm only doin' this because I owe Smith a favour, for not droppin' me inside when he could have done so."

The ex-criminal casually wiped away the discharge from his nostrils, with the cuff of his shirt and continued speaking.

"Now wench, remember that you're my sister and that your name is Hilda Jenkins. You were born and bred in a village in Cumberland, and you are now a widow, for your husband was a sailor who was drowned in a shipwreck of the China Coast. Do not volunteer any information about yourself, nor will you be asked very much, for every bugger in that house has something to hide." He paused.

"I'm to be your contact with Smith and nobody will think it odd that you should occasionally come to the conservatories to visit your 'brother.' As an outside worker, I can come and go as I please and I can easily post a letter for you in Stalybridge."

Hetty slowly inclined her head. However, it was quite obvious that Piggins was a very frightened man, but her intuition told her that he would probably remain silent and play his part, provided that no member of the household subjected him to hard questioning.

She smiled. "Now, brother, perhaps it is time for you to introduce me to my new employers."

The gardener conducted her to a door in the rear of the main house and hauled upon a bell-pull. A diminutive young housemaid answered and Piggins asked her to inform Mr Crowther, the butler and head of the household, that his latest employee had arrived.

The man who came to the door and ordered her to follow him inside was short and of stocky build, yet he possessed a gimlet gaze that seemed to pierce directly into her mind. The witches mental barriers immediately sprang shut and she knew instinctively that here was a man who would butcher his fellow human beings, without the slightest spark of remorse.

He took her into his small personal office, situated beneath the main stairway and ordered her to be seated.

"So you're Piggin's sister," he said, in a hoarse-sounding voice. "You are less hard-bitten in your appearance than some of those who seek employment in this house!" the head of the household remarked bluntly. "But that is perhaps to be expected, since you are a widow woman rather than an ex-jailbird. Very well, it matters little to me provided that you obey your orders to the letter and without question."

Again his chilling gaze swept over her. "There are parts of this house that are forbidden to ordinary servants, such as yourself, and are governed, at all times, by a strict set of rules; these rules you will learn from an experienced member of the staff, who will now conduct you on a tour of the house."

He paused, and flicked a speck of dust from his coat.

"I have given thought to the nature of your employment, and I have decided to assign you to the kitchen, where you will assist Mrs O'Day, the cook. Be sure that you do your work well, and in return, your life here can be pleasant and rewarding."

The butler rang a small hand-bell and a diminutive grey-haired woman entered the office. Crowther never spared her a glance.

"Rachel, give this woman the usual newcomers' tour of the house, then deliver her to Mrs O'Day!" Then, with a brief wave of his hand, he dismissed the two women from his presence.

The grey-haired woman said nothing to the wisewoman as she conducted her through the house, save what she had been instructed to say. Using short rapidly delivered sentences, she described the purpose and importance of every room and corridor through which they passed.

It immediately became obvious to Hetty, as she moved from room to room, that the Grange's grim external appearance bore absolutely no relationship to the house's pleasant and luxuriously appointed interior. Brightly coloured velvet curtains hung at every window, whilst expensive furniture and furnishings of crystal, silk and marble adorned every room in the main living quarters.

The wisewoman also noticed that gas-lighting had been installed throughout the house, and it appeared that Oldshaw had spared no expense in piping town-gas to his isolated residence.

Rachel conducted her to a door connecting the principle hallway of the house, to the much older east wing.

"Never attempt to pass through this doorway," Rachel said, with a hint of fear in her voice. "This wing is strictly forbidden to the entire staff, with the exception of Mr Crowther. The wing contains the master's workshops and laboratory. It's the place where he tests out the textile processes that have made him rich. Our master guards his secrets from the eyes of his competitors with great care, for the research staff who live in the east wing are allowed no contact with those of us who live here in the main house."

Rachel led her up a narrow back stairway to a small attic room, whose window looked out across the valley towards the distant mill-chimneys of Stalybridge and Ashton-Under-Lyne.

"This is your room!" Rachel said. "One of the best, your bed has a soft feather mattress and you have a gas light for your own personal use during the hours of darkness. Our master looks after us well. Good food and lodgings and a decent rate of pay. What other master was ever so good to his servants?"

The pair descended the stairway and followed a short passage opening into a large kitchen. At the far end of the room stood a big iron range and a plump woman in a white apron was slowly stirring a pot of soup standing upon one of the simmering plates. She turned and faced the wisewoman with her hands upon her hips.

"My kitchen help has arrived at last!" she said. "Thanks be to providence, for I've been on my own for the past three weeks, aye and without help from any of the other servants!"

The cook dismissed Rachel with a casual wave of her hand, and then pointed towards a teapot that stood on the edge of the range.

"Help yourself to a cup," she invited. "For you must be as dry as snuff after your journey here; so take a seat and rest awhile, before you don your working cloths and prepare to serve the staff dinner. The staff are the only ones who will be dining today, for the master is absent on business and the mistress is confined to her bed with a bad cold. Poor thing, she never seems well these days!"

"Are there children to be tended?" Hetty asked.

Mrs O'Day shook her head. "No my dear, the master and mistress are childless and servants are never allowed to bring their children within these walls."

"Sad, I say," the cook remarked wistfully, "Nothing like a few little ones for brightening up a house."

Mrs O'Day then became serious and pointed towards a small closet.

"You'll find a working dress and an apron in yonder clothing store. Then you had best set a dozen places in the servant's dining room. Very soon, twelve hungry workers are going to pile in here and start eatin' the master out of house and home!"

❧

Hetty spent the following week accustoming herself to the routine of the kitchen and household.

She rose at five o'clock in the morning, cleaned out the coal fired range and lit the fire. She then roused Mrs O'Day with a cup of tea, before assisting her in preparing breakfast for the servants that usually consisted of porridge, followed by fried potatoes and a little bacon.

About nine o'clock, Mrs Oldshaw's personal maid would arrive to collect a breakfast tray consisting of tea, thin-sliced bread and marmalade for her mistress.

She spent the remainder of the morning peeling vegetables, cleaning the kitchen and its numerous cooking utensils, and in helping the cook to prepare a substantial meal for the household staff. The afternoons passed in a similar manner, until the servants arrived for their final meal of the day, at about seven in the evening.

Crowther, the butler, never dined with his underlings, and the wisewoman always served his meals in the privacy of his own personal office. The sinister Head of the Household never uttered a single word, as he accepted the tray of food that Hetty brought three times a day, and he always dismissed her from his presence with a single casual wave of his hand.

The routine of the kitchen was occasionally broken by the arrival of May, the mistress's personal maid, who sometimes collected a light meal of poached fish, or some other form of invalid food, whenever Mrs Oldshaw felt inclined to eat something. However, the pace of work was leisurely and the two women were able to enjoy a pot of tea whenever the mood took them. Hetty remarked upon the unhurried pace of work, during one of their numerous tea-breaks, and Mrs O'Day had laughed.

"Aye, it's steady at the moment," the cook explained, "but we've plenty to do when the master is at home, especially when he entertains his Chapel friends for dinner."

Mrs O'Day's voice fell almost to a whisper. "I shouldn't mention it, but you're bound to find out sooner or later. The master, you see, has his own little whimsies and he's a fair devil for the boxin' and the cock-fighting. Loves it, he does."

She took a sip of her tea. "There's a big basement down below this house. It stretches almost the whole width of the building, so it does. That's where the master and his friends hold their fights. No harm in it I say, man like him can't be expected to get all his fun from preaching down in the Stalybridge Chapels."

She paused. "It's hard work then, lass, two full days and nights of solid work lookin' after the master's guests."

"You think a lot of the master?" the wisewoman remarked cautiously, and Mrs O'Day responded by nodding her head vigorously.

"I do indeed!" the cook answered quietly. "I wouldn't repeat this to just anyone, but I certainly owe Mr Oldshaw my life. When I was young, I served in many fine houses until, one evil day, I was tempted to steal money for the sake of a blackguard who sometimes shared my bed. I was caught, imprisoned, and thrown upon the street without a position or a reference. I would surely have starved or had to drown myself in Liverpool Bay, had not a friend of the master's found me and brought me to the Grange, some five years ago."

Tears filled the plump cook's eyes. "Do I think a lot of the master? You ask. I owe him everything and so do many who dwell beneath his roof."

Mrs O'Day emptied her teacup "Enough of idle chat," she said briskly. "Now we had best get back to work."

Later, in the privacy of her bedroom, the wisewoman pondered over Mrs O'Day's confession and she realized that she would have to pursue her inquiries with extreme caution; for it was obvious that the majority of the household staff would go to extreme lengths to protect the interests of their beloved master; however, she knew that some risks were unavoidable and she resolved to leave her room, in the dead of night, and examine as much of the house as possible.

On her first night abroad, she carefully perused the upper attic levels of the building, and, thanks to her witch's inner eye, she succeeded in identifying the bedrooms occupied by each member on the household staff.

In the following nights, Hetty silently extended her range until she had minutely searched every portion of the Grange, with the exception of the master and mistress's personal suite, situated on the first floor of the main house.

Yet, despite her extreme caution, the witch was almost discovered during one of her nocturnal forays.

She had been moving down the main stairway, when her foot accidentally depressed a creaking floorboard and she had immediately crept back onto the first floor landing, in case the sudden noise had been overheard. The precaution proved to have been very wise for, moments later, the door to the butler's under-stair office had swung open and Crowther had stepped out into the moonlit hallway.

Hetty had tiptoed into an unoccupied bedroom and taken refuge behind an antique screen occupying the far side of the room. With baited breath, she had listened to the butler's footsteps as the man ascended the polished main stairs, and bitten upon her lip as he passed down the carpeted passageway only a few feet from where she stood.

Crowther had returned some five minutes later, but he appeared to have been still suspicious, for his footsteps had periodically halted and it was plain that he was listening for any unusual noise. Hetty had finally heard the door of Crowther's room close, but she had waited a good hour before creeping back to the relative safety of her own room. During later night-time forays, the wisewoman had taken care to give the main stairway a wide berth.

Hetty discovered nothing unusual during her nighttime investigations of the Grange, yet the master and mistresses personal suite remained unexamined, and she therefore attempted to nurture a friendly relationship with May, the girl who was Mrs Oldshaw's personal maid. This proved to be fairly easy, for the servant frequently visited the kitchen on her employer's behalf and, unlike many other members of the staff; she seemed to enjoy a cup of tea and a good chat.

One day, the wisewoman assisted the maid in the laborious task of carrying Mrs Oldshaw's bathwater up into her employer's personal suite and it was in the course of this visit that Hetty had her first opportunity of viewing the mistress of the house.

As she entered the bedroom, the wisewoman caught sight of Mrs Megan Oldshaw propped up in a high-backed chair. The woman was almost completely covered by a heavy rug, and Hetty was able to see little more than her pale face and her thin white hands. She realized, at once, that the woman was suffering from some chronic lung infection, probably a common form of consumption, and had not long to live.

'Perhaps only a few months,' she thought, and she fought back an urge to offer the woman her skills, in a desperate effort to slow down the inevitable outcome of the disease. Hetty had immediate felt sympathy for the young mistress of the house, who could have been no more than thirty years of age, and who would never experience the pain and pleasure of motherhood and would soon be dead.

Despite her best efforts, the witch had been able to define nothing of a particularly unusual nature within the confines of the master-suite, or indeed in the remainder of the main house, and she was forced to conclude that if anything of a sinister nature existed within the walls of Westdyke Grange, then it unquestionably lay within the forbidden east wing; and she knew that she must somehow secure an entry.

Even so, her intuition told her that something might be gained by learning more about Mrs Oldshaw and her relationship with her husband. The wisewoman therefore carefully questioned the maid on the next occasion that she visited the kitchen, and whilst the cook was absent upon some other duty.

"What ails your mistress, lass?" Hetty enquired, as she poured out two cups of tea.

"She has consumption," the maid confirmed. "The master has engaged all of the best physicians, but to no avail and I don't think that she is long for this world!"

Hetty noticed tears welling up in the girl's eyes.

"Have you been long in your mistress's service?" She enquired.

"Aye, ever since I was a child," May replied. "I come to Manchester with the mistress when she married Mr Oldshaw. Folks said that he wed her for her father's money, for the master was but a mill manager at the time and it was said that he needed funds to start his own business. But they are wrong, for never did I see a young couple so much in love!" The girl sighed. "Then she contracted her disease and we moved here to Westdyke Grange, so that she could enjoy the cleaner air of the hills."

Tears were now running down the maid's face, but she continued her explanation.

"The master changed after he came here. He's still considerate to the mistress, aye, and to a fault, but he went cold inside and he's a different man to the pleasant gentleman who courted my mistress. All this prizefighting and the like ... he would never have countenanced it then!"

May pulled herself together and look of unease entered her eyes, for she probably realized that she had spoken too much for her own good.

She brushed away her tears and stood up. "Well, I mustn't stay here gossipin' about things that concern neither of us," she said, and quickly left the kitchen without even waiting to finish her tea.

ℒ

Hetty and the remainder of the staff of Westdyke Grange enjoyed another three weeks of leisurely employment, before Silas Oldshaw completed his business in Manchester and returned to Westdyke Grange, upon a dark and windy Friday evening.

Suddenly, the pace of work in the kitchen increased. On Saturday morning, the wisewoman found herself helping the cook to prepare a mass of light sponge cakes, refreshments for the master's invited guests to enjoy with their tea, when they arrived at the Grange, directly after the chapel services on the following morning.

Piggins also drove a light horse-van into Stalybridge and returned with two saddles of freshly killed lamb, together with a selection of sausages, kidneys and other offals, which the two women set about preparing for the next day's midday meal.

The wisewoman and Mrs O'Day rose before five o'clock on the following morning, and worked without respite until one in the afternoon, when the main meal of the day was ready to be served to Silas Oldshaw and his guests. A full hour of complete bedlam then followed, as servants bore away the fruits of the women's labours to the hungry guests in the dining room.

Afterwards, the staff arrived for their own meal, and the clock on the wall had turned three before the two kitchen hands were able to relax with a pot of tea. It was during this well-earned break that Hetty happened to glance out of the kitchen window and view Mr Silas Oldshaw for the first time.

Three men were examining a horse in the cobbled yard at the back of the Grange. One of the men was a short and massively shouldered individual with battered features and a shaven scalp. He held the horse's head whilst the other two men ran their hands over the creature's body. One of these men wore a tweed coat and leggings, having the appearance of a country gentleman or perhaps a local veterinary surgeon; however, Hetty knew instinctively that the third man was Silas Oldshaw, the industrialist and master of the household.

Oldshaw was much younger than the wisewoman had imagined and was certainly a year or two short of turning forty. He was tall and stood over six feet four inches and his lean build displayed the fine cut of his black church-going suit to perfection. She also noted his blonde hair and his handsome aquiline features showing few of the marks of oncoming middle age. Yet a cold chill ran down her spine, for her inner eye instantly warned her that she was viewing a man who was completely steeped in evil.

The cook noticed Hetty's interest in the man and smiled.

"Yes lass, that's the master right enough, he's out there with yon vet from Stalybridge--seems that his favourite coach-horse is in trouble again."

"God bless the master!" she said, and then frowned.

"I'll give you some good advice; lass. You see that broken-faced man holding the horse's head; make sure that you keep well clear of him. He's a bad lot. More than one housemaid has finished upon her back with her skirt over her head, whether she wished it to happen or no. His name's Bill Travis and likes to call himself Bill the Boar. He's Mr Oldshaw's pet prize-fighter and he drives the master's coach when he's not fightin' or training for a fight."

Mrs O'Day pointed towards a black four-wheeled coach that stood parked at the far side of the yard.

"Master's been known to come up from Manchester in yonder coach, sometimes without a single change of horses, it's no wonder that he often lames his animals like that poor creature over there!"

The stout cook shrugged her shoulders.

"Well, that's the master's business. Now I think that you'd best begin washing up the utensils, whilst I start carvin' up the remainder of the meat, for teatime will be upon us before we can blink an eye and everything must be prepared!"

※

The entire staff at the Grange were kept fully on their toes in coping with the needs of Silas Oldshaw's friends and business acquaintances who came visiting him at his home.

Hetty, however, only came face to face with the master on one occasion.

She had been sent, by the cook, to collect a net of carrots from the vegetable store that was situated close to the long range of glass-houses that Piggins normally tended.

She was hurrying from the store with the heavy net of carrots underneath her arm, when she rounded the corner of one of the conservatories and almost ran into the master, who was admiring his collection of palm trees through the panes of translucent glass.

He steadied her with his hand.

"Those vegetables are far too heavy for you to carry, my woman!" he said, in a smooth and cultured voice. "Drop them on the path and tell Piggins to bear them to the kitchen for you. Now back to your other duties at once!"

Hetty bowed and did as she was bidden, quickly hurrying back to the refuge of the kitchen. Indeed, she was glad to do so, for her questing inner eye had clearly defined a bottomless well of malevolence within the master's being, and this had touched her deeply; she now knew the man to be extremely dangerous, and realized that she could expect no mercy from Oldshaw, should he suspect the true nature of her mission to Westdyke Grange.

Hetty penned a report for Inspector Smith that very same evening and early on the following morning she visited her 'brother' in the conservatories with the envelope hidden in the bodice of her dress. Piggins accepted the letter with considerable trepidation; the wisewoman noticed the gardener was much more nervous than usual, possibly due to the fact that the master was in residence. Even so, he promised to post the letter in Stalybridge that same evening.

Hetty returned to her round of kitchen duties and was physically tired out when she finally sought the comfort of her bed. Sleep came hard for the wisewoman, for her inner eye constantly impinged upon her consciousness. As she dozed, she often found herself looking into the handsome face of Silas Oldshaw. Sometimes, the battered features of Bill Travis also drifted across her minds inner vision. In the end, she rose from her bed with the firm intention of taking a drug that would induce untroubled sleep, but as her feet touched the floor, she heard the distant rumble of a horse-drawn vehicle approaching from the direction of the gate-house.

The wisewoman looked out from her window and was surprised to see the master's four-wheeled coach pulling into the moonlit courtyard. The vehicle slowed down to a walking pace, disappearing into the cul-de-sac leading to the main door of the old eastern wing of the house.

Hetty's curiosity was aroused. She quickly donned a black working dress then slipped down the stairs and into the kitchen. She tiptoed over to the outside door, drew the bolts and stepped out into the darkened courtyard.

The wisewoman quietly flitted through the numerous shadows cast by the high walls of the house, until she reached the corner of the eastern wing; she then fell upon her knees and cautiously peered around the corner.

The cul-de-sac, which gave access to the eastern wing, was illuminated by a direct shaft of moonlight and Hetty had no difficulty in recognizing the coach that was now halted outside the open door of the building.

Two men stood alongside the coach as Travis climbed down from the driving seat and prepared to open the door of the vehicle. One of the men was Crowther; Hetty had no difficulty in identifying his gaunt features in the moonlight, but his powerfully built companion was a complete stranger to her.

Travis opened the door of the coach and a heavily veiled woman stepped lightly from the vehicle and accompanied the two men into the eastern wing.

The wisewoman would dearly have wished to continue her observation, but she was compelled to regain the shelter of the kitchen, with all haste, for the coachman suddenly took the head of the lead-horse and began manoeuvring the empty vehicle around in the cul-de-sac with the probable intention of parking it in the main portion of the open courtyard. Indeed, the wisewoman realized that she was extremely fortunate in avoiding detection.

Hetty returned to her bed, but sleep continued to evade her as she pondered upon the relevance of the scene that she had just witnessed.

The arrival of the veiled woman in the dead of night was a strange occurrence, but there might be a perfectly innocent explanation, she reasoned Yet her witch's inner eye strongly suggested that dark and malevolent forces were presently at work.

The wisewoman also knew that another person had witnessed the arrival of the veiled woman in the master's coach; for she had noticed a slight movement in the doorway of the eastern wing as the unknown woman was alighting from the coach. From the corner of her eye, the witch had caught a fleeting glimpse of a young woman peering around the edge of the door jamb.

Hetty turned the situation over and over in her mind and, by dawn, she had arrived at the inescapable conclusion that she must find some means of entering the forbidden east wing, in order to discover its secrets. However, she knew, from past experience, that the only doorway between the east wing and the main house lay at the foot of the stairwell, in close proximity to Crowther's office. She realized that she must find some alternative means of entry, but how?

The task, she knew, would not be easy, for her previous nocturnal forays had confirmed that all of the other doorways leading to the east wing had been securely closed off by solid brickwork and were now quite impassable.

"There must be a way!" she muttered to herself, as she rose to begin another day of hard work. "There must be a way and may the unseen forces help me to find it!"

❧

Exactly a week later, Silas Oldshaw boarded his coach for Manchester, to deal with some matters of business that had suddenly arisen and the household quickly settled down into its normally sedate working routine. It was during this period of relative calm that Hetty accidentally stumbled upon a discovery that eventually enabled her to penetrate the forbidden eastern wing of the house.

One morning, Piggins arrived at the door of the kitchen with a wheelbarrow loaded with autumn fruits, and Mrs O'Day announced that the time had now arrived to manufacture a stock of Jam for the coming winter. The cook took a bunch of keys from a hook on the wall and handed them to the wisewoman.

"Turn right at the foot of the stairs," she ordered, "and you will find a small door leading down into a cellar. This is where we store kitchen utensils that we only use on odd occasions. There you'll find the big copper pan that I use to make jam at this time of the year, fetch it up here and then we shall get to work on this confounded pile of ripe fruit."

Hetty opened the cellar door, lit a candle and descended into the basement by means of a set of rickety stairs. The cellar proved to be quite large and had probably been used as a larder at sometime in the past, for the walls were lined with rotting wooden shelves. The floor was also littered with discarded kitchen equipment and it took Hetty a good ten minutes to discover the copper pan that was the object of her quest. She noticed that another door was set into the far wall of the basement and probably led into an adjoining cellar, but although one of the keys that she carried appeared to fit the lock, it was quite solid from lack of use and refused to open. However, the witch's curiosity was now fully aroused and she resolved to return that very evening and explore the basement lying beneath the house.

Hetty waited until the small hours before entering the kitchen, and she descended into the seldom-used store-cellar. The wisewoman lit a candle and began soaking the rusty lock with melted lard that she has stolen from the kitchen pantry and allowed the lubricant plenty of time to penetrate the mechanism before attempting to turn the lock, but it refused to budge and it required a further two hours of patient work before it finally snapped open with a sharp click.

The door opened out into a short passageway giving access to a number of dark cellars. Dust lay everywhere and it was obvious that this portion of the basement had been disused for many years. The end of the passageway was closed off with a barrier of rough brickwork, and Hetty's knowledge of the house suggested that Mr Oldshaw's basement gaming-room lay on the far side of the obstruction. Another short side-passage led her in the direction of the forbidden east wing, and she was not surprised to find this passageway also blocked by another mass of brickwork.

The night was now well advanced and the witch knew that she must suspend her subterranean investigations without further delay. She therefore returned to the kitchen and washed the grime from her body, before returning to her room, in order to gain a little rest before the start of the next working day.

Hetty rested the following night, but she returned on two successive evenings armed with a powerful storm lantern, and she minutely searched the cellars lying closest to the forbidden eastern wing. Yet, despite her best efforts, she found no way of accessing the building that lay beyond the basement wall. She rested for the next three nights, then, encouraged by her witch's intuition, she returned for one last effort.

Once again, she found nothing. But as she searched a small closet, she felt a slight breeze brushing against her cheek. The draught of air appeared to be rising from the floor and falling upon her knees, she began carefully examining the rough stone flagged floor-surface.

The flagstones had been laid in mortar and the joints were often so tight that a knife could hardly have been inserted. However, the wisewoman discovered a single flag, about two feet square, with a number of rough-hewn slots cut through its surface and a light draught of air was blowing upwards from the apertures.

"An old stone grid!" the wisewoman muttered to herself. "And where there is a grid there has to be a drain. Perhaps it once cleansed the old east wing of the house and may now give me access to that damned place!"

Hetty returned the following night with a wooden hammer and a thin bladed chisel that she had found in the gardener's tool store. By the light of the lantern, she began cutting away the mortar joints holding the grid-stone in position. An hour later, she had succeeded in clearing away the mortar from the joints and the grid was loose in the floor.

The wisewoman took a deep breath, inserted her fingers into the slots in the stone and heaved upwards with all her strength.

The grid moved a little and the witch redoubled her efforts. Gradually, it slid backwards until a black hole was revealed in the centre of the floor.

Hetty rested for a while in order to regain her strength, and then she peered downwards into the hole with the aid of the light reflected from the powerful lantern. She immediately realized that she had discovered a very old sewer that had probably been built by the original owners of the old east wing. The sewer, she noted, was well constructed of rough hewn stone slabs and was approximately four foot square. It was also very shallow for the slabs of the existing basement floor now formed its roof. Fortunately, the sewer was dry and it smelt quite fresh and had obviously not been used for a great many years.

The first thing that Hetty noticed was that a current of air was travelling down the sewer from a westerly direction and she surmised that the duct must have an outlet somewhere in the gardens on the far side of the main house however, this was of little concern to her for the moment.

The wisewoman's curiosity was now irresistibly aroused, and, after lighting a candle, she lowered herself into the duct and crawled eastwards along its length until it terminated in a small circular stone chamber that must have been situated well below the floor of the forbidden wing. The chamber was about six feet in diameter and had probably once served as a collecting point for all the sewage from the original monastic building. The wisewoman looked upwards and she noticed that the top of the chamber was covered over by a line of rough-hewn wooden planks, which she could easily touch with her fingers if she stood upright and raised her arms above her head.

She gently pushed upwards and the timbers moved with ease and she knew that she would experience no difficulty in reaching the space that lay above. Even so, she realized that dawn must now be approaching fast, and that she must return upon another occasion to explore the forbidden east wing.

※

Hetty spent the following two days carefully making her preparations. She obtained a number of extra candles and a small lantern, which she added to the one that she already possessed. She also found a small wooden box that, if placed at the bottom of the circular space, would give her the extra lift that would enable her to climb out of the chamber.

On the third night, Hetty waited until the entire household was fast asleep and then she tiptoed her way down into the basement area. She made her way into the closet were the entrance to the duct lay, and there she paused for a moment and made her final preparations. She took the poisoned hat-pin from its wooden storage tube and inserted it into the lapel of her dress, then she lowered the two lanterns into the sewer, together with the wooden box, and carefully climbed downwards into the duct itself. The wisewoman inched her way towards the circular chamber, carefully moving the lanterns and the wooden box before her as she advanced. Finally, after a great deal of effort, she entered the chamber and lay motionless in the darkness. She listened intently for any noise that might issue from the room above, but nothing disturbed the absolute silence surrounding her. The witch also consulted her inner eye. Strangely, her highly tuned intuition told her nothing and she realized that she would have to be guided by her normal senses alone.

Hetty gently pushed upwards upon the underside of one of the planks that lay above her head. The timber moved with ease and she pushed it aside, followed by two of its neighbours. She listened for a while, then stood upon the wooden box and lifted her head and shoulders above the floor-level of the room above. Once again, she paused and listened for a good five minutes, before gathering up enough courage to light both of the lanterns.

After taking the precaution of leaving the smaller of the two lanterns burning in the base of the chamber, she quickly swung herself out of the pit and onto the floor above, and then she held the remaining lantern above her head, in order to gain a view of her immediate surroundings.

The cellar, into which she had emerged, was small and cluttered with long abandoned junk of every description. Empty wooden boxes and old wine-casks lay on every side, together with broken furniture and numerous decaying hangings that may once have graced the walls of some Georgian banqueting hall. Over everything there lay a coating of grime that must have taken long generations to collect.

'Where does this abandoned cellar lead to?' Hetty wondered, and she immediately began searching for an exit. The light from the lantern revealed a large door at the far end of the cellar, and she moved towards it and began examining it closely. The door was constructed from planks of solid oak, which the passage of time and generations of wood-lice had failed to destroy, but the hinges and the lock mechanism were completely rigid with corrosion and would never move again.

The wisewoman's spirits fell and she began to wonder if her painful efforts to enter the east wing would finally prove to be a failure. Then her gaze fell upon the base of the door and she noticed that a swinging trapdoor was let into the ancient timbers.

A useful facility, she surmised, that had probably been intended to allow vermin-hunting animals to gain easy access to the storage cellars where preserved food had probably been stored.

The trapdoor had once swung from leather straps, but these had long since perished and Hetty easily lifted the door aside, thus revealing a narrow exit through which she could squeeze with some difficulty. The wisewoman removed her working dress and most of her underclothing and then wriggled her way through the mouth of the trapdoor. Once through, she clambered to her feet and found herself standing in a corridor that was illuminated by a small gas-jet mounted on the wall of the passage. She quickly donned her discarded clothing and checked that the poisoned hat-pin was still secure in the lapel of her garment, before continuing her search.

The corridor terminated at the bottom of a flight of stairs that appeared to lead upwards to the ground floor of the east wing. She crept upwards, a step at a time, until she was confronted by a wooden door of modern design. Again, the wisewoman attempted to employ her witch's inner eye, in order to gain a foreknowledge of any danger awaiting her beyond the threshold, but her gift appeared to be strangely inoperative and she had no choice but to proceed without the valuable aid of her second-sight.

Biting her lip, she pressed the latch and allowed the door to gently swing open.

A gas-lit main hallway lay beyond, and this gave access to a pair of well appointed day-rooms that appeared to occupy much of the ground floor of the wing. To the rear lay three smaller rooms that were completely filled with stout workbenches, their surfaces littered with hanks of yarn, bolts of cloth and various pieces of complicated scientific equipment. In addition, the walls were lined with shelves that supported numerous bottles of variously coloured liquids, boxes of powdered chemicals and other types of scientific paraphernalia; the wisewoman immediately realized that she had entered the research laboratories where the rich industrialist developed and tested his newest discoveries.

The east wing was obviously much smaller than the main portion of the house and only one other ground floor room now remained to be explored. The room lay on the far side of the main hallway and the only access to it appeared to be through a large door that had been entirely constructed from wrought iron plates. Two keyholes were let into its smooth metal surface and a large brass knob appeared to operate a latch on the far side of the door.

Hetty placed both of her hands upon the knob and she had just begun turning it in a clockwise direction, when she heard a muffled footfall on the floor immediately behind her. Instinctively, the wisewoman's hand flew to the poisoned hatpin in the lapel of her dress, but the same instant, she felt the sharp prick of a knife at her throat.

"Remain still, witch!" a woman's voice hissed in her ear. "Or by the Prophet, I swear to kill you this very instant!"

Chapter 8

A flickering glow on the distant southern horizon was the first indication that the Bonny Barbara was approaching the copper-clad walls of Holy Ptah, and the temporary crewmembers of the narrowboat were in especially good humour, for they knew they were approaching the spiritual home of their race.

Even so, they had little time for idle pondering, for the river was now crowded with vessels of every shape and size and a careful watch had to be set in the bows and the person manning the tiller had always had to be one of the more experienced steersmen. Indeed, the river would have been even more difficult for them to navigate, had the overseers' galleys not been in close attendance; a fact that encouraged many vessels to give them a wide berth. Finally, on the thirty-eighth day out from the tragic Island of Plenty, the entire crew of the narrowboat were able to stand on deck and view the burnished copper walls of Holy Ptah for the first time.

The Holy City stood on the eastern bank of the river and was protected by enormous metal-clad walls that towered at least two hundred feet above ground level, yet these cyclopean walls were simply dwarfed by the numerous finger-like buildings springing upwards from the environs of the city, and whose spires almost pierced the crimson clouds rolling endlessly overhead.

On the western bank of the Life River, directly opposite the metal girt metropolis, there stood a huge and sprawling suburb, whose modest buildings were constructed from commonly used materials such as brick, stone and timber and erected in the normal fashion of the river-folk. This western suburb, Wilakin the navigator had carefully explained, was a civil settlement that housed a vast labouring population, and the sole purpose of this mass of humanity was to provide all of the basic services needed by the Dark Priests, that strange group of clerics who dwelt in virtual isolation behind their shining copper walls.

The two vastly contrasting settlements were joined together by a slender single-span bridge, made from some strange white -coloured metal that arched over the Great Life River, and stood a good three hundred feet above the waterway at the highest point of its massive span.

One of the overseers' galleys suddenly increased its stroke-rate and took up a new position ahead of the narrowboat. A sailor standing by the vessel's stern-rail executed a series of swift hand-signals, which the navigator carefully read before turning to Darryl who was standing by his side.

"Master, we are ordered to follow that craft to the mouth of the overseer's military dockyard, over on the western shore where a pair of towing-galleys are waiting to help us into our berth. There we shall be met by a representative of the Dark Priests, who is waiting to give you further instructions."

"Nothin' like feeling wanted!" the boatmaster reflected. "Anyway, they may have some fresh victuals waiting for us, for that final week of eking out the last of our food-stocks has left me with a fair appetite." He laughed. "I think that George is almost ready to start eating his boots, for he knows they're made of good narrs-leather!"

The Bonny Barbara and its two escorts swept beneath the great bridge, and as they emerged, the lead-galley abruptly changed course and headed for the mouth of a large dockyard lying about a quarter of a mile away.

Moments later, two swift towing-galleys passed their lines over to the narrowboat and began easing her towards the

entrance of the overseer's dockyard. Darryl now took over
the tiller from his twin sister and he followed the navigator's
steering instructions with the utmost care, until his precious
craft was berthed and under armed guard in the safety of the
overseer's dock.

A young man was standing upon the quayside. He wore a plain
light brown robe and held an intricately carved baton of office
in his left hand. A squad of eight heavily armed mercenaries
were drawn up at his rear. The young official ordered his men
to remain on the quayside and then he picked his way across the
nearest outrigger and stepped down into the cockpit of the boat,
where Darryl had just finished securing the tiller.

He grasped the boatmaster's hand in the common Water
Realm greeting.

"I bid you welcome to the City of Ptah and extend to you
the greetings of the Priests of the Ancient Lore. My name
is Paris. I am the personal envoy of Councillor Hemm, the
head of the High Council of the Priesthood. I am instructed to
inform that yourself, and the two other newcomers to the Water
Realm, who fare with you, will be received by my master at
noon tomorrow, in the Palace of the High Council. I will return
early in the coming morning, to conduct you thither!"

Darryl returned the envoy's greeting and was about to give
his acquiescence to the priestly summons, when the door of the
cabin suddenly swung open and his twin sister emerged. She
bowed to the young envoy, then turned and quietly addressed
her brother.

"I mean no disrespect to our guest and I will gladly offer
him refreshments from our remaining store of provisions,
but I must warn you that although he is not a member of
the Dark Priesthood, he still possesses considerable psychic
ability. Brother, you must shield your mind, for he knows your
thoughts as easily as reading a book!"

Paris threw back his head and burst out laughing.

"My lady," he said, with a smile. "Your knowledge is indeed

great, for only the most accomplished of seers could define the extent of my powers and done so before I attempted to make use of them." The envoy raised his arm. "I swear before the forces of the unknown that I will never seek to use such powers against you or any of your friends!"

He paused and looked the young witch directly in the eye. "You know full well, my lady, that I will never break such a powerful oath."

The envoy paused again and adjusted his robe.

"Councillor Hemm has much to discuss with you, and please do not be afraid. My master holds no animosity towards any of you, for he has known of your presence in the Water Realm, almost from the first day that you arrived. Indeed you would not be alive, at this moment, if he wished you ill!"

"You have known..." Darryl began, but the youthful envoy held up his hand for silence.

"All your questions will be answered on the morrow. In the meantime, you must remain aboard this craft, for here you will be quite safe and you will also receive the best of provisions from the dockyard kitchens."

The envoy adjusted his robe and prepared to quit the narrowboat.

"The dockyard overseer has been instructed to purchase your cargo of rare timbers at the full market price and to pay you, at once, in good solid discs. You will then have the means to pay off or retain your crew members, as you see fit."

The envoy bowed graciously towards the girl. "I am glad to have made the acquaintance of so beautiful a seer. Now I must return to my other duties!"

So saying, he rejoined his escort upon the quayside and quickly disappeared.

"What do you make of the man?" Darryl asked, once they were alone.

But his sister simply shrugged her shoulders. "I feel that we can probably trust him. He gave me the security of an almost unbreakable oath, when I warned you of his psychic powers, and my inner eye also suggests that he is a man of considerable integrity, but we may well be minnows amongst sharks, so we must remain on our guard!"

Half an hour later, three sweating cooks visited the vessel, laden with baskets of hot food and a large jug of Thoa-nut beer. The boatmaster immediately called out the entire crew and they enjoyed an excellent meal seated upon the deck of the narrowboat.

However, the crew members had barely finished their repast when the brown-robed assistant overseer of the dockyard arrived, accompanied by an adviser from the timber merchants' guild and a dozen common labourers. At the overseer's request, the Bonny Barbara's cargo of rare timbers was exposed for examination. For a full hour, the overseer and the merchant-adviser clambered about the hold, perusing its contents with care. Finally, they emerged from the hold and offered to pay the boatmaster a quantity of copper discs that was about equal to what old Agar-Marduk had expected the cargo to bring in the markets of Holy Ptah. Darryl accepted the offer without a moment's hesitation, and, for the remainder of the day, the dockside was a hive of actively, as the contents of the hold were carefully unloaded by the labourers and transported to the safety of nearby warehouses.

Darryl, meanwhile, was taken to the dockyard's main office, where the agreed sum in copper discs was counted out before his eyes, and presented to him in two strong leather moneybags.

The three laden cooks returned to the Bonny Barbara at dusk. Once again, the crewmembers dined upon the open deck, but this time with the aid of lanterns. At the end of the meal, Darryl produced one of the bags of discs and meticulously paid out the wages owed to each member of the crew. He also thanked them for their loyalty and offered to retain their services for the foreseeable future.

Wilakin the navigator immediately stepped forward then kissed the boatmaster's hands and swore to remain with the craft until all their journeying was over.

He was instantly followed by Whiteflower, the newest crew member, who repeated the same oath of loyalty also without hesitation.

The two blood cousins, Tess and Tom-Tess, were undecided, but agreed to remain and experience some of the wonders of the Holy City of Ptah, before deciding whether or not to take part in the next leg of the voyage.

Dromon, as expected, declined the offer of re-enlistment and declared his intention of briefly visiting Ptah before returning northwards, to the village of his birth, in order to begin life as a freehold farmer.

Once again, Darryl thanked the men for their services, then he and the tired crewmembers sought the comfort of sleep.

※

Dawn broke over the City of Ptah and the crew of the Bonny Barbara awoke and greeted another day.

They ate a light breakfast. Then Dromon, resplendent in his best garb and with a travel-pack slung loosely over his shoulder, descended the gangplank for the last time and waved goodbye before disappearing in the direction of the dock gates.

The two blood cousins followed shortly afterwards, leaving only five crewmembers aboard the narrowboat.

Darryl turned and addressed both his sister and the giant boat hand. "Well friends," he said. "The five suns are already high, so we had best get ready for our meeting with Councillor Hemm. Paris said that we should wear only common dress and carry no weapons. So let's get to it!"

The three newcomers were waiting upon the quayside when the young envoy arrived together with a bodyguard of soldiers.

Darryl and the boat hand were dressed in dark trousers and plain brown caftans and this simple garb drew no comment from the young official, but the man was visibly taken aback by the strikingly beautiful appearance of the youthful wisewoman. She wore a long figure-hugging dress of emerald green, leaving little to the imagination, matching to perfection the long flowing tresses of red hair covering her shoulders and back.

"In the name of all the Gods!" the envoy gasped. "Can all the women who dwell in the world beyond the barrier possibly be as fair as she?"

Suddenly and quite unexpectedly, a psychic message pierced the mind of the young envoy.

"No Paris... Indeed they are not. But as the priests of Dumteck say... Beauty of the form, without beauty of the soul, is but an empty and worthless gift!"

The envoy quickly regained his composure and led his charges towards an open passenger carriage that was drawn by four stout labourers. He chose not to comment on the mind-message that he had just received from the red-haired wisewoman, but he now realized that he was in the presence of a female seer with incredible latent power.

The three newcomers followed the envoy into the carriage and the escort of mercenaries took up station at the rear as the vehicle moved forward.

The carriage passed through the gates of the dockyard and joined a dense throng of traffic that was moving down a wide avenue running parallel with the western bank of the Life River. Paris pointed towards the base of the great metal bridge, lying about a quarter of a mile ahead of them.

"We must pass over the bridge," he said, "for it's the only means of entry into the Quarter of the Guardians, the portion of the Holy City that lies closest to the eastern bank of the river and where most of the Dark Priests reside. Fortunately, we shall experience little impediment from other travellers once we near the entrance to the bridge, for the lay-helpers, serving the Dark

Priests, will have crossed the river long before dawn and are already at their employment. All commercial traffic crosses by night, so we shall pass unhindered at this hour of the day."

Sure enough, the press of traffic eased considerably as they approached the bridge, and the carriage was almost alone as it came abreast of the heavily manned checkpoint standing at the great bridge's western portal, but Paris brandished his baton of office and both the vehicle and its escort passed onto the white-metal roadway without the slightest pause. The carriage had only travelled a short distance when some of the soldiers broke ranks and put their shoulders to the rear of the carriage, so as to help the vehicle in its laborious accent of the sharply curving slope, an incline that led steeply upwards towards the point where the bridge reached its highest point above the Life River. George coughed nervously and all of the newcomers stared uneasily at the many different types of vessels navigating upon the surface of the great waterway lying a dizzy three hundred feet below them. Eventually, the loftiest section of the bridge was reached, and one of the mercenaries hurriedly applied a brake to the rear wheels of the carriage, and slowly, the vehicle began its controlled decent towards the heavily guarded gateway piercing the mighty outer-walls and gave access to the interior of the Quarter of the Guardians.

Once again, a flourish of the envoy's baton ensured an uninterrupted passage through the ranks of the guards standing by the gate. The carriage passed through the shinning copper clad walls and emerged at the beginning of a wide avenue running directly into the very heart of the Holy City.

As the carriage moved onwards, the newcomers were held in awe by the immense buildings towering upwards on every side. The vast majority of the structures, the travellers immediately noticed, were constructed from huge blocks of stone resembling the ones littering the ruined cities of the The Ancient Dead. The very tallest of the structures, the ones that seemed to almost pierce the crimson sky, were invariably made from the same strange white metal that had been used in the construction of the great bridge spanning the Life River.

Smaller roadways branched off from the main avenue at regular intervals. These were inhabited by numerous groups of scurrying individuals whom Paris described as 'helpers,' namely the workers in modest technical and administrative grades, who could easily be identified by their bright blue uniforms. Occasionally, they noticed an isolated figure wearing a plain brown robe, whom they now knew to be an official holding the important rank of overseer and above. Of the black-robed Dark Priests, there was no sign, but Paris immediately explained that the 'Guardians,' as he generally called them, occupied the high towers and were seldom seen abroad in the streets.

In addition to the uniformed denizens, a great many parties of ordinary citizens, dressed in a wide variety of local Water Realm garbs, could be seen being shepherded along by the blue -uniformed helpers who were obviously serving as tour guides.

The visitors were numerous in the vicinity of a number of richly decorated high towers. These structures, the envoy casually explained, were chapels dedicated to the worship of the Ancient Lore; these shrines were the ultimate destination of most of the many pilgrims who visited the Holy City of Ptah.

The carriage had travelled about a quarter of a mile down the main thoroughfare, when the man-hauled vehicle slowed down and turned into a short avenue. It drew to a halt in the shadow of an immensely tall building constructed from the ubiquitous white metal. The structure, the newcomers immediately noted, was completely windowless and reached upwards towards the crimson sky like some gargantuan obelisk. Only a single entrance could be seen, a doorway of massive proportions set near the base of the building and reached by a short flight of stone steps.

Paris led the three travellers up the steps and into one of a number of circular chambers facing them as they crossed the threshold.

"Do not be afraid," he said. "You are now inside a simple transportation device that will deliver us to Councillor Hemm's place of work without further delay."

A door slid shut behind them and the envoy touched a small green panel with his baton of office. Instantly the newcomers experienced a sensation of complete weightlessness and they realized they were shooting rapidly upwards, on what seemed to be an invisible cushion of air. Each one of the travellers was startled by this new phenomenon and was immediately tempted to shout out in alarm, but the sensation of weightlessness lasted for only a few moments, and they suddenly found themselves standing motionless upon the floor of another circular chamber, similar in every detail to the one they had entered only seconds before.

A door in the front of the chamber slid noiselessly open and the group stepped out into a spacious room that was plainly furnished with a table and a few simple chairs.

"The Councillor will join us shortly," Paris explained. "In the meantime, it may interest you to view the City of Ptah from the highest room in its tallest building."

The envoy raised his baton and the walls and ceiling of the room glowed pink for a moment before turning completely transparent and below them, the entire city lay open to their scrutiny.

The high white-metal towers of the city were arrayed before them like pine trees in a plantation, whilst the encircling walls of burnished copper shone brightly in the filtered light from the five suns. The travellers peered out across the Holy City for a few moments and then looked above their heads at the rolling crimson clouds that appeared to be speeding across the sky only an arm's length above their heads.

The walls and ceiling of the room suddenly resumed their normal appearance.

"An impressive sight, my friends," said an unfamiliar voice from the farthest end of the room, and the newcomers turned in time to see the hooded figure of a Dark Priest emerging from a door that had silently opened in the far wall.

The man was tall, and must have stood a good seven feet in height, and he appeared to be of very slight build, a fact that was not disguised by the voluminous black robe covering him from head to foot. He waved his hand towards a group of chairs.

"Please be seated," he said. "A servant will arrive shortly with wine and refreshments, but until then we have much to discuss!"

He threw back his hood and gave the three travellers their first glimpse of the facial appearance of a member of the dark priesthood.

By Earth standards, the man seemed to be of early middle age, for his closely cropped brown hair was tinged with streaks of grey, but his light blue eyes possessed a strange opaque quality that was slightly disturbing to the beholder. In addition, a further physical characteristic singled him out from the commonplace run of humanity, for the priest had an extra-prominent forehead that was supported by a small ridge of bone, that sprang from the bridge of his nose and curved upwards like some medieval flying buttress.

"Look well," he commanded, in a resonating voice that seemed to demand immediate attention. "And you will realize that we Guardians do not belong to the same genus as you humans!"

The priest paused and seated himself before the three wanderers, with Paris at his side.

"Firstly," he continued. "I will tell you something of the Guardians and of the role they play in the maintenance of civilized life, within this reality that is sometimes described as the 'Water Realm.' Many aeons ago, this world was ruled by a great and incredibly advanced race, who are remembered here as The Ancient Dead. You have seen many relics of this race as you journeyed down to the Life River and beyond.

You will also remember the ruined city by the lake, close to where you emerged into this reality, and the bridge where you were attacked by river pirates on your voyage to Calar of the Mighty Walls. These are but a few of the physical reminders of this long disappeared people. In those distant days, we who are now called Guardians of the Ancient Lore or simply Dark Priests, were the servants of that ancient race who are said to have originated somewhere amidst the distant stars. Serve them we did, and for countless generations, until they finally quit this world for reasons that are difficult to fathom after such an immensely long passage of time. We remained as the Guardians of their greatest surviving achievement, the Life River, which allows trade to flow and for civilized life to exist in the Water Realm."

Myra's eyes narrowed. "Councillor, your words have now confirmed my suspicions that you have been keeping a discrete watch upon us ever since we arrived in this world. The help afforded us by the Dark Priest, on the battlements of Calar, and the timely arrival of the overseer's galleys at the doomed Island of Plenty, can hardly have been mere acts of chance."

The hint of a smile crossed the Councillor's face.

"We have known of your presence in the Water Realm, ever since your craft berthed at the home village of Thom Jak's, the wizard. It is also true that we have intervened whenever your destruction appeared to be inevitable, but we had our reasons and they will soon be revealed to you."

He paused. "I and the other councillor's, feel that you should now view the Great Cavern, lying far beneath the City of Ptah, and see for yourselves the machinery that powers the two-directional flow of the Life River. Only then will you fully realize the magnitude of the task we inherited from the Ancient Dead. A burden we have discharged for countless generations since the Old Ones disappeared into the abyss of space."

Councillor Hemm replaced his hood. "Refreshments will now be brought to you. Paris will then conduct you to the Great

Cavern and you will view undreamed of wonders. Afterwards, we will talk again!"

The door in the wall slid open and the Dark Priest quickly disappeared.

꿏

The three travellers dined upon cakes of plain Thoa-bread, then followed the envoy back into the transportation chamber. Once again, they felt the sensation of weightlessness as they hurtled downwards upon a cushion of air, until they found themselves inside another matching chamber. However, the sight which met their eyes, as they exited the chamber, almost took their breath away.

The newcomers found themselves standing upon a metal platform that was situated high upon the inner wall of an enormous natural cavern. Before them lay a huge void that was at least a mile in breadth and stretching away into the distance as far as the eye could see. The interior of the cavern was illuminated by panels set into the rocky walls and ceiling and threw beams of white light down upon the floor below. However, little of the cavern's natural floor remained exposed to view, for the base of the void was completely filled with a massive array of apparatus of unimaginable size and complexity. Rows of huge metal tanks marched onwards, rank after rank, until they disappeared into the far distance, whilst metal pipes and an indescribable tangle of multicoloured cables criss-crossed the cavern in every direction, supported upon white-metal gantries of considerable strength.

The newcomers stood mystified. Councillor Hemm had said that the Great Cavern contained machinery. Yet the mass of apparatus below them did not resemble anything which the Earth-born viewers had ever experienced within the bounds of their own reality. No steam cylinders hissed. No con-rods pounded. Indeed, not the slightest sound issued from the vast installation occupying the cavern floor, and the only movement to be seen, was that of a small number of Dark Priests who made their way, ant-like, between the tanks and the gantries.

Darryl strove to come to terms with the strange complexity of the scene lying before him, and he turned to question the envoy who was standing at his side.

"Tell me, if this is the engine house that drives the waters of the Great Life River, then where does it derive its power? Is it wind, steam, or something so unbelievable that our minds cannot possibly comprehend it?"

The envoy shook his head.

"The truthful answer is that no one knows. The very best of the Guardian Scientists, the Dark Priests who tend the machinery according to the knowledge inherited from the Ancient Dead, suggest that the power is somehow drawn from the molten core lying within the subterranean depths of our own world. Yet nothing can be proved, for compared to the Ancient Dead, we are like children groping in the darkness of an everlasting night!"

The party returned to the high chamber and Councillor Hemm rejoined the group and requested them to be seated and afford him their undivided attention.

"My friends," he began. "You have seen with your own eyes, the great installation driving the flow of the Life River. You now understand something of the enormous burden which the Ancient Dead laid upon the shoulders of their successors. The great cavern is free from interference, for it lies far beneath the ground, whilst the Holy City of Ptah is protected by a defence system, both material and occult, that can easily repulse the assault of any force existing upon this entire world. Indeed, nothing can remain alive within a day's march of this city, if we so wish it!"

The Councillor fell silent for a moment and gathered his thoughts before continuing.

"Unfortunately, not all threats to the continuity of civilization within the Water Realm are so easily countered. For long ages, The Guardians of the Ancient Lore, have worked diligently to maintain a balance of power between the differing races that depend upon the Life River, for their very existence. Only thus, could we ensure that civilized settlement could continue to flourish amidst the chaos reigning supreme on the remainder of our world!"

The Councillor paused again and then resumed his lecture, taking care to choose every word with the utmost care.

"We have maintained control by a variety of means, some of which you have personally witnessed, but our greatest weapon has always been the awe and fearful respect that most folk have for our priestly order, a mental hold that we are careful to maintain in the minds of the population. However, in recent years, this control has been much eroded by the brutalizing effect of the bitter wars upon our distant eastern frontier; wars that have inevitably resulted in the displacement of entire peoples who are far too desperate to fear even the terrible wrath of the Guardians."

George's massive frame suddenly stiffened in his chair.

"The pirate who survived the attack upon our boat, as we descended the Exit River," he interrupted, "claimed that his band was forced to leave the shelter of their clan-house and seek victims further afield, because large numbers of desperate newcomers had also begun plundering inside their traditional home territory. Aye and one of the robbers who held me captive in the City of Calar mentioned that his brothers had been driven from the river for the same reason."

The Priest inclined his head in agreement. "Yes, you are correct in equating these random acts of banditry with the growing levels of violence that I have just described. Also, please recollect that you barely survived the powerful Saxmen attack, which completely destroyed the Island of 'Plenty. An assault, that only five cycles ago, would have been deemed utterly unthinkable."

Darryl remembered the words of the drunken Stone-carrier, upon the night that George had fought the boatman in the riverside tavern. 'Towns and cities, from Calar right down to Holy Ptah seem to be overhauling their defences!' the man had said, and Darryl also recalled 'the forges of the armourer's continue to ring!' and his closing prediction: 'some great catastrophe was hanging over the world!'

The boatmaster was tempted to follow George's example and repeat the old Stone-carriers' testimony. However, he said nothing, and instead, put forward a question of his own.

He raised the palm of his hand, in order to catch Councillor Hemm's attention.

"Sir, do you know the root cause of this spate of warfare upon your eastern borders and creating this terrible chain of violence?"

"I do indeed," the priest replied. "It is the Hix! Ten cycles ago, they suddenly began emerging from their distant wastelands, and launched a series of irresistible attacks against the human clans closest to their borders. These clans-folk migrated west, into the lands of the Saxmen tribes. Many Saxmen warriors were also displaced and driven westwards, and these fighters are now threatening the cities and principalities that lie close to the banks of the Great Life River."

Myra looked enquiringly at the Councillor. "Have you given assistance to the clans-folk in their battles with the Hix?

"We have dispatched many troops of powerfully armed mercenaries to their aid," Hemm answered. "It is largely due to their efforts that the Hixian' warriors have not yet penetrated into civilized territory. We have also dispatched a number of scientists and seers from our own black hooded order, but the Hix are not human and are seldom totally devastated by our plagues and occult spells."

The young wisewoman looked the Councillor directly in the eyes.

"Why have you brought us here?" she asked.

"To help us make peace with the Hix," he answered at once. "You and your friends represent the only hope that we have of ending this ocean of bloodletting. If you bear with me, I will explain how this may possibly be accomplished."

The Councillor straightened his robe, before continuing. "Many years ago, we Guardians, together with most of the human races in the Water Realm, were in a state of perpetual conflict with the Hix. Sometimes, our wisest councillors dispatched envoys to treat with the Hixian' leadership in order to stop the killing, but they were always murdered, and their heads returned to us as a token of their hatred for us. A hatred that is deep and quite beyond our understanding."

The priest paused, and smiled at the twins.

"Then a seer possessing immense mental powers arrived in the Water Realm. Her name was Rose Littlewood and she is a direct ancestor of yours. She made a bargain with the Council of Guardians, that she would journey to the wastelands of the Hix that lie far to the east and attempt to negotiate a treaty with the Hixian' leadership that would end the conflict. In return, the council of the day agreed to tell her the location of the secret place where she could pass through the curtain and return to her own reality. Your ancestor succeeded. She returned with a promise of peace from the Hix, providing that half of the Thoanuts from the great eastern forests would be turned over to them, in exchange for quantities of the rare metals that abound within the Hixian' lands." Hemm sighed. "The agreement with the Hix held solid until ten cycles ago and it was of great benefit to all who dwelt within this reality. As for Rose Littlewood, she continued her journey and was never seen again!"

"My friends," he continued. "We wish you to retrace the steps of your illustrious ancestor, and make a new treaty with the Hix, in return for almost any concession lying within our power to grant. On your return to Ptah, we will divulge the same secret that was given to Rose Littlewood, and you will have the means of returning to your home reality."

Again, he paused.

"The route to the wastelands of the Hix passes through dangerous and difficult territory, but the ability of your little group to surmount danger, has been well proven in the course of your journey to Ptah. You must forgive us for not giving you greater assistance during your journey, but we needed to test your ability to survive a range of perilous situations and we only intervened on your behalf when your position became critical."

Councillor Hemm sat quietly for a full minute, before concluding his breathtaking explanation.

"I am the first member of our order, for long cycles, to request help from a traveller from another reality, but it is now my duty to do so. I beg of you in the name of all the forces for good, in the known and unknown portions of the universe. Please come to our aid!"

Councillor Hemm urged the three travellers to give his proposal their most careful consideration and returned them to the care of Paris, who installed them in a suite of comfortable rooms at the base of the tower; where they could rest and decide upon a suitable answer to the Dark Priest's plea.

The envoy was about to leave them to their deliberations, when George suddenly grasped him by the wrist. "Tell me," he asked. "How is it possible for some wandering seers from Earth, to successfully treat with the Hix, when all your native Water Realm adepts have failed so abysmally?"

"A necessary question," Paris replied. "The answer lies in the way in that individual Hix communicate with each other. They have the ability to speak and many are able to converse in the common Water Realm tongue. Indeed, a few brave and enterprising border clansmen seem to have met and spoken with isolated groups of Hix and succeeded in conducting a profitable trade with them. However, the Hix are accomplished

telepaths and normally prefer to converse with their fellows by
mind-power, alone, and have little need of the spoken word.
The Dark Priests they hate beyond understanding and shun
all mental contact with them. Whilst we Water Realm seers,
who are descended from human stock, appear to have lost the
telepathic ability to contact all but our own kind."

"One last question," George said, releasing the envoys
wrist. "If we refuse to journey to the wilderness of the Hix,
will we be killed out of hand?"

Paris appeared shocked. "In the name of the unseen powers,
never, you would be allowed to depart unharmed. Or offered
responsible positions in the ranks of the overseers, should
you choose to stay in Ptah. No Dark Priest would harm a
descendent of Rose Littlewood, whose memory they hold with
great affection."

The newcomers rested awhile and then began discussing
the councillor's proposal.

George was sceptical about the entire business and had
little confidence in the assurances of good faith given to them
by Hemm and his envoy. He stated that he would willingly
turn his back on the problems of the Dark Priests and take his
chances on the river.

Darryl, by contrast, was much influenced by the evidence of
the growing chaos witnessed during their voyage to the Holy
City. He worried over the possible fate of the people who had
shown them kindness and generosity, people such as Thom
Jak's the wizard and Agar-Marduk the merchant, and their
numerous families. However, time appeared to be an important
factor. Paris had mentioned that a round trip to the wastelands
of the Hix, was likely to take the best part of a year, and perhaps
much longer if unforeseen difficulties were encountered. The
boatmaster wondered if enough time would remain for them to
reach the exit portal that, Thom Jak's believed lay far beyond
the Southern Sea.

It was the young wisewoman who finally decided the issue.

"Remember," she said. "Only the Dark Priests know the exact location of the exit portal. Without their knowledge, we might well blunder around the furthermost reaches of the Water Realm for the remainder of our lives without finding our way home. We must have faith enough to trust the Guardians'and undertake this mission. We have no choice although I still share some of your fears. My inner eye has informed me that both Councillor Hemm and his envoy have told us the plain truth, yet my intuition has also warned me that Hemm is holding back some very important details, whose nature I cannot fathom. We must therefore remain forever on our guard as we journey into the lands of the Hix!"

Darryl pressed his finger upon a coloured panel knowing it would summon Paris to their quarters.

"Go to your master," he told the envoy. "Inform him that we shall depart for the wilderness of the Hix, at our earliest opportunity!"

✢

The following ten cycles were extremely busy ones for the travellers, for it was essential to make the most of the Water Realm's dry season and depart from Ptah as quickly as possible.

The first thing that Councillor Hemm did at their next meeting, was to enquire about the degree of success the twins had achieved in communicating with each other, by mind-power alone. Hemm had been visibly disappointed to learn that only the short distance transmission of basic feelings had been successfully accomplished. Even so, the Councillor had immediately declared that even this limited amount of psychic contact might well prove to be useful in an emergency.

He then made an unexpected suggestion that Paris, his personal envoy, should accompany the expedition until it reached the edge of the wastelands. The presence of a senior overseer, he argued, might help to clear away any bureaucratic problems they might encounter when passing through areas containing human settlement. Furthermore, the overseer's telepathic ability to maintain mind-contact with the young wisewoman might prove to be vitally important, should the group ever become separated.

The three travellers were also instructed in the handling of the tough little transport narr that were used as common beasts of burden by the clansmen dwelling far to the east. The newcomers were given the necessary lessons at a small stable on the western edge of Ptah, where the proprietor used the animals to carry vegetables to the city markets in pouches that were strapped to the creatures' backs. Their first experience in handling the transport narr was no great pleasure for the newcomers, for the creatures were stubborn and bad tempered when handled by complete strangers. The three travellers were often frustrated in their attempts to strap the pouches to the animals' backs, yet Paris harnessed them with ease and he sometimes even kissed their ugly faces. When questioned, he readily admitted that he was originally born into one of the narrs-folk clans, on the far western plain, and that he was quite adept at handling the unruly beasts.

A week before the day scheduled for their departure, the three wanderers returned to the Bonny Barbara in the company of Paris, in order to collect their weapons and other items of equipment needed during the long journey lying ahead of them. Darryl was also keen to meet with Wilakin and discuss the complete refitting of the narrowboat, which the navigator would supervise during the boatmaster's absence.

"I will personally check every plank and nail," Wilakin stated. "When you return from the wastelands, you will find your boat ready to ride upon the waters as though she was brand new."

Whiteflower was completely distraught by the news of their imminent departure and she flung herself down at the boatmaster's feet.

"Master," she cried. "Do not leave me here in this city of strangers. Allow me to accompany you and remain in your service!"

Darryl lifted the girl to her feet and began to insisting upon her remaining with the boat, but Paris interrupted his speech and addressed the girl.

"Tell me, are you indeed a child of the Kev, the tribe that dwells just south of the great Thoa forests growing far to the east of here?"

Whiteflower wiped away her tears.

"Yes sir, you describe the home of my people, who hunt the wild narr and hold their land against all enemies."

The envoy turned to the boatmaster and whispered quietly in his ear.

"Under normally circumstances I would advise you against taking yet another woman on so difficult a journey, but we are likely to pass through the territory of the Kev and a native-born guide would not come amiss."

Darryl paused for a moment and then inclined his head in agreement.

"If you think it wise, Envoy, then I will allow the girl to do as she wishes." He smiled. "Anyway she would make Wilakin's life a misery if we left her here!"

Early on the following morning, the travellers were summoned to Hemm's place of work high in the great tower, where they were met by the Councillor and a group of senior overseers including Paris, the envoy. Hemm welcomed them warmly, then pressed a blue panel and a large section of the wall immediately turned opaque and a huge relief map of the eastern portion of the Water Realm instantly took its place.

The Councillor then picked up a long pointer and laid it upon the map's representation of a city, which they all recognized as being Holy Ptah.

"We are here," he explained. "We wish you to leave here and journey to the territory of the Hix by the quickest and safest route."

Hemm moved the pointer south, until it touched the mouth of a substantial waterway that joined the Life River a little way below the Holy City. The Councillor then let the pointer follow the path of the river, as it wound its way eastwards.

"This waterway is the Red Bank River!" Hemm said. "In normal times, this river is the swiftest route to the wastes of the Hix. A fast passage boat takes its passengers as far as the small town of Hiram, which lies upon the fringes of the great Thoa forest. A mere fourteen days of hard marching would then be needed to bring a traveller to the territory of the first of the Hixian tribes."

The Councillor shook his head sadly.

"The town of Hiram is now in ruins and the surrounding territory is so full of hostile bandits and desperate refugees from the Hix that it would now take a veritable army to ensure the safety of anyone who attempted to travel by that route. Alternatively, it would have been possible to leave the line of The Great Life River and strike through the great Thoa forest to the Hixian heartlands, but the area is now a battleground with the armies of humans and Hix embroiled in combat."

Once again the pointer ascended the line of the Red Bank River, until it stopped at a small riverside town approximately three quarters of the distance from Ptah to the ruins of Hiram.

"This town is called Yam," the Councillor explained. "From here, a little-used trading road wanders eastwards until it enters the territory of the Kev and some other nomadic tribes."

Hemm looked seriously at the three travellers.

"Our intelligence gatherers suggest that it would be best if you followed this route, one that avoids the most southerly of the Thoa forests enabling you to enter the Wastelands of the Hix from the south, where the borderlands are believed to be quiet and presently free from major conflict."

The Councillor swung his pointer towards a group of brown-robed overseers who stood behind Paris.

"Those men are the best intelligence gatherers in our service and they categorically state that only the difficult southern route is still open to travellers. Unfortunately, it will take at least six of your Earth months for you to travel by this alternative route and the seasons of the year will have completed their full cycle before you return to Ptah!"

The Councillor lowered his pointer and allowed his gaze to rest upon the three travellers. "The first part of your journey will present you with no great problems, for occasional passage boats still run upriver to Yam and you will be well protected during your voyage by a strong escort of mercenaries. Only you three, together with Paris and that woman of the Kev, will march south from Yam, for the intelligence gatherers believe that a larger group would stir up the fear and animosity of the tribesmen through whom you must pass. You must travel under the guise of merchants, and you will be provided with plenty of copper discs and trade goods to give credence in that role, but your ability to survive will often rest upon the sharpness of your wits as upon any prearranged plan."

Councillor Hemm paused.

"Your escort of mercenaries will take up quarters in the town of Yam and await your return. If you do not re-appear after the space of a full year, they will return to Ptah and inform us of your presumed death."

George laughed, "Much to the regret of all!" He said with more than a hint of sarcasm in his voice.

"Yes, it will be to the regret of all," Hemm replied seriously. "For it might well mark the final crumbling of civilization in our world!"

The Councillor pressed the blue panel on the wall and the huge map disappeared.

"There is much to do". He added. "So let us continue with our preparations without further delay!"

The travellers' remaining days in the Holy City of Ptah'were spent in a veritable blur of actively, as equipment was checked and double-checked by Darryl and his giant boat hand. In addition, their combat skills were honed to perfection by the very best masters-at-arms to be found in the ranks of the overseers' mercenaries, whilst Myra acquired an even greater breadth of occult knowledge from the powerful seers of the Ancient Lore.

Finally, on the morning of the twenty-second day after the wanderers first set eyes upon the shining walls of the Holy City, the five members of the expedition to the wastelands of the Hix, boarded a broad-hulled passage boat that was due to sail from the busy quayside of Ptah.

Shortly afterwards, the three travellers stood at the rail and watched the high towers of Holy Ptah disappearing astern and Myra openly expressed the two questions occupying their minds.

"I wonder what dangers await us, and will we live to see those high towers again?"

Chapter 9

Hetty remained perfectly still, with the point of the knife resting only a hair's breadth from her jugular vein.

"Push open the iron door with your foot, witch," her captor whispered in her ear. "Move easily, or I will release your lifeblood in an instant!"

Hetty did as she was bidden and the iron door swung open upon well-oiled hinges.

"Walk slowly inside," the woman said menacingly, "and continue walking until you reach the far wall of the room."

The wisewoman obeyed and the light of the lantern, which she still held, told her that she was in a large windowless room containing only a single item of furniture, a large bench-like couch of strange design.

"Stand your lantern upon the floor," the woman ordered. "Then turn slowly until your back is hard against the wall and hold your arms high above your head. Try to snatch at that witch's needle hiding in your dress and your body will be lifeless before it hits the floor."

Hetty had no choice but to obey her captor, and, moments later, she heard the metallic click of the iron manacles as they closed upon her wrists.

The wisewoman blinked as a gas-jet upon the wall flared into life and for the first time she was able to see the woman who held her captive.

The woman was quite young. Not more than eighteen years of age, Hetty estimated, as she watched the girl moving across the room to light up a second gas-jet that was situated on the opposite wall.

The girl was small in stature, but the tightly fitting red dress that she wore displayed her youthful figure to perfection. She was dark-haired and the newly lit gas-jet also revealed her light brown features and the hazelnut shading of her eyes, a combination suggesting that the girl was probably of Middle Eastern origin. Hetty carefully scrutinized the girl's appearance and she recalled Darryl's rather vague description of the young woman, who had terminated the conflict at Hells Corner.

'Yes,' she thought. 'This could be the very person that I need to assist me in clearing my son's name!'

Hetty was about to speak to the girl, when one of the gas-jets suddenly flared up and the additional light gave the wisewoman an uninterrupted view of the room's furnishings and a disturbing sight momentarily diverted the witch's attention away from the young woman.

The centre of the room was dominated by a large flat-topped couch, whose surface was entirely covered by a layer of black silk upholstery. Straps hung from each corner of the couch and the only possible use for those leather fastenings would have been to restrain some unfortunate human being in a helplessly prone position, whilst that person endured some unimaginable form of torment. Hetty also noticed a number of dark stains on the plush silk coverings that had all the appearance of being dried blood.

The wisewoman almost cried aloud as her eyes fell upon the glass-fronted display case occupying the wall-space closest to the couch. A number of whips were on open display and the collection included riding crops, cat-o-nine tails and even an example of the cruel stock-whips used by the cattle herders of Southern Africa. Hetty had also to control the sudden wave of panic as she caught sight of the sets of chains and manacles hanging from the far wall, for she knew them to be the exact duplicates of the devices holding her at the mercy of her youthful jailer.

"Oh, witch, I see that you have just noticed the master's toys," the girl said quietly. "Perhaps he will strap you to yonder couch and use his whips upon your body. Yes, you would not be the first witch to suffer such torment. My mother once told me that witches were often flogged for their sins in the village of my grandparents!"

Hetty did not answer the girl at once, for her mind was occupied by what she had seen in the past few moments. Her first step, she concluded, was to conquer fear and she immediately whispered a spell that rendered her calm and in full control of her powers of reasoning. Her vague suspicions were now verified in full and her newly won calm almost deserted her. Silas Oldshaw was indeed a dangerous sadist; the eating house in Manchester, the commercial hotels, The Cleopatra Music Hall and whorehouse. All of these establishments, together with this very mansion-house and its staff of misfits and ex-criminals, existed only to provide the industrialist with an endless supply of young female flesh, and the means of sating his perverted lusts behind a cloak of outward respectability. The man's sadistically motivated instincts undoubtedly explained his virtual obsession with bare-knuckle fighting, a sport that often turned the participants into mind-damaged cripples? Even so, the truth was almost beyond belief!

'But how did this young girl become ensnared in Oldshaw's vile schemes?' Hetty wondered. 'Perhaps she is herself a victim of the industrialist's whiles and could be persuaded to abandon his service and become her ally?'

"My child," Hetty began. "How did someone of your tender years become involved with a twisted villain like Oldshaw?"

The girl walked over to the wisewoman and placed the point of the dagger to her stomach before relieving her of the poisoned hat-pin lying hidden in her dress. She then flung the pin into a distant corner of the room and twice she struck Hetty across the face with the palm of her hand.

"Witch, witch," she spat, and her hitherto excellent English-speaking voice began faltering as a result of her rage. "You, who are steeped in evil, you dare to question me? I am born of good family and I knew that you were approaching, witch..."

The girl paused for a moment and regained her self control.

"I knew that you were coming, witch," she repeated, "but I protected myself and I used my grandmother's spells to stop you from far-sighting me, you spawn of darkness!"

Hetty shook her head in order to throw off the effects of the girl's blows and she formulated her next sentence with great care.

"Were all of the wisewomen, known to your mother and grandmother, always the servants of evil?" she asked. "Did none of them ever tend the sick or charm away the fog of black despair from those who were broken-hearted?"

The girl hesitated.

"Yes, my mother once told me that her own life was saved by such a healer, when she was but a little child, within her home village upon the Bulgarian plain. But how do I know that you were not sent here by some demon? Perhaps you intended to kill my father and myself with that witch's needle of yours?"

"Child," Hetty replied, as gently as possible. "If I were truly a servant of the devil, would I not be the devoted friend of Silas Oldshaw, rather than his bitterest enemy?"

The wisewoman read deep uncertainty in the girl's eyes and she decided to risk her immediate destruction, in a desperate attempt to convince the girl of her own sincerity.

"Tell me child, do you remember a day when a man called Stovepipe Arkwright and another person, perhaps your father, were dispatched by your master to ambush and injure a young gentleman, as he passed through a hamlet that people rightly call Hells Corner?"

The girl was visibly surprised and shaken by the wisewoman's statement and Hetty instinctively pressed her advantage.

"The young gentleman defended himself and killed Arkwright, but could easily have died by the hand of the other man, had you not intervened and led away this second assailant. The young man is my son and I thank you with all my heart for saving his life!"

The young woman shook her head in disbelief.

"How can you know of this?" she asked.

"My son told me everything, before he fled from the law," Hetty replied. "For he is now wanted for the murder of Stovepipe Arkwright and will certainly be hanged if he is taken!"

The wisewoman took a deep breath.

"It's my belief that Oldshaw is somehow forcing you both to carry out actions that you yourselves would never willingly contemplate. Let us talk with your father and perhaps we can find a way of releasing you from Oldshaw's clutches."

The girl hesitated and then slowly nodded.

"My father is sleeping, but I shall wake him and tell him everything that you have said, and then he can decide what is to be done with you!" She turned and left the room by a small side-door.

Hetty remained manacled to the wall with fear and apprehension probing at her mind, for she knew that her life now hung by a slender thread. Finally, after what seemed like an eternity, the side-door reopened and the girl returned, accompanied by a short but powerfully built man of about forty years of age. The man was shaven-headed and he possessed a bull neck that gave him the overall appearance of a fairground wrestler, yet his eyes sparkled with intelligence and the wisewoman's inner-eye could define no malevolence in the man. He stared at the wisewoman for a full minute, and then uttered a few short sentences to the girl in a language that Hetty completely failed to recognize. He then turned and quickly disappeared through the side-door.

The girl smiled and released the wisewoman from the manacles.

"My father believes you speak the truth and he will listen to your suggestions in the comfort of our quarters. Not in this chamber of Shaitan!"

The wisewoman was conducted to an adjoining room that was small and simply furnished. A table, a few chairs and a pair of feather mattresses occupied two corners of the room, and this was obviously where both father and daughter lived and slept.

Hetty was offered a chair and provided with a beaker of strong wine to help her to recover from her recent ordeal.

"My name is Amina," said the girl, "and my father wishes to be known simply as Mechmet. He has no knowledge of English so I will translate. Now, witch, we will discuss everything that is of mutual concern to us."

$$\mathcal{Y}$$

Hetty was tired to the bone, for the task of washing up the dishes from the staff's midday meal only served to increase her bodily fatigue.

The discussion with Amina and her father, during the previous night, had been long and difficult and she had been unable to gain a single hour's rest before beginning her daily chores in the kitchen. Even so, she had gained the satisfaction of knowing that her scheme to clear her son's name had taken a considerable leap forward.

The father and daughter, she had learned, were political refugees from somewhere inside the boundaries of the Ottoman Empire and had been discovered and befriended by Silas Oldshaw, whilst he was engaged upon a business trip to Lower-Germany.

The pair had apparently been living under the threat of assassination and the industrialist had offered them a free passage and safe accommodation at his property near Stalybridge, in exchange for what Oldshaw had described as, 'discrete caretaking duties.' However, much to their horror, the fugitives had found themselves looking after their master's private torture chamber and ministering to the hurts of the unfortunate prostitutes who were brought here, by coach, from Manchester, in order to satisfy Oldshaw's perverted lusts. The pair had strenuously denied personally hurting the girls and had declared that Travis the coachman and Crowther the sinister butler had willingly aided their master by playing the role of torturers assistants.

"To what extent are the women injured?" the wisewoman had asked. And she was told that all had suffered from the brutal application of the master's favourite whips, a practice leaving them covered in welts and shallow cuts. She had also learned that Oldshaw's victims eventually became shocked and exhausted from the effects of being strapped to the couch for up to two days at a time and from the frequent sexual assaults delivered by the industrialist and his two sad acolytes.

On three separate occasions, the girls had been so badly used that Amina and her father had feared for their lives. Oldshaw had also become worried and had given orders for the women to be placed in his coach and taken to a discreet nursing home were their hurts could be healed by skilled hands.

The refugees had also questioned Hetty to some length. She freely admitted that she was a police spy and divulged many of the details of her mission within the walls of Westdyke Grange, but she revealed nothing of her experiences inside the Cleopatra Music Hall, or the means enabling her son to escape to the Water Realm. Instead, she claimed that he was hiding in the depths of the Pennine hills.

Finally, Amina had asked the two questions concerning them all.

"How can we help to clear your son's name? And how in the name of the Prophet, can my father and I leave the service of that monster Oldshaw?"

"You can remove the charge of murder from my son's shoulders, by telling the police everything that happened at

Hell's Corner upon that cursed afternoon when Arkwright met his death," Hetty had replied. "As for yourselves, if the police are willing you can both turn Queen's evidence and help to bring yonder villain to justice. You would not be punished for your involvement in that devil's schemes and you would certainly be allowed to go upon your way unmolested."

"Unmolested by your police, perhaps," Amina had retorted, "but we are both targets for the Ottoman Empire's assassins and our public appearance in court would surely tell them where to find us."

"Give me time to get in touch with my police contact," she had argued. "Perhaps they can give you protection from the killers hunting you."

"No," the girl had retorted instantly. "We would be as good as dead!"

Hetty had continued to argue for a full hour, until the couple eventually agreed to allow the wisewoman time to contact Inspector Smith and discover the level of anonymity and protection the police were prepared to extend to the two fugitives.

The wisewoman shook her head and almost dropped a soiled dinner plate, as she remembered the strain of the long discussion and the hurried return to her bedroom with dawn already breaking over the horizon.

Hetty finished the dishes and then pretended to be suffering from a headache; at Mrs O'Day's suggestion, she returned to her room to rest for an hour before involving herself in the labour of the afternoon.

Safe in the solitude of her bedroom she wrote a letter to Inspector Smith describing her recent discoveries and explaining the situation regarding Amina and her father. Furthermore, she suggested the policeman should meet her as soon as possible, in order to discuss what their future course of action should be in the light of the aforementioned events. She proposed that Inspector Smith should arrive by carriage, four days hence, and wait for her, an hour after midnight, in a ruined stack-yard lying about half a mile from Westdyke Grange. Hetty then sealed the letter and returned to her duties in the kitchen.

Later that afternoon, Hetty left the kitchen in order to fetch a selection of vegetables from the root store lying close to the conservatories, and there she found Piggins busily sorting out the piles of potatoes and carrots. She handed him the letter and urged him to post it in Stalybridge that very same evening. The gardener, however, was reluctant to make the journey and Hetty was forced to bribe the man with one of the half-sovereigns that she had so prudently sewn into her dress.

"Stir yourself!" she ordered, as she handed over the gold coin. "Make sure that you get this letter into the post as quickly as you can or the inspector will be far from pleased with you."

Hetty knew that she must find a safe way to leave the estate and return without being seen. The wisewoman therefore denied herself another full night's sleep and when the day's work was completed, instead of seeking her bed, she took a strong restorative draught and then tiptoed down to the basement of the house. Once there, she lowered herself into the old sewer and followed it in a westerly direction, leading her away from the house and towards the duct's original point of discharge, and she prayed that it would be out of sight of the main house.

She was fortunate, for the sewer widened slightly as she advanced, thus allowing her to progress swiftly and with relative ease. Her prayers were doubly answered for when she reached the mouth of the duct, she was relieved to discover that it was camouflaged by a clump of elderberry bushes lying in a small depression not fifty yards from the outer wall of the estate. The wisewoman then returned by the same route and sought out the well-earned comfort of her bed.

The following morning, Hetty began making the preparations for her meeting with the inspector. Crossing the formidable boundary wall should have presented the witch with an insurmountable problem. However, she had foreseen the difficulty and the answer was already at hand. Scrap timber, for lighting the cooking range in the kitchen, was always piled at the rear of the house and one of the oddments was an old but still serviceable ladder of about twelve feet in length that was light enough for the wisewoman to move without too much difficulty. Knowing this, Hetty had avoided breaking it up for firewood and the time had now arrived to make use of it for another purpose. On the night before her meeting with Inspector Smith, the wisewoman had crept out of the kitchen door of the Grange and hid the ladder in the clump of elderberry bushes near to the mouth of the sewer. Crossing the open grounds of the house with the ladder over her shoulder represented a considerable hazard for the wisewoman, for she could have been glimpsed from one of the upstairs windows, but, once again, a calculated risk paid off for the wisewoman and her nocturnal escapade remained undetected by the other occupants of the estate.

The following day was wet and overcast with frequent bands of rain sweeping over the Pennine uplands and the kitchen, where the two women worked, had to be illuminated by flaring gas-jets for the entire day. The depressive nature of the weather lowered Mrs O'Day's spirits and the cook hardly spoke a word. Hetty, by contrast, was satisfied by the timely arrival of the mist and rain, for she hoped that it would discourage the other occupants of the Grange from wandering abroad after dark and would hide her own nocturnal movements.

The damp and misty weather persisted into the evening, encouraging most of the household staff to seek their beds at an early hour and the house was quiet and in pitch darkness by eleven o'clock, when the wisewoman left her room and crept down into the basement.

The witch then began the long crawl through the disused sewer and made rather slower progress than on the previous occasion, for she was hampered by the need to drag an old bed-quilt behind her as she worked her way along the duct. It was therefore almost midnight by the time she reached the shelter of the elderberry thicket obscuring the mouth of the sewer.

Hetty paused and listened for a good five minutes, in order to make sure that she was quite alone in that portion of the grounds and she also allowed her inner eye to probe the pitch darkness. Satisfied that no other human being was nearby, she pulled the old ladder from its hiding place in the thicket and carried it to the base of the boundary wall. The wisewoman then whispered a strengthening spell before pushing the ladder upwards until its head was level with the double row of hooks crowning the parapet. Hetty made sure the ladder was securely grounded, and then slowly ascending the rungs, dragging the old quilt behind her as she climbed; once her knees were level with the parapet, she flung the quilt over the hooks, before swinging her body onto the crown of the wall. The witch then squatted perilously on the top of the wall for a few moments, until she had fully regained her breath, and then undertook the most difficult part of her scheme. She repeated the strengthening spell, and then heaved the ladder upwards, until it was balanced across the crown of the wall. Then, with a final effort, she lowered it down the external face of the boundary wall until its heel was firmly grounded on the other side. Hetty was then able to climb down to safety, after first freeing the protective quilt from the dangerous hooks.

The wisewoman rested for a moment before hiding the ladder and the quilt in a patch of brambles and then struck out across an open meadow, in the direction of the ruined stack-yard where she prayed that Inspector Smith would be awaiting her arrival.

Hetty need not have worried, for a light one-horse carriage stood motionless in the shadow of the stack-yard wall. The witch tapped gently upon the carriage door and was relieved when it swung open and the familiar voice of Inspector Smith bid her enter.

The policeman closed the door and helped her to remove her soaking wet shawl then poured her a stiff measure of whisky from a small flask. At that very moment Hetty became aware of another shadowy figure occupying the opposite corner seat of the coach.

"Who the devil have you brought with you, Inspector?" she said. "Is our business not private and confidential?"

"Easy lassie, finish your drink, for it will drive out the chill from your bones."

He paused. "The information in your last letter included matters that are well beyond normal police concerns. The two refugees, whom you stated were in Silas Oldshaw's employment, seemed like the kind of people whom our national security authorities would like to know about. I have long had the honour of being a close friend of a man who serves with British army intelligence and is sitting opposite you. For the sake of prudence, you may simply refer to him as Captain Wilson and the darkness of this coach will ensure that his appearance will remain a complete mystery to you. He will now explain everything that he wishes you to know."

Captain Wilson coughed in order to clear his throat.

"My dear lady, the inspector has informed me of your son's unfortunate predicament and has also mentioned some of the relevant details concerning your attempt to clear his name."

He coughed again.

"I feel that we can be of considerable service to you in this matter and you can rest assured that the warrant for your son's arrest will be quietly torn up, provided that you carry out a small service on behalf of your country."

Hetty was elated by the offer but was also naturally suspicious. "What kind of service might that be?" she asked.

"We simply wish you to convey an offer of asylum, from the British Government, to those two people in the east wing. If they agree, you must conduct them secretly out of that house and place them in our keeping. Say, not later than three nights hence!"

"What is the real identity of that man and woman?" the wisewoman asked. "You must tell me if you wish me to do as you say, for I will have no truck with evil doings, not even in the name of Queen and country."

Captain Wilson remained silent for a full minute and then answered. "Dear lady, your cooperation is essential for the furtherance of our plans. I will therefore tell you all that you wish to know, provided that you give me your solemn undertaking that you will not repeat my words to any other person."

Hetty immediately gave her assurance and the agent began to speak.

"The man whom you know as 'Mehemet' is certainly Mehemet Collona, or to give him his correct title, 'Mehemet Bey' who, until two years ago was the governor of an important frontier district in the Ottoman province of Bulgaria.

Mehemet Bey was born an Albanian but he also had much Italian blood in his veins; he entered the Turkish civil administration at an early age and won high office through sheer hard work and ability. Some five years ago, he was made the governor of an extremely troublesome district in Bulgaria, where both of his predecessors had suffered assassination. Mehemet Bey, however, managed to pacify the inhabitants through governmental efficiency and the absolute honesty of his administration. Unfortunately, his purging of corrupt officials made him a great many enemies and these men eventually brought about his ruin and disgrace. The Bey was a widower with a single surviving daughter, the girl Amina.

"The pair fled across half of Europe, hounded by Ottoman assassins, until they were apparently befriended by Silas Oldshaw, and the rest you know."

The wisewoman was still not completely satisfied.

"Why should Her Majesty's Government and army go to such inordinate lengths, simply to succour a stray Muslim and his daughter?"

"I am not empowered to divulge further information," the captain replied, "save that a man of Mehemet's experience and ability could tell us a great deal about the situation within the European provinces of the Turkish Empire and also give us important details about the men who currently hold power in many of the strategic areas of the Balkans. His enemies also know this. Therefore, you may inform the Bey, that Her Majesty's Government will provide the most secret of accommodation for himself and his daughter and their safety will be our most important consideration!"

The witch slowly bowed her head.

"I will do as you say, Captain Wilson, for I know instinctively that you hold the couple's well-being close to your heart. Nor would I willingly harm the interests of our kingdom. Three days hence, if the two parties are in agreement, I will lead them out through the old sewer and place them into your keeping."

Inspector Smith offered the wisewoman a further nip from his flask.

"You'll be glad to know, lassie, that we shall raid the Cleopatra on the very same night that yon two refugees are rescued. We shall close the place down, aye, and there'll be no grand reopening, for the magistrates will also revoke its license to trade. Also, that group of dishonest policemen from the local station, who allowed that whorehouse to exist, will be quietly dismissed from the force."

"The girls, what will happen to them?" Hetty asked.

"Och, those who might be wanted by the constabulary will be arrested and charged, but the rest will be allowed to go upon their way, for there's no sensible point in filling every cell in Manchester with the whores from the Cleopatra, when there's thousands more walkin' the streets."

The Inspector paused and seemed to lose a little of his self-assurance.

"The unfortunate part of this business, lassie, is that we shall have to leave that devil Oldshaw free and unpunished, for we need the Turkish authorities to believe that Mehemet and his daughter have disappeared for good and are probably dead. Aye, freedom from prosecution is the bribe that we shall offer to Silas and his two henchmen, in order to ensure that our villainous trio keep silent about the fugitives. A Justice of the Peace, who is also a local preacher, will put this offer to Oldshaw. He will also try to ensure that Silas gives up his interest in prize fighting and the mistreatment of young girls in yon house of his!"

"Don't take it amiss, lassie," he concluded, "remember, your son's good name and reputation are now safe, and in three days from now, you can return to your home and to your other responsibilities!"

Anger rose within the witch's breast, but her keen logic triumphed over her other emotions.

"Very well, Inspector," she said quietly. "It seems inevitable that we must allow yon devil to escape the consequences of his sins, but I will not hide my disappointment. The man is a sadistic tyrant and the occasional remonstrations of a local preacher will not prevent him from ill-using other poor women in the future."

"Well, that's about the long and short of the matter lassie," the inspector said.

"But now to business and as quickly as possible, for my watch says that it's close to two o'clock and that you must soon return to the house. The captain and myself will be waiting at the mouth of the sewer from midnight onwards, three nights hence.

"We will bring better ladders than the one that you have been forced to use and the captain will bring along three trusted agents to assist us if it becomes necessary. But first, lassie, you must discover if yon Turkish pair are willing to accept our offer of asylum. Then send Piggins to the White House hotel in Stalybridge, where I will take up residence and have him give me a single word: yes or no."

The wisewoman repeated the inspector's instructions and bade the two men goodnight, before beginning the return journey back to her accommodation in Westdyke Grange.

An hour later, she was resting in the temporary comfort of her bed.

"Matters are coming to a head," she muttered to herself, as the warm blankets enfolded her body, "Not before time either, for I cannot wait to depart from this house of evil!"

꤮

Hetty rose from her bed, on the morning after her nocturnal meeting with Captain Wilson and the inspector, only to find that several of the household staff were already hard at work. The master, she was informed by a flustered housemaid, had unexpectedly arrived back from Manchester, at daybreak, and every effort was being made to ensure his comfort. She quickly aroused Mrs O'Day and the two kitchen women were soon engaged in lighting the cast iron range and in preparing a selection of dishes, in case the master should require an early breakfast. As the day progressed, the tempo of work in both the kitchen and the main house increased considerably, as was always the case when the Industrialist was in residence.

Silas Oldshaw's unexpected arrival worried the wisewoman considerably as she undertook her chores, for she knew that tonight she must again penetrate the east wing and convey the captain's offer of asylum to the two fugitives. The task would have been difficult enough under normal circumstances, but she knew that she must now face the risk of accidentally running into the master, or one of his unsavoury minions, as she emerged from the sewer and entered the forbidden east wing.

Fortunately for the witch, a number of Oldshsaw's business colleagues arrived from Stalybridge in the late evening and the two women were ordered to leave refreshments in the drawing room, for a conference was in the offing and it was likely to last for most of the night.

A little after midnight, Hetty passed through the sewer and carefully entered the eastern wing of the house and successfully made contact with Mehemet Bey and his daughter. The witch then outlined Captain Wilson's offer of a safe asylum, which the pair accepted without a moment's hesitation. She also gave them the precise details of the escape route the three of them would take in approximately forty-eight hours time. Hetty then crept back through the sewer and sought out her bed in the main house.

The following day, the kitchen routine was the same as the one preceding it, but the household staff-members, who visited the kitchen, gradually lost their strained appearance once they became accustomed to having the master back in residence. After breakfast, Piggins arrived at the kitchen door with a basket of freshly cut cabbages and the wisewoman had no difficulty in giving him the message of acceptance that he was expected to deliver to Inspector Smith that same evening.

Darkness fell and Hetty enjoyed the luxury of a full and uninterrupted night's sleep.

But in her state of deep slumber, she completely failed to hear the clatter of Oldshaw's carriage, as it crossed the cobbled yard and drew up before the door of the east wing.

Hetty entered the kitchen on the morning of what she fervently hoped would be her final day at the Grange and she was in good spirits as she undertook her kitchen chores.

Mrs O'Day remarked to the wisewoman that she appeared to be happier than she had been for many a day and she asked her companion if she was expecting a birthday or some other type of celebration. The witch, however, merely laughed and continued with her work.

Evening came, and the witch returned to her room and began making the final preparations for her departure. All of her clothing save the thick dress that she wore, could safely be abandoned, for all of the items had been purchased from itinerant garment dealers and were quite untraceable. She took the added precaution of going through the pockets, in case anything had been overlooked that might give away her true identity. Her drugs, potions and spare cash she packed safely in an oilskin pouch that she secured inside the bodice of her dress, then, once the house was quiet, she slipped down into the basement and entered the sewer. The wisewoman worked her way along the duct until she reached the chamber lying beneath the floor of the east wing, and she was mightily surprised to find Amina awaiting her arrival.

The girl reached down and helped the wisewoman to climb out of the chamber; as she did so, the witch noticed that the girl was extremely upset and that tears were running down her face.

"Oh, wise one," she said between sobs. "I do not see how my father and I can flee with you. Last night, that vile creature, Bill Travis, arrived from Manchester with another poor girl in his coach. That trio of demons have injured her so terribly that I fear for her life."

"Gently lass, gently," the witch said in a soothing voice. "Now take your time and tell me if all three of them are still here in the east wing."

Amina shook her head.

"No, the girl lost her senses after the last beating. The master and Crowther departed for the main house, leaving only that hell-spawned coachman to let them know when she recovers her senses. Father is also within the torture chamber, helping the girl as best he may."

"We must remove that damned coachman!" the wisewoman declared.

"Father is a good wrestler," the girl interrupted. "Perhaps he can break the man's spine."

"No, no, lass," Hetty replied, drawing the oilskin pouch from the bodice of her dress. "Crude violence ain't always the best way of settling these matters."

The witch took a small vial of colourless liquid from the pouch and placed it in the palm of the girl's hand.

"Put this draught into a measure of beer or wine and give it to yon bastard Travis," she instructed. "But get hold of yourself, for he mustn't suspect that you're trying to poison him."

"This is poison?" Amina said, staring at the vial.

"No, lass," Hetty replied. "Simply a powerful sleeping draught that will knock yon creature out in two minutes and keep him dead to the world for a good twelve hours. Now lass, do your part, and for all our sakes. Stay calm!"

Amina returned a few minutes later with a fleeting smile upon her face.

"Witch, your potion worked well. Come and you will see him sleeping like one of the dead."

The wisewoman followed the girl into the industrialist's private torture chamber and the first thing that met her eyes was the senseless figure of the coachman, who was slumped in a chair like a discarded rag doll. She also noticed that Mehemet Bey was bending over the recumbent form of a young woman who was lying prone upon the padded couch. Hetty moved closer and she bit her lip as she realized the degree of torment that had been inflicted upon the women's body. She was lying face down upon the couch and the wisewoman could easily see the criss-cross pattern of cuts and welts that covered her back, buttocks and upper thighs.

The injured woman groaned and moved slightly as Mehemet released the straps securing her to the couch and Hetty cried out in horror as she caught sight of the woman's face, for she found herself looking into the pain-twisted features of Marsie, her friend from the Cleopatra Music Hall.

The wisewoman quickly examined her unfortunate friend and then asked Amina to fetch a mug of water. She took two vials of powder from her pouch and stirred them into the liquid. Supporting Marsie' with her arm, she encouraged her to drink the entire draught.

The Cockney girl opened her eyes and recognized her friend from the Cleopatra.

"Gawd sakes," she whispered. "They all said that I'd come to a bad end, looks like they might be right."

"You'll not finish your days here," the witch retorted. "You're young and strong and I'll get you to safety, even if it's the last thing that I do!"

Marsie' lapsed into unconsciousness and Hetty turned to address the girl who stood at her side.

"I was goin' to take you and your father out through the old sewer, even though it would have been a tight squeeze for such a big man; but we cannot pass with the girl encumbering us. I have given her a draught that will strengthen her and keep her sound asleep for a good two hours--more than long enough for your father to carry her across the grounds of the house and to the group of friends who are waiting to aid our escape. Providing that your father is strong enough to bear the load."

"Father could carry this woman from here to Istanbul without tiring," the girl replied, "but is it possible for us to pass through the grounds of this place without being seen?"

Hetty shook her head. "I don't know lass, but we must try. I will take the lead and you and your father must follow as quietly as you can."

The girl turned and quickly translated the wisewoman's instructions to Mehemet Bey, who cradled the injured girl effortlessly in his arms. The party then made their way to the front door of the east wing and began their escape from Westdyke Grange.

Fortune favoured them from the very beginning, for the door-key was still in the lock and they passed out into the yard without difficulty. However, a few lights still burned in the main house and their passage across the rear of the building was made even more hazardous by the fact that moonlight was illuminating the cobbled yard.

The witch paused at the corner of the east wing and listened intently. She also made use of her inner eye to probe ahead and detect any unwanted human presence.

Satisfied that all was clear, she signalled for the others to follow her. Carefully, they began crossing the dangerous rear yard, making as much use as possible of the long shadows cast by the towering bulk of the house. Finally, after many heart-stopping moments, they reached the comparative safety of the landscaped grounds without the slightest sign of being detected.

Ten minutes of careful movement brought them to the shelter of the boundary wall, where Inspector Smith was waiting, together with Captain Wilson and three tough-looking young men. Hetty quickly explained the reason for her change of plan to Inspector Smith and the other officer and requested the men to take Marsie' away from the Grange, along with the two fugitives. She begged the inspector to lodge her friend in a place of safety and send to Elfencot for Jenny, whom she knew would tend her injuries with great expertise. The policeman instantly agreed to the witch's requests, but he was utterly astonished when she declared her intention of returning to her domestic employment at the Grange. He began to protest, but Hetty instantly silenced him.

"You are not my master!" she hissed. "Now listen to my words. Hell on earth will shortly break out when Oldshaw returns to the east wing only to find out that his two overseas helpers have apparently absconded with his plaything for the night. If I also disappear, then I will be exposed as having served as their accomplice and Silas Oldshaw will then rightly blame me for everything that has occurred. He will undoubtedly use his great wealth and influence to discover my true identity and exact his revenge. A further consideration, Inspector, is that if I disappear tonight, then I will undoubtedly expose my 'brother' Piggins as yet another traitor in their midst and no further information would be gained from that quarter. My revised plan is to return undetected to my post, then depart openly when the time is right and give that bastard Oldshaw no opportunity of suspecting me of depriving him of his future nights of pleasure!"

"A dangerous course of action, lassie," the policeman said reluctantly. "But there's much in what you say. Yet I council you to take care--yonder man is as unpredictable as a snake and you have already taken enough risks to my mind!"

The wisewoman said no more; instead she briefly shook hands with the newly rescued fugitives and disappeared in the direction of the elderberry thicket hiding the mouth of the disused sewer, and concealing her return route to the perils of Westdyke Grange.

Hetty completed her long passage of the sewer and hauled herself up into the basement of the main house. She carefully cleared away any of the fragments of mortar that had fallen into the base of the duct and gently lowered the masonry grid back into its original position in the basement floor. The wisewoman had no doubt that Oldshaw would order a complete search of his property, once the disappearance of the fugitives had been noticed, and that the old sewer system would be re-discovered and carefully examined. She also scattered dust and grime over the floor of the basement cubicle in order to help disguise the position of the grid, and then she exited the cellar leaving as little disturbance as possible.

The wisewoman did not return to her bedroom immediately. Instead, she entered the kitchen and lit a candle before removing her soiled outer garments. She tore away all the buttons and clasps that were not inflammable and then opened the fire-door of the cooking range and thrust the discarded clothing onto the still-glowing coals. Hetty closed the door and opened the damper to its fullest extent, thus allowing the resulting draught of air to fan the coals into life and burn away the evidence of her subterranean journeys.

Hetty knew that a great deal still remained to be done before she could return to the comfort of her bedroom, and she wasted not a single moment. She placed the oilskin pouch, containing her collection of toxic potions, upon the kitchen floor and in close proximity to the cooking range. Afterwards, the wisewoman took a desert spoon from a utensils drawer and emptied the contents of the vial containing a red liquid into the bowl of the spoon. She added a little water and then boiled the mixture briskly by holding the spoon over the flame of a candle, until only a few grains of white powder remained. She poured the powder into a tiny glass vial and sealed the mouth of the container with a cork, then, with a smile, she held up the vial and viewed its contents in the light of the flickering candle.

"Silas Oldshaw!" she muttered to herself as though uttering a curse. "You will never be given the opportunity of sending your evil minions from the slums of Manchester to seek out the wisewoman of Elfencot. Nor will you use another woman as cruelly as you did my friend Marsie.' The revenge that I will shortly wreak upon you will be for her sake as much as my own!"

Hetty opened the door of a store cupboard and took out one of the many blocks of rough household soap used to scour the floor and the kitchen equipment. She took a sharp knife and dug out a hole in the soap-block that was just large enough to hold the vial. Hetty then inserted the vial and covered the aperture with a fragment of soap, which she smoothed down with her dampened thumb until the surface of the block had a uniform appearance. She completed the task of concealment by marking the block of soap with a scratch from her fingernail before hiding it beneath its fellows in the cupboard. Finally, the witch cast the oilskin pouch upon the hot coals within the range, followed by the contents of the remaining vials, and watched as the heat destroyed the dangerous liquids. She then took the empty vials, the buttons and clasps from her discarded clothing and her reserve of gold coins and dropped them down through the hole in the staff privy and into the mass of liquid sludge lying in the cess-pit beneath.

Afterwards, Hetty washed the grime of the night from her body, before returning to her room to await the inevitable hue and cry that would result when Silas Oldshaw eventually discovered the loss of his pet fugitives together with his latest victim.

ﾡ

Hetty was dozing when she heard the sound of voices drifting up from the yard that lay far below her bedroom window. It was still dark as she rose from her bed, but looking out of the window she was able to make out a number of shadowy figures, bearing lanterns, moving about in the yard and the surrounding grounds.

The wisewoman lit a candle and looking at the clock and she realized that it was almost time to begin her daily chores. She quickly dressed and was descending the stairs when she ran into one of the housemaids.

"Thank heavens you're up," the girl said breathlessly. "Mr Crowther says you're to brew tea and prepare sandwiches for the men searching the grounds and the surrounding countryside!"

"What on earth has happened?" Hetty asked, pretending to be completely ignorant.

"Why, last night, thieves broke into the master's private workshops in the east wing and tried to steal all his secrets," the girl gasped. "Some of his business rivals, I expect. The master thinks that some of them may still be in the vicinity and he's ordered the men of the household to conduct a close search. Hurry, for Crowther is demanding that refreshments be available for the men as soon as humanly possible."

The girl rushed away and Hetty entered the kitchen and immediately shook down the ashes and relit the cooking range. She placed a cauldron of water to boil on the hob, before hastening to wake Mrs O'Day.

The women set to work and prepared platters of cheese and cold meat sandwiches, which they served to the men as they began drifting into the staff dining room from first light onwards.

Crowther was amongst them and it was easy to observe the signs of the repressed anger distorting his features. He still clasped the walking stick, that he had so recently used to beat the shrubs growing abundantly in the grounds, and so tightly did he grip the head of the stick that his knuckles were completely white and bloodless. The butler uttered not a word as he drank his mug of tea; then he angrily banged the container down onto the dinner table and urged the men to resume their search.

The dining room soon emptied and the two women cleared away the used crockery and prepared a cauldron of stew, placing it upon the hob to simmer, for there was no telling at what hour the men would return for their midday break.

At exactly twelve noon, Hetty happened to glance out of the window of the kitchen and she noticed that Silas Oldshaw was standing in the middle of the yard with his hands on his hips. Before him stood Crowther with his normally immaculate house-suit covered in dirt and clay. Another member of the staff stood at his side, a wiry individual, who, it was whispered, had once been an accomplished housebreaker.

Between the men lay an old ladder that Hetty instantly recognized as the one she used to climb over the boundary wall little more than three nights ago; with it lay the old quilt that had protected her from the hooks.

Hetty's heart gave a lurch, for she realized that she had quite forgotten about the two items of equipment that she had left hidden in the elderberry thicket and close to the mouth of the disused sewer. The presence of the two articles lying at the industrialist's feet suggested conclusively that he now knew of the subterranean duct running beneath the Grange and he also knew that some trusted member of his household staff had assisted in the escape of the trio from the east wing.

"A foolish oversight," the wisewoman muttered, as she chided herself for her dangerous stupidity. "Now I must push along with my plan to encompass yon bastard's downfall, before I'm eventually discovered."

A little before one o'clock, Crowther entered the kitchen and informed the two women that every person employed at the Grange would be expected to attend a meeting in the staff dining room in exactly fifteen minutes time, when they would be addressed by Mr Oldshaw himself.

The butler departed and the pair removed their kitchen aprons and entered the dining room. Other members of the staff began arriving and the room was filled with visibly worried individuals by the time that Silas Oldshaw finally appeared.

The master was dressed in a light blue waistcoat and trousers and he carried a heavy walking stick with a polished brass handle. The industrialist's face was purple with rage and the witch had no need of her inner eye to realize that he was in a diabolically evil temper.

Oldshaw's gaze swept over the entire gathering. "You will all have heard by now," he began in a loud voice, "that my research quarters in the east wing were entered last night by my enemies, who appear to have departed scot-free. However, I have reason to believe that assistance was afforded them by at least one member of this gathering."

The industrialist paused and a buzz of whispered conversation ran through the company. He let a few more seconds pass and then brought his walking stick down with a crash upon the surface of the dining table.

"Remember this," he exploded. "I dragged most of you out of the gutter and I promise you, if this informer who hides in our midst is not quickly found, then I'll toss the lot of you back into the slime without a moment's hesitation!"

Oldshaw paused again and Hetty swiftly glanced across the room at Piggins, who had turned a deathly white, and she fervently prayed that the gardener would keep his nerve.

Once again, the walking stick descended upon the top of the table. "You may now eat," he hissed. "And this afternoon, your belongings, your own persons and the complete interior of this house will be searched in order to discover clues to the identity of our traitor."

He paused for the final time. "Search diligently, my servants, or you may all be enjoying your last meal at Westdyke Grange!"

Mrs O'Day wept uncontrollably as the two women served the midday meal to a subdued gathering in the dining room.

"Onto the streets again," the cook moaned. "Oh, a hundred curses upon the ungrateful creature who would betray so good a master."

Hetty attempted to console the woman as she waited for the search to begin and she fervently hoped that all the precautions she had taken during the previous night would be sufficient to conceal her true identity.

The search, when it began, proved to be as nit-picking as Silas Oldshaw had promised. Firstly, the entire staff was split into pairs by the butler. The couples were then detailed to undertake a stripped-down search of another pair of individuals drawn from a different portion of the house. Hetty and Mrs O'Day were confined to the kitchen and carefully searched by a pair of upper housemaids, whilst they themselves carried out a similar duty upon the persons of the two old female skivvies who normally tended the fire-grates and helped in the garden.

Once the personal searches were completed, the entire staff was then ordered to begin a search of the house and its contents. Mattresses were turned, carpets were lifted, and every nook and cranny of the house was energetically probed in case it should prove to be a hiding place for some incriminating object.

Oldshaw stalked about the house as the staff laboured and his unabated rage was plain for all to see. Once, he poked the wisewoman viciously with his walking stick, as she was kneeling upon a carpet in the mistresses' music room, in order to examine its upturned edges. He poked her again as she rose and ordered her to check the interior of the upright piano standing in the corner. It was whilst she was examining the inside of the instrument that fate intervened and gave her the ideal opportunity to destroy the industrialist and all of his evil works.

A clatter of hooves sounded from the yard. Moments later, a sweating horse-messenger was ushered into the music room. The man handed Oldshaw a brown envelope, which he tore open and Hetty watched with interest as the master quickly scanned the single page of writing that it contained. Oldshaw was visibly shaken by the information contained within the letter, for the heavy stick fell from his hand and he groaned aloud. Even so, the man rapidly regained his composure.

"Travis. Travis!" he roared at the top of his voice, and he continued to repeat the summons until the startled coachman arrived from the other side of the house.

"Get that bloody coach ready as quickly as possible," he ordered. "Take me down to Stalybridge railway station as fast as you can, for I must get to Manchester without delay. Crowther can deal with affairs here. Now I must go upstairs and say goodbye to my wife."

Hetty smiled to herself as Oldshaw rushed from the room, for she guessed the letter contained news of the expected police raid on the Cleopatra, and the man was probably hurrying to Manchester in order to ensure that several incriminating mouths remained firmly shut.

The witch knew that she must move quickly and she pretended that a sharp splinter from the inside of the piano had lodged beneath her fingernail. She declared her intention of visiting the kitchen and drawing the splinter with a pair of tweezers that were always kept ready for such a purpose. Mrs O'Day, who was engrossed in checking a window-sill, raised no objection and Hetty swiftly made her way to the kitchen.

The wisewoman found herself quite alone as she entered the kitchen and momentarily taken aback by the mess, for cooking utensils and items of furniture were strewn around the floor,for the searchers had done their work and moved elsewhere. The contents of the store cupboard had also been scattered around the floor, but the witch had no difficulty in finding the soap block containing the hidden vial, and she quickly extracted the tiny glass container and placed it in the pocket of her work-gown. She then made her way back to the main hallway where she was relieved to find only a young housemaid poking at the underside of the lower stair carpet with a short stick.

Hetty walked over to a hatstand in the vestibule and pretended to look for objects hidden behind the mirror. As she did so, she secretly slipped the vial from her pocket and carefully scattered the contents around the interior of the master's favourite topn hat, lying on the hatstand along with a pair of kid gloves. The witch then visited the outside privy and consigned the empty vial to the sludge filled cess-pit.

Hetty returned to the music room and rejoined Mrs O'Day in the fruitless search that was destined to continue until almost midnight.

A few minutes later, Silas Oldshaw descended the main stairs and crossed the hallway to the vestibule. He paused for only a moment to slam his favourite top hat upon his head, before beginning his hurried journey to Manchester.

Most of the grains of white powder that Hetty had poured into the top hat, evaporated harmlessly, due to heat from his scalp. But a few fatal grains found their way through the industrialist's blonde hair and allowed the terrible brain poison to enter the pores of his skin.

Oldshaw was only slightly confused when he entered a first-class carriage of a train bound for Manchester, but he was little more than a mindless dribbling vegetable by the time the engine drew into Piccadilly Station.

The once hard-headed industrialist was lodged in the local bedlam, where he was examined by numerous doctors. Five days later, he was removed to a private hospital specializing in the accommodation and care of the permanently insane. Thus did the wisewoman of Elfencot extract her revenge.

Hetty overslept on the following morning and small wonder, for like the rest of the staff, she had been worn out by the almost paranoid searching of the previous day.

She was soon joined in the kitchen by Mrs O'Day. Despite the late start, the two women were soon able to prepare a heavy breakfast for the household staff when they duly arrived for their first substantial meal since yesterday's lunch.

The butler did not order a resumption of the search, but detailed all members of the staff to begin clearing up the chaos caused by the fruitless rummaging of the previous day. Hetty and the cook therefore spent every spare moment stowing away scattered utensils and repacking spilt foodstuffs.

A little before midday, a messenger arrived in all haste from the industrialist's Manchester household, bearing an urgent letter for Mrs Oldshaw. He was shortly followed by the mistress's physician and a minister from her chapel in Stalybridge.

By midafternoon, a rumour was spreading throughout the household that some dreadful affliction had befallen the master, and the exact details of the matter were quickly provided by Mrs Oldshaw's personal maid, who had been at the bedside as the physician attempted to calm her distraught mistress.

It was an extremely worried group of servants who gathered in the staff dining room for their evening meal, for the fate of the ex-criminals who made up the vast majority of the household staff had always been closely bound to the fortunes of their master. Some had undoubtedly loved him and a number of the maids were weeping openly into their handkerchiefs, and few in that company had much of an appetite for the rich brown stew that was placed before them.

During the night, Crowther and Travis the coachman packed their belongings and disappeared under cover of darkness, and only one person witnessed the departure of the master's two evil accomplices. Hetty stood at her attic window and watched the two men as they crossed the moonlit yard. Before they melted into the night the wisewoman had extended her right arm in their direction and uttered the words of an ancient death-curse.

Perhaps it was the men's lifestyles rather than the witch's curse that brought about their demise only weeks after their departure.

In any event, Crowther was fatally stabbed by an irate pimp in a Cheapside brothel, after the ex-butler roughly handled one of the whores; whilst the coachman suffered a fractured skull after being kicked in the head by an overworked dray-horse in the city of Bristol.

The worst fears of the remaining servants proved to be quickly justified, for several of the mistress's close paternal relatives arrived by coach upon the following day.

The desperately sick woman was soon persuaded to accompany them to one of their country residences, where she could be lovingly tended by members of her own family; a family that would soon add the immense Oldshaw fortune to their own already considerable wealth.

A steward was immediately detailed to oversee the closure of Westdyke Grange. Exactly one week later, a sad and sorry group of unemployed servants, carrying their few possessions, turned their backs upon their former place of work and trudged through the falling rain in the direction of Stalybridge.

Hetty, bringing up the rear, turned upon her heel and took one last look at the dark outline of the Grange and she swore a solemn oath before rejoining her companions.

"Never, as long as I live, will I ever return to that accursed pile, where so many evil acts have been contrived and committed. I wish for nothing more than to leave this place and return to the peace of my home in Elfencot."

The first storms of early winter had begun sweeping over the bleak Pennine hills, soon after the wisewoman had returned to her cottage in Elfencot. The winter that followed proved to be extremely hard, with blizzards frequently sweeping down from the high crags and covering the valley with snow for weeks at a time; but Hetty sheltered comfortably in the warmth of her kitchen and only ventured abroad when she was called out to tend some sick person in the surrounding district.

Hetty's appearance had gradually returned to normal, for she regained her normally voluptuous figure and her artificially dyed hair slowly regained its natural red hue whilst growing longer with every passing week.

She was now quite alone, for Jenny Bowyer had returned to her witch-mother's cottage in the Forest of Dean once the wisewoman had been able to resume her healing duties at Elfencot. Even so, she was forced to admit that she sometimes missed the young girl's company, but the witch's spirits improved as winter slowly gave way to spring and the ewes began giving birth to their lambs as the new grass sprang up green upon the lower slopes of the Devil's Tor.

Hetty was planting the last row of potatoes in her garden when a familiar voice addressed her from the other side of the hedge.

"Good day to you, lassie. I trust that you be keeping in good health?"

The wisewoman kicked the soil over the last of the tubers and turned to catch sight of Inspector Smith's head peering over the top of the hawthorn barrier.

She smiled. "Inspector, why has it taken you so long to visit me? I expected you to come to my house before the turn of the year, at the very latest!"

"Aye, well, lassie," the policeman slowly replied. "I've had a muckle o' work to attend to. Firstly, I had to clear up all the loose ends of yon Oldshaw affair, then a gang of London housebreakers arrived in Manchester and fair ran me ragged until I put the lot behind bars."

The wisewoman leaned her spade against the wall of the cottage and brushed the soil from her apron.

"Spring's a busy time for us country folk, Inspector, for the land must be cultivated and crops planted, but tomorrow will do for the remainder of the work in my garden, so come into my cottage where we may talk in private."

Hetty made the inspector comfortable in her sitting room, then excused herself and repaired to the kitchen where she washed herself thoroughly with hot water taken from the kettle on the hob. Afterwards, she visited her bedroom and donned a simple floral patterned dress that she had embroidered to help pass away the long winter evenings.

The wisewoman returned to the kitchen and prepared a tray of light refreshments that she carried to her waiting guest in the sitting room.

"Eat heartily, Inspector," she invited as she filled two cups with strong tea. "For you must be famished after your long journey from Manchester."

"Aye it's a good journey, lassie, but I feel sure the information that I'm carrying will justify the effort. I will start with the least important. Yon Piggins is safely removed from the north of England, for one of my police associates found him a gardening job far away in the County of Cornwall. As for yon pair who ran the Cleopatra brothel, why lassie, I investigated them deeply and found them to be implicated in a crime of blackmail and they'll be guests of Her Majesty's Prisons for the next six years. Even so, lass, it would be for the best if you don't show your face in Manchester for quite a while."

"And my good friend Marsie?" the wisewoman enquired as she refilled the policeman's teacup.

Smith uttered one of his rare chuckles.

"Och yes, she fares well and is likely to do much better in the future. For she's married a young mining engineer, by proxy. Some old school friend of Captain Wilson, I believe, and the lassie is now bound for New Zealand and the chance of a far better life."

"May all the powers of the unknown aid her!" Hetty said, well-wishing the friend that she would never see again, and she leaned over to the inspector and gently brushed his wrist with the tips of her fingers.

"Now my good friend," she said in little more than a whisper. "I think the time has now arrived for you to complete your portion of the bargain that we struck in this very room. Please give me the exact location of the portal that will allow my children to escape from the Water Realm and return to the reality of their birth."

Hetty leaned a little closer, allowing the bodice of her dress of swing open slightly, thus presenting the policeman an excellent view of her ample bosom, but the red-bearded man simply gave another of his rare chuckles and lay back in his chair.

"Och lassie, you can keep your lovely melons to yourself, for I'll tell you all that I can without further encouragement." He paused. "Well lassie, you may recall that I once told you of my grandmother, Meg One Eye, who practiced the art of healing on the Island of Sky that lies close to the western coast of Scotland. I also told you that I learned much occult knowledge from that old woman. Aye, she taught me spells, incantations and the preparation of potions and the like. Yet grandmother was a seer of great power and knowledge and she was far too wise to entrust her deepest occult secrets to a feckless young child. But granny liked a drop of whisky to keep out the winter cold. One evening, when she was well drunk with the strong spirit, she held me in her arms and told me the location of the portal and some of its secrets."

He paused again and drew a deep breath.

"A little to the west of Sky, there lies a small island, which the fishermen never visit because they believe it to be unlucky. The island has no name, but it's easily recognized by a circle of tall standing-stones upon its northern promontory. At the base of the cliff, in the shadow of the standing-stones, there lies a cave containing the portal that you so desperately seek!"

"Perhaps this island is merely the product of an old women's imagination?" Hetty suggested, but Inspector Smith shook his head.

"I once passed close by yonder island on a trading smack and I viewed the stone circle with my own eyes. Aye and I also noticed a black smudge at the base of the cliff that must be the cave of which my grandmother spoke. Grandmother also told me in her drunkenness that a distant ancestor of hers once sailed to the island to open up the portal and rescue a powerful witch from The Land 'O' Muckle Water. Granny was drunk and her speech was difficult to understand, but I ken that she named the seer as Rose Littlewood. Perhaps yon woman was of the same blood as yourself?"

Hetty grasped the policeman and kissed him full on the mouth in order to show her gratitude.

"Yes indeed, Inspector!" she affirmed. "Rose Littlewood was born in this very cottage and she was the only person ever known to have visited the Water Realm and lived to return. Now I am quite certain that your island cave holds the portal that I so desperately seek."

Inspector Smith stood up and drew a small leather pouch from his pocket and handed it to the wisewoman.

"One last thing before I depart. Captain Wilson is grateful for your help in rescuing yon pair of refugees, and he's charged me with the delivery of one hundred gold sovereigns as payment for your services. You will need every penny of this when you fare north to retrieve your children, for the cost of such a venture will not be cheap!"

The inspector reached for his overcoat, but Hetty caught his arm.

"The day is almost done, my friend," she whispered softly, "and only a single hour of daylight remains. Leave the villains of Manchester to others and spend a night in the arms of a loving and grateful woman."

The policeman laughed.

"My duty awaits me in Manchester, but my old granny told me never to spurn a witch's offer of love. So lead me to your bed, lassie, and without another moment's delay."

Moonlight struck through the bedroom window as Hetty lay awake in the arms of her sleeping lover. She was content; for she now had the means of rescuing Darryl and Myra, her beloved children, from perpetual exile in the Water Realm. Years must elapse before this could be accomplished and now she must exercise patience and let the necessary occult energy build up within her.

"I must rest and allow my powers to grow ever stronger," she concluded. With that thought in mind, she slipped into a deep and dreamless sleep.

Chapter 10

M yra stood in the tall bows of the big passenger craft and watched with interest as the vessel approached the small river-port of Yam where their expedition would shortly disembark.

The young witch heaved a sigh of relief, for she was heartily glad the long river voyage was coming to an end, for well over a hundred darkenings had come and gone since the wisewoman and her companions had boarded the river craft at the Holy City of Ptah. During that time the travellers had never once been allowed to visit the shore and feel dust of dry land beneath their feet.

"I am charged with keeping you safe from all danger!" Overseer Camdar, the commander of their military escort, had repeated whenever the newcomers had requested a few hours of exercise ashore at one of the night-stations. "And this is what I intend to do, even if you must suffer confinement aboard this spirit-cursed scow!"

George had often raged at the officer for his inflexibility, but the man's caution was far from misplaced for the passenger craft suffered a savage attack on only its tenth night out from Ptah.

The vessel had been moored close to the bank for the night when a group of armed men suddenly assaulted the exhausted bow-haulers who were encamped upon the adjoining towpath. Simultaneously, a number of fast pirate boats darted out from the opposite shore and discharged a wave of fighting men onto the upper deck of the stationary vessel. The travellers were confined below in their quarters and George raged with frustration and fingered his long axe as the sounds of combat reached them from above. However, the noise of battle had quickly faded and Camdar had soon joined them with human blood still running down the blade of his drawn gill.

"The pirates are all dead," he had announced. "Sixteen of my troops have given their lives to protect you, so do not expect me to make their sacrifice worthless by allowing you to be killed during some stupid excursion ashore!"

The travellers had then resigned themselves to viewing the riverside scene from the upper deck of the slow-moving passenger craft.

The vessel often passed through long stretches of peaceful countryside, where farmers could be seen toiling amidst fertile acres and where fat meat narr grazed quietly in paddocks of soft crimson moss. Women had frequently come to the towpath and refreshed the sweating bow-haulers with jars of cool water and sold them hunks of fresh Thoa-bread, which they carried in deep baskets. Indeed, one could almost have believed that peace and security extended throughout the length and breadth of the Water Realm. Yet the craft had also passed through territory that had been recently devastated by bands of raiders, where farmsteads, villages and small towns lay burnt out and lifeless and where the bleached bones of their former inhabitants lay pitiably scattered down to the water's edge. The travellers had viewed many such scenes of ruination and they became ever more convinced that the threat of terminal chaos, as described by Councillor Hemm, was close to becoming a stark reality.

Myra knew that George and her brother had been bored almost to tears by their long confinement aboard ship and had spent many hours in practicing combat drills with Camdar's mercenaries in order to relieve the tedium of the voyage. The young wisewoman seldom joined them and had chosen to remain in her cabin in order to finish translating the grimoire of her witch-ancestor, Rose Littlewood.

One hot afternoon, the young witch heaved a deep sigh of relief and looked down upon the fully completed translation lying upon the desk before her and took stock of its contents. Most of the grimoire, she had long realized, was concerned with the spells, potions and magical incantations that were the stock-in-trade of every practicing witch. Many of the aforementioned spells and potions had their origins in Rose's home reality of Earth, but a great number had obviously been gleaned from the wise-men of the Temple of Dumteck or learned from the Priests of the Ancient Lore in Holy Ptah.

Myra already possessed much of the knowledge, which the grimoire contained, but she resolved to gain as much additional information as possible from the newly translated volume and commit it to memory for possible future use.

The young wisewoman had also carefully translated a small number of brief and often distorted passages, in which her ancestor had attempted to describe some of the many dangers and pleasures that she experienced during her long trek through the Water Realm. However, these passages were not arranged in any sort of regular chronological order and often made no sense at all to the young wisewoman. Myra even wondered if the strain of making so terrible a journey had not adversely affected her predecessor's powers of reason. Yet she knew the grimoire must inevitably contain information that would help to ensure their survival.

One tattered page had contained a short poem referring directly to the Hix and the young wisewoman had taken great care with its translation for it obviously contained crucial information.

If you seek the Lords of Hix
In Lands where others fear to tread
Then be you Fey or Earth-land's born
Or join the frightful Bloodless Dead

Myra had pondered long and hard upon these few lines of bad poetry, until she was quite sure that she fully understood the prophetic warning contained in the words of the short verse.

"Be you fey," she concluded, was undoubtedly a reference to herself and her twin brother, who carried the fey blood of the Littlewoods in their veins, and possibly George who was "Earth-land's Born." She was now convinced that only herself, Darryl and George would be able to cross into the wastelands of the Hix with any hope of survival. The girl Whiteflower and Paris the envoy would have to remain at the Hixian border and await their return.

Myra had smiled as she closed the grimoire, for she knew that many dangers lay ahead before they even reached the wastelands of the Hix, where their small party would be forced to divide, and she resolved to tell the others of her discoveries as soon as they docked at Yam. The bow-haulers were singing loudly as they pulled their floating charge towards its berth at the quayside of Yam and the men were undoubtedly elated by the prospect of receiving their hard-earned pay. But Myra had no wish to be entertained by their music; instead she turned and made her way back to her cabin in order to finish packing the last of her belongings. Soon, old Camdar would form up his mercenaries and escort the party ashore and she would again experience the welcoming feel of land beneath her feet.

"I greet you, Port of Yam," she said with a laugh. "Now let us see what range of pleasures you can offer to a jaded traveller such as myself."

※

In terms of pleasure, the riverside town of Yam offered little. Indeed, almost half of its buildings were abandoned or in disrepair and few of its remaining citizens were to be seen on the streets, as the newcomers marched through the settlement protected by the massed ranks of Camdar's troops.

About an Earth mile from the town and close to the river bank, there stood a deserted fort that was protected by thick walls of timber and sun-dried brick. A spring of fresh water bubbled up in one corner of the fort and old Camdar resolved to take up residence there with his mercenaries and use it as a base camp for the travellers' expedition to the land of the Hix.

The next few days were spent in repairing the defences of the fort and mounting the terrible fire-throwing engines of the overseers on top of its thick walls. The toiling mercenaries also cleaned out its deserted buildings and hauled a year's supply of food and equipment from the river boat lying moored alongside the quay.

In little more than five days, the fortress was fully supplied and garrisoned and capable of withstanding all but the heaviest of attacks.

Meanwhile, the five principal members of the expedition undertook the difficult task of familiarizing themselves with the dozen locally bred transport narr that were to serve as beasts of burden during their long overland journey. The animals proved to be quite as obstinate as the ones used for training in the City of Ptah and a good four days of strenuous effort was needed before the bad-tempered beasts were prepared to obey the orders of their new masters.

The travellers also undertook a short course of physical exercise, under the direction of the mercenaries' master-at -arms, for it was necessary to re-accustom their limbs to the rigors of hard land travel after their long sojourn aboard ship. Finally, on the evening of the seventh day, Darryl carefully inspected every item of their equipment, in person, and afterwards he declared the expedition to the land of the Hix was now ready and would leave the fort at first light on the following morning.

The red glow of the Water Realm dawn was beginning to stain the sky when the five travellers and their dozen heavily laden transport narr passed through the gates of the fort. The entire company of the overseer's mercenaries was drawn up in review order on both sides of the gate, and they roared out a loud cry of acclamation as the little expedition passed through their ranks.

Old Camdar raised his gill in salute.

"May the Gods go with you!" he cried. "And may they bring you back to us with your mission accomplished. So, for the time being, we wish you farewell!"

The little column advanced at a steady pace and the fort, together with its garrison of mercenaries was soon left well behind.

Whiteflower had travelled this old trade route in the past and she had immediately taken the lead in order to act as the expedition's guide. Darryl followed close behind, holding the bridles of the leading pair of transport narr, whilst Myra and Paris goaded on the main body of the fractious pack animals with long sharpened sticks. George brought up the rear with the shaft of his massive long handled axe resting upon his shoulder as he marched.

The first two or three miles of the journey was accomplished with relative ease, for the road was in a good state of preservation with its surface hard and unpitted. Then the condition of the route suddenly deteriorated and the line of the road was often almost completely obscured by scattered rocks and mounds of drifting red soil. The pace of the advance slowed as the laden animals experienced increasing problems in negotiating the difficult road-surface, whilst the progress of their masters was also rendered arduous by the added weight of the shoulder packs, which each of them carried in addition to their personal weapons.

By midmorning, the full heat of the five suns was cutting through the rolling crimson sky and beating mercilessly down upon man and animal alike and the pace of the march slowed down to a crawl. Eventually, after about four hours of constant effort, the expedition reached the shelter of a thicket of stunted Thoa-trees and Whiteflower declared that it was essential to rest the pack animals in the shade of the branches and wait for the fierce midday heat to abate.

The travellers threw off their heavy shoulder packs, and watered the transport narr before settling down to rest beneath the shelter of the largest Thoa-trees.

The boatmaster lay down alongside Whiteflower and offered her a drink of weak beer from his flask.

"Here lass!" he said. "Take the dust of the day from your throat and tell me how far we must travel before the going becomes easier for both the pack animals and ourselves."

Whiteflower took a sip of the bitter liquid and laughed.

"Not for many a day, my master. Years ago, when the road was frequently used by caravans to bringing goods to Yam and other parts of the Water Realm, my people, the Kev and the men of the other tribes, used to clear away the windblown debris and keep the road in good repair. The clans-people did this so that the iron ore we used to hew from the rocks, and the black pitch welling up from the ground in parts of our lands, could be exchanged for the medicines and fine clothing that came to us from elsewhere in the Water Realm. Those days are over--the road lies abandoned and only few hardy travellers pass along this route to barter bunches of medicinal herbs with the clans who dwell close to the old route. That is why I advised you to carry only herbs and medicines, as trade goods, on the backs of our transport narr; any other form of cargo would have been looked upon with suspicion by every tribesman crossing our path."

Darryl frowned. "So we have no choice but to continue our slow rate of progress until we sight the Hixian' borderlands?"

The blonde girl shook her head.

"Not necessarily, Master. The road loops and turns and we can save a great deal of travelling time if we leave the route at the neck of one of the loops, then strike across open country and rejoin the road with a great saving in both time and effort. The danger is that we may blunder into the territory of some family or clan who resent our intrusion. Such an unfortunate misadventure would doubtless cost us our lives.

"We could also save many darkenings of hard travel if we cross the Green Desert, but the aera is waterless and covered with poisonous plants and the bones of many men remain to mark out the route."

"The intelligence gatherers in Ptah said nothing of these dangers," the boatmaster said with a frown, but the girl simply laughed and playfully pinched the man's cheek.

"Old stuffy men, poring over maps and reports from inside their dusty chambers; they know nothing. I am Whiteflower of the Kev, who has wandered this hard land since I was able to walk and all of my knowledge lies at your service. Now, Master, I beg you to sleep for a while, for a hard afternoon's trek lies ahead of us and you will need all of your strength before the coming of night."

The full heat of the five suns had waned somewhat by midafternoon and the little expedition resumed its march along the old trade route. The road surface improved and the caravan advanced at a much faster rate than in the morning. Unfortunately they soon entered an area that had recently experienced a considerable amount of earth movement and the road was completely lost in a mad jumble of shattered rocks and uprooted Thoa trees. Whiteflower declared it was essential to cross this belt of devastation before nightfall, in order to draw water for the transport narr.

Soon the travellers were threading their way through a veritable maze of boulders and broken tree stumps and were often forced to heave the transport narr bodily over the obstacles barring their path. Yet their progress was pitifully slow, and despite their best efforts only a glimmer of sunlight remained when they finally reached open ground.

Whiteflower raced ahead, and standing upon a tall rock she surveyed the surrounding countryside in the hope of sighting the ruins of the old way-station where she expected to find water.

"This way," she called out, pointing into the gathering darkness. "I can see the way-station for it lies only a little way ahead of us, but we must hurry, for we shall never find it once the light is gone!"

The members of the expedition redoubled their efforts and soon they were driving their complaining charges through a broken gateway and into the shelter of the station's ruined wall. Despite their personal exhaustion they immediately set about tending the narr and watering the thirsty animals from a spring welling up in the middle of the station yard.

Whiteflower produced a bundle of dried tree branches and carried them into a dilapidated and roofless building standing in the middle of the enclosure. The girl quickly lit a fire in a still serviceable hearth and a stew made from dried narrs-flesh was soon simmering in an iron cooking pot.

George, axe in hand, took first watch at the door of the enclosure, whilst the remainder of his companions gathered around the fire and waited for the dried meat to soften in the boiling water.

Paris distributed a ration of Thoa bread to each of the travellers and turned to the young clans-woman sitting by his side.

"Our first day's march was exceedingly hard!" he observed. "Will the going always be like this?"

The girl laughed. "Finding it tough, are you? Oh, temple creature. Well never fear, man-of-books. During the next few days, we shall travel over a section of the road that remains in a reasonable state of repair. Also you will become accustomed to the hard toil of marching overland as the journey progresses, and you will find it less harrowing, once your muscles become hardened by the rigors of the trek."

"Are we likely to meet some of the clans-folk who live in these parts?" Myra asked as she retrieved a food bowl from her travelling pack.

Whiteflower shrugged. "I cannot say. Perhaps we shall meet a group of the hunters who stalk the wild narr, or possibly find a small isolated clan living in one of these ruined way-stations. Even so, I expect us to be received hospitably by the people who dwell close to the road, but robbers are to be found everywhere in these turbulent days, so we must be ever upon our guard and always keep our weapons close at hand."

The girl tasted a spoonful of the stew and declared it to be palatable.

"Eat and then sleep!" she ordered. "The night is short for tired travellers and we have much distance to cover on the coming morrow!"

The travellers made good progress during the next four days, for Whiteflower was proven correct when she declared that a well-preserved section of the road lay ahead of them. Even so, the members of the expedition had to treat the little transport narr with care and avoid driving them excessively hard, for their bird-jointed hips were liable to become inflamed through overuse if the creatures were made to trek for long periods. Paris, the Dark Priest's envoy, was often to be found rubbing the creature's hip-joints with soothing oil whenever the caravan stopped for a rest beneath some convenient clump of Thoa trees. The man seemed to have a strange empathy with the normally bad-tempered animals, who obeyed his every order without the slightest hesitation.

One evening, as the travellers rested around the cooking fire, the young wisewoman had paused to congratulate the overseer for his skill with the creatures. Paris replied that he spent much of his childhood as a narr-rider; that had been in the days before his telepathic gifts had been recognized by the Dark Priests, who immediately conscripted him into their service.

"Do you wish that you were still tending the breeding narr in the village of your people?" George had asked, but the man shook his head and explained that entering the service of the priests was an opportunity afforded to but few, and his selection had brought great honour to both his home village and to the clan that bred him.

"But I sometimes miss the stinking creatures," he admitted with a sigh. "For life in the service of the Priests of Ptah can become exceedingly dull and tedious and I often hanker for the open air of the plains and the warm beat of the five suns upon my face!"

"Would you ever be allowed to return to your native clan and live out the remainder of your life as a common herder?" George asked, as he passed a warm sleeping robe to the envoy.

"No," Paris replied, drawing the garment around his shoulders. "The servants of the Dark Priests may retire to the villages of their birth only if they achieve low rank during their careers, but those who attain high office must live out the remainder of their lives behind the walls of Holy Ptah. Such men possess too many of the priests' secrets to be allowed to dwell in freedom amongst ordinary men."

He laughed. "Had the present crisis not been so grave, then I would certainly not be here with you now!"

The envoy lay down and drew the night robe over his head.

"Sleep, man with two axes!" he said, with a hint of finality in his voice. "Sleep and let us replenish our strength for the morning's march!"

On the evening of the sixth day of their trek, the newcomers made their first contact with the tribes-folk dweling beyond the Red Bank River.

The column had been making good progress along a level and well-surfaced portion of the track and both men and animals were still in a fairly fresh condition when they came within sight of the supposedly abandoned way-station where they intended to spend the night.

The first indication that other people were currently occupying the station came when Whiteflower noticed a thin column of smoke rising from behind the walls of the ruined structure. She instantly halted the column whilst they were still out of darter range of the gate. The girl threw back her head and uttered a high-pitched piercing cry that echoed across the boulder-strewn plain before eventually dying away in the far distance. Whiteflower's identification call was immediately answered from within the way-station by a similar cry that differed slightly in cadence.

She gave a visible sigh of relief. "Yonder call was that of a family of wandering narr-hunters who are on friendly terms with my Kev kinsmen. We may now advance to the gateway and treat with them for a space at their campfire."

The caravan covered the remaining distance to the gate and was met by a short barrel-chested tribesman dressed in rough garments made from crudely prepared narrs-skin. Whiteflower raised her hand in salute and then took a bunch of dried herbs from her backpack and bowed to the man before placing the present in his outstretched hands.

"Birthing herbs," Myra whispered to her brother. "They help to ease the pain of childbirth and make the delivery of babies much easier. The plants only grow on the banks of the Life River and they must be a priceless gift to tribes-folk such as these."

The chief narr-hunter was obviously delighted with Whiteflower's gift, for he ordered the other members of his family to welcome the newcomers into the station and help them to unharness and tend their complaining beasts of burden, once they were safely within its walls.

The family of narr-hunters, it later transpired, numbered eighteen souls in all. Six were fully grown male hunters who were all armed with darters of an extremely unusual design, being heavy single-shot weapons, each capable of bringing down a fully grown narr with a solitary well-aimed dart. A dozen women and children, similarly clad in poorly cured skins, made up the remainder of the extended family of nomads. None of the adults was of an advanced age and Whiteflower quietly explained that narr-hunters who became too old to keep up with the remainder of the family, during their frequent forced marches, were left behind to die upon the open plain.

"Life is often extremely hard for these people," the young tribeswoman explained. "The wild narr frequently migrate over long distances and these hunters must often travel swiftly if they are to obtain a regular supply of food."

"Are all the inhabitants of the eastern plains forced to endure such a hard and uncertain life?" Darryl asked, as he watched a group of children scavenging for the few clumps of edible moss that clung to the station walls.

"Indeed not," the girl replied sharply. "Most of the clans are in permanent occupation of their own stretches of territory and are able to supplement their diet by rearing domestic narr and cultivating a few crops in their small gardens; but should a clan be forced from its land through conflict or lack of resources, then its members have no choice but to become wandering narr-hunters like these unfortunate folk."

Whiteflower pointed towards the carcass of a freshly killed narr that was being spit-roasted over the embers of an open fire glowing in the middle of the compound.

"It appears that hunting has been good today. This evening, we shall be the guests of these hospitable people and we shall eat our fill of the sweet roasted meat. Afterwards, you may sleep in safety and I will treat with the chief hunter in the hope of trading a few more bundles of dried herbs for a sack of preserved narrs-flesh in order to supplement our rations."

The girl shook her blonde hair. "Now I must bid you farewell for a short time and wash myself at the spring, for I would be clean when I dine with these people."

The newcomers ate in the company of that poor but hospitable family of nomads and slept soundly throughout the night with their hosts standing guard over them. At first light they rose, breakfasted upon the remains of the roasted narr and bade farewell to the hunters before resuming their journey eastwards. However, the caravan had progressed less than an Earth mile before Whiteflower abandoned her place at the head of the column and sought out the boatmaster, who was urging on a particularly bad-tempered transport narr.

"Master," she began, laying her hand upon Darryl's wrist. "I was unable to persuade the chief hunter to part with any of his precious reserve of dried flesh, for he and his family are facing a long and hard trek in order to keep up with their migrating prey. Even so, he gave me some information that may well save our lives. He warned me that a band of robbers are plundering and murdering the clans-folk who dwell close to this road, and they were last seen about three days march ahead of our present position. The chief believes them to be far too numerous and well armed for us to defeat, should they attack our expedition when we pass through their territory. Master, I know the road ahead of us turns and executes a considerable loop to the north. We are close to the base of that loop and therefore have the opportunity of striking across open country for three days, in order to traverse the base of the loop and regain the road where it turns again in an easterly direction. Also, crossing the base of the loop will save us a total of about ten days of hard travel."

"Do we have a choice, lass?" the boatmaster said with a worried look upon his face. "I've become used to trekking along this road and have no wish to push out into that waterless wasteland if it can be avoided."

Whiteflower shook her head.

"We could push on and hope the band of robbers has moved away from the road in search of a new territory to plunder, but I honestly beg you to refrain from taking such a dreadful risk. Master, the wastelands are a grave to the inexperienced traveller, but I was born in the midst to these very plains and you are reasonably safe whilst I am acting as your guide."

Darryl kicked a divot of the red moss high into the air and watched its flight until it fell back to the ground.

"Well, if we must strike through the wastelands, the sooner that we are about it the better. I'll inform the other members of the expedition of my intention to deviate from the route, the next time that we pause to rest the narr."

The caravan made good progress along the old trade route and reached the next way-station well before evening. And the water bubbling up from its spring proved to be every bit as sweet and pure as Whiteflower had promised and the entire company drank their fill of the liquid and washed the travel dust from their bodies before seeking the solace of sleep.

Paris, who was standing the final guard duty of the night, woke the travellers a good hour before dawn. Every member of the expedition rose and quickly breakfasted upon dried narrs-flesh. Afterwards, they filled every container they possessed with fresh water from the spring, for they knew they would need every drop of the precious liquid during the cross-country journey lying ahead of them.

At first light the caravan departed from the way-station and began its long trek across the open plain. The newcomers quickly discovered that movement across the plain was far from easy, for patches of wild red moss often grew well past ankle height and impeded the movement of both the men and their laden pack animals. The ground was also criss-crossed by dry gullies that filled with rainwater during the wet season, and by the numerous pot-holes and patches of sinking sand barring their path. Indeed, the newcomers would have made very little progress without the guidance of the blonde-haired tribeswoman.

The expedition advanced for miles into the open wasteland until they were engulfed by the seemingly endless sea of crimson moss, with both the newcomers and their animals being constantly subjected to the pitiless heat of the five suns lying upon them like a heavy weight.

The daylight hours seemed never-ending to the struggling travellers, whose only respite from the toil of the march was the few short stops that Whiteflower allowed enabling them to catch their breath and to water the tough little transport narr.

Darkness fell, but the members of the caravan groped their way forward for a further hour before Whiteflower declared herself to be satisfied with the first day's progress and called a halt for the night. The travellers released the pack animals from their burdens and tethered them close to clumps of edible moss where they could graze and regain their strength for the brutal toil of the following day. Meanwhile, the temperature fell and the newcomers swathed themselves in their warm sleeping garments and huddled around a small fire made from dead moss. A stew of dried narrs flesh simmered over the flames and Whiteflower bulked out the soup with a few handfuls of the same wild moss that was the staple diet of the transport narr. Unfortunately, the moss gave the food a bitter flavour that was hard upon the palates of the travellers and Whiteflower laughed as she watched her companions struggling to swallow their portions.

"Forget the taste and eat every morsel," The tribeswoman ordered. "The moss has a disgusting flavour, but is nutritious and contains a drug that will stop your joints from becoming inflamed by the toil of the journey. Sometimes, my clans-folk have survived for weeks at a time by simply chewing upon that bitter plant. Now, my friends, put your heads down and sleep whilst you may."

The second day of the trek across the wasteland largely resembled the first. Unfortunately, as nightfall approached, the weakest of the transport narr sank under the weight of its burden and neither an extra ration of water nor the encouragement of Paris, who was its drover, could persuade the creature to rise and resume the advance. Paris wished to continue with his attempt to succour the animal, but Whiteflower pushed him aside and cut the creature's throat with a single stroke of her knife.

"Save only the food and water that is part of its load," she ordered sternly. "Cut a good portion of flesh from its haunch to serve as our evening meal. Leave the herbs and medicines that it carries to rot with its carcass, for the weight would kill the remainder of our narr, if we should be so foolish as to burden them with an extra load. Now move swiftly, for very little daylight remains!"

The sky darkened, but the caravan struggled onwards for a further two hours before Whiteflower paused and ordered the travellers to make camp in the shelter of a narrow gully. Soon, they were all crouching around a small fire and roasting the haunch of meat cut from the unfortunate pack animal.

For the first time, Whiteflower appeared unsure of herself and said not a word as she carved the haunch of meat into individual portions. After they had eaten she stood up and addressed the company.

"Master and friends," she began. "I must confess to you that I have become unsure of our exact position, for many of the features in this barren landscape have been altered by falling rain and flash floods. I know the old trade route lies a good days march ahead of us, but the way-station, containing a well of clean water, may lie a mile of two in either direction when we reach the road. It is therefore essential for us to find the road well before tomorrow's darkening, and give ourselves ample time to discover the way-stations possition before night falls, for we must reach the water supply that we and our animals need to survive."

She paused and drew a deep breath.

"I suggest that we rest here for only a portion of the night and resume the march a good four hours before daylight. We must give most of our remaining water to the transport narr or they will not live to reach the road. This will allow us only a single mouthful before we march and another to keep us going when the heat becomes intolerable."

The girl burst into tears and flung herself at Darryl's feet.

"Master, I have failed you. I fear that I have been foolish in overstating my ability as a guide. I humbly beg your forgiveness."

The boatmaster opened his mouth to reply, but Myra quickly reached over and helped the girl to her feet.

"You have no reason to blame yourself," she said. "For my inner eye tells me that everything will be well, providing that we strive to do our best during the hard trek that surely lies ahead. I have no doubt that we shall be sleeping in comfort at yonder way-station tomorrow night!"

Darryl joined his twin sister and gently wiped away the blonde girl's tears.

"Aye, tomorrow we shall rest peaceably. Now let us waste no more time with useless doubts and recriminations, for the night advances and we must all rest whilst we may!"

彩

Whiteflower shook each of the travellers into full consciousness and urged them to prepare to resume the march as quickly as possible, although the night was pitch black and the Water Realm dawn was still several hours away. The members of the expedition groaned and massaged new life into their cramped muscles, before rising from their sleeping robes in order to help the tribeswoman to load the packs of trade goods onto the backs of the complaining transport narr. Once the loading was completed, the girl supplied each of the travellers with a single meagre mouthful of water before giving almost all of the remaining liquid to the laden pack animals. Once she was satisfied that the preparations for the day's march were completed, she took her customary place at the head of the caravan and gave the order to resume the trek.

The caravan advanced for hours through the bitterly cold night and each member of the expedition would have given a king's ransom for the privilege of returning to their warm sleeping robes, yet they gritted their teeth and carefully felt for each foothold upon the treacherous ground as they moved through the inky darkness. Indeed, some of the travellers would certainly have become separated from their fellows and lost in the night, had the tribeswoman not lit a torch and held it high in the air as a point of reference at the head of the column.

The travellers groped their way forward, across the numerous dried watercourses and the many other obstacles littering the darkened wasteland, until they began detecting a slight reddening in the sky and they knew the Water Realm dawn was close at hand. Rapidly, the light strengthened until they were able to make out the surrounding landscape and Whiteflower was able to discard the torch that she had carried ever since the beginning of the day's march.

The bitter chill of the night quickly departed from their bodies with the rising of the five suns and the members of the expedition stepped out with new vigour as their faces were caressed by a warm and pleasant breeze. Yet the strength of the sun's rays increased as the hours past and by midday, the heat was so intense that even the simple act of breathing became an energy-sapping chore.

George, the Herculean boat hand, was the first of the newcomers to reach the point of near exhaustion, for the weight of muscle making him a formidable adversary in battle, was simply an added burden during this blistering cross-country trek. The boat hand accidentally stubbed his foot on a hidden rock and tumbled to the ground. Despite his best efforts, he was quite unable to rise until Darryl grasped his hand and hauled him back onto his feet. Fortunately, the young giant still had a hidden reserve of strength and was able to resume the march without a pause.

Paris was the next member of the expedition to experience difficulty, for the envoy simply passed out and fell by the side of the transport narr that he was leading. Whiteflower halted the caravan and helped Myra to revive the exhausted man with a tiny draught of water; she then shared out the remaining liquid amongst the rest of the company.

Myra knew that the time had arrived for her to bring her witch skills into play, and after causing the men and animals to be drawn around her in a circle, she uttered the words of a powerful strengthening spell and issued a measure of a strong pain relieving drug to each of the travellers before allowing the march to continue.

The caravan struggled onwards across the trackless waste and for a while the heat seemed less oppressive and fresh energy began flowing through their tired bodies, but the elemental power of the five suns gradually ate into and finally dispersed the protective powers of the witch's spell and the members of the expedition were once again fully exposed to the full rigors of the march.

By the middle of the afternoon, both humans and animals were reaching the point of complete physical collapse and Whiteflower was desperately scanning the horizon for a glimpse of the old trade road that was their initial objective, Darryl forced his tired limbs to carry him to the head of the column where he joined the blonde-haired scout and together they peered into the far distance.

"Nothing, Master, nothing!" the girl said. "We should have reached the road by now. I cannot believe that we have not found it!"

The boatmaster placed his hand upon the tribeswoman's shoulder.

"Courage lass," he replied. "The pace of our march has slackened over the past hour and we may still have some way to go."

Once again he peered out across the expanse of crimson moss and his eyes lit upon a faint dark line, which seemed to run across the face of a low hill about a mile ahead of the advancing column. Darryl immediately drew the girl's attention to this unusual feature and she let out a single heartrending sob from her parched throat.

"It is the road, Master. May all of the unseen forces be praised, if we press on we shall reach the road and then we must find the way-station if we are to survive."

The other members of the expedition received the good news and advanced with renewed hope. Soon the ruined culverts and broken bridges lying along the line of the road could be clearly seen as the caravan drew closer and the sharp eyed boatmaster eventually spotted a rectangular building standing in the shadow of the low hill. He embraced his youthful guide and pointed towards the structure

"There's the way-station, lass--directly ahead of us. Soon we shall drink from the cool waters of the well lying within its walls. Lass: we must all pay homage to your skill as a navigator. You, alone, have ensured our survival by your intimate knowledge of this confounded wasteland."

The girl thanked Darryl for his kind words and tugged urgently at his sleeve

"Come, Master," she urged. "The way-station is further off than you think and we must reach it before the daylight fails. We must not be numbered amongst the multitude of travellers who have died of thirst within a stone's throw of water. Come master; let us continue the march with all possible speed!"

✻

The day was almost over and only a single hour of daylight remained when the caravan finally approached the entrance to the way-station. Unfortunately, access was denied by a door made from tough Thoa timber. Whiteflower paused and called for Darryl and his witch-sister to join her at the head of the column, then turned and addressed the twins.

"A few of these way-stations are still occupied by their original owners, who cling to their property in the hope that traders will once again return to the road. Such men live isolated lives and are understandably wary of strangers. I will therefore advance alone and bargain for shelter with the proprietor, should the place prove to be occupied."

"My inner eye tells me that yonder place is indeed occupied, aye and by exactly six souls!" Myra gasped from her parched throat. "And all of them are very nervous, so take the utmost care, or you may get a darter bolt in your body for your trouble."

The tribeswoman left her friends and slowly walked towards the door of the station with the palms of her hands extended to show that she was quite unarmed. As she walked, she noticed that a number of darters were pointing at her from weapon slits in the station walls, but she bit her lip and continued to move forward. The girl halted about thirty paces from the gate.

"I am Whiteflower a child of the Kev," she announced. "I am guide to a merchant from the river-lands who wishes to obtain protection and sustenance within the walls of your establishment. For this service he is willing to pay you handsomely with the very best of medicinal herbs."

She paused and a man's voice answered her from within the wall.

"I am the proprietor of this way-station and I am prepared to supply you with ample water and shelter, for the reasonable price of two narr-loads of herbs."

"You thieving son of a whore!"the girl shouted, despite the painful dryness in her throat. "Two bunches would be enough for what you offer, yet you have the nerve to ask for two whole narr-loads?"

"For you and your companions, two loads is cheap indeed my girl," the man replied. "I can see that your caravan has just emerged from the wastelands and you must therefore be in desperate straits for water. It would be a simple thing for me to deny you aid and wait for you all to die of thirst and take your entire cargo at no cost to myself!"

"You are wrong!" the girl shouted angrily. "We would rather kill our transport narr and burn our goods to ashes, than let you profit from our unjust deaths."

Whiteflower half turned and pointed towards Myra who was standing alongside her brother.

"Yonder woman is a witch who possesses great occult powers; before she dies, she swears that she will lay a terrible curse upon you and your family, one that will bring misfortune to your kin for many generations to come. Her inner sight reveals that you are six in number, and she declares that her spell will strike you all, if you are callous enough to leave us to die in this wasteland!"

There was a long pause and the man behind the wall spoke again, but this time in a much subdued voice.

"I am a trader who must do the best for his family in these troubled times. I will ask for only twenty bunches of herbs and a well-wish from your seer, in return for food, water and lodgings for seven darkenings within my way-station. If my terms are acceptable to you, then my sons will open the gate and my wife and daughters will tend to your every need."

Whiteflower agreed to the man's terms and the gate swung open. An old man wearing a turban appeared upon the threshold and called for them to enter. Darryl was still suspicious and wished to enter the station first, sword in hand, in case of treachery, but his twin sister forestalled him.

"Have no fear!" she said quietly. "My inner eye tells me that yonder man is sincere and will keep his word and his threat to watch us die of thirst was but a traders bargaining ploy."

The young witch stepped forward and taking Whiteflower by the hand, she led both the tribeswoman and the caravan into the safety of the way-station.

Darryl lay back and relaxed upon one of the comfortable bunks lining the walls of the way-station's simple but adequately appointed hostelry. As he rested, the boatmaster recalled the expedition's entry into the way-station that had taken place only a few short hours ago.

Ulf had greeted them inside the gate and he turned out to be a small elderly gentleman with a red beard. He wore a rather worn robe woven from narrs-wool and he sported a bright blue turban, which he later explained was the traditional garb of a way-station proprietor. Ulf had immediately demanded payment of his fee of twenty bunches of medicinal herbs, after introducing the newcomers to his plump and jovial wife and his grown up family comprising two sons and two daughters. The proprietor's family had supplied the thirsty travellers with cool sweet water freshly drawn from the station's well and allowed them to bath in a cistern filled to the brim with the life-giving liquid. The five newcomers had sighed with delight as it cooled their sun burnt skin and revitalized their dehydrated bodies. Afterwards, they had dined to repletion upon a vegetable stew that was flavoured with herbs and fragments of dried narrs-flesh.

Darryl had subsequently engaged the proprietor in conversation and it transpired that his caravan was the first to call at the station for over three years. The boatmaster had wondered how the man had survived in business with so little commercial traffic now using the route. When asked this question, the proprietor had sighed loudly and stated that he and his family had been forced to become farmers in order to survive. The spring inside the way-station, Ulf had explained, could be relied upon to produce copious supplies of fresh water and the proprietor, together with his sons and daughters had diverted much of the liquid and used it to irrigate an area of soil lying inside the walls of the establishment.

"Much of the land enclosed within these walls is highly fertile," the man had explained, and he declared that two crops a cycle could easily be obtained, though not without much hard labour on the part of himself and his family. Ulf's two sons, it also transpired, were competent hunters and occasionally brought the carcass of a wild narr back to the way-station to enliven their diet with a little fresh meat.

Ulf was unquestionably proud of his family's success at adapting themselves to the practice of husbandry. Yet the old station proprietor admitted that he sorely missed the days when the caravans from the river-lands called regularly at his establishment and traded their wares to the numerous clans-folk who once dwelt hereabouts.

"Where are those clans-folk now?" Darryl had asked, before retiring to the hostelry to rest in the comfort of his bunk.

"Dead or scattered to the winds!" Ulf had replied. "That would have been our fate also, but for our fertile garden, our stout boundary walls and deadly skill with our darters when bandits approach."

The boatmaster then ceased to question the old man and had retired to his bunk in the station's hostelry where he now lay and the last thing that he heard was the distant call of a wild narr as he slipped into a deep dreamless sleep.

♆

On their first full morning at the way-station, the travellers awoke and enjoyed a leisurely breakfast at a bench outside the door of the combined kitchen and dining room. The kitchen was a smoky establishment occupying a wing of the station proprietor's dwelling, and was itself conveniently situated close to the main gate at the western end of the complex.

Upon completion of the meal, Darryl wiped his mouth and declared his intention for the caravan to resume its march no later than the day after tomorrow. Paris however, said that he had earlier examined the transport narr, which were stabled close to the hostelry where the travellers had spent the night, and said that two of the animals were now quite lame. He also added that the remaining animals needed several darkenings rest before they would be fit to continue the trek or they would certainly die on the march. Darryl cursed when he heard the news, but he realized the inevitability of the situation and he accepted the need to remain as the guests of the station proprietor for a further week at the very least.

Most of the members of the expedition were happy at the prospect of a period of rest and recreation, but Myra remained uncharacteristically tense and in low spirits. She pushed away the remains of her breakfast and quietly informed the gathering that her witch's intuition had warned her that a period of extreme danger lay ahead of them and their very survival would soon be under threat.

"Are we to come under attack from some enemy from yonder wilderness?" the boatmaster asked. "Or must we expect treachery from our hosts?" But the young wisewoman simply shook her head and stated that any threat was likely to be of an elemental nature and that was all she knew.

The travellers spent the remainder of the day resting and tending their animals and Ulf proudly showed the newcomers his carefully tended gardens that provided his hard working family with a sufficiency of fresh vegetables. The garden also provided a valuable surplus that could be dried and bartered to passing narr-hunters, or simply held as a necessary reserve of food to support his family in hard times. Much hard labour was certainly required to make the gardens constantly fruitful, for the way-station had originally been constructed on the gentle lower slopes of the hill dominating the complex, and the gardens, together with the hostelry, the narr stables and a number of store buildings, lay just within the upper rear wall of the station.

A large manually powered pumping system had to be frequently operated by the members of Ulf's family, in order to lift the irrigation waters from the well in the centre of the way-station yard, to the gardens lying at a slightly higher elevation.

"Aye, we spend many hours each day pushing those confounded handles," the station proprietor said with a sigh, "but we must do it if we wish to continue living in this place." The five travellers viewed the blooming and productive gardens and could only agree.

The company had just finished taking breakfast, on the fourth morning of their stay at the way-station, when they felt the atmosphere about them grow suddenly cold and clammy. Whiteflower immediately stopped dead in her tracks and stared over the walls in the direction of the southern sky. Moments later, a mass of dark cloud began rolling in from the south and quickly obliterated all of the light radiating from the five suns. A sharp wind arose, whipping up the dust lying in the enclosure and bringing a bitterly cold chill to the bodies of the travellers.

Whiteflower gave an anguished cry.

"May all the unseen powers aid us? The Devil's rain is almost upon us. Quickly, run for the hostelry, where we sleep, for it possesses a strong roof and will give us the best protection that we can find."

"Hurry," she cried out, taking to her heels. "The rain from hell will soon strike and we had best not be in the open when it does!"

The little group had hardly reached the shelter of their accommodation building when the rains struck like a hammer blow; the newcomers to the Water Realm were aghast at the sheer weight of water falling from the inky black sky. Indeed, no rainfall experienced inside their native reality came within even a fraction of equalling the frightful deluge that cascaded down upon the roof of the dormitory. The thunder of the rain made normal speech quite impossible and Whiteflower drew her fellow travellers together into a tight group in order to converse with them.

"The Devil's rain comes out of the lands far to the east and strikes with very little warning," she cried. "Anyone who is unfortunate enough to be caught in the open will be beaten into the earth and drowned where they lie, whilst many others will be swept away by the incredible torrents of flood water that sweeps across the plains. Entire villages are often crushed by the force of the storm, but fortunately this way-station is built upon rising ground and we may yet survive the worst impact of the Devil's rain that is yet to arrive."

The tribeswoman pointed towards a number of two-tier bunks occupying the far wall of the hostelry.

"If the water enters this building, then we must take shelter on top of those bunks and hope that it does not rise far enough to drown us."

Myra placed her mouth close to Whiteflower's ear.

"Does the Devil's rain come to plague your people every cycle?" she asked.

The girl shook her head. "No, its visits to these western lands are extremely rare events and have never struck this particular portion of the wilderness since my grandfather's grandfather was a child. Indeed, if it came more frequently then human life could not be sustained here."

She pointed towards the packs filled with trade goods that had been borne by the transport narr and she gave orders for them to be piled for safety upon some of the highest bunks. She also suggested that everyone would be well advised to seek similar shelter for themselves.

The travellers did as they were bidden and cowered upon the top tiers of the bunks as the violence of the storm increased. Soon, water began flooding into the dormitory until it would have reached the thighs of anyone standing in the middle of the room and jets of water squirted down from the ceiling as the rain penetrated every minuscule chink in the stout stone flagged roof. Inevitably, the single small oil lamp illuminating the room was extinguished by a splash of water and the travellers were left stranded amidst the roaring darkness.

Time passed and the fugitives cowered in helpless terror upon their frail refuges as the increasingly violent rainstorm raged only inches above their heads. Even the normally fearless boat hand bit upon his lip until the blood ran down his chin.

Myra was the first of the company to succumb to the sheer horror of the situation, for the young witch's highly tuned senses were crushed by the elemental power of the storm. She began to scream uncontrollably and tried to bury herself beneath the sleeping cloths lying on top of the bunk, like some kind of panic-stricken animal. Paris, the telepathic envoy, was also shaken to the depths of his being by the terror radiating from the girl's mind. He found fresh courage and dragging himself across the narrow void between their bunks he clasped the helpless young wisewoman to his breast and held her tightly as the storm raged. The other members of the party were also cowed into near helplessness by the terrible product of nature beating and howling above their heads. The boatmaster began striking the side of his bunk repetitively with his fist, whilst tears ran down George's face for the first time since his early childhood.

The storm raged for what seemed like a veritable infinity to the frightened and cowering travellers. Then it ended as abruptly as it had begun.

Whiteflower slipped down from her refuge on top of a bunk and, after much effort, managed to light a lamp allowing the little group to view their immediate surroundings. The dormitory was flooded to a depth of about three feet and Darryl was submerged up to his knees as he swung himself down to the floor, but the waters were receding quickly and the flood water only reached up to the ankles of his comrades as they joined him at the door of the chamber.

The boatmaster opened the door of the hostelry and, one by one, they joined him in the open air.

The Devil's rain had disappeared as suddenly as it had arrived and the light of the five suns was again beating down from the crimson sky and illuminating a scene of utter devastation. The way-station was built upon the lower slopes of the hill and the flood-waters were fast receding from the walled enclosure where the five travellers stood. However, they were horrified to see that the torrential rains had done their worst, for the entire boundary wall of the station had subsided completely, and all that remained of the main gateway and the dwelling accommodation occupied by Ulf and his family were a few tangled piles of debris protruding from an expanse of mud and slime. And the travellers knew their hosts had not survived the visitation of the Devil's rain.

Darryl concentrated his mind upon their present situation and was relieved to note that the stable building was still intact and an immediate inspection proved that the resilient transport narr had survived and were in reasonably good condition. A storehouse standing close to the eastern wall had also escaped and a quick search of its interior revealed an abundance of dried provisions that had been stacked high enough to escape the worst of the floods.

"We shan't starve in a hurry," Darryl remarked, as he examined a basket of dried seeds. "But how can we possibly continue our march to the lands of the Hix? For the trade route must be quite impassable to land travel."

"The situation may not be as bad as it first seems, Master." Whiteflower said as she salvaged a sack of root vegetables from the water. "The Devil's rain is sometimes local in its effect, but capable of flooding the plains almost to the distant uplands of my own people. We must climb the hill behind us and view the extent of the flooding."

The travellers crossed over the heaps of rubble where the boundary wall had once stood and began clambering up the slopes of the hill. A task proving to be far from easy, for the ground was slippery with mud and the five companions were often forced to grasp hold of the clumps of the crimson moss that had survived the flood and haul themselves bodily upwards.

Darryl was the first of the climbers to reach the crest of the hill and he openly cursed the view meeting his eyes. Glistening flood-waters lay on every side and they stretched away as far as the distant horizon; only low hills and stretches of high ground stood clear of the waters and they resembled groups of isolated islands scattered across some endless primeval sea.

Suddenly, the boatmaster's mood changed and he burst out laughing and slapped his thigh with glee, whilst his companions were taken aback and stared at him as though he had taken leave of his senses.

"My friends," he shouted. "We need not endure the hardship of trekking under the heat of the five suns, or take the risk of being ambushed every time we pass a pile of rocks. No, the flood waters, brought by the Devil's rain, has given us a fresh route to the land of the Hix. We will salvage timbers and iron nails from the wreckage of yonder way-station and build ourselves a stout craft that will carry us to the hills of the Kev, which lie beyond the flooded plains. Aye and we will scour the ruins for strong Thoa-ropes and the cured hides of wild narr and make ourselves a sail that will carry us to our destination without effort; providing that we are granted fair winds and no more than our share of good luck!" The boatmaster leapt from the summit of the hill and splashed through the mud and slime in the direction of the devastated way-station.

"Come, my comrades!" he shouted. "Come with all haste and let us begin building the vessel that will carry us to the land of the Hix."

Chapter 11

Whiteflower uttered a cry of pleasure and relief as she came within sight of the village of her birth. and the four members of the expedition, upon hearing her exclamation, hurried forward and joined her at the head of the party. The village of the Kev appeared to be a substantial settlement protected by a high stockade spanning the mouth of the deep canyon in which the village lay. On both sides of the entrance to the canyon, and beyond, there reared a range of jagged hills, that, as Whiteflower had earlier explained, acted as a natural boundary between the sparsely populated western plains and the Wastelands of the Hix.

Darryl heaved a sigh of relief and he placed his hand upon the young tribeswoman's shoulder and gave it a gentle squeeze.

"You must be glad to set eyes upon your home after all your wanderings, aye and happy to see your friends and relatives again?"

The girl replied with a nod and the boatmaster smiled with satisfaction as he gazed upon the nearby village; for the journey from the flood destroyed way-station to the jagged hills of the Kev had tested both his ability to be a leader of men and also his skill in making the logical decisions required to ensure the expedition's survival.

Indeed, his authority had not always been accepted without question. For example, his decision to build the makeshift craft that had successfully borne them almost as far as the foothills of the Kev had been strongly contested by the knowledgeable

Whiteflower. The tribeswoman had insisted that the expedition's safest course of action was to bide their time and hope the floods would quickly recede, thus allowing them to resume their land journey without too much delay. Darryl, however, had overruled the girl and driven the party unmercifully for the space of fourteen days, until they succeeded in completing a spacious sailing raft, which they named Floodrider.

The boatmaster reflected upon the care he had taken whilst supervising the loading of the craft, for all the food that could be salvaged from the destroyed way-station had been loaded onto the raft, together with the trade goods normally carried upon the backs of the transport narr. Finally, he had taken the utmost care in accommodating the tough little animals in a specially constructed pen, which the travellers had built in the stern of the craft.

Twenty-one days after their arrival at the ill-starred way-station the expedition had cast off and sailed westwards, assisted by a strong and favourable breeze.

The voyage, the boatmaster recalled, had presented the travellers with few problems, for the direction and strength of the wind remained constant and Floodrider was never becalmed for a single day or even threatened by a dangerous gale.

The company of five had quickly fallen into a regular routine as the days passed by. They had kept the craft under full sail during the hours of daylight and with the onset of night; they moored themselves to one of the numerous temporary islands standing above the waters of the flooded plain. Once secure, they were able to make camp for the night and enjoyed almost perfect security. Darryl, however, had always ensured that an alert guard was set during the hours of darkness and that the craft was underway again as the first glimmer of light began illuminating the morning sky.

On two occasions, the craft had sailed past islets sheltering groups of human survivors, who begged pitiably to be taken aboard and conveyed to the dry land, but the travellers had hardened their hearts and given them no assistance, for the craft was already overloaded and there was no telling how long their supplies of food would have to last.

Shortage of food, however, had never proved to be a problem, for groups of wild narr were often found stranded upon patches of dry ground. They were easily killed with a few well-aimed darter bolts and they provided the travellers with a frequent supply of fresh meat.

Neither Darryl, nor any of the other members of the little expedition, were surprised when Myra and the envoy Paris had become lovers during the course of that raft's voyage over the flooded plain; for they had been quite obviously drawn to each other, ever since the Devil's rain, when they had clung desperately to one another for comfort. The pair now slept openly together and the boatmaster made no objection, for he knew quite well that the Littlewood wisewomen brooked no criticism from anyone over their choice of partners. Darryl however had learned much from his nearly fatal sexual encounter with the aristocratic woman on the Isle of Plenty and had been determined to remain celibate until the expedition reached the borderlands of the Hix, even though Whiteflower had openly expressed her willingness to satisfy all of his sexual desires. Even so, the boatmaster had refused her offer as gently as possible, for he knew that George's amorous needs could not be similarly met and he well understood the dangers that could arise from stirring up unbridled jealousy.

After twenty darkenings of comfortable voyaging, Floodrider had finally reached dry land with the jagged hills marking the home territory of the Kev tribesmen visible on the far horizon. Whiteflower's village, however, was only reached after an overland march of some ten days' duration, along the furthest extremity of the old trade route; and the travellers had thankfully sighted the high stockade protecting the main settlement of the Kev from attack and which the caravan was now rapidly approaching.

A deep ditch filled with sharp stakes fronted the stockade and the only route into the settlement appeared to be across a wooden bridge spanning the ditch and giving access to a heavy gate situated in the middle of the high timber stockade.

The caravan was almost a hundred paces from the gate when a flight of darter bolts hissed from loopholes in the stockade and thudded into the ground a few feet ahead of the leading transport narr. The warning was obvious and Whiteflower ordered the caravan to halt before advancing alone to the edge of the ditch.

"Iram, Chief of the Sword Clan of the Kev," she called in a loud voice. "Do you not recognize Whiteflower, your eldest daughter? I have returned from the river-lands with a cargo of the finest medicinal herbs to cure our people of their many ills. I also beg you to extend the friendship and hospitality of the Kev to the comrades who travel with me."

The door in the middle of the stockade was immediately thrown open and a powerfully built man with a shaven head strode over the bridge and embraced the young tribeswoman.

"Welcome home, my daughter," he said, with deep emotion in his voice. "The days have been many and long since you quit the land of the Kev, in search of adventure. You are welcome and I insist upon the honour of having your friends as my personal guests within my own house. The door to the village of the Kev is open and we beg you all to enter!"

The caravan moved forward across the bridge and passed under the doorway before entering the main village of the Kev tribesmen. The travellers immediately found themselves in the midst of a large settlement that appeared to be comprised of at least two hundred well-built stone cottages together with numerous workshops and storehouses. The entire village was constructed around a wide public square flagged with slabs of the same rough hewn local stone that appeared to serve the Kev as a general building material.

The village itself, the travellers quickly noticed, lay in the throat of a deep canyon and dark cliffs of smooth rock, towered above them for a good five hundred feet and completely dominated the entire floor of the valley in which the settlement lay.

Whiteflower laughed as the newcomers viewed the massive product of nature with some considerable awe.

"My friends, this canyon is the impregnable refuge of the Kev and the door through which you passed is the only possible point of entry. Any foe who attempts to cross this smooth and treacherous range of crags, in order to penetrate our stronghold is sure to fail and plunge to his death. Within this canyon we keep herds of meat narr and we also raise food crops in a great number of sheltered gardens." She laughed. "We even tend a sizeable grove of Thoa trees and are able to bake cakes made from our own Thoa-nut flour. We are in no danger of being starved into submission by a numerically superior enemy."

"Does this settlement ever come under attack from the Hix?" George asked, "for we must be very close to their borders."

Whiteflower shook her head.

"Long ago, they tried to storm this stronghold and failed with great loss, but they have recently begun to raid our outlying hamlets and most of our tribesmen have withdrawn into this stronghold, bringing with them their wives and families and all their possessions. Here they are safe!"

The caravan halted before the spacious house of the clan chief and Whiteflower's father ordered some of his followers to attend to the transport narr. He then invited the travellers into his house and begged his new guests to take refreshments and recover from the fatigue of their journey. The women of the household swiftly served the newcomers with roasted narrs-flesh and hunks of freshly baked bread. After they had eaten their fill, the little group was conducted to the chieftain's personal meeting hall where Iram regaled them with foaming tankards of Thoa-nut beer.

The boatmaster then quietly took the chieftain into his confidence and disclosed the fact that the true objective of the expedition was to make contact with the Hix and attempt to negotiate an end to the bitter warfare threatening to destroy all civilized life in the Water Realm. Iram was amazed and stated his firm opinion that any attempt to treat with the Hix must end in the certain death of the would-be negotiator. However, he offered the services of six of his most experienced warriors. These men, he stated, would guide the three chosen ambassadors through a deep pass in the hills of the Kev and deliver them to the borderlands of the terrible Hix. He also agreed to take Paris into his own household and protect him until the expedition returned in safety, which he though very unlikely to occur. In addition, Iram offered to exchange the caravan's cargo of herbs for a shipment of the rare metallic ores extracted from the surrounding hills; a commodity the transport narr would carry during the return trek to the riverlands, if the pretence of being simple merchant traders was to be maintained. Iram, however, restated his belief that the three white-skinned ambassadors would never return from the wastelands of the Hix and would not require a cargo of rare metals, or indeed any other substance.

Darryl expressed his wish that the expedition should set out for the lands of the Hix on the following day, but Iram shook his head vigorously and said that two of his most competent scouts were absent from the village and three days must elapse before all necessary preparations for their departure could be completed.

Furthermore, he suggested that the boatmaster should bridle his impatience and make the best of this unexpected period of rest and relaxation, for the route through the mountains of the Kev was both hard and dangerous.

The chief's residence was spacious and well appointed, and the travellers were provided with individual sleeping chambers, each one being furnished with a comfortable bed and plenty of soft sleeping fabrics. A sweat-house was also situated at the rear of the building and the travellers were able to indulge in the luxury of a steam bath before retiring for the night.

Darryl was the first of the chieftain's guests to seek the comfort of his bed and he was fast asleep whilst the other travellers were still sipping Thoa-nut beer and gossiping with their host and his family. However, the boatmaster's slumbers were eventually disturbed by a slight movement in the pitch darkness of his sleeping chamber. Within a split second, Darryl was wide awake and groping for the fighting knife that he always kept within easy reach of his right hand, but another strong hand grasped his wrist.

"Gently, Master," Whiteflower whispered. "Surely you would not slay the woman who is your sworn slave!"

The bed fabrics rustled and moments later, the young tribes-woman's naked body was pressing tightly against the boatmaster's muscular frame.

"In Heaven's name!" Darryl gasped. "Your father must be sleeping in a room only a short distance from here. What would he do if he found me in bed with his daughter, whilst I was a guest under his own roof?"

"He would probably laugh and compare us to a pair of rutting narr." The girl chuckled. "We woman of the Kev give ourselves freely to the men we desire, unless we have been bonded for life by the tribal mating ceremony."

Whiteflower giggled.

"Do you remember my younger sister, the tall girl with the long hair who helped to serve your food? She is now in your giant friend's bed and fulfilling his every desire."

The girl pressed her small but firm breasts against Darryl's chest and then allowed her fingertips to glide gently down his abdomen until they brushed against his rapidly engorging member. Despite his best intentions, sheer lust began dominating the boatmaster's mind.

"Lass, lass." He groaned, and he drew away slightly. "Do you wish to make love to me when you know, full well, that I may disappear into the wastelands of the Hix and never return?"

The girl said nothing, but answered the boatmaster's question by plunging her head beneath the bed fabrics in order to slip his fully erect member into her mouth. Darryl tried to protest, but he was only able to utter a single groan as Whiteflower's tongue began to gently lave his throbbing organ, and, with a sigh of pleasure, he allowed himself to sink into a veritable sea of sensual ecstasy, which he knew would last until the coming of the Water Realm dawn.

*

Darryl took a piece of rag from his pouch and wiped the sweat from his brow and he bitterly cursed the heat radiating from the five suns and beating mercilessly down upon him.

Two days ago, the three newcomers and their escort of half a dozen heavily armed Kev warriors had entered Skeleton Gorge, the almost impassable route leading through the jagged hills of the Kev and giving access to the wastelands of the non-human Hix.

The going was extremely hard, for nothing resembling a road or even a rough track existed to help the travellers negotiate the gorge. Indeed, the nine members of the expedition, together with their two laden transport narr, often experienced great difficulty in crossing the deep ravines and the loose scree slopes that frequently impeded their progress.

The travellers were often forced to rest in the shadow of the great boulders that littered the floor of the gorge and the boatmaster was given ample time to reflect upon the three pleasurable days he had so recently spent as a guest in Iram's hospitable household, and upon the exquisitely delightful nights when he had lain in the arms of Whiteflower, his friend and lover.

The boatmaster vividly recalled the scene, when, four mornings ago, the expedition had departed from the stockaded village of the Kev, and he remembered the tearful face of the young tribeswoman as she bade him a safe journey and a swift return. Myra and Paris had also parted company; however, neither of the telepaths showed any outward sign of emotion as the caravan drew away from the village. Any feelings of regret that might have passed between the couple were conveyed exclusively by the medium of their interlocking minds and were thus quite beyond the ken of the tribes-folk who had gathered to watch the expedition departing upon it perilous mission.

George, by contrast, had hardly spared his long-haired bed friend a passing glance as the march began, but Darryl had sorely missed Whiteflower's company as the expedition skirted the lower slopes of the Kev hills and the boatmaster felt strangely ill at ease, knowing that the ever dependable tribeswoman, who had guided them through so many perils, was no longer leading them at the head of the column. However, matters of sentiment had quickly begun to pale into insignificance, as the expedition entered Skeleton Gorge and its members were forced to concentrate wholly upon the task of traversing the fearfully dangerous terrain.

A little after midday, the column began crossing a particularly difficult and extensive scree slope and the marchers were forced to pick their way with extreme caution, due to the instability of the material underfoot. Darryl had also begun to worry about the effects of the fierce heat upon the two transport narr and the strain which this portion of the march must be putting upon the creatures fragile hip joints, for the laden pack animals were constantly slipping as they picked their way across the loose scree.

It was obvious that their escort of Kev warriors was becoming ever more nervous with every passing hour. However, by mid-afternoon, the column had succeeded in drawing clear of the murderous scree slope and entered a delightful tree-lined dell that was watered by a small spring that gushed from a cleft in the towering cliff face.

The wiry old tribesman, who was acting as the expedition's chief scout, ordered the other five members of the escort to take up defensive positions then joined the three travellers, who were watering the pair of transport narr and ministering to their numerous minor cuts and abrasions.

Myra placed her hand upon the swollen hip joint of one of the creatures.

"I don't think this poor animal can go any further," she said. "I can administer a pain-relieving draught and lay a strengthening spell upon the beast, but it will only delay its final collapse for a little while longer."

The chief scout nodded.

"Our purpose will be well enough served if yonder narr keeps going for a few hours longer, for beyond the next rise is The Mine of the Two Fools, a place where we can shelter for the night. There we can kill this crippled animal and use its body for food. The remaining beast will carry all that you need, until you finally quit this gorge and enter the Wastelands of the Hix, a journey that will take you a further two days of marching over slightly easier terrain."

The chief scout looked uneasy and rubbed his chin.

"Neither I nor any of my men are prepared to venture further than The Mine of the Two Fools. We will take you there and guard you throughout the coming hours of darkness. In the morning, we will begin the return march to our village, whilst you three white-skinned adventurers will doubtless continue to the land of the Hix in order to seek out your destiny."

He turned towards the young witch and bowed his head.

"We beg you, do not lay a curse upon us for not accompanying you to the borders of the Hixian' lands, for we have wives and children to consider and only madmen would be willing to guide you further!"

Myra smiled and touched the old man lightly upon the cheek.

"You are all brave men and have done your duty. Tomorrow, when you depart, you will go with a wisewoman's blessing to speed you on your way."

The witch eased the lame narr to its feet.

"The hours of daylight are passing swiftly," she said, "so let us depart without further delay!"

☙

Smoke from the remains of the cooking fire hung beneath the stony roof of The Mine of the Two Fools before finding its way out into the open air. The fumes presented no inconvenience to the travellers sitting with their backs to the wall of the mine and were hardly noticed by the two Kev warriors who stood guard at the entrance to the tunnel with their darters at the ready.

The Earth-born travellers and their escort were replete with food, for the injured narr had been killed and the choicest portions of its body had been roasted and eaten by the members of the expedition who were now resting within the mouth of the mine.

Darryl turned to the old scout who was seated nearby and who was occupied in picking his teeth with a shard of narr bone.

"Tell me, if you will, why this place is called The Mine of the Two Fools."

The scout laughed grimly.

"It's a tale of oft repeated greed!" he said. "Two friends once ventured deep into Skeleton Gorge in search of rare metals and they discovered a rich vein of copper in the midst of these very rocks where we now take our rest. The partners mined out as much of the ore as could be transported on the backs of the dozen or so strong narr, which the pair owned, and they bore it back to the home village of the Kev. In those days, the merchants from the river-lands still traded regularly with the folk who dwell in the Kev hills and the partners were able to exchange the ore for a chief's ransom in medicinal herbs and other imported goods; most men would have been satisfied with this stroke of good fortune and would never have ventured so close to Hix territory again during the remainder of their lives."

The old man paused and uttered a deep sigh.

"Yet greed is a terrible master and the two fools chanced their luck, once again. They and their transport narr were never seen again, and that is how this mine gained its name!"

The old scout moved uncomfortably.

"We are the first humans to visit this place for many a long cycle, so you can understand why my men wish to depart from here as soon as possible!"

Darryl thanked the old man for the information and then sought out the comfort of his sleeping robes.

He could not have slept long before he was awakened by an irresistible sense of dread, and he instinctively quit his makeshift bed and knelt beside his twin sister, who was resting only a few feet away. The girl was moaning and twisting violently in her sleeping robes and the young man had to shake her for fully half a minute before she regained consciousness and opened her eyes.

The young witch gathered her wits and struggled upright until she was in a sitting position.

"I had a terrible dream," she said. "I saw colours. Flashing lights and rippling bands of colour and shapes that I could not properly make out, let alone understand. This was no ordinary dream, for my inner eye tells me the visions originated somewhere outside my own being. Brother, I am frightened, for I believe the Hix are close and are attempting to penetrate my mind. I recall a verse that I translated from the grimoire of Rose Littlewood."

> When thy mind knows mortal fear
> Amidst the hills of sharpest stone
> Then know the monstrous Hix are near
> And wandering in your memory

Darryl held his sister tightly.

"Myra, lass," he whispered. "You must not give in to your fear, or we are all lost. Much is happening that is far beyond our understanding, but think on lass, only you can make contact with the Hix for I have not the powers to do so. If you lose your wits then we are surely lost!"

The wisewoman nodded in agreement and settled down again with her brother holding her hand for comfort.

By and by, the exhaustion brought on by the previous days march began to weigh upon them and soon the twins were slipping into a deep and satisfying sleep.

ꙮ

It was still dark when the old scout shook Darryl and his sister into wakefulness.

"Dawn will soon be upon us," he declared. "We of the Kev must prepare for our departure at once, for we shall begin the return march to our village as soon as there is light enough to see, whilst you three adventurers must continue alone to the land of the Hix in search of your destiny!"

The three Earth-born travellers packed their belongings and breakfasted upon grilled narr steaks. Soon, the first red streaks of the Water Realm dawn began to colour the sky and the six Kev scouts said their final goodbyes, then shouldered their packs, took up their weapons and disappeared through the entrance of the mine on the first leg of their homeward march. The remaining trio soon followed, but they struck out in the opposite direction towards the mouth of Skeleton Gorge and the lands of the Hix.

At first the going was fairly easy and they were even able to make use of the shade that was provided by the numerous stunted Thoa-trees dotting the bottom of the gorge. Unfortunately, a little before midday, the party ran into yet another of the many areas of difficult scree slope. This served to impede their progress and only about three hours of daylight remained by the time they reached the firm ground lying close to the mouth of the gorge.

Darryl was in the lead and he almost blundered into a small pool of water lying upon the edge of a thicket of Thoa trees.

He cast aside his pack and knelt down to taste the water but the giant boat hand restrained him.

"Hold on a moment," he advised. "We no longer have Whiteflower to tell us what is safe to be consumed and what is poisonous. But I still have the magical spoon that your mother gave me when we left our own reality and I can use it to test this water."

George took the witch's spoon from his pack and dipped it into the pool then watched carefully in case the talisman turned a warning black, but the spoon remained bright and silvery.

"Sweet as new milk!" the boat hand declared. "Now we can drink our fill with confidence!"

The little group rested for a while and Myra tended the remaining transport narr that was growing weaker and obviously approaching terminal collapse.

Darkness was only two hours away when the expedition resumed its march, but they had only covered a few hundred yards when the young wisewoman's vision was blanked out by a curtain of blood red mist and she fell screaming to the ground as a wave of totally alien thought penetrated her mind.

"You are soon to die — humans." It seemed to say with a hint of sadistic mirth. "We shall come soon and rend your bodies apart and use your flesh for our evening meal."

The wisewoman lay petrified with fright upon the hard bare rock and her whole body shook uncontrollably, but Darryl was at her side in a moment and the limited telepathic link existing between the boatmaster and his twin sister enabled him to instantly grasp the situation.

"The Hix are getting into your mind, lass," he said, as he cradled the girls head and shoulders in his powerful arms. "Don't give in to the terror that is flooding your mind, compose yourself and try to thrust a return message into the brain of the creature that's causing you so much grief!"

Myra shook her head and drawing upon her reserves of mental energy she flung out a message, which she prayed would be received and understood by her psychic tormentor.

"Who are you--Who threatens me with destruction? Identify yourself without further delay!"

The red mist cleared from the wisewoman's eyes and she sensed a welter of surprise and confusion emanating from the brain of her adversary and she had ample time to steel herself against the pulse of black hatred that she sensed would follow.

"You are a dark priest--We will take you alive and chew the flesh from your bones whilst you still live--We will--"

Myra easily blocked out the stream of incoming invective and gaining confidence in her mental powers. She framed a message and cast it forth with all her strength.

"Fool,How could I be a female and also a member of the dark priesthood? My name is Myra Littlewood and I am a seer who was born in the lands that lay beyond the great portal.
I come in peace with only two others to accompany me--My mission is to mediate an end to the warfare tearing your reality to shreds, as did my honoured ancestor, Rose Littlewood, who visited the lands of the Hix many years before I was born --Now tell me if I may advance and also be a guest in your lands?"

Many nerve-wracking moments passed before she received a reply, but now the mental communication was soft and bereft of murderous threats.

"Myra Littlewood--The Hixian Prime will be informed of your mission and you will received their decision within the space of two darkenings--Meanwhile, you will make camp

in your present location and wait. We will be close by and watching—To convince you of this we ask you to stand by the pool and view the hillside above you—I bid you farewell for now, Myra Littlewood."

The psychic voice died away and the wisewoman with her companions climbed to their feet and carefully examined the crag-side towering above them. At first they saw nothing. Then a huge bulky figure stepped out from behind a boulder lying about a quarter of a mile from where they stood. Another appeared and then more, until at least two hundred spear-carrying Hixian' warriors were to be seen standing on the face of the barren slope. For the space of a full minute, they stood quite motionless and then disappeared from sight in the space of a single heartbeat.

The boatmaster helped his mentally drained sister to regain the shelter of the thicket and brought her a beaker of cool water from the pool.

"Well lass," he remarked. "There's nothing more that we can do but bide here and wait to find out what yon creatures have in store for us!"

Chapter 12

The three travellers set up camp by the side of the pool and spent the following two days resting and ministering to their last remaining transport narr, which quickly recovered most of its original strength and vitality.

The newcomers, however, remained worried and ill at ease, for they understood perfectly well that their lives now hung in the balance and they could do little more than wait and see what fate held in store for them. Even so, George and the boatmaster took the precaution of keeping their personal weapons close at hand, for they were determined to sell their lives as dearly as possible, should the Hixian' leadership resolve to order their destruction.

Two darkenings passed and on the morning of the second day the travellers looked out and noticed a single unarmed Hixian' standing upon the hillside about two hundred paces from their camp. Myra immediately placed her left hand upon her forehead, for she felt a slight disturbance in her brain that she now identified as the precursor of a telepathic communication from a member of the Hix.

"Greetings—Seer from beyond the portal."

Said a silky smooth voice within her mind.

"My identifier is Z3*554. I have been instructed by the Hixian Prime—To allow you entry into our lands and convey you to The Heart of Emerald. There you will be given an opportunity to fully explain the purpose of your mission— The Prime, however, will not guarantee you a safe return!"

A break occurred in the Hixian's telepathic communication, but another slight disturbance in the young witch's brain heralded its immediate re-establishment.

"Turn loose your last surviving pack animal—You will have no further need of it—Collect all of your possessions —We will come for you presently!"

The telepathic communication immediately ceased and Myra quickly repeated the message to her two companions.

"We must do as the Hix command," the boatmaster said and he immediately stepped over to the tethered transport narr, then he cast loose its halter and sent it leaping down the gorge propelled by sharp slaps upon the rump.

The twins began packing their personal belongings into their shoulder packs together with their remaining food supplies, but George hesitated and looked worried.

"What did that bloody ogre mean when he said the prime would not guarantee our safe return?" he asked.

The wisewoman shook her head.

"It probably means that if the Hix have no liking for our words, they will simply kill us out of hand!"

The boat hand pondered for a moment upon the witch's words then forced a reluctant smile.

"Well, if I'm to finish up inside the belly of one of them gargoyles, then I hope the ugly bastard dies of the gripes as a result!"

Exactly one Earth hour later, a single Hix appeared from behind a pile of rocks.

The creature slowly advanced towards them and came to a halt only a few feet from where the little group stood and the Littlewood twins took the opportunity of viewing the newcomer at close quarters. The creature closely resembled the two Hixian' warriors whom they had killed in the City of the Dead. The very same dark pupil-less eyes stared out from the apparition's triangular shaped head and its massive shoulders were supported by a heavily muscled torso. Most of its body weight was carried by a pair of legs that could have been fashioned from the trunks of small Thoa-trees, and the creature's entire body was covered by the same hairless dark blue skin. The boatmaster noticed one striking difference: this Hixian' warrior possessed only one single multi-jointed arm and a small rudimentary stump was all that hung from the creature's right shoulder.

Once again, Myra experienced the same mental disturbance that preceded the last telepathic communication.

"It is—Z3*554—Who stands before you—I am able to speak a little of the tongue, which is mouth-spoken by most of the humans who dwell in the Water Realm—I am willing to communicate in this manner if it will bring better understanding to your two companions whose mind powers are small!"

Myra concentrated her mental energies and dispatched her reply.

*"Yes--Z3*554--Mouth-speak would serve us best!"*

The Hixan' opened its cavernous mouth and began speaking in a high-pitched squeaky voice that seemed almost laughably incongruous coming from the throat of such a monstrous apparition.

"I give you my greetings--You who cannot mind-speak. Your means of conveyance will arrive in a moment and you will reach Heart of Emerald after an overland journey that will take exactly two and twenty darkenings. We know that you possess only limited reserves of food and water but we shall supply all of your needs once your stocks are exhausted--I cannot guarantee that your journey will be pleasurable to you, but you will reach the Heart of Emerald unharmed!"

Z3*554 had hardly finished speaking when a dozen other Hixian's appeared from over the brow of the hill bearing three improvised litters. Each litter was borne by two of their number, whilst two more relief bearers trotted alongside each of the conveyances. The group halted alongside the three travellers, who were each invited to embark upon one of the litters and make themselves as comfortable as possible upon a layer of freshly picked moss covering the base of the crude conveyances. The white-skinned humans did as they were bidden and the strange column began advancing towards the northern mouth of Skeleton Gorge.

The multi-jointed arms of the bearers, together with their massively strong legs, enabled the litters to be carried forward at a steady rate. Even so, it proved to be a far from gentle ride for the occupants, who were often thrown violently around as their Hixian' porters negotiated the difficult terrain. Indeed, the newcomers were frequently forced to hang onto the sides of the litters to avoid being catapulted out of their conveyances and onto the hard rocky ground over which they travelled.

On one occasion, George's shoulder pack was flung out of the litter and was returned by one of the Hixian's, who unceremoniously thrust it back into the giant boat hand's arms, accompanied by a stream of irate squeals carrying the undoubted suggestion that he should take better care of his property.

Darkness was fast approaching by the time the column won clear of Skeleton Gorge and Z3*554 gave orders for the expedition to halt and make camp for the night upon what appeared to be the edge of the Hixian' wastelands. Nearby, grew a clump of low shrubs covered with silver-red leaves, which the Hixian's began to devour ravenously, thrusting both leaves and twigs into their cavernous mouths. The newcomers watched in amazement as this crude food source was masticated into a digestible pulp and swallowed by the massive creatures. Within minutes, the Hix has sated their huge appetites and were soon fast asleep, with the exception of a pair of sentries, who stood guard with their long spears held at the ready.

Darryl managed to force a laugh.

"Yon creatures would be the perfect draught animals for drawin' barges along the Lancashire canals," he observed, as he gathered an armful of twigs to fuel the travellers' cooking fire.

"Aye, and cost nothing to feed," the boat hand added. "Just turn 'em loose at the end of the day near some thicket and let 'em fend for themselves!"

The young witch was far from amused by the men's comments, as she sprinkled fragments of dried narrs-flesh into the stew that she was preparing.

"How dreadfully shallow you both are. You suppose these Hix to be no more than primitive animals, but you are quite wrong!"

She paused and began stirring the soup with a wooden spoon, as she did so she gave the two men a long look containing more than a hint of sadness.

"How much you non-telepaths miss with your limited faculties," she remarked. "You cannot hear the song our Hixian' bearers were singing as they carried us out of Skeleton Pass. Nor can you listen to the improvised poetry they recite to each other as they march. Our guide, Z3*554, is a telepath of considerable power and he is able to communicate with his kind across the vast wastelands occupied by these people. I know the letter 'Z' that prefixes his identifier is only given to telepaths of the highest order, this he told me by mind-speak."

"Aye sister," the boatmaster replied. "Small minded and weak is what we now are, George and me, and the weapons lying in our packs have been rendered as worthless as toys. For the success or failure of this expedition and our very lives, now depends upon your great intellect and formidable witch-powers. Yet situations can change and a time may well come when the cold steel, wielded by two simple boatmen, may once again prove to be our only salvation."

The wisewoman gently placed a hand upon her brother's shoulder.

"Forgive me, Darryl," she said. "I should not have spoken to you as I did. I have a deep love and a great regard for you both, but the new knowledge that is swamping my brain is hard to digest. I must try to inform you of everything that I learn by the practice of mind-speak for there must be no secrets between us; for dangerous hidden knowledge might well fester like a sore and harm our close relationship."

She gave the boiling stew one last stir and ladled the steaming brew into three wooden bowls.

"We must eat and then gain all the sleep we possibly can," she said, "for the Hix have informed me that we have many long miles to cover in the course of the coming morrow!"

※

The three travellers slept soundly upon the beds of soft moss cushioning their litters and were roused a little before first light by their monstrous guards, who simply nudged the sides of their impromptu beds, with their feet, until they were sure their human charges were fully awake. They breakfasted upon strips of dried narrs-flesh and draughts of cool water and had hardly completed their brief meal, when Myra received a telepathic message from Z3*554, telling them to board their litters for the day's march was about to begin.

The Hixian' bearers took up the litters and carefully picked their way across the final stretch of mountainous territory, but once the creatures felt the soft moss of the plain beneath their feet, they immediately fell into a shambling trot that consumed the miles as the expedition advanced into the vast and undulating Wastelands of the Hix.

The hours passed and the five suns reached their zenith in

the crimson sky, but the bearers hardly slackened their pace for a second, save for a few moments when they paused to allow a new shift of bearers to grasp the poles of the litters.

Dusk was beginning to fall and the jagged hills of the Kev were but a faint line upon the southern horizon when the Hix suddenly halted for the night close to a large thicket of shrubs and, once again, the creatures began dining upon a surfeit of silver-red leaves.

The travellers climbed out of their litters and began gratefully exercising their cramped limbs. A few minutes later Z3*554 joined them and informed them that the march would be resumed at first light on the following morning. He also led them to a tiny spring of sweet water that welled up from the ground in the densest part of the thicket and he advised them to fill their water containers to the brim, for no drinkable water was to be found during the next four days of hard marching.

The leader of their escort then departed, leaving the trio to prepare their evening meal and get as much rest as possible before the march was resumed with the coming of dawn.

The daily routine of the march was established during the first two days of the newcomers' journey into the wastelands of the Hix, a routine that was destined to be repeated for the next twenty darkenings as the trio were conveyed ever deeper into the heartlands of their monstrous hosts. Yet odd events did occur that startled and sometimes frightened them, but these isolated events often enabled them to learn a great deal about the Hix and their strange non-human lifestyle.

Perhaps the first thing the travellers noticed was the fact that individual members of their Hixian' escort often differed from one another in physical appearance. For instance, the pigmentation of their skin ranged from a light pastel blue to a dense blue-black. The travellers also noted that whilst all of the Hix were massively built some were undeniably stronger than others. A few of the Hix were a good head shorter than their fellows but possessed huge barrel chests, a characteristic suggesting that these individuals were capable of performing immense feats of physical strength. This was proven on one occasion when a large rock barred the passage of the litters and one of the barrel-chested spearmen thrust the obstruction aside as though it weighed practically nothing. However, an event occurred during the fourth day of their march that shocked the newcomers to the bone, but considerably aided their understanding of the creatures who were their hosts and protectors.

The column had been marching for about three hours and the five suns were high in the sky, when they came upon the carcass of a wild narr that had died upon the open plain and had now reached a high state of putrefaction. Upon sighting the dead animal, the bearers had instantly grounded the litters and flung themselves upon the carcass like a pack of hungry wolves; within the space of a single minute, the Hixians' succeeded in tearing apart and consuming every scrap of the rotting material. The young witch and her companions were horrified and disgusted by what they had witnessed and they mentioned this fact to Z3*554 when they next made camp for the night, and the leader's explanation proved to be extremely informative.

The Hix, it transpired, were natural vegetarians whose normal diet consisted of the silver-red leaves and soft twigs of the ubiquitous shrub that thrived in even the most inhospitable portions of the wastelands. However, their powerful grinding teeth and extremely efficient digestive systems enabled them to utilize the same mosses upon which the wild narr browsed and also enabled them to derive sustenance from the toughest forms of vegetation, should the need arise. Even so, the harsh environment of the wastelands had accustomed the Hix to consuming any form of nutrition coming within their reach, be it the putrefying body of a dead narr, or indeed any other creature. Nothing was ever allowed to go the waste. By contrast, a fresh Thoa-nut picked straight from the tree was a delicacy much esteemed by the Hix and isolated families had been known to travel great distances in order to sample the flesh of a single fruit.

Food soon became a personal concern for the travellers, for by the seventh day, their meagre food supplies were swiftly becoming exhausted. As promised, Z3*554 provided them with a variety of roots and plants, which he believed would supplement their remaining food rations and furnish his human charges with sufficient nutrient to sustain them until they reached The Heart of Emerald. Most of these offerings had a flavour rendering them far from appetizing, whilst some tasted positively revolting, but all of the new food sources proved to be harmless when tested with George's spoon and were acceptable additions to Myra's evening pot of broth.

During the seventeenth day of the march from Skeleton Gorge, the expedition reached an area where the familiar groundcover of shrubs and crimson moss gave way to a wide expanse of barren earth, where the only vegetation to be seen was a type of bright blue thorn bush growing in scattered profusion as far as the eye could see.

The column suddenly halted and Myra clasped her hand to her forehead as she felt Z3*554's thoughts entering her mind.

"Myra Littlewood—We are now close to the place that we Hix call 'The Land of Poison' because the slightest scratch from one of those blue thorn bushes inevitably results in a painful death—No Hix would willingly enter this place but the Hixian Prime wishes you to reach The Heart of the Emerald as soon as possible—We will carry you across this terrible place in order to save three days of travelling time, even though it may cost some of us our lives—Instruct your friends that your bearers will now tie you all to your litters —Do not be afraid—It is for your own safety—For if you were to be thrown out of your conveyances and into the thorn bushes, then it would surely mean your deaths!"

The young witch passed Z3*554's warning to her friends and

the Hixian' bearers bound each of the travellers to their litters with a surprising gentleness belying their grim appearance.

The bearers then took up their burdens and began crossing the deadly terrain.

Both the bearers and the spear carrying guards picked their way between the deadly bushes with extreme care, whilst ahead of them moved a pair of scouts who marked out the safest line of advance by scraping a series of lines in the soft dust with the butt ends of their spears.

Z3*554 remained close to the young witch's litter at all times and Myra had no difficulty in reading the mood of deep anxiety emanating from his brain.

Evening approached and the column made camp for the night in a small area that remained free of the lethal blue bushes, but the members of the Hixian' escort made no attempt to feed upon any of the sparse clumps of moss that managed to survive between the thorn bushes, they simply huddled together in a group and awaited the coming of dawn.

The march was resumed as soon as it was possible to see with reasonable clarity. By late afternoon, the blue shrubs had begun thinning out noticeably and the Hixian' bearers responded by increasing the speed of their advance.

Z3*554 leaned over the wisewoman's litter and informed her that the expedition would soon be clear of The Land of Poison, but only seconds later one of the outlying spear-carriers gave a dreadful shriek, then collapsed to the ground and lay writhing in agony. Another of the Hix moved forward to his assistance, but he screamed pitiably before also folding up in pain.

Myra clasped her hands to her head as she received the full blast of the telepathic command that Z3*554 flung out to the surviving Hixian' warriors.

"Hix—Ignore your fallen comerades—Who have wandered into an area strewn with the sharp seed pods of those accursed blue plants—They are now beyond assistance—

Follow the scouts and let us be gone from this place!"

The column moved forward leaving the bodies of the dead spear carriers behind them and within minutes they had successfully drawn clear of the deadly blue bushes. The expedition paused and the bearers took a well-earned rest, whilst Z3*554 visited each of the litters in turn and released the bonds securing their human occupants. The Hixian' leader moved to the head of the column and after a while he addressed the three travellers, using Myra as a conduit for his thoughts.

"In two darkenings we shall reach The Heart of Emerald and you will meet with—the Hixian Prime—The council of wise leaders who ensure the well-being of our race. Tonight, you will sleep upon ground that is free of those evil blue plants and you will also be given flesh from a freshly killed narr to cook over your fire, as is the custom of you humans —I will now continue tending to the needs of my warriors."

The wisewoman's empathy with Z3*554 began to fade, but Myra concentrated her mental powers and re-established contact with the Hixian' leader.

"Tell me more about the leadership that you call the Hixian Prime and the nature of this place you call The Heart of Emerald?"

The Hixian's reply immediately began forming itself in her mind.

"I am not empowered to answer your questions—But I will confide to you, that your party are the first humans to visit The Heart of Emerald and speak with the Prime since your ancestor—Rose Littlewood—Passed through The Land of Poison on a similar mission to your own—A great

many darkenings ago.—| council you to remain patient and
everything will soon be made claer to you."

The mental contact was broken off abruptly and Myra was
left standing beside the litter. "Remain patient," the wisewoman
muttered to herself after relaying the Hixian's message to her
companions. "A hard thing to do, when you know that your life
lies in the hands of strange beings of whom you know little."

Myra made a witch-sign with her hand and muttered a good
luck spell. She then quickly reboarded her litter as the column
prepared to resume its march.

⚘

For two further days the column moved as swiftly as possible
across the open wilderness. On the third day they breasted a
low ridge and found themselves looking down into a shallow
bowl-like depression that must have been a good five miles in
circumference.

The travellers dismounted from their litters and were
immediately rooted to the spot in amazement, at the sight of the
huge non-human structure lying in the base of the depression.
A mile wide sheet of some deep green glass-like material
obscured the bottom of the great cavity and on its fringes they
could easily make out a huge number of Hixian's, who moved
hither and thither like an army of gigantic ants.

The surface of the canopy shone in the light of the five suns
and the rippling beams of bright light were constantly caught
by the strange material and flung back towards the crimson
sky. Deep apertures pierced the rim of the great canopy and as
the members of the expedition advanced on foot, they could
see many groups of Hixian' workers entering the structure
with great bales of the silver-green food plant carried upon
their broad backs. Other workers accompanied them carrying
a diverse collection of commodities, whilst the toilers entering

the structure were matched by an equal number of workers who emerged carrying containers filled with excreta and other types of waste products.

The group halted before one of the large cave-like apertures and the travellers realized their bearers and the accompanying spearmen had all disappeared, leaving Z3*554 as their sole escort. The Hixian' envoy spoke directly to the group in his strange high-pitched squeaky voice.

"Before us lies a subterranean route leading into the very centre of this complex that we called The Heart of Emerald-- And safe within their underground council chamber meets the Hixian' Prime, the gathering of our wisest leaders, who make all of the decisions that directly affect the future of our race --- I will conduct you to the vicinity of their meeting place and you will be given ample time to rest and refresh yourselves before the Prime summons you to their presence."

Z3*554 led then through a gaping hole in the huge rim and down a lofty passageway that seemed to give access to the interior of the Hixian' complex.

The newcomers anxiously viewed their surrounding as they advanced and the first thing they noticed was that the walls of the passageway was slightly concave and appeared to be lined with a red material that seemed to have all the hardness of Portland cement. However, the passageway remained well lit, for the ceiling of the thoroughfare was formed by the underside of the great green canopy that enclosed the entire complex and the light of the five suns filtered through to illuminate their progress.

The passageway was a good twenty feet in width and easily allowed free movement for the numerous Hix who passed them in both directions. Many of the Hix were carrying red cylinders of about two feet in length, which they gently cradled in their arms. They often disappeared with their burdens into the side galleries branching off on either side of the main passageway.

Myra managed to steal a glance into one of the galleries and she was surprised to see long rows of the cylinders lying upon a thick bed of soft red moss.

Z3*554 apparently noticed the young witch's interest and he offered an explanation using mouth-speak, so the entire party could understand his words without difficultly.

"You are mystified by what you see --- Young Seer --- So allow me to enlighten you. Human creatures reproduce their kind by way of the womb --- But we the Hix are hatched from eggs that are laid by certain of our people. The red cylinders, that have caught your attention, are these very receptacles of life which are resting in their incubation chambers --- They will develop in the warmth, that percolates through the green canopy, for the space of two hundred darkenings --- And when each breaks open --- Another of our race will enter this world and see the light of the five suns for the first time."

The witch paused for a few moments in order to digest this surprising piece of information, and then she asked two further questions.

"Are all of your kind incubated beneath this single canopy, and how are your children raised to adulthood?" Their ponderous guide slowed down and conducted them into a short side-passage that was closed off by a door made from the strongest Thoa-wood.

He unbolted the door, flinging it wide and motioned them to enter and they gasped at the sight that met their eyes. The chamber was about one hundred paces in circumference and completely occupied by a seething mass of small hairless creatures that mewed pitiably as they chewed upon the flesh of the freshly husked Thoa-nuts strewn around the chamber in profusion. Only their heavy jaws and stout limbs enabled the newcomers to recognize them as the young of the Hixian' race.

"This will answer your questions. You are now standing inside one of the many rearing centres serving the reproductive needs of our various tribes. Even so, a few isolated Hixian' clans still reproduce their young by warming their eggs in the light of the five suns during daytime--And protecting both the eggs and the young from the cold by the heat of their own bodies during the hours of darkness."

"You are the first humans to view a Hixian' rearing chamber since Rose Littlewood visited this very complex, many cycles ago."

"How do they survive such conditions?" Myra enquired. "And what happens to the weak and sickly?"

"They die and their bodies become food for the remainder --- Only the strong and fit are welcomed as warriors in the fighting ranks of our clans --- And this is as it should be --- for only the strong can survive the hardships of life in the cruel wilderness that lies beyond the green canopy."

Z3*554 led them back to the main passageway and they plunged ever deeper into the heart of the strange complex. After about half an hour's steady progress, the passageway began to angle downwards and the green glow from the canopy suddenly disappeared. The travellers realized that the passageway had given way to a long tunnel that plunged ever downwards into the solid rock upon which the Hixian' breeding complex stood. A few lamps were suspended from the ceiling and the newcomers had to advance carefully to avoid tripping up in the semi-darkness.

The little group had progressed for about a mile when they found their way barred by an enormously heavy door that was constructed from huge blocks of Thoa-timber.

Z3*554 then turned and addressed all of the travellers in the common Water Realm tongue.

"Beyond this door lies the current quarters of the Hixian' Prime -- I can accompany you no further -- But I will remain here and await your return should the leadership see fit to spare your lives -- I council you to act with humility -- Yet hold nothing back from those who dwell beyond this point for they greatly respect straightforward honesty -- Do as I advise and you may stand some chance of accomplishing your mission!"

Their huge guide turned and faced the massive door and

Myra winced as she caught the backwash of the immensely powerful mental signal that Z3*554 projected through the timberwork. The door slowly opened and the three travellers stepped nervously over the threshold.

The chamber they entered was roomy and adequately lit by the many lamps hanging from its ceiling of rough-hewn rock. The walls were likewise unadorned, but the harshness of the bare stone was relieved the some degree by the many skilfully worked tapestries that hung at intervals around the subterranean chamber, an artistic touch that seemed somewhat at odds with the generally austere appearance of the rest of the complex.

Yet it was the six strange figures seated upon a row of stools at the far end of the chamber who immediately dominated the newcomers' attention.

The creatures were definitely members of the Hixian' race for their bodily appearance displayed all of the common characteristics of their species, but they were much smaller in stature than any of the Hix who had escorted the travellers to The Heart of Emerald and their heads appeared to be much larger in relation to the remainder of their bodies.

Two of the creatures were of an advanced age and their skin was wrinkled and hung in folds from their lean bodies, but one of their number was far younger in age and rising from his seat, he clearly addressed the newcomers in the common Water Realm tongue.

"My greetings to you, who are visiting us from another reality," he said, in a voice that was completely devoid of emotion. "My identifier is Prime Three and I am the nominal head of this small group of natural leaders, whose task it is to order the affairs of the majority of the vast Hixian' race. We are informed that you have been charged by the Dark Priests to seek peace terms on their behalf."

He pointed towards Myra.

"Speak and we will listen!"

The young witch's mind was in turmoil, but she forced herself to remain calm and in a quiet voice she began to speak. She stated her belief that the priests were quite sincere in their wish to restore peace to the Water Realm and were prepared to surrender both territory and vast wealth in order to bring this about.

"How many of your finest warriors have been slain by the fire weapons of the priests' overseers?" she asked. "And would not the return of peace relieve the Hixian' clans of the heavy burden of supporting this terrible conflict?"

Prime Three listened silently to her words, and then he released a high-pitched hiss, which the wisewoman knew to be the Hixian' equivalent of a burst of mirthful laughter.

"Young seer, your words suggest that our inroads into the human lands are creating difficulties for the Dark Priests!"

He loosed yet another loud mirthful hiss.

"Perhaps their human subjects are not so easily controlled through superstition and fear, when an even greater object of terror begins to threaten their very existence ---- Perhaps an escalation of the conflict would serve our ends far better than allowing the priests a period of peace in which to regain their strength."

The Hixian' leader concentrated his almost mesmeric gaze upon the face of the young wisewoman.

"We are currently considering the wisdom of launching most of our forces at the weak border separating the Saxmen lands, from the settled principalities that lie beyond Holy Ptah. Tell me young witch -- How long would it take before the Water Realm relapsed into anarchy -- If our offensive succeeded in reaching the Great Life River and putting an end to the movement of water-borne trade upon which human civilization depends?"

The wisewoman met Prime Three's gaze. "You paint a grim picture," she replied without flinching. "We know well enough that a great misfortune would befall humanity if the great river no longer carried its burden of commerce. But an even greater calamity would fall upon the Hix, if some priestly scientist in Holy Ptah discovered a way of destroying this great incubator and the installations where you rear your young in such vast numbers. Is the present bout of murderous warfare to continue until both the Hix and the Dark Priests go down into mutual ruin? Perhaps your disagreements can be settled by...."

The young witch's mind was suddenly buffeted by the outpouring of mental anger issuing from the minds of all the Hixian's present and she pressed the palms of her hands against her head in a futile attempt to block out the burning pain piercing her temples. George fell groaning upon his knees, but Darryl managed to ignore the pain and he stepped forward and supported his twin sister in his arms.

The torrent of anger that had sprung from the creature's minds and which seemed to last for an eternity, ceased as suddenly as it had begun.

Prime Three stood up and stretched out his arms towards the newcomers, and they began to feel a soothing warmth sweeping over them as the effects of the terrible outpouring of mental energy began to dissipate.

"Forgive us, we had assumed that the Dark Priests had explained the nature of the bitter rift that has long existed between those malevolent beings and we of the Hixian' race. The suggestion that we might find it in our own interest to negotiate a peace with our dark enemies inadvertently caused us to release the torrent of mental anger causing you so much pain."

He pointed towards a door that was set into the wall at the far end of the chamber.

"A comfortable anteroom as been prepared for you and there you will find ample food, drink and comfortable bedding material. Rest, and when you return to this chamber, we will attempt of resolve the age-old enmity that has existed between the priests and ourselves ---- I bid you to retire and take your rest!"

֍

A huge attendant entered the chamber and led the three

travellers into a small side room where a table was laden with a selection of welcome provisions. Freshly split Thoa-nuts, dried edible fungi and a wide variety of other foodstuffs. The travellers were hungry and they fell upon the refreshments with a will, but only after each item had been carefully tested with George's poison-seeking spoon.

A pile of narrs-skins lay in a corner of the resting room and the trio wrapped themselves up in the comfortable material and despite the gravity of their situation, they quickly fell fast asleep.

The travellers were awakened by the same attendant re-entering the chamber carrying a steaming platter of newly cooked do-fowl.

"Eat your fill!" the huge attendant invited, using the common Water Realm tongue. "And I will return presently to conduct you back into the presence of the Hixian' Prime."

The newcomers immediately cast off the sleeping material and relieved themselves into a wooden tub that had obviously been provided for that purpose. Afterwards, they ate their fill of the do-fowl and then prepared to resume their negotiations with the Prime.

The attendant conducted them back into the council chamber and the three newcomers noticed at once that changes had been made whilst they had slept. A comfortably upholstered couch had been placed in the centre of the room and the same six Hixian' councillors were now seated in a semi-circle around the couch that had obviously been procured for their comfort.

"Be seated," Prime Three commanded. "And I will aid our discussions by relating to you the origins of the deep division's lying between the Dark Priests and ourselves.

"Once--Long ago, this entire reality was a young and pristine world, where rolling plains of purple moss stretched from horizon to horizon; a vista broken only by isolated groves of wild Thoa trees. Within the shelter of these groves lived the ancestors of our Hixian' race, simple creatures who dwelt in small family groups, who browsed upon herbs and collected the wild Thoa-nuts that fell to the ground in plentiful quantities whenever the wind blew strongly.

"Perhaps our race, if given enough time, would have developed naturally and possibly founded an advanced civilization ---- Yet this was not to be ---- For one accursed day, a predatory race of giants, who are commonly remembered as the Ancient Dead, arrived here from some benighted corner of space and time and made this reality their home.

"As for the primitive Hix, our ancestors, they were totally exterminated, save for a few selected specimens; from these few survivors were genetically bred a race of powerful slaves who were strong of body and could derive sustenance from the roughest of herbage. These slave Hix toiled for their masters for countless generations and turned their pristine homeland into the world that you now call The Water Realm -- However, their masters were a supremely greedy race and the resources of this reality alone were insufficient to satisfy their needs, and other worlds were also systematically plundered for materials."

Prime Three paused and pointed towards the couch upon which the travellers were seated.

"One of these worlds was the planet Earth, from which you are all sprung. Long ages ago, great lumbering beasts once roamed the surface of your planet and browsed amidst the hot rainforests of this young world. These egg-laying animals were killed in great numbers by hunting parties from this reality. The carcasses of these great animals were brought back through the very same portal by which you entered the Water Realm and processed into food for consumption by the Ancient Dead, in the city that now lies in ruins at the head of the Exit River. Ages came and passed and the great beasts were hunted to extinction and were naturally replaced by smaller creatures bearing their young alive and some of them eventually evolved into the forerunners of your own race."

The Prime bowed his head slightly and then continued.

"By now, the ancient rulers of this reality were becoming lazy and too slothful to direct the labour of their own slaves. Therefore, they took a few members of your own evolving race and used their vast scientific knowledge to endow these creatures with great intelligence and they also sought fit to equip them with considerable psychic ability -- These mutated Earthlings were then given the task of overseeing the everyday running of the paradise, which the now extremely effete ancients had created for themselves--These new super-human creatures are presently known to all the other inhabitants of this reality as 'The Dark Priests.' In time the priests grew tired of serving their decadent masters and broke into open revolt. After a bitter struggle, they triumphed and drove the ancients back into the void. We, the Hix, the lowest of slaves, also wished for our freedom, but the priests were born to administer and rule and were not prepared to grant this; so we withdrew into the forests and wastelands leaving the great works of the ancients to fall into ruin.

"The civilization of the Ancients crumbled to dust -- All save the portions of the Water Realm bordering the Great Life River. The accursed priests caused this area to be re-populated by the descendants of a small trickle of humans, who occasionally found their way to our reality through the portals that remained open after the last of the ancients disappeared into the endless void -- In this fashion, did humankind become the new servants of the priests and have inevitably become our enemies."

"You must hate us for robbing your people of their birthright." George said, nervously fidgeting on the corner of the couch.

"Hate you!" Prime Three exclaimed. "We do not hate you. The humans who dwell in the Water Realm are but simple creatures that are manipulated by the will of others. If the human populations who inhabit this portion of our world were not under the control of the Dark Priests, why then we would negotiate separate peace treaties with their various rulers and regard them henceforth as our brothers!"

"Then our mission here is futile!" Myra said, with a shake of her head, "for you will never consider a cessation of hostilities that includes the priests."

"Not under normal circumstances, young witch," Prime Three replied, after taking a short pause for consideration. "Yet one possibility exists--It has been our long-term objective to succeed in closing down all of the portals joining our reality to the planet Earth, thus denying the humans who currently dwell within the Water Realm the supply of new blood that keeps their race strong and vigorous in an environment that is foreign to their race and quite unsuited to the health of their species."

Once again, the Prime took a short pause.

"Your ancestor, Rose Littlewood, once negotiated a treaty between the Dark Priests and ourselves. We surrendered great tracks of the vastly important Thoa forests, and much else – In return, we received full control of a small and relatively unimportant portal from your world lying in the territory of the white-skinned Northmen and close to the waters of the Northern Sea. -- This portal is now blocked by an immense wall of solid masonry and protected by magical wards set by a renegade shaman of great power."

Prime Three looked the wisewoman straight in the eye and spoke slowly and with great clarity.

"Witch – Only one portal now gives access to our world from the planet Earth ---- It is the very one you employed to gain access to the Water Realm -- We wish it to be closed forever.

"If the Dark Priests crave peace, they must agree to give us this last portal, together with the nearby lake. They must also surrender the ruined city and all of the crimson plains stretching from the northern bank of the Exit River, down to the outskirts of the City of Calar ---- We will then close this last remaining portal and the drift of fresh human stock from your home reality will cease forever."

Myra was silent as she considered the implications of the Prime's words and then she spoke.

"You are offering the priests a choice between the imminent extinction of their human subjects, by warfare, or alternatively requiring them to agree to a blockade that will slowly rob their human subjects of their vigour and reproductive capacity?"

"Precisely," Prime Three answered. "We are certain that our strategy will eventually lead to the supremacy of the Hixian' race within this reality and we shall regain what was rightfully ours before the coming of the Ancient Ones."

"I wish to ask you a question!" George said, the moment the Hixian' leader had finished speaking. "Why do you not simply ignore the humans and their priestly masters and simply expand into the regions lying far beyond the wastelands your people presently occupy?"

The three travellers felt the cold aura of dread exuding from the minds of the six Hixian' Councillors at the very moment they understood the young boat hand's suggestion.

"What you propose is simply not possible," Prime Three answered in reply. "For, to the east, lies a great desert inhabited by life-forms that are terrible to contemplate, which the Ancients probably imported from the many realities they ruled and plundered. The finest army that we could raise would not survive there for long, even if we were foolish enough to order an advance into that wretched desert."

Prime Three stood up.

"Perhaps it would be best if you were to return to your rest chamber and discuss our offer to the Dark Priests. We will await your reply. Finally, do not fear for your personal safety. Whatever the outcome of our negotiations, you will be allowed to quit our lands in good health and without any harm coming to the three of you -- I give you my word!"

The travellers re-entered the rest chamber and refreshed themselves with cool water from an earthenware container standing in the corner of the room.

Afterwards, Myra turned and faced her companions.

"It is my belief that we should return to Ptah and inform the Dark Priests of the peace terms that we have negotiated with the Hix. We should advise their acceptance without a moment's hesitation."

Darryl, however, appeared unenthusiastic. "Are we not betraying the birthright of all the human beings living in the Water Realm? After all, do they not belong to the same race as ourselves?"

Myra shrugged her shoulders.

"Perhaps, but only if one accepts the theory that humanity cannot survive within this reality without a constant supply of fresh blood from the Planet Earth. Yet we know that diverse groups of humans have managed to exist in remote corners of this strange world without degenerating into weakness and impotence. The white-skinned Northlanders are a good example. I consider it quite possible that humanity will continue to exist here without an endless supply of stud bulls from our own reality."

She waited for a moment for her words to sink into the minds of her companions and then she continued to speak.

"It is my belief that in the fullness of time, the human population of the Water Realm will cast off the tutelage of the Dark Priests and become responsible for their own destiny. It is also my belief that a free population of humans will either come to amicable terms with the Hix, or find the will to resist them unaided."

The wisewoman paused.

"This was also Rose Littlewood's view for she mentioned it in her grimoire, which I have successfully translated."

The huge boat hand appeared to be satisfied with Myra's

explanation, but Darryl's face still wore a worried expression.

"If the Dark Priests relinquish all control over the territory north of the Exit River, then will not our narr-herding friends in the Fruitful Valley be left at the mercy of the Hix?"

"Have no fear of that!" Myra said to her brother in a soothing voice. "My witch's intuition tells me that the Prime's bargaining position is not set in stone. I believe the councillors will accept much less territory providing they gain their main objective: control of the portal through which we entered this world."

The young wisewoman combed her long red hair and arranged her dress, then pointed towards the door of the rest chamber.

"Come, gentlemen!" she said firmly. "Let us rejoin the Prime and see if we can bring this negotiation to a satisfactory conclusion without further delay!"

$$\mathcal{Y}_{\ell}$$

Many hours elapsed before the trio re-entered the rest chamber, for the negotiations with Prime Three and the other members of the Hixian' leadership had been protracted in the extreme. The Hix had argued over each simple point at issue and the travellers were dog tired by the time a comprehensive settlement had been finally worked out. However, the newcomers were more than satisfied with the eventual outcome.

The Hixian' leaders had agreed to evacuate most of the great tracts of Thoa forest they had recently conquered from the humans who occupied the borderlands.

In return, the Hix would be given control of the mouth of the Portal, the nearby City of the Ancient Dead and the lake upon which it stood. After a protracted bout of haggling, the Prime had relinquished its claim to the remaining territory north of the Exit River and had agreed to accept a seldom-used overland route between the main Hixian' homeland and the area close to the portal; a route that would be demilitarized and free from all forms of conflict.

Myra delved into her medicine bag and drew out a vial of powder that had strong restorative properties and she stirred it into a beaker of water. She drank deeply and ordered her companions to consume a similar draught before dining upon the badly cooked leg of wild narr provided for their refreshment.

Afterwards, the trio sought the comfort of their sleeping skins and they knew no more until roused from their sleep by the huge attendant, who requested them to re-enter the council chamber for a final meeting with the Hixian' leadership.

The council chamber was empty, save for the figure of Prime Three who stood alone in the centre of the room.

"Your business here is now completed!" he said. "Word has already gone out to all Hixian' warriors who are fighting beyond our borders to cease all offensive activities and to defend themselves only if attacked. You must now return to Ptah with all speed and explain the terms of the new treaty to the Dark Priests. Once they agree, then the final details of the agreement can be left to our respective underlings."

Prime Three advanced and touched each of the travellers upon the shoulder.

"In the name of my race, I thank you for the considerable risks that you have undertaken and also the suffering you endured, in order to secure this peace treaty. We will send you back to human occupied territory by the fastest and safest route possible and your return journey will begin at once."

The Prime paused.

"Do you wish to ask me any further questions before taking your leave of us?" he asked.

"I have one question, Prime Three." Myra said. "We have friends who await our return in the lands of the Kev. I may not be able to contact them by the power of my mind due to the great distances involved. How can the seer who accompanies them be told that we shall not be returning by the expected route?"

"This can easily be accomplished, "the Hixian' leader replied. "We can unite the power of our minds and your mind-message will easily reach into the brain of the seer in the distant lands of the Kev."

Prime Three closed his eyes and the same instant the wisewoman experienced the now familiar disturbance in her brain.

"Quickly, send your message now."

Myra concentrated all of her reinforced mental powers and cast a thought-message across the vast wastelands of the Hix and over the high mountains to the village where Paris, her former lover, slept under the roof of the Kev chieftain.

"Paris--I know that you can understand my thoughts--I am contacting you from the land of the Hix, in order to tell you that our mission has been successful and that you need await our return no longer--You must now endeavour to make your own way back to Ptah--Alone and un-aided--I give you my love and wish you good fortune and-- "

The mental contact between Prime Three and herself suddenly disappeared like a snuffed out candle.

"Enough," said the voice of the Hixian' leader in her mind, "A further expenditure of your mental powers would require you to rest for a long period--But that cannot be--For you must travel at once with your friends."

George interrupted by rapping upon the side of the bench.

"One thing mystifies me, Prime," he said. "You and the other council members are obviously much weaker than any of the Hixian' warriors who brought us to this place and some of your number are also physically disabled into the bargain. Tell me, how did you and your fellows survive your upbringing in the rearing chambers of the Hix where the weak are always killed and eaten?" Prime Three released a mirthful hiss.

"A good question, human. As you have obviously been told, only the strongest may survive the rigors of the rearing chambers and become warriors in the fighting ranks of the Hix. Even so, a small number of physically weak individuals do manage to reach adulthood -- But only through the possession of superior intellectual ability and enhanced psychic powers, which they use to protect themselves against their brutal siblings -- These gifted ones are specially trained to become administrators such as Z3*554, the Hixian' guide who brought you here to The Heart of Emerald. Some very few who display exceptional mental powers may be granted a Prime identifier and become a member of the council that leads the entire Hixian' race -- I am such a survivor!"

Prime Three stated that no time remained for answering further questions and he handed the wisewoman a roll of parchment inscribed with a number of intricate symbols.

"We know that you must travel far in order to reach the portal enabling you to return to your own reality. Only a few Hixian' families still manage to exist in the far-flung regions. But if you ever need their assistance, then show them this parchment and it will obligate them to give you all the help and protection that lies within their power."

He pointed decisively towards the door of the chamber where Z3*554 was standing.

"Go now -- Earth-folk -- The light of the five suns will soon illuminate the wilderness of the Hix and you have far to travel before they set ---- Go, and may you all live to feel the warmth of the single mighty sun, which is said to light your own planet!"

Chapter 13

The return journey to Holy Ptah was accomplished within the space of one hundred darkenings, and little over a cycle of Water Realm time had elapsed before the travellers found themselves, once again, within sight of the shining copper walls of the Holy City. Even so, the journey had not been accomplished without much effort and a good deal of danger.

The newcomers had taken leave of the Hixian Prime and led away from The Heart of Emerald by Z3*554, who had been detailed to command their escort and protect them until they were clear of Hixian' territory and reunited with forces loyal to the Dark Priests.

The escort had consisted of no less than one hundred experienced fighters and once again, they were carried along in litters borne by relays of warriors.

The first leg of their return journey, from The Heart of Emerald to the beginnings of the great Thoa forests, had been accomplished swiftly and with comparative ease, for it lay across the wastelands of the Hix and few natural barriers existed to delay their progress. However, once they had passed beneath the shadow of the great Thoa trees, their progress was frequently impeded by fallen timbers often supporting an almost impenetrable mass of prickly creepers. Fast-flowing streams had occasionally slowed their progress and were crossed only with reluctance by the water-hating Hix.

Eventually, the travellers had been forced to abandon the

litters and henceforth they had followed the Hixian' advanced guard, on foot, as it strove to force a passage through the tangled undergrowth.

The forest, however, had provided them with an abundance of nutritious food, for fallen Thoa-nuts lay on every side and the Hix often struck fresh ones down from the trees with their long spears.

After four days spent struggling through the woodlands, the expedition had encountered a number of broken ruins that, sometime in the past, had marked the easternmost boundary of human occupation. On the sixth day of their woodland trek, they encountered an abandoned road that ran in a westerly direction and allowed the expedition to pass through some of the densely wooded areas without undue difficulty. Finally, after a further ten days of hard marching, the great stands of Thoa trees had begun thinning and stretches of the common red moss began taking their place and Z3*554 had informed them that they were approaching the western edge of the great forest.

Signs of former human habitation became ever more frequent as the trees thinned. Deserted farmhouses, surrounded by untilled fields, were often encountered, whilst ruined hamlets strewn with the bones of their former inhabitants became a familiar part of the landscape.

The forest road joined a larger highway and there was much evidence of the bitter conflict that had recently taken place between the Hixian' and human armies.

The decomposing corpses of slain warriors lay in substantial numbers upon the road verges and many of the opposing fighters were locked together in the final embrace of death with their shattered weapons still in their hands.

As the expedition reached the open plain, they came across the site of a bitter battle where the unburied corpses could be counted in thousands. So great had been the slaughter that each member of the expedition had to clamber across a veritable field of dead Hix that must have stretched for a good half a mile across the open plain. The Hix showed few signs of mutilation, but tiny poisoned darts were protruding from the bodies of the slaughtered warriors and this grizzly evidence showed they had encountered one of the human mercenary units whose principle weapon was the deadly perm.

For fully half a mile beyond the dreadful barrier, was spread a carpet of human and Hixian' corpses mangled and twisted by sharp weapons that were normally used in hand to hand combat; the travellers had no choice but to carefully pick their way across the dreadful scene of carnage.

However, it was quite obvious that the overseer's mercenaries and their local allies had suffered a major defeat at the hands of the Hix, for many of their technically advanced war engines lay smashed and the bodies of their highly skilled operators were strewn around them like common chaff. The magnitude of the disaster was further emphasized by the corpse of a Dark Priest, whose body was pinned to the ground by a sheaf of long Hix spears.

After a further two days of hard marching, the expedition had finally made camp alongside a major tributary of the Red Bank River. Z4*554 had told them that a small force of the overseer's mercenaries was holding a rearguard position about a mile downstream from their present location. The Hixian' leader said he believed that one of the young officers, who commanded this detachment, possessed limited telepathic powers. He had suggested that Myra should use her own telepathic abilities in order to contact him and to arrange for a safe passage through the mercenary's lines for herself and her two companions.

The young witch had quickly succeeded in merging with the officer's mind and an arrangement for a safe conduct was soon made. Afterwards, the trio and Z3*554 made their farewells and, within the hour, the travellers were secure within the ranks of the overseer's mercenaries.

The officer who was in charge of the rearguard had

fortunately been instructed to keep a good lookout for the returning expedition and he placed them aboard a small fast galley that transported them down a tributary of the Red Bank River to the fort at Yam and greeted with immense relief by old Camdar who was still in command of the garrison. The overseer had commandeered the first sizeable river craft arriving at the nearby river-port and the three travellers, together with their strong military escort, had proceeded downriver until they came, once again, within sight of the Holy City of Ptah.

Myra was almost weeping with joy as the river craft drew alongside the wharf serving the city's bustling business district. The moment she stepped ashore, she felt as though a great burden had been lifted from her shoulders, for she had been perpetually conscious of the fact that the success or failure of the mission had rested upon her largely untried psychic abilities. Even so, she suppressed her feelings and was perfectly composed when she descended the gangway with her two companions.

A military escort awaited them on the quay and they boarded a man-hauled passenger cart, which they knew would take them into the sacred portion of the city and to their expected meeting with Councillor Hemm and possibly other influential members of the dark priesthood.

Once again, they crossed the great metal bridge spanning the Life River and soon they were moving swiftly along one of the holy cities main thoroughfares, which, as ever, was unbelievably crowded with blue uniformed helpers engaged in the seemingly endless task of shepherding the huge throng of visiting worshippers between the various chapels dedicated to the veneration of the Ancient Lore.

The man-hauled vehicle eventually turned into the familiar side-avenue leading to the travellers' immediate destination: the colossal metal tower housing the main headquarters of the Dark Priests. They were met at the door by a brown-garbed overseer, who led them inside the structure and up one of the weightless elevators to the chamber of Councillor Hemm. He greeted them with obvious pleasure.

"Welcome back to Holy Ptah!" said the priest as they crossed the threshold.

"I must congratulate you upon your successful mission to the lands of the Hix and also upon your safe return."

"I think it would be advisable for you to withhold your congratulations until we have fully explained the nature of the peace we have negotiated with the Hixian' Prime, on your behalf," the young wisewoman answered quietly. "For the terms may not be to your liking!"

The councillor gesticulated towards a comfortable couch that was situated in the centre of the room. "Be seated." He said. "Then take your time and tell me everything that has passed in the land of the Hix."

The trio obeyed and for a full Earth hour, Myra related every single detail of the journey and of the hard negotiations she and her companions had conducted with the Hixian' Prime. Finally, she lapsed into silence and awaited the councillor's reply.

"You have all done well," Hemm said after a short pause, "for you have certainly obtained the very best terms that we could have expected from the Hix. In accordance with this new agreement, we shall immediately dispatch numerous envoys to the borderlands with instructions to thrash out local territorial agreements with their former enemies. We shall also begin making the necessary arrangement needed to transfer the last remaining portal into the Water Realm, to the control of Hixian' officials. Once again, in the name of the Priesthood of the Ancient Lore, I thank you all for your assistance in securing this peace!"

The Littlewood twins received the priest's words and maintained a tactful silence whilst the old man ordered refreshments, but George fearlessly blurted out a pair of extremely thorny questions.

"Councillor, you must have considered the possibility that

our new treaty may begin an unstoppable chain of events, leading to the abolition of the rule of your dark priesthood in this reality. Or will you only countenance this treaty until such times as you are able to devise some revolutionary new strategy for defeating the Hixian' tribes?"

The councillor shook his head.

"We will never break this treaty with the Hix, for its success is vitally important to the Water Realm humans who are currently dependent upon us. If we eventually lose control of our subjects, then so be it. All races must change and evolve or be cast upon the dunghill of time. We Priests of the Ancient Lore are no exception to this rule!"

Hemm paused for a moment before continuing.

"The priesthood is deeply in your debt and the time has now come for us to repay it as best we may. We promised to give you the location of the portal to your own native reality, if you survived your mission to the lands of the Hix; this promise I will now honour."

The councillor took a deep breath.

"A vessel faring south along the Life River from the City of Ptah will reach the northern border of the mighty Empire of the Kaa-Rom after only four days' sailing. Yet this same vessel will need to plough the waters of the river for at least half a cycle before reaching the Southern Sea where the great waterway terminates. This sea also forms the southern boundary of Kaa-Rom influence. Beyond this great body of water lies a mountainous region that is sparsely inhabited by fierce warrior clans who are constantly fighting with each other.

"In the midst of a mighty range of mountains, there stands a gigantic spire fashioned from the white metal of the ancients and is said to tower above the highest natural peaks. At its base is a deep cavern containing the portal that leads to your own world!"

Hemm stopped speaking for a moment and allowed his gaze to sweep over the three travellers.

"The journey from Ptah to the high mountains lying beyond

the Southern Sea is long and dangerous. It must be accomplished within exactly five cycles after your arrival in the Water Realm, for the curtain separating our realities will be at its weakest and it may possibly be crossed by those who possess the necessary occult powers. You must therefore reach this southern portal in less than three cycles, for two full cycles have already elapsed since you first trod the soil of the Water Realm...."

"You say that we can reach the Southern Sea in about half a cycle!" Darryl interrupted. "That will give us well over two cycles for crossing yonder sea and trekking inland to the portal. Presumably we have time to undertake the journey at our leisure?"

Councillor Hemm shook his head. "Not necessarily, my friends," he replied. "The distances involved are considerable and many obstacles lie in your path.

"Firstly, you must cross the mighty Empire of the Kaa-Rom, a vast stretch of territory, ruled with a rod of iron by Claudius Rufinius, the Legate who currently holds the baton of First Tribune. The Empire is governed from its capitol, the great City of Deva, and resembles no other state in the Water Realm, for its administration is so highly centralized that even the simplest personal undertaking appears to require a stamp of authority. Common citizens have few rights and can be conscripted into the army or used as forced labour without any redress; only members of the nobility and high ranking military officers may question the actions of the First Tribune's all-pervading civil service and only at the risk of life and limb."

The young witch caught the priest's attention.

"Would I be correct in thinking that the Dark Priesthood maintains its usual ability to influence the policies of this First Tribune and his administrative minions?"

"Unfortunately, no," the councillor answered hesitantly. "We have less influence inside the boundaries of the Empire than in almost any other portion of the Water Realm. True, the rules governing the flow of traffic on the Life River are generally observed by the various leaders of the Kaa-Rom. We also staff a network of maintenance depots close to the river's edge that are seldom entered by imperial officials. But we hold no special privileges within the hinterland of the Empire, where the Guardians of the Ancient Lore is but one of the many religious sects that are tolerated by the First Tribune and his government."

The young witch continued with her same line of questioning.

"Is it correct that the empire was founded by a company of Roman soldiers who blundered through the eastern portal and into the Water Realm almost two thousand cycles ago?"

"Yes indeed!" Hemm replied. "They descended the Exit River and settled close to the present city of Calar, where their discipline and fighting efficiency enabled them to maintain themselves in the midst of a hostile population. The newcomers had the impudence to levy a tax upon the traffic using the Life River and the priesthood was close to ordering their annihilation when they thought of a use for these new intruders. In those days, the land from Holy Ptah to the Southern Sea was occupied by a particularly savage race who described themselves as the 'Kaa,' after an obscene deity to whom they frequently offered blood sacrifices, whilst the eastern portion of their territory was often infested by parties of raiding Hix who sometimes penetrated almost as far as the Great Life River itself. The priesthood succeeded in persuading these Romans to abandon their settlement in the north and occupy the rich river-lands lying to the south of Ptah, thereby securing the Life River from savage incursions."

Hemm paused and the hint of a smile crossed his lips.

"Unfortunately, the outcome of this strategy was not entirely what the priesthood had predicted. True, the Romans married local women and settled down to become model citizens; as expected, they pushed the Hix back into their wastelands and also drove the brutal Kaa beyond the environs of the river, for these Romans possessed superb fighting efficiency."

The councillor paused and shook his head.

"Then something happened that we had never foreseen. About six hundred cycles ago, the Romans and the Kaa suddenly ceased their endless conflict and united to form the Kaa-Rom Empire, creating the greatest military and political human force in the entire Water Realm. Even today, many members of the priesthood hate this union; for it inevitably resulted in a vast reduction of our influence in the southern regions, but the Empire continues to be tolerated due to its skill in maintaining social order and its help in ensuring the security of the great river upon which we all depend."

George shifted uncomfortably on the couch.

"Are you saying that you cannot protect us during the remainder of our voyage to the Southern Sea?" the giant boat hand asked somewhat abruptly.

"We cannot put you under the protection of the overseers' war-galleys as we did when you foolishly ventured ashore at the Island of Plenty," the priest retorted sharply. "But we have discovered a means enabling you to reach the Southern Sea without unduly risking your lives." Hemm paused.

"As I explained earlier, we maintain a series of depots along the southern line of the great river. These establishments hold reserves of construction material, working boats and squads of men whose task it is to remove sunken vessels and other obstacles to safe navigation. Our order often dispatches vessels from Ptah to resupply these depots and also transport members of the priesthood to the various shrines of the Ancient Lore'that are located in Kaa-Rom territory.

"It is suggested that we should commission your vessel, the Bonny Barbara, to carry construction materials to the furthest of our maintenance depot located close to where the Life River meets the Southern Sea.

"Whilst aboard your craft, you will all wear the uniform of the overseers and your craft will sail under the pennant of our order. The fact that you are in the service of the priesthood should help excuse your unfamiliar white skins and the strange lines of your Earth-built vessel and possibly save you from undue molestation from the Imperial authorities."

"Is it possible for my vessel to navigate safely across the waters of the Southern Sea?" Darryl enquired anxiously, but the priest shook his head at once.

"No. Strong winds often sweep across the surface of the sea and your small boat would not survive. You must abandon your craft at the furthest maintenance depot and pass overland to the sailing port of Ostia that is only a short distance away. We hope to be successful in obtaining passage for all three of you on one of the cargo sloops crossing the Southern Sea and trading with the clans-folk upon the opposite shore."

The councillor frowned. "We can give you no further assistance, once you reach that southern shoreline, for long ages have passed since any member of our order has ventured into that barbarous land. I have not the slightest doubt that you will need to use all of your combined wits to survive in that most inhospitable country. We cannot even accurately say how long it will take you to complete the journey through the mountains and reach the base of the great metal spire were the portal is situated. Time may therefore be of the essence and you had best sail from Holy Ptah as soon as possible!"

Councillor Hemm summoned a uniformed attendant by pressing one of the coloured panels situated in the metal wall.

"Your escort will now take you to the dockyard where the skeleton crew of your craft, the Bonny Barbara, are eagerly awaiting your return. You have much to consider and I will summon you again when plans for your departure are further advanced. In the meantime, may the unseen powers give you wisdom and happiness."

ༀ

Wilakin eagerly grasped the boatmaster's hand as he stepped

onto the deck of the Bonny Barbara.

"Greetings, Master," he said with tears in his eyes. "I prayed to every deity in the Water Realm that you would be allowed to return safely from your perilous journey to the east. The craft awaits your inspection, but my gaze has never left the dockyard staff and I feel sure that your vessel is as sound as the day it first entered the water."

The sailing master also welcomed Myra and George back aboard and the returning trio were also greeted by Tess and Tom-Tess who chattered away like a pair of startled do-fowl.

Later, the three travellers and the sailing master crowded into the tiny cabin of the narrowboat and discussed the prospects of the forthcoming voyage to the Southern Sea.

Wilakin appeared to be more than a little worried about the projected trip and he rubbed his chin thoughtfully.

"I must admit that I have never ventured farther than Ptah in the whole of my sailing career," he said slowly. "But I have often talked to mariners who have ventured as far as the river's junction with the Southern Sea. All of them stated that the waterway south from Ptah is particularly easy to navigate and is almost free from pirates, due to the constant vigilance of the Imperial authorities. However, the same civil and military establishments are said to be very intrusive and merchant craft using the waterway are sometimes boarded and searched on the pretext of 'hunting for pirates' although such an interference with the movement of trade is strictly forbidden by order of the Dark Priests. Astute merchants are said to keep a few bolts of good cloth handy for use as a 'gift' to ensure a swift search and a quick end to the unwelcome molestation. The imperial government maintains havens where boat crews can find a night's lodgings ashore, but these establishments are invariably expensive and a mariner can find himself paying substantial sums in fines and taxes to the officials who run these hostelries. Small wonder that most traders find it advisable to keep to the water as much as possible. However, we shall be sailing beneath the pennant of the Dark

Priests and this should save us from many such difficulties. We should also be able to put into the priests' maintenance depots when we need supplies or a night ashore and this should enable us to avoid the attentions of prying officials."

Darryl nodded in agreement. "Aye, we shall certainly avoid putting into strange shores if it can be avoided. That business on the Island of Plenty has persuaded me to do my sightseeing from a good distance and I resolved, in future, to keep a good stretch of water between myself and any possible danger!"

The boatmaster turned and looked Wilakin straight in the eye.

"You have served me well, sailing master. Any debt that you owed me has long been discharged. You are under no obligation to face further perils on my account, but if you are determined to remain in my service, then I will reward you by making you a gift of the Bonny Barbara once we reach the Southern Sea, for you will have earned its price many times over."

Wilakin knelt and grasped the boatmaster's hands.

"I willingly and gratefully accept your offer," he said. "Furthermore, I will cherish your craft for as long as I live. I will paint your name on the boat's hull and you will be remembered in the Water Realm for as long as your craft ploughs the water."

"What of those two youngsters, Tom and Tom-Tess?" Darryl asked. "Do you suppose they would be prepared to crew for us on the voyage, in return for a substantial sum in discs?"

"Without a doubt," the navigator answered. "Master, that pair would sail to the land of the dead if you asked it of them!"

George raised his hand for attention.

"What of that quantity of scrap copper lying behind the bulkhead in the bows? Shall we need to sell it in order to pay for the supplies used during our voyage to the sea?"

The boatmaster thought for a moment. "No, for we still have a sizeable sum in hand from the sale of the rare timbers we shipped from Calar. Also, one of the overseers at the priests headquarters said that any craft sailing under the pennant of the Dark Priests has the right to draw supplies, free of charge, from any of the maintenance depots lying along the line of the Life River. No, we will leave the metal in its hiding place for use should some unforeseen emergency arise."

The occupants of the cabin fell silent and Darryl waited for a moment before pushing the door open with his foot.

"Darkness is falling, my friends, so let us drink and dine to repletion in that little tavern standing by the dockyard gates. Move your bulk, George," he said with a laugh. "Let's go and see if the proprietor's Thoa-nut beer is still the very best to be had in the whole of Holy Ptah!"

Six darkenings after the expedition returned to Holy Ptah, an envoy arrived at the Bonny Barbara with orders for the three travellers to accompany him to the main city, for Councillor Hemm awaited them with important news.

Once again, the newcomers crossed the great bridge in a man-hauled passenger carriage and very little time elapsed before they were rising weightlessly upwards in the elevator leading to the highest levels of the towering headquarters building.

Hemm greeted them as they entered the council chamber and invited them to enjoy the comfort of the now familiar couch.

"My friends," the councillor began. "I have summoned you here so that I may personally inform you that preparations for your departure to the southern lands are now almost completed and there appears to be no good reason why you should not sail within the space of two darkenings." He paused and adjusted his gown.

"We began the necessary preparations for your voyage to the south even before you returned from the land of the Hix. The first thing that we did was to despatch a priest belonging to our order, to the south, on one of the fast packet galleys that occasionally ply the southern portion of the Life River. The priest will be well ahead of you and warn the priest-technicians who are in charge of our maintenance depots of your imminent arrival and order them to give you all possible assistance. This priest has long experience of serving the order within the borders of the Kaa-Rom Empire and his final task will be to find a trading vessel in the port of Ostia that he considers capable of transporting you across the Southern Sea.

"He is also charged with making all possible preparations for your journey into the barbarous lands beyond that distant sea. He will meet you at the southernmost of our maintenance depots and watch over you until you disappear over the horizon."

"How will we recognize this priest?" George asked.

"Have no fear on that account," Hemm answered. "For he will approach you, once you have completed your journey."

The councillor's voice then became grave.

"Everything possible has been done to ensure your safety. In addition, a trusted overseer, who has had long experience within the imperial lands, will join your vessel before you sail and he will serve as your personal adviser. I will now give you a few final words of warning. Should the fates force you ashore inside imperial territory, then you must keep your wits about you and endeavour to get word of your predicament to the nearest of our maintenance depots and our servants there will try to bring you aid.

Also, beware of all Imperial noblemen who have elongated eyes and lashes joining over their noses, for these strange physical characteristics are peculiar to pure-blooded members of the old Kaa aristocracy. These creatures are best avoided if possible, for they have successfully assimilated much of the culture of their Roman countrymen, whilst retaining a talent for perfidy and extreme cruelty that was all too common amongst their nomadic ancestors."

The priest then addressed the young witch.

"Women are not generally allowed aboard the transport vessels of the order and your presence might be enough to draw the unwelcome attention of the Imperial authorities to the craft. It would be fitting if you were to don the robe of an adept of the healing god Dumtek; it will be assumed that you are travelling to one of their many temples under the good offices of the priesthood."

The Councillor handed the wisewoman a leather bag fastened at the neck by a thong. "This bag contains a selection of uncut diamonds. These are little more than baubles in the Water Realm, but they may serve you well enough if you successfully return to your own reality. I suggest that you divide them among yourselves and sew them into your clothing so they cannot be lost."

Councillor Hemm stepped forward and grasped each of the travellers by the forearm in the common Water Realm greeting.

"For the last time I thank you for the services that you have rendered to all of humanity dwelling within the Water Realm. Even as I speak, the dockyard workers are beginning to load the stores and cargo aboard your craft, now you must leave and begin making your own preparations for your departure. So, for the last time, I give you the blessing of our order and wish you all a safe return to your own reality and to your homes on the planet Earth!"

⁂

A fiery red Water Realm dawn was breaking as the Bonny Barbara was shepherded out of the dockyard and into the south flowing stream of the Great Life River by a single towing galley. Wilakin stood in the bows and controlled the delicate operation, whilst the boatmaster stood at the tiller and guided the craft out into the flowing current.

Darryl, like all of the other members of the crew, with the exception of Myra, now wore the brown uniform of the overseer's marine personnel, but beneath this outer clothing they all wore their padded battle gear, for the boatmaster had ordered the crew to remain armed and protected at all times, in case the vessel should be unexpectedly attacked.

The overseer, who was to serve as their adviser, had come aboard the vessel on the previous evening and his first action had been to hoist the black pennant of the Dark Priests from the makeshift mast that had been rigged in the bows.

Poldaar, as the man was called, was a surly individual with few words to spare for the boatmaster and almost none for the remainder of the crew.

"Not worth his victuals!" the boatmaster had decided as his craft dropped the towing line from the galley and began ploughing its way unaided along the line of the Life River.

The narrowboat spent the first evening of the southern leg of the voyage, tied to a stout mooring post close to left bank of the river and none aboard were surprised when the newcomer elected to sleep alone in the bows of the craft. Yet Poldaar's knowledge of the Empire proved to be invaluable and this was demonstrated on the fourth morning out from Ptah when the vessel slipped into Kaa-Rom territory.

Traffic upon the Imperial portion of the river was lighter than any the travellers had experienced whilst navigating upon the waters in the vicinity of Holy Ptah and the task of the steersman was also much less exacting. Darryl was considering the wisdom of handing the tiller over to one of the less-experienced members of the crew when two light galleys suddenly put out from the western bank of the river and headed directly for the Bonny Barbara.

Poldaar was at the boatmaster's side in a flash.

"Ignore them!" the overseer said sharply. "Those confounded boats are just a pair of government cutters hoping to frighten some merchant into giving them a handsome bribe. Their captains are not senior enough to risk serious trouble by boarding one of the priests' craft. They'll simply take a good look at the pennant at our masthead and push off to pester another boat."

The cutters closed ominously and then suddenly turned away and disappeared from view in a matter of minutes.

"Told you so!" the overseer muttered as he turned to retrace his steps to the bow. "These minor officials are cowards to a man; they won't risk the wrath of the priests simply to win a bit of cloth or the odd copper disc!"

On the sixth day out from Ptah, the narrowboat passed a substantial riverside town. The young witch stood upon the deck and admired the temple colonnades and the many public buildings whose classical lines clearly showed their Graeco-Roman architectural ancestry. Even so, a few such cultural diversions were quite insufficient to stop a feeling of mind-grinding boredom from gradually taking hold of the crew as the long days spent aboard the craft began turning into weeks. Indeed, this was hardly surprising, for the boatmaster remained adamant that the crew of the Bonny Barbara should not be allowed to risk their lives by going ashore for recreation.

Darryl often steered the craft onwards throughout the hours of darkness and when he allowed the vessel to anchor for the night, it was always at a safe distance from the shore. Occasionally, the narrowboat put into one of maintenance depots in order to take on supplies and to give the crewmembers two or three days rest. The depots were invariably Spartan establishments surrounded by high palisades of sharpened timbers and manned by squads of dull uncommunicative technicians, and the travellers were generally glad to be riding upon the current of river within a very short space of time.

Sixty darkenings out from Ptah, the travellers noticed that numerous small riverside towns were being sighted on both banks of the river, sometimes two or three in the course of a single day's sailing, they also noticed that every one of the settlements was surrounded by carefully tended groves of Thoa-trees, together with well built farmhouses and neatly laid out fields. One morning, Myra approached Poldaar, who was standing in the bows of the craft, and asked him the reason for this sudden change in the appearance of the landscape.

The overseer spat over the side of the boat in a casual fashion. "This portion of the Imperial domain is almost completely given over to soldiers settlements," he answered reluctantly and without taking his eyes from the river. "The Empire employs many pure blooded Rom soldiers to guard its frontiers and to keep order within the realm. When these men have completed their term of service, about twenty cycles on average, they are given land to farm in one of these veterans' settlements. Afterwards they spend the remainder of their lives breeding yet another generation of soldiers to serve in the legions of the First Tribune. The settlements that we are currently passing, were all established centuries ago. Nowadays, the new veterans' colonies are founded as far away as possible, often in the east and in close proximity to the Hixian' border!"

The overseer spat again. "You won't find any slaves on the holdings of these Rom veterans like you do on the estates of the nobles, only hard-working countrymen who will instantly leave their families and rejoin the eagles if their generals order it. And that, my lady, is where the military strength of the empire lies!"

"But what of the Kaa?" the witch asked. "What part do they play in this Imperial scheme of things?"

"As always, the Kaa drive their herds of narr over the vast plains of moss lying far to the west of this river. A plain stretching from the shores of the Southern Sea, to the grazing ranges of a few scattered families who dwell far to the northwest. Some of their clans occupy ranges lying to the east of the Life River and many of their warriors serve the First Tribune as swiftly moving light infantry. It is also said that a few of their nobility have abandoned their nomadic style of existence and occupy some of the landed estates surrounding the Imperial capital of Deva, that we shall reach in about thirty darkenings from now if we continue advancing at our present rate of progress."

The overseer spat over the side for one last time and watched as the glob of spittle struck the water.

"You have probably been warned to keep well clear of folk with elongated eyes and extended lashes. This is good advice and you had best take heed of it!"

With that, Poldaar turned his back upon the young wisewoman, leaving her with much to consider.

The Bonny Barbara continued its steady progress towards the Southern Sea, but as the vessel advanced, the crew began noticing yet another gradual change in the appearance of the surrounding landscape. The riverside towns became larger, but less frequent, whilst the neat little farmhouses surrounded by groups of small fields, had slowly given way to imposing mansion houses that were frequently surrounded by large tracts of arable farmland and massive groves of Thoa-trees.

Myra was the first of the travellers to notice this change and she mentioned her observations to the dour overseer as he occupied his usual position in the bows.

"Lady," he answered. "We are now only ten darkenings away from Deva, the Imperial capital. What you are now seeing are the estates of the great families, who, for centuries have served in the court of the First Tribune."

He pointed towards one of the great fields to where a gang of about fifty men were harvesting some type of leaf vegetable.

"Those are a few of the slaves of the Legate Gius Quintillius and it is said that his estate provides much of the wealth that he squanders upon pleasure-girls in the dens of the capital."

Once again, he gesticulated towards the group of labouring slaves. "You can be sure those poor creatures don't lead easy lives!"

The young wisewoman nodded and then she remembered something about the ancient Roman Empire that she had learned in the course of her limited education in Elfencot.

"Tell me, Poldaar. Does the Rom have arenas where men and animals are killed for the amusement of the populace?"

The overseer paused for a moment before answering.

"Not anymore, lady; such spectacles were staged here many long centuries ago, but it is said that the Dark Priests objected to such a pointless waste of human life and forced the First Tribune of the day to declare the practice illegal."

Poldaar's voice fell to a whisper.

"But it is widely rumoured that some members of the nobility still carry out this bloodthirsty practice in the deepest secrecy!"

The overseer turned his back upon the young witch. "Your brother was correct in keeping to the river," he said finally. "Keeping clear of the Imperialists is far the best policy."

The following evening, the narrowboat anchored safely offshore and Darryl ordered his two fellow wanderers, together with Poldaar and the navigator, to assemble in the vessel's tiny cabin.

"In eight darkinings from now," He began, "we shall reach the outskirts of Deva, the capital of the Kaa-Rom Empire. The passage is not without hazard, for Poldaar tells me the river is crowded with shipping at this point, and that Imperial cutters skim about like a swarm of water fleas, and trading vessels are often detained for months at a time without any reason being given. We do not wish to suffer any such inconvenience and our friend has devised a way of avoiding this, he will now speak!" The overseer stood up and almost banged his head upon the low roof of the cabin.

"There are two maintenance depots in the vicinity of Deva," he said. "One lies on the western bank of the river and close to the northern outskirts of the city, whilst the other is again situated on the western shore, about half a day's sailing beyond the southernmost environs of the capital."

He paused.

"My plan is to anchor overnight at the northern depot, then cast of at first light and run past the city, keeping well to the centre of the river to avoid any prying government cutters. As darkness draws near, we can either put into a quiet wharf for the night or hope that the Imperial officials overlook us, or take the risk of running onwards to the nearby southern depot providing the night is reasonably clear and boat traffic on the river is fairly light. That is my best suggestion!" he said, before regaining his seat.

Darryl ran his eyes over the little gathering.

"I have considered Poldaar's plan and it seems to give us our best chance of getting clear of this dammed city without trouble, but if anyone here has a better suggestion, then let's hear it?"

The cabin remained silent.

"Very well!" the boatmaster said with an air of finality. "The overseer's plan is accepted. Now let's all get some sleep whilst we have the chance."

Precisely eight darkenings later, just as Poldaar had predicted, the Bonny Barbara docked at the Dark Priests' maintenance depot lying on the northern outskirts of the Imperial capital. Darkness was already falling fast and Darryl ordered the crew to eat a hearty meal and to gain as much rest as possible within the warmth of their sleeping robes, for the overseer had told him the narrowboat must cast off a good hour before dawn, thus enabling it to take up station near the centre of the river before the fast-flowing current carried his vessel abreast of the city proper. The crew immediately did as they were bidden, but the extremely anxious boatmaster moved about his craft for a while longer, checking upon the serviceability of the rudder and the other gear so vital upon the morrow. Finally, exhaustion overcame him and he was also forced to seek the comfort of his bunk.

One of the depot guards awoke the Bonny Barbara's crew at the prescribed hour and the narrowboat was soon nosing its way out into the dark waters of the Life River.

Darryl stood at the tiller with the sailing master at his side both ready to respond instantly to the directions that Poldaar yelled back at them, from his perch high in the bows of the vessel.

The red Water Realm dawn found the Bonny Barbara close to the centre of the river and being carried along by the current at an extremely fast rate. The light strengthened and as the travellers gazed over the water, they were instantly struck by the sight meeting their eyes.

Well clear of a jumble of suburban dwellings, stood the outer defensive walls of the City of Deva. True, they were not as high as the mighty cyclopean walls of Calar, yet they followed the line of the Life River for as far as the eye could see and there was little doubt that the long snaking rampart protected a huge city with a teeming populace. Beyond the walls, the travellers could make out rank upon rank of houses, palaces and temples that seemed to continue forever into the far distance. The narrowboat's crew, however, had little time to admire the view, for this portion of the river was alive with a veritable swarm of shipping and they had to keep a sharp lookout in order to avoid running down some luckless trading boat.

Government cutters scurried about like sheep dogs marshalling their charges on the planet Earth and they did not appear to have any interest in the narrowboat, all save a single large galley with an eye painted upon its prow. The craft advanced until it lay only a stone's throw away from the narrowboat's stern and Darryl immediately drew a leather bag filled with copper discs from beneath his jerkin and he was preparing throw the bribe onto the deck of the following vessel, when Poldaar grasped his wrist.

"Yonder vessel belongs to one of the military cohorts policing the streets of the capital, and it would be extremely dangerous to try bribing any of their officers. The witch and I have already considered the possibility of this situation arising and it would be advantageous if you were to summon her without further delay."

Darryl turned and was about to call out his sister's name, when the young wisewoman joined him in the stern and every member of the crew gasped in awe at the witch's appearance.

Her red hair was combed out into long tresses that fell down her back in a crimson cascade, whilst the clean classical lines of her face had been carefully accentuated by the skilful application of a make-up brush. In addition, the intricately patterned ritual shift of a priestess of the healing god Dumtek clung to her like a second skin showing off her lithe figure to perfection.

"State the nature of your business," shouted an armoured and helmeted figure in the bows of the police galley.

"We are a transport craft chartered to the service of the Dark Priests!" Poldaar called in reply. "We carry materials for their maintenance depots and are also charged with delivering this healer to the house of a member of the nobility who dwells close to the Southern Sea. And whose son and heir is dangerously sick!"

"Your vessel is of strange design," the armoured policeman shouted back. "And at least two of your number appear to be white-skinned Northlanders. It is therefore my duty to conduct your craft to the police dockyard for further examination!"

Myra took a single step forward and simultaneously transmitted a wave of sympathetic mental energy in the direction of the armoured figure in the bows.

"Look at me well, officer of the guard!" she called, in a loud but carefully controlled voice. "Do I resemble a bloodthirsty river pirate, or am I a healer going about her business? I fervently entreat you to allow me to continue with my mission of mercy, or do you wish to be answerable to the First Tribune if I am too late to save the poor young nobleman's life?"

The official stood still for a moment in thought and then he shouted out an order to the galley's helmsman. Moments later, the craft sheered away in the direction to the city, much to the relief of all aboard the Bonny Barbara.

For the remainder of the morning the current continued to carry the narrowboat past the enormous Imperial city. However, by midafternoon, the craft had left the capital's long defensive walls astern and dusk found the narrowboat clear of the southern suburbs and navigating through open countryside.

Darryl had spent most of the day at the tiller, and, as the light of the five suns began to fade, he handed the helm over to the giant boat hand and joined Wilakin and the dour overseer in the bows of the narrowboat.

"What shall it be?" the sailing master enquired. "Shall we select a quiet wharf or some other secluded spot to spend the night, or do we continue to advance throughout the hours of darkness?"

"A hard decision to make," Poldaar remarked as he carefully scanned the river. "But the traffic on this portion of the waterway appears to be very sparse and few vessels of any size seem to be heading in a southerly direction. My advice is to steer towards the western shore, to where the current is the slackest, and push on throughout the night until we reach the next maintenance depot."

Darryl also looked out across the river and he noted that a pair of small timber carriers appeared to be the only other craft currently heading south.

"Very well!" he declared. "We shall do as you say, Overseer, but we shall keep torches burning in the bows to aid our vision and every single member of the crew will stand watch throughout this night. There will be plenty of time for us to rest once we reach the shelter of the priest's maintenance depot. Now let us get those torches in position for darkness will soon be upon us and we don't want to be running blind!"

꒰ꕤ꒱

Night found the narrowboat being carried along by the flowing waters of the Life River, with every member of the crew peering unceasingly into the darkness aided by the flickering beams of light cast by the torches set high in the bows.

Darryl stood at the tiller with his twin sister constantly at his side and both of them waited in anticipation for the dark hours to pass and for the red light of the Water Realm dawn to once again illuminate the river.

Sometime, in the middle hours, the boatmaster felt the young witch's hand tighten upon his arm. "My inner eye warns me that

danger lies ahead," she whispered. "We had best find shelter!"
But Darryl replied with a grim laugh.

"Would that we could, lass, but we have no hope of finding
a safe anchorage in this pitch darkness. All we can do is to
continue as we are and hope that fortune favours us."

It was Wilakin, standing in the bows, who had the first inkling
of the impending disaster and he shouted desperately for the helm
to be put hard over at the very second he spotted the dark hull of
a towing galley entering the pool of light cast by the flickering
torches. The vessel ahead of them was crossing close to their bows
with a light passenger barge in tow and there was absolutely no
means by which the crew of the Bonny Barbara'could prevent
their craft from ramming the second vessel.

Moments later, the bow of the narrowboat tore through the
light timber-works of the passenger barge, flinging most of
its occupants into the water. The sailing master immediately
ordered the narrowboat's crew to cast lines over the side
and to save as many of the unfortunate vessel's compliment
as possible, before they were all swept to their deaths by the
current of the Life River.

A score of bedraggled figures were pulled from the water
and lay coughing upon the deck and Myra quickly moved
amongst them administering draughts of a restorative cordial
and tending the survivors who had sustained injuries in the
course of the collision.

Darryl noticed at once that some of the survivors were
undoubtedly persons of quality, for their few remaining
garments were made from the finest fabric available, but he
was also disturbed to see them sporting the elongated eyes of
the native Kaa. However, there was little time for speculation
for the towing galley had by now come about and it proceeded
to manoeuvre carefully until its stern was in close proximity to
the narrowboat's bows.

A line was cast from the galley and it was quite obvious
that the vessel wished to take them in tow. But Darryl was

uncertain of his best course of action and he hesitated before giving the order for the line to be secured. His mind, however, was made up by one of the survivors, who staggered to his feet and confronted the young boatmaster.

"My name is Creon of the house of Klee and I am a senator in the court of the First Tribune. I ask you to allow our galley to take you in tow and to deliver myself and the other survivors to a quay that is nearby on the western shore!"

He clasped a talisman that hung from his neck by a copper chain.

"I swear that I will not harm any of you and that your craft will be allowed to go on its way in peace upon the morrow!"

Darryl nodded and gave orders for the towing line to be secured, but his sister laid a hand upon his arm.

"This is not wise, brother!" she said. "My witch's intuition tells me that yonder nobleman intends to trick us."

"That's my feeling also," Darryl replied. "But if you look carefully you'll see that yon galley is full of armed men and I spotted a loaded catapult on her bows as she came about. We cannot put a knife to the throat of a great Imperial nobleman and hold him hostage, whilst we are still deep in Kaa-Rom territory, so I feel that we should do as the man says and hope for the best."

The witch reluctantly agreed with her brother's logic, but a deep feeling of foreboding still clouded her mind as she turned and walked away.

Dawn was breaking as the narrowboat came to its mooring at the small river quay serving the landed estate of Creon of Klee. The nobleman was seated amongst the other survivors who were also recovering from their ordeal and the three travellers were able to gain their first clear view of their unexpected guest.

The senator was extremely tall for an inhabitant of the Water Realm and he stood a good six Earth feet in height. His body was strong and well muscled due to a strenuous regime of physical exercise, but his features were thin and angular and the newcomers were disturbed by the lines of cruelty rigidly etched into the man's face.

The nobleman stood up and approached the newly rigged gangway with the obvious intention of disembarking from the craft, when he suddenly turned and faced the three travellers.

"Come ashore all of you!" he said in a voice that was more of a command than an invitation "Come and enjoy my hospitality for the remainder of the day. Food will be brought to the quay for the enjoyment of your crew, whilst you three travellers visit the Villa of Klee and enjoy many of the comforts that it has to offer."

"We thank you for you kind offer," Darryl replied. "But our vessel is on charter to the Dark Priests and we must resume our journey without further delay."

"No, no!" Creon insisted. "You must rest yourselves adequately before you depart; your journey will be all the swifter as a result!"

Out of the corner of his eye, Darryl noticed that soldiers from the galley were closing in around them and he could see no alternative but to go along with the nobleman's intentions and hope for the best.

"Go and prepare yourselves!" he whispered to his sister and the giant boat hand.

"Pack the most needful of our artefacts in your travelling packs and we shall be fully armed and protected when we depart. This we shall explain as being a custom amongst the Northland folk."

The boatmaster also turned to Wilakin who stood at his side and instructed him to cut the narrowboat loose from its mooring and attempt to reach the nearest of the priests' maintenance depots, should the three newcomers fail to return from Creon's villa by the next darkening.

The travellers were armed and protected by their padded battle gear when they boarded the slave-hauled carriage that was to convey them to the nobleman's villa.

George fingered the long-handled axe that he held between his knees, whilst Darryl had loosened the sword 'Kingslayer in its scabbard. Myra, however, remained deeply worried, for her inner eye warned her that a long period of danger and suffering lay ahead of them.

The carriage rocked and swayed along a stone paved road for a short period of time and came to a halt in the courtyard of an extensive range of single storied buildings occupying the entire side of a low hill.

The newcomers were greeted by an old man who was dressed in a white toga and appeared to be the bailiff of the establishment. The man led the trio through a spacious colonnade and into a wide atrium that was surrounded by a number of rooms. The bailiff opened one of the doors and ushered them into a comfortable day-room and he bade them rest until it was time to attend a banquet that was being prepared in their honour. He then bowed his way out of the room and promised to return for them at the appointed hour.

The trio took their rest upon sumptuously upholstered couches and even enjoyed a period of fitful sleep due the exertions of the previous night. Several hours had elapsed before the white-robed retainer arrived to conduct them to the celebratory banquet.

The bailiff led them through a number of antechambers, whose walls were decorated with elaborate wall paintings and into a lofty dining hall lit by torches burning in cressets fixed high upon the walls.

A long wooden table occupied the centre of the hall and it was laden with every conceivable type of delicacy available in the Water Realm.

Creon sat at the head of the table accompanied by a woman whose sallow complexion suggested that she was far from being in the best of health, and Myra instantly noticed that she was the only person in the room who failed to sport the elongated eyes and the extended lashes of the native Kaa.

About forty other individuals occupied the long sides of the table and three empty chairs stood at the far end directly facing the nobleman and his escort.

Creon pointed towards the vacant chairs.

"Be seated, my friends," he said. "Before we begin enjoying the victuals that are set before us, I will take the opportunity of introducing you to my wife Livia, who, as you have probably noticed, is not in the best of health, due to the birth of our son, an otherwise happy event that took place some thirty darkenings ago. The others who dine at my table are kinsmen and retainers who are sworn to my service."

Creon then stood up and raised his arms above his head.

"I call upon Kaa, God of the Kaa!" he shouted out in a loud voice. "To bear witness to our feast and to grant us luck and good fortune until we meet again at this table!"

The senator had hardly finished uttering his prayer before the entire gathering fell upon the piles of food like starving animals. Exquisite delicacies were thrust into gaping mouths and swilled down gluttonous throats by tankards of strong Thoa-nut beer carried to the table by relays of female slaves.

The heaps of food quickly disappeared and the slave girls cleared away the remnants before returning with small dishes filled with sweet red berries, which, Creon explained, came from the slopes of the western mountains and were delivered to Deva by relays of swift runners. The berries were quickly despatched and yet more tankards of beer were served to the diners along with bowls of perfumed water and napkins, which they used to wash the residue of the feast from their faces and hands.

Suddenly, a hush fell over the gathering as a number of burly slaves entered the hall bearing wooden platters with the contents hidden from view by thick red coverlets. The nobleman rose to his feet as the platters were placed upon the long table and the hint of a smile crossed his features.

He turned and faced the newcomers.

"My friends!" he said, allowing his gaze to sweep over the entire gathering. "I have a special present for our guests." And he nodded towards the male slaves, who immediately swept away the red coverings and exposed the severed and bleeding heads of the crew of the Bonny Barbara.

The three travellers gasped in horror and their hands instinctively sped towards their weapons, but at the very same instant, they each felt the prick of a dagger upon the nape of their necks and they were curtly ordered to remain still by the armed guards who now stood directly behind them. Moments later, the newcomers' arms were securely fastened behind their backs with stout cords rendering them quite helpless.

Creon took a long draught of strong beer from his tankard.

"Did you enjoy your reunion with your friends?" he asked his features twisted with cruel pleasure. "They were fortunate and died swiftly, but you three may not!"

"Tell me!" he continued, "were you all stupid enough to expect me to forgive you for running down my personal barge and drowning my maternal uncle and two of my cousins? Can you really have believed that I would not have sought revenge for the deaths of my other retainers who manned the barge?"

Myra was the first of the travellers to reply to the senator's tirade.

"You are a fool,Creon. You have placed hands upon the servants of the Dark Priests. You will certainly be punished for this sacrilege and you may well die from the shaking death before this present cycle has elapsed."

Creon made a sign with his left hand and a guard who stood closest to the young wisewoman struck her heavily across the face.

"Foolish woman, am I so stupid as to incur the wrath of the dark order? I can assure you: those meddling priests will learn nothing of this incident. The soldiers who executed your crewmen also sent your craft of the bottom of the Life River with a great rent in its stern. Many craft, together with their crews, have disappeared forever beneath the waters of the river and even if the overseers find your boat and salvage it, then it will have all the appearances of being crushed and sunk by a larger vessel such as a Stone-carrier."

Creon then turned his attention to the former boatmaster.

"I must give you my thanks for the large quantity of copper that we discovered inside the secret compartment within the bows of your craft. It will be melted down into bullion and make a splendid addition to my fortune."

He paused and the cruel twist of his lip became even more pronounced.

"Now, you pair of Northland warriors, the time is drawing near when you shall both die in a manner affording my friends a little after-dinner entertainment. Meanwhile, this priestess of Dumtek will tend my wife's ailments and I may be tempted to spare her life, if her skills prove to be useful!"

He slammed his empty tankard down upon the hard surface of the table.

"Guards!" he shouted. "Do your duty and convey the two male prisoners to the death pit."

The guards dragged Darryl and the giant boat hand out of the hall and down a long flight of stone steps taking the pair well below the foundations of the villa and into a circular chamber containing several rows of upholstered seats. In the centre of the chamber was a rectangular pit some fifteen Earth feet in depth. The pit was a good twenty paces in width and about forty paces from end to end. Two short flights of steps gave access to the pit at either end and each of the stairways was closed off at the bottom by a stout iron portcullis that could raised and lowered by means of two small winding engines.

The travellers were forced to descend one of the flights of steps and were made to enter the pit by the guards, who prodded them menacingly with the points of their spears. The iron grill was then lowered, thus blocking off any possible escape route, but only after one of the guards had quickly cut their bonds with a sharp dagger.

The two prisoners had only a few moments to become accustomed to their surroundings before the senator's entourage entered the chamber and occupied the rows of seats closest to the lip of the pit. Darryl looked up and noticed that his sister was seated close to Creon and she now wore a light iron collar around her neck and was secured to a short length of chain, which the nobleman held in the palm of his hand.

Creon leaned forward and addressed the two prisoners.

"You are now guests inside my death pit and you are expected to die with style for the pleasure of myself and my retainers. You will be given back your own weapons and you will shortly face your first opponents, namely three Hixian' captives who are armed with their traditional spears." He laughed. "You had best fight well, for they are hungry and have been promised your flesh to eat if they succeed in killing you both. If you manage to kill the Hix, then you will face Maximus of Deva and Iron Club, who are my resident gladiators."

The senator smiled broadly.

"If you succeed in killing both of my gladiators, then you will be allowed to take their places as my pet fighters and you may live a while longer!"

Creon turned to his guards who stood nearby.

"Enough," he shouted. "Give them back their weapons and let the match commence."

The sword Kingslayer and the target-shield Gutripper were flung down to the former boatmaster, whilst George caught his long-handled axe in midair and then picked up his cleaver of Sheffield steel and clipped it to his belt.

"Bastards sunk my boat!" Darryl muttered as the pair prepared for the inevitable combat. "Sunk it in the middle of that bloody river the bastards have!"

George turned and grasped his companion by the shoulder and looked him straight in the eye.

"Fuck your bloody boat!" he cursed. "Any second now we'll be fighting for our lives and we'll be dead in a flash, if all that you can think about is yon tub of yours!"

Darryl bit his lip and nodded in reply and both men concentrated their attention upon the opposite end of the pit, where three shambling Hixian's were being goaded down the steps by the spears of the guards.

George carefully eyed their opponents and he noticed that one of the Hix was much larger than his companions and seemed to be their leader.

"Yon big Hixian' seems to be the boss," he said. "If we can get rid of him quick, then the other two might not present much of a problem."

Darryl inclined his head in agreement.

"I don't doubt that you're right. The best thing we can do is to charge the devil's before they can line up with their spears levelled, aye and cut yon big sod down before his two mates can aid him."

"Right!" the boat hand replied. "Get ready...NOW!"

The pair covered the length of the death pit in a matter of seconds and closed upon the leading Hix. Unfortunately, the huge creature reacted instantaneously and lunged at Darryl with his spear, but the ex-boatmaster dropped upon his knees and half parried the spear-thrust with his upraised target. Gutripper saved his life, but the spear-point drove onwards, tearing a deep gash in Darryl's left shoulder. A split second later, George's axe bit into the huge Hixian's skull and the creature's brains were spattered along the wall of the pit as it fell.

The two remaining Hix quickly suffered the fate of their leader, for Darryl sprang to his feet and buried Kingslayer in the chest of his second adversary, whilst the giant boat hand smashed the head of the remaining creature with a mighty sweep of his axe, but only after receiving a deep spear-thrust in his hip.

Myra observed the blood trickling from the wounds suffered by her fellow wanderers and she addressed the nobleman who was chewing idly upon the leg of a roast do-fowl.

"I beg you, return my bag of remedies and allow me to tend my wounded friends," she said quietly. "It would present a poor spectacle if the men facing your resident gladiators are too weak to defend themselves through loss of blood!"

Creon cleared his mouth by spitting a mass of half chewed do-fowl into the witch's face.

"Very well!" he replied. "Tend their wounds, but be swift or I'll have the guards put a whip to your back for delaying our pleasure!"

A guard took hold of the wisewoman's chain and led her into the death pit, where she quickly staunched the flow of blood from the men's wounds with two padded dressings taken from her bag of remedies. She also gave the two men draughts of a restorative cordial and recited the words of a strengthening spell in their ears.

"Good luck!" she whispered as she refastened the men's battle garb. "Fight well and try your best to survive, for our situation may not be hopeless. Did you notice that Wilakin's head was not amongst those of our poor crewmen? Perhaps he escaped the guards and may somehow bring us succour. I must go now, for this accursed audience is becoming restless and baying for more blood."

Myra had hardly resumed her place at the senator's side when a loud cheer erupted from the audience as Creon's resident gladiators descended to the floor of the death pit and stepped over the bodies of the unfortunate Hix.

One of the men wore the traditional helmet and body armour of a Roman soldier of the Caesarean period. Upon his left arm he bore a large rectangular body shield that was ornately decorated with strips of burnished copper and in his right hand he carried a gladius, a type of short stabbing sword often used by the professional fighters in ancient Roman.

His name, Maximus of Deva, was chanted over and over again by the bloodthirsty audience who stared eagerly into the pit of death.

The swordsman's companion was squat and extremely broad shouldered and wore only the minimum of body armour over his powerfully muscled body. He carried an iron shod club upon his shoulder that was only a little shorter in length than George's long-handled axe.

The boat hand spat upon his hands meaningfully as the Earth-born pair strode towards their latest opponents.

"Best if you take yon swordsman," he hissed to his companion. "And I'll see if I can chop yonder club-swinger down to size!"

The combatants rapidly closed together and the two ex-boatmen commenced what proved to be the most dangerous close-quarters combat of their lives.

Darryl and the Devan gladiator clashed in a blur of rapid sword play in which the swift footwork of the Earthman, alone, saved him from the darting gladius of his heavily armoured opponent. Meanwhile, George and the squat club-wielding fighter circled each other for a full minute before club and axe clashed together in midair.

The men sweated and grunted with effort as they fought for their lives and a good five minutes elapsed before the Devan swordsman slipped upon the blood of a dead Hixian', a mishap causing him to momentarily lose his balance. Darryl instantly seized his opportunity and stepped inside the man's guard and dashed the spiked boss of his target into the gladiators face before drawing Kingslayer's sharp edge across the man's throat.

George, meanwhile, experienced the greatest difficulty in countering the lightning club-work of his squat opponent and he almost lost his life when the shaft of his axe suddenly shivered in his hands. Fortunately, he escaped the inevitable coup-de-grace by ripping the steel cleaver from his belt and hurling the weapon at the man's chest with tremendous force. The club-man reacted swiftly and deflected the flying cleaver with the butt end of his club, but the sharp edge of the weapon severed the gladiator's left hand before burying itself in the wall of the death pit. The giant boat hand grasped the crippled club-wielder by his neck and left thigh and bent the unfortunate man's spine across his knee until it snapped with a sickening crack.

A pregnant hush fell over the audience lasting for the space of several heartbeats. And the entire chamber rang to the cry of acclamation at the white-skinned Earthmen's amazing feat of arms.

Creon turned to the young wisewoman who was seated at his side with tears of relief running down her face.

"Woman!" he said. "You may attend to your friends' injuries. Care well for them, for they will provide a deal of profit and amusement for myself and my household."

He paused and gave Myra a cold stare causing the witch's stomach to twist with fear.

"Remember this!" he said. "You will live and remain unmolested for as long as that pair of fighters survive, but you will die when the last of them perishes in the pit of death. Now, woman, go quickly and do your duty!"

✍

Myra lay back upon her sleeping couch and watched the first red rays of the Water Realm dawn creeping into the chamber she occupied in Lady Livia's personal apartment. She was tired and craved sleep, for she had spent the whole of the previous night tending her mistress, who was currently enduring one of her frequent bouts of ill health. Yet sleep evaded her for she was constantly worried by the situation existing in the household of Senator Creon and the dangerous way it was impacting upon herself and her companions from Earth.

A full cycle had elapsed since George and her twin brother had managed to survive that terrible gladiatorial contest in the senator's death pit. Since that day, Darryl and the giant boat hand had been regularly matched against the very best professional fighters to be found in the Empire of the Kaa-Rom. So far Darryl had killed six men in single combat, whilst George had slaughtered nine in the same number of contests, for it had often been Creon's whim to pit him against two opponents at the same time.

Fortunately, the two Earthmen had escaped serious injury and the hurts which they had received, had been easily treated during the witch's daily medical visits to the senator's gladiatorial school, an establishment lying in a secluded wing of the villa and not far from the barracks housing the estate's force of agricultural slaves.

Myra recalled the feeling of disgust that she had experienced when she first encountered the sickening stench emanating from that miserable barrack block where the unfortunate creatures dwelt, when they were not tilling the farmlands for the benefit of their master and his extravagant household.

By contrast, the quarters occupied by the gladiators were comfortable and clean. The food was also plentiful and of excellent quality for Creon required his playthings to be at the peak of fighting fitness at all times. The gladiators, however, were afforded little freedom and a dozen picked guards patrolled the high wall enclosing their training compound, in case any of the doomed fighters should try to escape.

Darryl and George were the only combatants to be regularly housed within the compound. A few other gladiators had arrived after being purchased from other masters, but none had survived longer than a single brutal contest within the senator's death pit and the Earthmen had watched their bodies being dragged away for burial. Only the two luckless wanderers could be seen undertaking the daily combat exercises beneath the watchful eye of Yam-Yy-Beel, the senator's chief master-at-arms.

Myra turned restlessly upon the couch as she gave thought to her mistress condition. The wisewoman had immediately diagnosed that Lady Livia was suffering from one of the chronic post natal problems often suffered by human females in the Water Realm. Unfortunately, her condition was almost incurable and likely to prove fatal within a cycle or so. Myra had spent a great deal of time with the woman and had gradually gained her confidence and she had learned that Lady Livia was desperately unhappy and quite untroubled by the prospect of her imminent demise.

Livia, it transpired, was born and raised here on the estate of Klee at a time when the property had been owned by her father, a leading official at the court of the First Tribune.

Her marriage to Senator Creon had been little more than a matter of cold political expediency. Creon had eventually gained control of the estate of Klee upon the assassination of her father, and it pained Livia greatly to see the friends and retainers of her childhood being gradually replaced by her husband's uncouth relatives, spongers who had drifted in from the distant territories of the nomadic Kaa.

On one occasion, when the noblewoman had been under the influence of a powerful sedative, she had openly declared that her husband's cruel treatment of the estate's force of slave labourers was driving them into a state of complete desperation. She feared that Creon was inexorably pushing them into open revolution, if only to obtain the release of death for themselves and their families.

"Goad the gentlest narr," the noblewoman had muttered as she lay under the influence of the powerful narcotic, "and it will strike back at you, and harder than you ever thought possible!"

Once again, Myra turned over upon the couch and tried to clear the concerns of the household from her mind, hoping to take some temporary comfort from the oblivion of sleep; but some indefinable power seemed to be probing at the boundaries of her consciousness.

The wisewoman considered visiting her medicine bag in order to procure a sleeping draught that would enable her to gain a few hours of much needed rest. But the strange mental irritation continued and seemed to come from some external source and she decided upon a quite different course of action in the hope of identifying the disturbance. She lay back upon the couch and concentrated upon an insubstantial point lying deep within her consciousness and slowly the chamber and her immediate surrounding faded from view as she slipped into a deep self-induced trance.

"Myra ... Myra .... MYRA!"

A weak voice began repeating within her mind.

"Tis I -- Paris, who seeks to make contact with you--Myra, reach out to me--Now--If you feel my presence within your brain."

The young wisewoman drew upon her reserves of mental energy and she strove to unite her mind with that of her former lover.

"Paris, I hear your words--Are you near?--Are you safe?"

The reply came almost immediately.

"Yes my love--I am safe in the cabin of a fast passenger galley lying anchored upon the Life River--Only a small distance from where you and your friends are held captive!"

Myra had now established a solid link with the overseer's mind. *"How did you know that we are improsined in Creon's villa?"*

"Wilakin was fortunately in the cabin of the Bonny Barbara when the senator's murderers began killing the crew and he managed to slip over the side undetected and escape the slaughter. He eventually came ashore and made his way to the nearest of the Dark Priests' maintenance depots amd word of Creon's treachery was immediately despatched to the priests in Holy Ptah. Whiteflower and I myself had returned to the Holy City by this time and ordered aboard a galley, which the Dark Priests were despatching to your aid, for they knew that my telepathic powers would be invaluable in organising

your escape my love -- You must now take careful heed to my thoughts -- Aboard this galley are secreted one hundred picked mercenaries, who, when the time comes, will seize and hold the senator's riverside quay and bring you to the safety of this vessel. But first the three of you must break clear of Creon's villa and reach the vicinity of the Life River and--"

Myra broke into the envoy's train of thought.

"How is that possible? George and my brother are presently under heavy guard in the gladiator's compund, whilst I am usually confined to the quarters of the Lady Livia."

There was a short pause before the envoy replied.

"We have an agent within the estate of Klee--His name is Gius Lupus and he holds the position of head blacksmith to the estate. Lupus is said to be extemely clever and he will doubtless be able to devise some means of organising your escape. You must contact him and give the code-word 'pulla-plant' and he will answer 'on my plate'--Now, a word of warning--We cannot remain at anchor for very long without attracting the attention of the river patrols--So you must plan to make your escape no later than four darkenings from now. I shall wait in my cabin throughout the hours of darkness and be ready to receive your thoughts within my mind--Long may you live in my heart--My love--And now farewell."

The mental contact disappeared and Myra lay back upon her couch and mulled over the situation. Gius Lupus certainly appeared to hold the key to her future and that of her friends. But how was she to make contact with the blacksmith without arousing the suspicion of the other members of the household...how?

ℒ

The clang of heavy hammers upon metal and the glow of charcoal fires told the young wisewoman the workshop she was now entering contained the forge of Gius Lupus, the head blacksmith. In her hand she held a delicate wound-probe that she had deliberately snapped in two halves, a regrettable sacrifice, but a necessary one if she was to have a plausible excuse for contacting the smith without arousing any suspicion.

Myra crossed the threshold and was immediately confronted by a red-headed giant whose body was burnt black by the smoke from the forge fires.

"Would you be Gius Lupus, the head smith?" she enquired. She received a sharp nod in reply and opened the palm of her hand in order to show him the broken instrument.

"I was told that you are probably the only man on the estate with sufficient skill to repair this much valued instrument of mine. Can you help me?"

Lupus took the pieces and examined them carefully.

"This is work best suited for a jeweller, Mistress!" he remarked. "But I will attempt to undertake the repair. If you will please follow me into the small forge where I do most of the intricate work."

Myra followed the smith into a small workshop lying at the rear of the main forge building and she felt the blast of heat radiating from the hearth as the Herculean smith began pumping the bellows.

"This heat is enough to dry up a bodies' throat!" she remarked. "What would I not give for a cool salad of 'pulla-plant' and a beaker of beer to wash it down."

The smith never missed a stroke as he began hammering at the broken ends of the wound-probe.

"Right enough, Mistress," he answered. "I too fancy some of that salad, 'on my plate!"

The blacksmith's voice then fell to a whisper.

"How might I serve you, Mistress." he enquired.

Myra quickly explained the situation to the smith, who ran his fingers through his red beard for a while before replying.

"It will be extremely difficult to release your brother and his friend from the gladiatorial training compound," he said, "as the fighters are guarded at all times by at least six armed men; the only way is to create a violent diversion by encouraging the slaves to break out into open revolt upon the very night chosen for the escape."

Once again, the smith ran his fingers through his beard.

"Two of the blacksmiths who work at the forge are perfectly loyal to me and the three of us should be quite sufficient to overpower the remaining compound guards, once their compatriots have been drawn away to deal with the rioting slaves."

The young wisewoman seemed doubtful. "Are you quite sure that the agricultural slaves will rise at your command?" she enquired. "For it must mean certain death for them. Even if they gain control of this estate and start a much wider slave uprising, they must eventually fall beneath the weapons of the First Tribune's legions."

"Have no fear, lady," he replied "Most of the slaves here will welcome death like an old friend. Better to die in battle than permanently endure the torments of such a heartless and cruel master as Creon of Klee."

The smith tossed the broken wound-probe in the palm of his hand.

"Return for your instrument the day after tomorrow and we will finalize our plans. In the meantime, you must warn your two comrades to make ready and prepare to flee for their lives,when the time comes!"

꒰⟡꒱

Darryl and the giant boat hand lay fully dressed upon the cots within their sleeping quarters with the thin sheets hiding their bodies from the prying eyes of the guards and obscuring the broken chair-legs, the only weapons available.

The two men waited patiently in the darkness and let the hours pass until the quietness of the night was broken by a scream of mortal agony that might well have issued from the throat of a tormented animal rather than a human being. Moments later, the night became alive with the howls of men in combat and the sharp sound of clashing arms. The pair remained quite still beneath the sheets and neither man budged, even when a guard thrust a lighted torch into the chamber to check upon their continued presence. The men only cast aside the coverings and stood upright when they heard a panic-stricken voice ordering most of the guards to seize their heavy spears and hasten to the rescue of their outnumbered comrades, who, it appeared, were battling desperately to contain the agricultural slaves who were now in open revolt and rampaging across the estate of Klee with the savage intention of butchering their oppressors to the last man.

Minutes later, the two men heard a strangled cry from the direction of the exercise yard and the door of their chamber was suddenly flung open and they heard the voice of Lupus the smith calling from the threshold.

"Quickly now!" the metalworker shouted. "We must make for the armoury of the gladiatorial school and retrieve your personal weapons, then you must hasten to Lady Livia's quarters in the villa where your sister is waiting for your arrival. Come, you must move with all possible speed if you wish to continue living!"

The smith, helped by another metalworker, quickly broke down the door of the armoury with their heavy striking hammers. The two boatmen swiftly armed themselves and followed their companions into a wide expanse landscaped gardens lying between the gladiatorial establishment and the wing of the villa containing the apartment of the Lady Livia.

All around them the night was alive with the noise of conflict and pillars of flame were beginning to leap skywards as the escaping slaves carried fire and slaughter across the estate of Klee. Fires were also taking hold in the main portion of the villa and it was obvious that the slaves were desperately determined to wreak vengeance upon their former masters before coming face to face with their own inevitable deaths.

Suddenly, a group of ragged scarecrows emerged from the darkness bearing spades, hoes and other makeshift weapons and they closed with murderous intent upon the four men.

"Freedom for all!" Lupus cried. "Freedom for all! Do not kill your fellow revolutionaries!"

The group of escaped slaves instantly recognized the smith's words of identification and quickly melted back into the night without threatening any further harm.

Moments later, the group arrived outside the wing of the villa containing the apartment of the Lady Livia and they gained entry by forcing a small side door.

They entered a narrow service corridor and Lupus almost fell over a tiny servant girl who was cowering upon the threshold.

The smith grasped the girl by the neck of her robe.

"You are in no danger, girl," he grunted, "providing that you lead us at once to the white-skinned healer who tends your mistress."

The girl whimpered with fear but she led them down a side-corridor and into a tiled bathroom that was brightly lit by a single blazing torch. And an extremely macabre sight met their eyes.

Myra was kneeling by the edge of a small sunken bath and the young wisewoman was supporting the head of the Lady Livia, whose naked body was half submerged in the crimson bathwater. As the four men moved closer they noticed that the veins in the noble woman's wrists had been opened by the bloodstained scalpel lying by the edge of the bath. Myra carefully felt for the slightest sign of a pulse in the noblewoman's throat and then allowed her lifeless corpse to slip beneath the water.

She rose to her feet and joined her companions.

"This was always the traditional way for a Roman woman

to seek death," the wisewoman explained. "And it is still a common practice amongst the Kaa-Rom females. Livia had no wish to witness the destruction of her family home and the butchery of her loved ones. Her children lie dead from poison in the next room and she begged me to assist her in this final ritual. This I have done!"

Uncontrollable anger began flooding Darryl's mind and he grasped his sword ever more firmly.

"Yon bastard Creon is to blame for causing all this suffering, I vote that we seek him out and make an end of him?"

But the giant boat hand grasped him by the shoulder with a vicelike grip.

"Hold hard, Master," he said, with an icy coolness in his voice. "Our task is to reach the river-landing and continue our mission. There are plenty of other vengeful souls abroad this night and there's little chance of him escaping with his life. Come, let us depart at once!"

"Well said George!" the young wisewoman remarked. "Your mind has grown much stronger since we began this trek, that long axe of yours no longer rules your brain and you have learned how to reason sensibly."

The fugitives quit the villa that was now burning in several quarters and plunged back into the dark Water Realm night. At first, they had to carefully pick their way through the villa's extensive gardens, but they were eventually able to discover the road leading down to the riverside quay. At this point Lupus called a halt and addressed his white-skinned companions.

"My friends, we can be of no further service to you, this good metalworker and myself will now return to the struggle and we bid you farewell forever."

The two doomed blacksmiths then turned their backs and disappeared into the night, leaving the three travellers to grope their way onwards in the direction of the Great Life River. Suddenly, they heard a loud clash of arms and found themselves completely surrounded by a troop of heavily armed soldiers. The four travellers were preparing to fight desperately for their lives when a familiar voice issued from the ranks.

"Put up your weapons, my friends!" said Whiteflower of the Kev. "Cool Thoa-nut beer awaits you aboard our galley lying by the quayside. Put up your weapons and rest easy, for you are now safe and amongst friends!"

Chapter 14

Geor(e grunted with effort as he hacked his way
through the thick tangle of Thoa-shrubs impeding
the expedition's progress as they attempted to follow
the course of one of the broken highroads--yet another legacy
of the Ancient Dead.

The giant boat hand slashed through the last remaining branches
and then clipped his trusty steel cleaver back onto his belt. He paused
and viewed the long stretch of open highroad leading unerringly
towards the looming mass of the distant southern mountains.

He turned to Darryl who was following close behind and
clearing away the severed branches from the path of the other
members of the expedition.

"Thank providence for a clear stretch of road," he said. "I thought
that I was destined to hack my way through that tangle of shrubs for
all of eternity. At least we can now see where we are bound!"

Darryl nodded in agreement and pointed towards the far-
off mountain range. "Aye and it's good to view the crags
harbouring the portal leading back to our own reality, for I am
heartily tired of following false trails that lead nowhere and
always in great danger of losing our lives."

"Let's hope that you're right," replied the giant boat hand.
"Anyway, the stream over there will make a good place to
camp for the night. For the five suns will set in about half an
hour, if I'm any judge!"

George swept together an armful of dry brushwood and lit
a fire close to the stream. Soon, a pot of soup was simmering
over the flames, and as darkness fell he was joined for the
evening meal by Darryl and his witch-sister, together with
Paris, Whiteflower and their four surviving porters.

The travellers ate their evening meal in silence and their minds drifted back to the moment of their swift nocturnal departure from the quayside of the estate of Klee, followed by the long and tedious journey, by galley, to the place where the Great Life River joined its waters to those of the Southern Sea.

The tired wanderers also recalled the journey overland to the seaport of Ostia and the weeks spent in virtual idleness whilst the agents of the Dark Priesthood put together a trading expedition to the lands beyond the Southern Sea--an expedition whose real task was to find the only portal holding the power to return the three white-skinned travellers to their own native reality.

It was during their stay in Ostia that the travellers bade farewell to Wilakin the navigator, who had served them so well ever since the Bonny Barbara had sailed from Calar. The wanderers agreed that Wilakin had long discharged any debt owing to them and they could no longer expect the man to take further risks on their behalf. The sailing master had reluctantly agreed to leave their service and they had watched him depart upon the return journey to Holy Ptah, where he was to assume the ownership of a fine trading vessel, which the Dark Priests had promised to provide for him now that the Bonny Barbara lay on the bottom of the Great Life River.

As they ate, some of the wanderers recalled their ghastly voyage aboard the small sail-driven cargo vessel that seemed hardly capable of surviving a single hour upon the storm torn waters of the Southern Sea. Indeed, all of them shuddered at the memory of the frightful period when the expedition had fruitlessly searched for a route that would take them from the seacoast to the distant southern mountains where the portal was said to be situated. The travellers also recalled the bouts of bitter disappointment that each of them had suffered, when a promising route had petered out in the midst of a vast quaking swamp or had simply become completely lost in the dense jungle-like Thoa scrub covering much of the landmass of this inhospitable region of the Water Realm.   .

The expedition had numbered over two hundred souls when it had first departed from the shores of the Southern Sea--porters, guards, merchants and the like--but desertion and the deadly poisoned darts of the treacherous southland natives had now reduced its numbers to a mere handful.

The travellers had almost given up hope of finding the southern portal in time to reach their own world, for only one hundred darkenings remained before the end of the five-year cycle, when the curtain between the two realties thinned sufficiently for the wanderers to cross the barrier and return home. Yet fortune had finally favoured them, for twenty darkenings ago, the expedition had stumbled upon a small hamlet that was quite deserted, save for an old man who was sick and almost dead from lack of food.

Myra had treated the man's illness and the wanderers had given him all the provisions they had to spare.

When questioned about the portal, the man had told them that an abandoned shrine did indeed exist in the depths of the southern mountains, about ninety darkenings of hard marching from the hamlet where he now dwelt.

The old man had recalled that once, in his distant youth, he had penetrated deep into the southern mountains and in the far distance seen the spire of shining metal that was said to mark the spot where a mighty and powerful shrine existed.

The sacred place, the man had said, could be reached by following an ancient highway--a route that could be encountered if one quit the hamlet and marched due south for the space of only one darkening. But the oldster had also warned them against undertaking such a journey, for he declared that the same southern mountains were the home territory of an isolated clan of Hixian' warriors who invariably killed all who entered their craggy homeland.

The travellers had been instantly elated by news of the metal spire that Councillor Hemm had already mentioned during their briefing in the City of Holy Ptah. Myra also recalled translating

a verse from the grimoire of Rose Littlewood, which almost
certainly referred to the same spire.

Where the shining needle climbs
Above sheer peaks of hardened stone,
Witch-Wife pause and sing your rhymes
Then tread the path which leads to home.

"Don't you see?" the wisewoman had exclaimed excitedly.
"My ancestor has described the landmark showing the position
of the portal. This man has verified her words and has also given
us details of the route that we have been seeking for so long."

The travellers then held a swift consultation and had agreed
to find and then follow the nearby road, for it seemed to hold out
the best prospect of reaching the portal before their window of
time expired, leaving them trapped within the Water Realm for
a further cycle of five years. That had been twenty darkenings
ago, and they were now wending their way along the ancient
highroad described by the old man. A road leading toward
a spire of white metal that pointed towards the crimson sky.
Perhaps they would survive. Perhaps they would live and once
again tread the soil of their native Earth!

§   §

The small sail-driven fishing boat pitched and tossed as it
drove before the wind in the direction of the small treeless
island several miles from the northern shore of the Isle of Skye.

Hetty sat in the bows alongside Inspector Angus Smith, her
friend and lover, and keenly searched the coastline of the rocky
islet for a first glimpse of the narrow cove affording the only
possible landing place. But her eyes alighted upon nothing
more than wave swept rocks and barren slopes covered by
heather and ling.

The wisewoman winced slightly as her inner eye began

picking up a strange aura of menace that seemed to emanate from some ill defined spot beyond the sea-girt coastline.

Angus laughed quietly and without humour.

"Can ye feel it lassie? Do ye catch the ill feeling that place casts abroad and makes fishermen keep well clear of yonder island, even though good catches can be made close to its rocks?"

"Aye, you're right," she replied. "Yet I feel much more than that. I also feel a similar power to that radiating from the portal beneath the Devil's Tor; a power pulsing outwards whenever the curtain grows thin and when a crossing between the two realities can be attempted."

"Our two crewmembers feel it also," he said, nodding towards the two fishermen who were now steering the craft towards an almost imperceptible gap in the rocks marking the mouth of a small cove. "You can see the fear that's graven onto their features. Small wonder that it took five golden guineas in order to persuade yon pair to transport us to this island, aye and to get a firm promise from them to return for us in a month's time once our mission is completed, even though they be close kinsmen 'o' mine!"

The fishermen skilfully steered the craft into the cove and beached it upon a bank of fine shingle that acted as a landing place. A few yards above the high water mark there stood a small cottage, whose sod roof was still largely intact, despite having endured a long period of neglect. The door-space, however, was quite open to the winds and its tiny windows were likewise uncovered.

"That's the cottage where my old grandmother used to stay when she dwelt on this cursed islet," the policeman said as he began helping the fishermen to unload their personal belongings and the boxes of provisions they would need to stay alive.

"It's broken down a bit," he continued, "but once we've patched up yonder roof and stopped up the door and window spaces with some old blankets; then it will afford us shelter enough for the duration of our stay!"

After a good hour of hard labour the couple's stores and

belonging were safely stacked in a corner of the tiny dwelling and the pair climbed a nearby headland in order to watch the fishing boat putting back out to sea.

As they watched, the policeman paused and drew his companion closer to his body.

"There they go!" he said with a laugh. "Nigh scared out of their trousers, but we are of the fay kind and don't fear the unknown forces as much as they. Come lass, let's away back to the cottage, we shall be fine and warm once we get a driftwood fire burning in the hearth and ..."

The witch twisted away from his embrace.

"The stone circle," she said. "The place of power--I must see it at once, and also the cave that you say lies close by."

Angus nodded patiently. "Plenty of daylight still remains lassie and both of those places are near, so let's go at once."

Hetty followed the policeman up a narrow path that was overgrown with heather. After a few minutes' climbing, they breasted a rise and the witch gained her first view of the ring of standing stones occupying a small hillock on the opposite side of the island. The pair splashed their way across an area of swampy ground. As they drew near to the circle they realized that many of the great stones monoliths had given way to the elements and were leaning over at crazy angles, whilst others had collapsed completely and were lying prone upon the mossy earth.

The two lovers reached the circle of stones and strode over to a flat slab of the same material that occupied the centre of the site.

"It is here where all the power is centred!" the witch said, laying her hands reverently upon the surface of the stone. "It is from here that I must call to my daughter who dwells beyond the curtain, and it is from here that I must conduct the ritual that will open the portal and allow my loved ones to return to the reality of their birth.

Now, Angus!" she continued impatiently. "You must show me the cave."

An ancient stone-flagged path led from the shrine to the

edge of a nearby sea-cliff and disappeared from view. The pair moved cautiously forward and peered over the edge of the cliff. A narrow path, hewn from the rock face, led downwards to the mouth of a cave some ninety feet below the edge of the precipice.

Hetty shuddered and the policeman held her close to his body.

"I feel the power pulsing from yonder cavern," she whispered. "It is a power that fills me with terror!"

She stepped back from the edge of the cliff.

"Come, let us leave this place and return to the cottage. There we can find warmth and food and comfort in each other's arms."

✣

A few half-burnt fragments of driftwood collapsed amongst the dying embers in the hearth. The tinder-dry wood immediately caught fire and briefly illuminated the two lovers who lay naked upon a heather-filled pelisse occupying the centre of the cottage's single room.

Angus raised his head slightly and the flaring driftwood enabled him to view his lover who lay close to the edge of the improvised mattress. He leaned over and allowed his fingers to caress her breasts before moving down her body to gently stroke the dense thatch of red pubic hair that was still damp from their recent bout of violent lovemaking.

Hetty gently rotated her hips as the questing fingers moved inwards.

"I wonder," she whispered softly, "if many other couples loved and then rested here, as we do?"

"They did indeed, lassie!" Angus replied. "The laird's agents used to ask only a small rent for this island. There's good feeding for the sheep, the fish are plentiful and potatoes grow well in a plot of ground lying beyond the cliffs. But the families who settled here never stayed for long; they always returned to Skye bringing tales of strange happenings. My old grandmother One-Eyed Meg was the last person to use this cottage. She used to come here occasionally with a crippled fisherman for company, to listen to 'The Song of the Wind,' as she used to say."

Hetty drew back her hips and her lover's fingers slipped from her body.

"Oh Angus!" she said with a hint of sadness in her voice. "I must ask a great service of you. When the time comes for me to open the portal, I shall have no choice but to conduct the ritual from the stone altar lying in the centre of the ancient circle.

"If I should be successful, then my children will return to this reality by way of the cave that opens out onto the cliff face. Someone must receive them when they emerge from yonder cave and lead them up that dangerous cliffside path to safety.

"My children may emerge into warm sunlight or into the teeth of one of the gales that blow upon a stormy night. This I cannot tell--all I know is that you and I are the only people on this island and I must ask you to undertake this dangerous task for me."

Angus laughed aloud and playfully tweaked the witch's left nipple.

"Have no fear," he said with confidence. "I spent half my childhood climbing about the sea-cliffs in search of gulls' eggs and the like. I will retrieve your kin without even breaking a sweat. Play your part within yonder stone circle and I will do the rest." He reached out and took the wisewoman in his arms.

"Time enough for making our plans when the sun rises," he said. "Now let us spend the remainder of the night enjoying the comforts of love."

The nine remaining members of the expedition rounded a sharp bend in the ancient highroad and released a collective groan of disappointment as they viewed yet another mountain valley opening up before them.

The travellers had continued following the ancient highroad until it entered the southern mountains, and for many weeks they had followed the route as it wound its way through a seemingly endless succession of mountain valleys, but the wanderers' situation was now becoming desperate, for only thirty darkenings remained before the time came when they must reach the portal and cross the thinning curtain into their own reality.

It was Paris who first caught sight of the spire.

The party was resting for a few minutes before resuming their journey and the envoy had taken the opportunity to scan the distant horizon of jagged peaks for any sign of their objective. As he did so, he noticed a brief flash on the horizon, a flash that could only have been caused by a beam of sunlight striking through the rolling crimson clouds and reflecting from some object made from polished metal. He concentrated his gaze upon the same portion of the horizon and once again perceived the same metallic flash.

Whiteflower was known to have keener eyesight than any other member of the expedition and Paris called her over to him and asked her to scan the same section of the horizon.

Again they witnessed the metallic flash.

"I see it," the girl cried excitedly. "And I believe that it's the great metal spire that we seek. It's almost obscured by yonder crag with the twisted peak, but it appears to be the marker we have been searching for so desperately!"

"Thank providence for its mercy," Darryl exclaimed as he joined the group.

"It appears this road is running in the general direction of yonder spire, but it lies at a great distance and we shall be forced to march with all speed if we are to reach it in time to pass through the portal."

He looked skywards and viewed the position of the five suns and then pointed towards a mass of ruins clinging to the verge of the highway some distance to the south.

"The remnants of some old way-station," he surmised "We shall reach the place before darkness if we move at once and its walls will give us valuable shelter once the cold night winds begin blowing."

The expedition made good progress and succeeded in reaching the cover of the ruins well before the Water Realm night was due to fall. The little group was able to make camp inside a building whose roof was still largely intact and a rapid meal was quickly prepared, from their stock of dried provisions; afterwards, they settled down to enjoy the temporary oblivion of sleep.

The first glimmers of dawn were beginning to penetrate the ruins when Myra suddenly shocked her companions into full consciousness with her cry of warning and the travellers awoke to find the young wisewoman on her knees and holding her head in both hands.

"The Hix," she called out. "The Hix are close by. I hear them as they converse with each other by mind-speak; they know that we are here and will be upon us in a very short space of time."

Darryl and the mighty boat hand instantly sprang to their feet and grasped their weapons, but the witch ordered them to lay down their arms and remain still.

"Weapons are of no use to us now!" she stated calmly. "I must attempt to contact the Hix and beg for their assistance. Brother, take that parchment, which the Hixian Prime gave to you and show it to the first warrior who enters this building."

The young witch knelt upon the floor, then gathering her mental energies she flung a message towards the nearby Hix.

"We come in peace and are travelling under the protection of the Hixian Prime--We bear the parchment as an assurance that you will not harm us--You are also instructed to give us all the assistance that we require."

The reply entered her brain almost instantaneously.

"If you are telling us the truth--Witch--Then come out of your shelter--All of you--Otherwise we will atack and kill you all."

The young wisewoman stood up, drew the knife from her belt allowing it to fall to the ground.

"Disarm yourselves!" she ordered. "And then we must venture outside and meet the Hix. It is our only chance!"

One by one, the members of the party quit their temporary night shelter and stood in a little group upon the ancient highroad as the light from the five suns strengthened and illuminated the ancient ruins and the surrounding crags. After a while, a single Hixian' warrior bearing his familiar long spear emerged from the rear of the old buildings and cautiously advanced towards them with his weapon held at the ready. He drew near to Myra, who was holding the Hixian Prime's parchment before her and he inspected it carefully. After a short pause he grounded his spear and raised his hand in greeting.

"Have no fear."

A voice spoke within the wisewoman's mind.

"I have now seen the Prime's parchment and it requires me to place myself and my family at your disposal—My identifier is Q22 and I am leader of our numerous family group—Our settlement lies close by and we invite you to visit us and refresh yourselves—Before suggesting how we can be of service to you."

Myra quickly explained the situation to her companions and they readily agreed to accept the Hixian's hospitality. They re-entered their night-shelter, gathered together their belongings and returned to the highway where an escort of about thirty heavily armed Hixian' warriors awaited them. The warriors took up a defensive posture on either flank of the newcomers' tiny expedition and the entire body moved off in a southerly direction along the ancient highway.

After a little while they quit the road and entered a small side-ravine. It contained a spring of fresh water and the travellers were able to make out the dark mouths of a number of caves that evidently provided safe accommodation for the Hixian's extended family group.

The newcomers were quite used to the grotesque appearance of their hosts as a result of their journey to The Heart of Emerald, but their remaining porters were obviously terrified and the young wisewoman had to cast a calming spell in order to allay their fears.

The travellers, however, noticed that many of the village's inhabitants were of a much slighter build than their massive warrior escorts and did not carry any form of weaponry; these creatures, the newcomers quickly learned, were egg-laying 'breeders,' the nearest Hixian' equivalent to the human females of Earth. In addition, numerous adolescents mewed and grovelled in the dust of the ravine and avidly consumed anything that could be remotely considered as being edible. It became immediately clear to the travellers that the social organization of this isolated family of Hix was quite different from anything they had observed during their visit to the main Hixian' homeland in the eastern wastelands.

Q22 pointed towards a pile of freshly gathered Thoa-nuts and the obvious inference was for the travellers to satisfy their hunger and thirst. The Hixian' leader stood patiently by whilst they completed their repast before he communicated mentally with the wisewoman in order to discover their future requirements.

At Myra's request, the members of the expedition grouped themselves close to Q22 who was also joined by some of the Hixian elders and using her mental powers, the wisewoman was able to act as the communications link in the strange conference held between such vastly different forms of intelligent life.

Q22 demanded and received a full and truthful account of everything that had happened to the newcomers ever since their arrival in the Water Realm, including every detail of their mission to the members of the Hixian Prime who held court within The Heart of Emerald, only then did they move onto current matters.

Myra began explaining their need to reach the base of the spire of white metal as soon as possible in order to stand a chance of crossing the curtain leading to their own world. Then, and only then, did the young witch's inner eye define fear in a member of the Hixian' race, and she even noticed that Q22's head twitched slightly when she repeated her demand for urgent help in the name of the Hixian Prime.

The creature's answer was slow in reaching her brain.

"Witch woman—We must follow the commands of the Hixian Prime—And aid you with all the means at our disposal —But we ask—Cannot you forget this return journey of yours and live out your lives—Happily—In our world?"

Myra replied at once.

"No--No--Certainly not--We are absolutely determined to return to our native reality--And we cannot do this without the help of you and your people."

The Hixian' leader replied at once, but Myra defined the sadness in his communication.

"Our family will spare no effort in assisting you in reaching your goal—But many of our warriors will die in protecting you—From the unspeakable horrors that we must inevitably encounter during this dreadful march—Many of our breeders will perish when no one lives to bring them food—Our family will face hardship and grow few in numbers."

Q22 leaned forward and placed a huge hand upon Myra's shoulder and began caressing it with surprising gentleness.

"Remember the courage and loyalty of the Hix—When you dwell—Once again—In the comfort of your own reality—Now come witch-woman, who's thoughts reach the minds of others—Let us waste no time and begin our march without further delay."

꧁

During the following fourteen darkenings, the expedition marched ever southwards in the general direction of the shining metal spire, but the travellers were now under the protection of thirty hand-picked Hixian' warriors. However, the original members of the expedition now numbered only five; the remaining porters, who had remained loyal until they had reached the village of the Hix, had chosen to travel no further and elected to draw their pay and return to the coast under a safe conduct from the Hixian family elders. Indeed, their departure had proved fortuitous; for the route chosen by Q22 was difficult in the extreme and the few belonging the travellers still possessed had been divided up and carried by their massive protectors.

After leaving the village, the expedition had followed the line of the ancient highway for a further two darkenings, but on the morning of the third day, they branched off onto a side-track leading them through a gap into the mountains and then back onto the highway with the saving of at least a full darkenings march. The detour came as no surprise to the travellers, for Q22 had previously warned them that time-saving diversions, often hazardous, would be required if the expedition was to reach the portal before their fast-approaching deadline expired.

A few darkenings later, the highway swung due east and their guide led them away from the road and along a path taking them up into the highest reaches of the southern mountains. As they climbed, the air began to thin and the temperature plummeted until crimson icicles could be seen hanging from rocky ledges and a thick layer of frost crunched beneath their feet as they advanced.

The newcomers' teeth chattered and they drew their narrs-skin cloaks tightly around their bodies as they marched. Yet it was their Hixian' escort who suffered worst from the cold, for the great creatures appeared to have little resistance to low temperatures and they could be seen struggling forward in a pitiable condition.

The expedition was forced to spend two full darkenings at high altitude and both humans and Hix huddled together in the darkness in an effort to conserve every last vestige of warmth. Dawn came after the second darkening spent in the high mountains and the members of the expedition rose to their feet and prepared to resume their painful march, all save two of the Hixian's who had frozen to death during the night. Yet even in death the unfortunate pair continued to serve a purpose, for their bodies were torn apart and used as an emergency food source by their surviving kinsfolk.

Hours later, the expedition reached the bottom of a steep valley where they rejoined the highway and continued to follow the ancient route as it snaked its way ever southwards towards their intended goal.

Finally, a day arrived when the travellers emerged from the mouth of a steep pass and found themselves viewing the great metal spire from what appeared to be fairly close quarters, for the edifice towered above them and seemed to be almost touching the rolling clouds overhead.

"Three more darkenings!" said the voice of Q22 within the wisewoman's mind, "and we shall confront the last great obstacle standing—Between ourselves and the shrine lying —At the base of the great metal spire—The area upon which the spire stands is entirely surrounded by a great circular valley—A valley that is hot and humid—And contains a forest that is home to trees and plants—Found nowhere else in the Water Realm—."

For a moment the witch almost lost contact with the Hixian's mind, for Q22 suddenly and quite inadvertently transmitted a wave of naked fear.

"This forest is inhabited by strange creatures that are totally alien to this world—Many of them are dangerous in the extreme and more hideous than anything that your imagination can conceive—We must cross this terrible valley —And I am warning you now—So the ordeal will not come as a complete surprise!"

Myra passed on this fresh knowledge to her fellow travellers and it served to dampen the elation they had all experienced as a result of their latest viewing of the spire.

George, however, managed a laugh.

"What does it matter?" he asked, as he shouldered his long -handled axe and prepared to resume the march. "We have already survived a great many dangers and the ones lying ahead need not scare us unduly. I think!"

"I hope that you're correct," the young wisewoman replied. "But anything with the power to frighten the Hix cannot be treated lightly. Q22 has also told me that only a single hour of daylight remains and we must make camp for the night before descending yonder cliff and entering the 'Forest of Oblivion,' which is the Hixian's name for that terrible wooded valley lying before us. Q22 also suggests that we check our weapons carefully, for he feels sure that we shall have much need of them before we climb the cliff lying beyond the forest and finally arrive at the foot of the great spire."

The members of the expedition were soon occupied with their normal evening tasks as the Water Realm night closed upon them, and Paris sought out Whiteflower, who was scraping the red soil from some edible roots a Hixian guard has given to her.

"Have you given thought to the future?" he asked gently. "What do you intend to do once Darryl the swordsman passes through yonder portal and returns to his own reality?"

The girl was surprised by the nature of the question and almost dropped the knife that she was using to clean the vegetables.

"I shall be at my master's side when he returns to his own world. I will never leave him and I will stay with him until the moment death parts us!"

"That was the answer I expected you to give," replied the envoy. "Love blinds you to the fact that you can never cross the portal without subsequently destroying your own life and possibly blighting the future of the man whom you adore." He paused. "Remember, lady, like most other Water Realm humans, you have a light red skin-colouring due to your ancestors' long exposure to the environment of this reality. Consider, not one person in your lover's world will resemble you and you run the risk of being regarded as an aberration of nature, a freak to be pointed out and scorned by all who see you!"

"Darryl would not care!" Whiteflower said, with tears running down her cheeks.

"Perhaps not," the envoy replied. "But the years will pass and the passions of youth will inevitably cool, and you will run the risk of becoming a loveless stranger in a totally alien world!"

The girl broke down in tears.

"What of you, envoy?" she said, with a touch of anger in her voice. "Will you have the heart to turn your back upon your witch-lover, once you reach the vicinity of the portal?"

"Yes child!" Paris answered sadly. "And for the same reasons, in addition, I am bound by my sworn duty to the Dark Priests. I must return to Holy Ptah and inform them of the success or failure of this mission to the southlands."

"Does the wisewoman know that you intend to abandon her?" the girl asked.

The envoy nodded. "Yes, she knows and understands. It

was she who suggested that I should speak with you and make the situation clear. She believes that it would be best for all concerned, if you and I were to turn back at some point and return northwards with some of the Hixian' guards as escort and ..."

"No, no," Whiteflower interrupted angrily. "I will not give up my master. I will follow him to his place of birth and I will accept whatever fate the Gods may wish to bestow upon me. Now leave me in peace, slave of priests!"

She turned upon her heel and walked away, leaving the envoy shaking his head in resignation.

※

The campsite was still shrouded in darkness when the travellers were aroused from their sleep by their Hixian' escort and they hardly had time to pack their belonging and swallow a little food before being urged to resume the march.

The expedition struggled onwards through the darkness for what seemed like hours and they were only allowed to rest when the first glimmers of sunlight heralded the arrival of another Water Realm day.

The light strengthened and soon they were able to look over the edge of a precipitous escarpment and down into the depths of the Forest of Oblivion lying far below. The travellers realized at once that the escarpment was no creation of nature, but was another artefact of the Ancient Dead, for the huge cliff was reinforced and held in place by a colossal wall of the ubiquitous white metal. However, the passage of time and numerous earthquakes had attacked it unmercifully and the travellers were able to make out a great tear in the metal wall, extending downwards until it disappeared into a vast multicoloured jungle. Twisted shards of the same white metal and long jumbled lengths of metallic cable also hung in haphazard fashion from the damaged wall and the tangle of debris seemed to resemble the roots of some gigantic uprooted plant. About a mile from the edge of the escarpment there stood a massive white metal pylon that reared up from the valley bottom and was topped with the remains of a tubular roadway that appeared to be exactly level with the edge of the escarpment. Beyond the first pylon there stood others extending in a long line until they disappeared into the mists rising from the forest.

"It would appear that we are viewing the remains of yet another of the great bridges constructed by the Ancient Dead," Paris said knowledgeably. "It must have sprung from the area where the wall of the escarpment is torn away and then carried across yonder valley upon that line of pylons to the vicinity of the great metal spire. The bridge's tubular roadway must have collapsed, due to the passage of time, and its remains lie buried amidst that mass of vegetation in the valley bottom."

"What you say is probably correct, envoy," George agreed. "But why did the ancients build such an enormous structure in the first place?"

Myra immediately slapped her travelling pack.

"In this receptacle I keep the grimoire of my ancestor Rose Littlewood, and she seems to have answered your question in the final page. Unfortunately it's couched in yet another of her complicated riddles and I cannot grasp its full meaning. As I recall, it goes like this..."

The old ones came and cast a span
Across a vale where terrors vie
So they, alone, could tread the path
To lands beyond the rolling sky
But venture forth, and love will die.

"Strange words, indeed," the envoy commented. "But I think we can assume the Ancient Dead nurtured yonder Forest of Oblivion and introduced its savage and dangerous inhabitants. The ancients doubtless intended the valley to act as an effective barrier between the general population of the Water Realm and the portal that must have been of great value to them. However, they would need safe access for themselves and their servants and that appears to be the reason why they originally constructed the bridge."

"Aye, that would seem to be the case," Darryl said in agreement. "But the bridge is now gone and we must pass through that bloody jungle if we are to reach the portal. Yet do we stand a reasonable chance of making such a crossing?"

"I believe so!" the young witch answered decisively.

"I have communicated at great length with Q22 and he informs me that his family has occasionally hunted in the fringes of the forest, but only when driven to do so by sheer starvation, for many of the plants in yonder forest are poisonous and a simple touch is enough to kill. Three ferocious carnivores are also present in great numbers. The forest is home to a huge creature that moves on two legs and known to the Hix as K1. The beast is much feared because it can swallow a Hixian warrior in a single gulp. K2 is a snake-like predator that drags its victims into the depths of the swamps and devours them. But the creatures which the Hix fear the most are the K3, and I had a great difficulty in gaining an accurate description of them, save that they are small, ferocious, hunt in groups and move so fast that even the quickest warrior cannot outrun them."

The girl studied the look of near despair upon her companions' faces, and she managed to force a smile.

"Do not be alarmed," she said. "The Hix know of a route that will take us directly to the base of the spire and its one that can be travelled with a fair degree of speed..."

The girl paused and indicated that she was now receiving a mind-message from Q22 and moments later she turned her attention back to her comrades.

"Come," she ordered. "Our guide grows impatient and

requires us to continue the march without further delay!"

&

Q22 shook the young witch's shoulder and made sure that she was fully awake before addressing her in mind-speak.

"Come wisewoman—It will soon be time for the rising of the five suns—We must move without further delay—For a dangerous portion of the forest lies before us—And I wish to be through it well before the next darkening!"

Myra struggled to her feet and immediately began rousing her fellow travellers; a task that proved to be far from easy, for each member of the expedition was now suffering from the physical effects of the journey.

Almost five darkening ago, Q22 had guided the expedition to the mouth of an ancient inspection duct that led the travellers downwards until they reached the soft leafy floor of the Forest of Oblivion. The Hixian' escort had immediately formed up into a tight defensive screen and thereafter protected their charges with the greatest possible dedication, as the expedition passed beneath a thick canopy of high tree branches that filtered out most of the light from the five suns.

The first of their protectors had perished on the third day of their march through the forest, when a long worm-like creature lunged out from a patch of stinking marsh and dragged the Hixian down beneath the slime in the space of little more than a second. Another warrior had died when the trunk of a long dead tree was accidentally disturbed by their passage and fell, squashing the unfortunate spear-carrier like an overripe fruit, whilst a third was badly crippled and abandoned to his fate after stepping upon the spines of a poisonous plant. Small wonder that the expedition's progress was slow and undertaken with great care, for danger was lurking on every side. Fortunately,

Q22 had been able to follow the general line of the ancient bridge and the expedition was often able to pass, in near perfect safety, through long sections of the tubular roadway that had long ago crashed to the ground due to some powerful cataclysm and now lay in ruins upon the valley floor.

Myra succeeded in rousing her comrades from their slumbers and they slowly rose to their feet and began consuming the rich and nutritious purple fruit the Hix had picked from nearby bushes. Fortunately, hunger was not one of their problems for the forest contained ample sources of food that could be procured without undue difficulty.

As the expedition was preparing to resume its march, Myra began to feel the strange sensation in her head warning her that Q22 was about to enter her mind.

"You must warn your people that today's journey will take us through an extremely perilous section of the forest —An area known to be the main breeding ground—Of the terrible creature that we call—K 1—We must move slowly and with great care—To avoid disturbing one of the females—If we are unlucky and are attacked—Then we must fight for our lives."

The mental contact was broken and the expedition resumed its march and began entering a particularly dense portion of the forest, where the strange cries of unfamiliar animals echoed through the thick canopy of vegetation above their heads. Occasionally, they caught sight of massive herbivores, whose long necks enabled them to browse upon the tender foliage growing upon the upper branches of the tallest trees; animals whose ancestors had probably originated upon the planet Earth in some long forgotten age. But some of the other creatures, whom they briefly sighted, had a totally bizarre appearance suggesting an origin in some distant and unbelievably strange reality.

Biting insects were also present in this part of the forest and the travellers often had to brush them away from unprotected portions of their bodies as they marched. Unfortunately, the Hix were even more susceptible to their painful attentions and were obviously suffering terribly from their agonizing bites. The warriors were also much annoyed by the clouds of cloying vapour rising from the rotting vegetation lying underfoot and crushed with their massive feet as they advanced through the forest.

All day, the expedition struggled onwards and night was drawing near when Q22 halted the column and once again the wisewoman felt the Hixian entering her mind.

"Wisewoman—We have come across a female—K1— Who is broodding a clutch of eggs—The creatures usually continue sitting—Come what may—We will try to slip past her—Keep a sharp lookout—For if her mate is nearby—He will attack at once!"

The young witch passed the message on to her comrades and the march was resumed without further delay.

Soon, the travellers became aware of a series of long menacing snarls issuing from the nearby undergrowth and as they advanced, they caught sight of the head of a fearsome creature staring menacingly at them from the shelter of a shallow depression in the ground. They shuddered with horror when they saw the long rows of sharp carnivorous teeth within its monstrous jaws. The rear of the column was almost beyond sight of the brooding monster, when an even larger specimen of the same genre burst out of the trees and attempted to seize one of the Hixian' guardsmen who had closed in to protect the travellers with their long spears. George acted instinctively' and leaping forward, he drove the head of his long-handled axe deep into the creature's forehead before the animal had time to grasp its intended prey.

The ex-boat hand then cursed as he watched the monster

disappearing back into the jungle with his favourite weapon firmly embedded in its skull.

"A shame that I lost my trusty axe," he remarked, as he drew the steel cleaver from his belt. "But I won't need my war-axe when I'm home and crewing on a canal boat!"

Evening came and the members of the expedition took refuge in a fallen section of the ancient bridge that snaked its way southwards through the steaming tangle of the forest, and the travellers were much heartened when Q22 mentioned that the most arduous and dangerous portions of the forest now lay behind them. He also told the wanderers that most of their route now lay through long-collapsed sections of the ancient bridge structure. The stout metal, he asserted, would protect them from the vicious animals dwelling outside in the tangled undergrowth and they would no longer be harassed by stinging insects and threatened by poisonous plants.

The following day found the expedition picking its way through the massive tubular sections that seemed to stretch endlessly before them. Indeed, so complete were many segments of this ancient roadway that not a single beam of light penetrated from without, and the travellers were forced to rely exclusively upon a strange blue light radiating from long lines of translucent globes hanging from the metal ceiling high above their heads.

"Bloody kind of the old devils to leave us some light," George remarked to the envoy as they marched. "But how the hell do they keep burning after all this time?"

Paris shook his head. "The knowledge of the ancients was so great that we are little more than forest insects by comparison!"

The ex-boat hand simply nodded and asked no further questions.

✥

Day followed day, darkening followed darkening and the expedition advanced with considerable rapidity through the tubular remnants of the old bridge structure. However, they were sometimes forced to endure the terrors of the jungle, for in a few places, the ancient roadway had been completely destroyed and they had no choice but to trek through the forest until they found the beginning of the next complete section.

One afternoon, the travellers emerged from a section of the roadway and found themselves staring at a massive cliff made from the same white metal. The cliff stretched upwards until it towered a good thousand feet above the valley floor. As Myra looked upwards in awe, she felt Q22 entering her mind.

"Wisewoman—Half a day's march beyond yonder wall—Lies the base of the great metal tower—And also the shrine that you have come so far to find—."

Myra impatiently halted the Hixian's transmission and inserted a question of her own.

"Q22--It is good to confront the final barrier--But how can we ascend that cliff of smooth, white metal?"

The warrior pointed with the head of his spear towards a rent in the metal wall running diagonally across the face of the cliff, all of the way upwards from the base of the precipice that lay shrouded by tall trees, to the upper lip of the barrier standing silhouetted against the crimson sky.

"That is the way you must go—Wisewoman—Yonder tear in the metal—Is wide enough to serve you as an ascending pathway—Upwards—To the vicinity of the shrine—The way will not be easy—But the rent is home to a mass of vegetation that will serve you as hand and foot holds and enable you to make the climb—Tomorrow at dawn—You must begin the ascent—We Hix will accompany you no further—But will wait here for several darkenings—In case you fail to successfully make the climb and must return—Rest now—For tomorrow will be hard!"

The expedition made camp for the last time in the terrible Forest of Oblivion close to the mouth of the final length of road-section that would give them shelter during the coming night. The travellers built a cooking fire and began roasting the carcass of a young animal that had fallen to the spears of their Hixian' escort. As the light grew dim, the members of the expedition fell to satisfying their hunger and afterwards most of them sought the comfort of sleep.

Myra and Paris, however, continued to sit by the fire and hold hands far into the night, for they knew they must part forever with the coming of the next Water Realm dawn.

Yet neither of the lovers was unduly sad, for they both understood their individual responsibilities. The young Myra had to use her special occult powers to protect her friends and comrades, whilst Paris knew that he must return to Holy Ptah and report everything he had experienced and observed to his masters the Dark Priests.

Eventually, the two lovers quit the still glowing coals and made love beneath their sleeping skins one last time.

No tears were shed, for the couple knew that time and distance did not hold the power to extinguish a love enduring until the day they died.

ॐ

Whiteflower and the three travellers from Earth bade a final farewell to Paris and their faithful Hixian' escort, then, as the morning light from the five suns began to strengthen, they started the long and arduous climb out of the terrible Forest of Oblivion.

It soon became clear that the tear in the white metal cliff-face had been caused long ago by some titanic cataclysm that had struck this portion of the Water Realm.

The shock had evidently caused the lower lip of the tear to lean sharply outwards, allowing soil and rocks to erupt to the surface. This had eventually created a steeply angled pathway to the top of the cliff. It was a frightening route, which the travellers knew they must successfully ascend before the coming of the next darkening.

Darryl took the lead with Kingslayer held at the ready for they had been warned by Q22 that dangerous life-forms might well be encountered during their climb. Whiteflower came next, closely followed by the wisewoman, whilst George brought up the rear with his trusty steel cleaver grasped tightly in his right hand.

At first the ascent was easy, for the overhanging lip of the tear was a good Earth mile in width and the climbers had no difficulty in picking their way between the trees and shrubs that had established themselves in the debris spilling out from behind the damaged metal wall, but as they climbed ever upwards, the metal lip began to narrow and soon they were struggling along a crazy pathway that was only a few feet wide and almost impassably choked with vines and creeping plants.

Even so, the travellers had completed over half the ascent by the time the five suns reached their zenith in the sky and their rate of climb had also begun to increase as the lip of the tear began to broaden once again.

Darryl called a halt and together with his three companions he wandered over to the edge of the lip and stared downwards into the multicoloured mass of the forest lying far below them. Perhaps the four climbers let down their guard for a few moments as they took in the breathtaking view, for none of them noticed the three nightmarish life-forms that suddenly broke from a nearby patch of scrub and hurtled towards them at breakneck speed.

It was George who first spotted the creatures and the former boat hand had hardly time to shout a brief warning before spinning around upon his heel to engage the first of the outlandish life forms with his steel cleaver. 'Outlandish' was the perfect word to describe the fearsome creatures, for they were each about the size of a large dog and were propelled along the ground at great speed by a mass of threshing tentacles growing from the underside of their black cylindrical bodies. The apparitions also possessed huge mouths that occupied almost the whole front portion to their torpedo-like bodies, crude gaping apertures that were murderously armed with long rows of sharp serrated teeth.

At the very last moment the former boat hand sidestepped the first of the attackers and split the creature in half with a single massive blow from his cleaver, whilst Darryl, at almost the same instant, fell upon one knee and delivered a single murderous cut with Kingslayer opening up another of the apparitions from one end of its torpedo-like body to the other. Tragically, the last remaining monster evaded Whiteflower's sword stroke and laid open the tribeswoman's chest and abdomen with its razor sharp teeth. Too late, the wisewoman's dagger hissed through the air and buried itself in the creature's side. And too late was the stroke from George's cleaver sending it spinning down into the forest below. For Whiteflower of the Kev now lay upon the ground with the lifeblood draining from her body in a veritable torrent.

The three surviving travellers were at her side in a moment, but Myra did not even bother to take the medical bag from her shoulder, for it was obvious that the stricken girl had only moments to live.

Whiteflower had just sufficient strength to turn her head and address her lover for the last time.

"Remember me!" she said, in little more than a whisper. "Keep me in your thoughts ... and ... I will ... still live ..."

The girl's body gave a shudder, and with a sigh, the last breath left her body.

Darryl stood transfixed, as though suddenly turned to stone.

"In the name of creation, no ..." he muttered. "This cannot have happened ... We were going to live out our lives together in Elfencot. We ..."

The young wisewoman moved quickly. She instantly delved into her medicine bag and drew out a vial containing a drug known to counteract the effects of mind-numbing shock and she forced the vial between her brother's lips.

"Swallow this potion," she commanded, "and recall that we still have a long way to go, if we are to complete this climb before darkness falls!"

"Aye, listen to your sister!" George added, firmly gripping the ex-boatmaster by the shoulder. "You must take hold of yourself and continue to climb. Else you will never live to see your home again and Whiteflower will have died for no purpose. Come man, put one foot in front of another. And climb!"

Darryl shook his head and wiped the hideous creature's body fluids from the blade of his sword, then turned and faced his two comrades.

"Do not fear for my sanity!" he said, to their considerable relief. "My wits have returned. Come, we must bury Whiteflower's body as quickly as possible and then continue upon our way!"

The three survivors used their weapons to excavate a grave and buried Whiteflower's body exactly where she fell, as was the custom amongst the Kev. Afterwards, they heaped rocks upon the grave to keep of scavenging animals and resumed their climb with all possible speed.

Once again, the path narrowed and became thickly choked with vegetation and it was almost pitch dark by the time they reached the crest and staggered away from the edge of that terrible precipice.

In the near darkness, the exhausted travellers blundered into the midst of a group of sharp boulders that afforded them some rudimentary shelter and soon they were fast asleep. All save Darryl, who remained on guard and wept quietly for his lost lover, until sheer fatigue clouded his brain and he too fell into an exhausted slumber.

The travellers awoke at dawn and were amazed at the sight meeting their eyes as the light of the five suns broke through the rolling crimson clouds.

About half an Earth mile from the group of sharp rocks that had sheltered them throughout the hours of darkness, there stood a huge plinth cast from some dark stone-like material. This massive erection supported the base of the enormous white metal spire that had long been their goal and appearing to reach up above them as far as the turbulent Water Realm sky.

The three survivors stood motionless for several moments as they viewed the ancient wonder confronting them, but their reverie was suddenly broken when the young wisewoman let out a gasp and clasped the palms of her hands to her temples.

"Mother awaits us on the far side of the barrier," she cried. "I am reaching out and touching her mind. The portal we seek is very near, or such a strong mental contact could not possibly be achieved."

She fell upon her knees, concentrated her formidable psychic powers and flung out a message in the general direction of the spire.

"Mother!" She called. *"Mother--Mother--Should my thoughts reach you--Then contact me if you are able--Mother --Mother--"*

"Mother--MOTHER!"

The words echoed faintly in some remote corner of Hetty's mind as she lay slumbering in the arms of her lover.

"Mother--Mother-- MOTHER!"

The call was repeated over and over again, until the witch was forced to open her eyes and take heed to the message that was taking shape in her mind.

"Mother--Mother--It is Myra--Your daughter--If you can hear me--Reach out--Reach out to me--"

Hetty was now wide awake and shook the red-haired policeman who lay at her side.

"Myra is calling to me from across the void. They must be very close to the mouth of the return portal. I must attempt to contact my daughter without delay; for there is much to be done before my kinsfolk are returned safely to their own reality."

The witch closed her eyes and projected a psychic message towards the nearby cave in the cliffs containing the exit portal from the Water Realm.

"My daughter--I will be brief--For we must conserve our mental energies--Position yourself as close as possible to the portal--And in twelve earth hours--I will attempt the ceremony that will part the curtain separating our twin realities-Assist me as far as your powers will allow--Reach out to me now--If you receive and understand my message--My daughter!"

The reply entered Hetty's mind almost immediately.

"Mother--I will do as you say--Until later--I bid you goodbye."

The light of dawn was now entering the cottage and enabled the wisewoman to gather together a collection of accoutrements that she packed into a leather satchel. She worked carefully and methodically, for each precious item would be needed to carry out the desperately difficult magical ritual that lay ahead.

Meanwhile, Angus Smith prepared the storm lanterns and

the climbing ropes that he intended to carry down the cliffside path to his intended rescue station inside the mouth of the cave.

The sun was high in the sky before the pair had completed all the necessary preparations and the red-haired witch straightened her back and turned once again to address her companion.

"We have worked well and have time in hand!" she said softly. "So let us return to the comfort of our bedsheets, for I feel a terrible cold gathering within me and I must feel the warmth of your love!"

The policeman opened his mouth and was about to make a comforting reply, when the wisewoman silenced him by placing a finger to his lips.

"Come!" she said. "Please do not say another word. Instead, let your love give me the strength that I so desperately need, my dearest, for I know that a fearful ordeal awaits me. And I am so terribly afraid!"

༺ ༻

Hetty's words were fresh in her daughter's mind as the young wisewoman turned to face her two companions.

"We must move at once," she said urgently, "and discover the shrine holding the entrance to the portal. Mother will soon begin the ceremony that will tear open the curtain for our return. My inner eye tells me the shrine lies in very close proximity to the base of yonder spire and we should reach it without further delay."

Darryl and George immediately assented and the little party began advancing towards the spire as fast as the broken ground would allow, but the five suns were high in the sky before Myra pointed towards a small white metal structure lying in the shadow of the dark plinth supporting the great spire.

"It is there, within that building," she said, gasping from the physical exertions of the march. "My witch's intuition tells me that we are now very close to our goal!"

The trio advanced at an even faster rate and soon found themselves standing before the boxlike metal structure that appeared to be protruding from the base of the spire. An open doorway, about twenty feet in height, offered a way into the building and Myra stepped across the threshold without a moment's hesitation.

Her two companions immediately followed and the travellers found themselves standing in a large room whose walls were made from the white metal of the ancients. A large semi-circular opening could be seen in the far wall and appeared to lead into a long tunnel whose walls were lined with the same metallic substance.

The wisewoman moved closer to the opening and she saw that the tunnel was illuminated by the same light-source that had enabled them to travel down long sections of the old ruined bridge in the Forest of Oblivion.

A strange and almost transparent blue-green haze seemed to dance fitfully, hither and thither, in the mouth of the tunnel. She stopped and ordered her companions to go no further.

"We have found it!" she said quietly. "We have found the portal that will lead us back to our own world. I must contact mother at once and assist her in opening yonder curtain, but there is one last thing that I must do before I cast my mind across the void!"

She slipped the travelling pack from her shoulder and opened one of its pockets revealing a small package that was wrapped in narr-skin. She opened the folds of the soft material and revealed three bracelets of burnished copper, each being encrusted with a score of beautifully cut jewels.

"These precious stones," she said, "together with the Dark Priests' diamonds, carefully hidden amongst the remedies in my medicine bag, will ensure that each of us has a prosperous future in our own reality, if we succeed in winning through the curtain. Quickly now, stow them away upon your persons!"

Her companions stood rooted to the spot in amazement.

"How did you come by such a collection of priceless gems?" Darryl asked, as he stuffed several of the pieces into the pocket of his narrs-skin trousers.

"From the Lady Livia!" she answered as she spread a length of cloth upon the floor in front of the shimmering portal. "Before she entered her bath for the last time, she begged me to accept her personal adornments, for she could not bear the thought of them falling into the uncouth hands of slaves, or worse, coming into the possession of her hated husband!"

The witch turned her back upon her companions and knelt down upon the length of cloth.

"Now my friends, I am about to contact my mother and the two of us will begin the ritual that will part the curtain and allow us to return to our own native reality. Stand away from me and do not interfere with the ceremony under any consideration, but you must both obey me without question when the time comes to move forward and enter the portal."

The young witch drew deeply upon her mental resources and cast out a message to her mother whom she knew would be waiting on the other side of the curtain.

"Mother!--Mother!--Can you hear me?--Are you ready to begin the opening ritual?"

The answer entered her head almost immediately.

"Yes my daughter--I am lying upon the ritual stone that is situated in the centre of an ancient stone circle--Close-- Very close--To the mouth of the cave from which you must all emerge if you successfully cross the curtain--The sacred fire burns before me--And in a moment I will begin flinging my energies against the fabric of the curtain--Thus opening the way for your return-- My daughter--Be ready to aid me with the power of your mind-- Should I call for your assistance--Once you have passed through the portal--You will be greated by a man who is my trusted friend

and lover--Do as he says and he will lead you to safety--Now I bid you farewell--My beloved daughter!"

Hetty's consciousness disappeared from the young witch's mind and she turned her attention to the shimmering curtain that had suddenly begun to thin and lose some of its colour. She also began sensing the agonizing pain her mother was beginning to suffer as the older woman began prying open the portal separating the two realities. For a single minute that seemed to stretch into hours, the young wisewoman watched as the curtain gradually faded away until only an opaque disturbance remained to donate its presence. Suddenly, Myra sensed a violent increase in the level of agony that her mother was enduring, and a split second later she picked up the faint echo of the command which the older woman had cast over the void.

"Quickly now--My daughter--HELP--Help me to sweep aside this curtain!"

Myra responded instantly. She summoned up her entire reserve of mental energy and flung it against the failing barrier. For a moment the curtain maintained itself against the massive psychic assault and then collapsed entirely leaving the portal between the two worlds open and completely unguarded.

The young witch leapt to her feet and sprang towards the mouth of the tunnel.

"Follow me!" she called out to her companions. "The way is now clear. But the portal will close presently, so we must run for our lives if we are to reach our own reality in safety!"

The travellers fled down the tunnel for a good quarter of an Earth mile and they eventually began gasping for breath and the pace of their advance slowed.

As she ran, the wisewoman noticed that odd patches of the blue-green haze were beginning to re-form close to the walls and ceiling of the tunnel and she realized that the portal would soon become impregnable again.

"Faster!" she gasped to her companions. "Faster or we are surely doomed!"

The trio made one final effort and managed to redouble their pace and a few seconds later they passed out of the lighted metal tunnel, only to find themselves groping blindly down a dark and narrow underground cave, where rivulets of water trickled down slime covered walls of solid rock.

Myra collapsed upon the soaking wet floor.

"We have passed through the portal!" she gasped out to her companions as soon as she had gathered enough breath. "We are now upon the planet Earth and within our own reality. Now we must find the man who mother said would guide us to safety!"

"Ye already have, lassie!" said a voice from the darkness and the sudden flaring of a storm lantern revealed the be-whiskered features of Angus Smith.

"I bid ye welcome," he continued. "Hetty has instructed me to take you from this subterranean place and lead you up the steep cliff face to the relative safety of the island lying above our heads. But 'twill be no easy journey, for a storm of no natural making is raging over the sea and will seek to pluck us away to our deaths as we ascend the cliffside path. Come now, if you are sufficiently rested and let us depart!"

The returning wanderers followed the lantern-bearing policeman down the length of the cave until their ears began to be assailed by a frightful roaring sound echoing eerily from the rocky walls of the cave.

"It is the storm!" Angus explained. "The night sky is pitch black out there and it's shot through with streaks of violet light. Never in my ..."

"Mother, Mother!" Myra suddenly cried, clasping the palms of her hands to the sides of her head. "My inner eye tells me that something terrible is happening to her. We must go to her aid with all speed!"

The young wisewoman would have darted forwards,

towards the sound of the sea, had Angus not restrained her with his hand.

"Easy lassie!" he said. "I'm as worried as yourself, but the mouth of the cave lies just ahead of us and we must rope ourselves securely together if we are to stand any chance of ascending yonder path, for it clings precariously to the side of the cliff and we must proceed with care."

The policeman produced a long coil of rope and secured the travellers to the cord at five yard intervals. He then fixed the end of the length of rope to the rear of a stout leather belt that he wore about his waist. He completed his preparations by lighting an additional storm lantern and passed it to George. He then bade the little group to follow in his footsteps with the greatest care.

The party advanced in single file to the mouth of the cave and for the first time they viewed the open sea that seethed, roared and flung itself against the rocks below like a mad beast. They also felt the rip of the screaming gale and the beat of the rain that poured from the dark sky in torrents.

Slowly, the wanderers followed their guide out of the mouth of the cave and began carefully ascending the narrow pathway leading torturously upwards to the relative safety of the cliff top. As they climbed, they kept tight against the rock-face in order to escape the worst effects of the howling gale that sought to tear them away from the path and send them spinning into the seething cauldron of water lying far below them. Gradually, they worked their way upwards, grasping at each crack in the rock that gave them support and making full use of the pegs and loops of rope that Angus had previously driven into the rock-face to aid them in their dangerous climb.

On one occasion, the young wisewoman slipped on a patch of moss and would have been flung into the abyss, had her twin brother not caught her by the shoulder and dragged her away from imminent disaster. Minutes later, a tremendous gust of wind tore the lantern from Angus's grasp and tossed it into the sea like a discarded toy. Finally, after what seemed like hours, they breasted the head of the path and fell exhausted upon the rain-soaked heather that grew in abundance at the cliff's edge.

The travellers rested for a few moments, in order to regain a little strength, then, led by the young witch, they quickly made their way to the circle of great stones situated in the centre of the island. And the returning wanderers were struck temporarily dumb by the terrible sight that met their eyes.

Hetty Littlewood, the wisewoman of Elfencot, lay dead upon the altar slab that was situated inside the stone circle. Within her lifeless hand she still grasped the empty vial of poison that she used to end her life.

Myra was the first member of the group to fully regain their senses. After closing her mother's eyes, she took hold of the remaining lantern and shone its light upon the ancient symbols that had been carved, long ago, upon the sides of the altar slab.

After a while, she lowered the lantern to the wet earth and began sobbing out the reason for their sad bereavement.

"Long, long ago," she explained with difficulty and with many pauses, "those evil beings whom we call The Ancient Dead used their vast knowledge to create this portal, allowing their servants to reach our home reality and pillage its resources. The fiends must have placed great value upon this portal, for they created the Forest of Oblivion to keep unwanted strangers away from the entrance to the world they so mercilessly plundered."

She paused for a moment to wipe away the rivulets of tears and rainwater coursing down her face.

"But that precaution alone did not serve to allay their jealous fears. So the evil ones drew upon their immense occult knowledge and placed a terrible curse upon all who sought to tread their portal without receiving their expressed permission. The half-mad Rose Littlewood knew this and the last poem in her grimoire carried a dreadful warning."

The young witch paused and recited the verse from memory.

The old ones came and cast a span
Across the vale where terrors vie
So they, alone, could tread the path
To the lands beyond the rolling sky
But venture forth and love will die.

Once again, the young witch brushed the tears from her eyes and looked directly towards her twin brother.

"Any stranger who sought to pass through the portal would pay a terrible price: the swift and inevitable death of a loved one. It was Whiteflower who paid the dreadful toll, the very moment we crossed the Forest of Oblivion and drew near to the base of the great metal spire guarding the entrance to the portal exiting the Water Realm!"

Myra choked back her sobs before continuing.

"Mother read the warning carved upon this very altar-stone and she knew that a second life would also be forfeit, once she had completed the opening ritual within this ring of standing stones. And the victim would have been selected from amongst our number as we cleared the mouth of the portal. Yet she loved us all dearly and she cheated the curse by offering up her own life instead!"

Darryl stripped the tattered narr-skin tunic from his shoulders and used it as a shroud to cover his mother's body.

"Come!" he said to his three companions. "We must hold our grief in check a while, for we must ensure no other living being makes use of this portal, the source of so much sorrow and suffering. Come, my friends!" he said, turning his back upon the altar with its sad burden. "We have much to do before we can dream of rebuilding our own lives!"

Epilogue

Exactly one year later, to the very day. George, the former boat hand, and the Littlewood twins stood motionless upon the deck of a small fishing boat and from a safe distance they watched the detonation of the huge gunpowder charges obliterating every last trace of the cave that had once acted as their return route from the terrible Water Realm.

A few hundred yards from their stern lay another small craft. Angus Smith was standing by its mast and he watched grimly as the last broken fragments of what had been the circle of great stones were taken from the vessel's hold and flung over the side, together with the finely powdered remnants of the inscribed altar-stone.

The dust from the explosion gradually settled and nothing could be seen of the old cottage that had once stood by the shore, the dwelling that had sheltered Angus Smith and his old grandmother, for its walls had been levelled to the ground by order of the three wanderers. For the wealthy trio had recently purchased the island to ensure that it remained totally bereft of human habitation and strictly forbidden to all mankind.

Yet one human being still remained upon that fay isle. Buried deep in the rocky soil, in the exact centre of the island, lay the body of Hetty Littlewood, the wisewoman of Elfencot. By her left side lay the burnt remains of a witch's grimoire that had once belonged to an equally wise ancestor, together with a spoon that had the power to detect poison. To her right hand, wrapped in a soft narrs-skin tunic, rested Kingslayer, the peerless sword that had successfully guarded the life of her fearless son.

Presently, the wind freshened and the two boats disappeared over the horizon, abandoning the Island to the seals, the screaming birds and the ever-present sound of the unquiet sea.

About the Author

Alan Lawton was born in 1938 in the Pennine village of Micklehurst. He was educated in a small secondary modern school and left without qualifications of any sort. As a youth he worked in the farming and textile industries before serving in the RAF Regiment.

Alan moved to the Isle of Man in 1962 and was largely engaged in agriculture until the early 1970's when he entered the construction industry as a common labourer and began a long programme of self improvement. He subsequently qualified as a bricklayer and graduated from the Open University with a good honours degree. He later undertook research for a Liverpool University history project and also compiled family histories.

He became interested in creative writing at an early age and won the Olive Lamming short story competition for 1979. He now lives in quiet retirement with Hilary his long time partner and occupies himself with writing, light gardening and doing the cooking.